PLAYING DEAD

Rory McCormac

ARROW

Published by Arrow Books in 1996

1 3 5 7 9 10 8 6 4 2

© Muiris O'Scanaill 1993, 1996

First published in Ireland by Immel Publishing Ltd
as *Snapshot*

This edition published by Arrow Books Limited
20 Vauxhall Bridge Road, London SW1V 2SA

Random House Australia (Pty) Limited
16 Dalmore Drive, Scoresby, Victoria 3179

Random House New Zealand Limited
18 Poland Road, Glenfield
Auckland 10, New Zealand

Random House South Africa (Pty) Limited
PO Box 2263, Rosebank 2121, South Africa

Random House UK Limited Reg. No. 954009
ISBN 0 099 607 212

Typeset by Deltatype Ltd, Ellesmere Port, Cheshire
Printed in Great Britain by BPC Paperbacks Ltd,
a member of The British Printing Company Ltd

For Cormac, Ruairi and Alex, and for Mamo
who would have loved all the fuss, but just missed it.

I

I read the letter with disbelief at first, as though it might be a joke. Then I read it another couple of times and, by the end of the third reading, I was sitting there, grinning inanely at the two sheets of cream A4, shuffling them back and forth so that I could alternately beam at the heading which, in majestic curlicues, read:

> *P.R. Steele M.V.B., M.R.C.V.S.*
> *Carrickpedder House,*
> *Knockmore-on-Sea,*
> *County Galway*

and see the signature, which, though equally stylish, was totally illegible, a couple of inches of ECG tracing.

Lately, even I had begun to doubt that my fledgling Veterinary Locum Services would ever get off the ground, but after six barren months, this was all that the incurable optimist in me needed. I'd be run off my feet. Turning clients away apologetically but firmly . . .

I had discovered early on that I wasn't a 'company man' and, as time passed, found it more and more difficult to accept the rigid hierarchy of the large practice in which I was a junior – the senior junior actually, whatever that meant. We assistants were called 'juniors', to make us feel that we were already embryonic partners. Quitting hadn't been easy – the job had been hard enough to land in the first place. John

Cunningham and Partners (all eight of them), with their state-of-the-art facilities, top specialists, impressive client list, and the range of species represented by their patients, gave young graduates an opportunity to gain experience not readily available elsewhere; consequently, the Partnership always had the pick of the available assistants and, though I say so myself, employed only the cream. But now I wanted out, to try being my own boss for a while, to look around the country, find some place that I really wanted to live, not the stultifying midlands county town in which nothing ever happened unless it was ordained by the Functions Sub-committee of the Town Council or the Chamber of Commerce. Normally such a search would have entailed moving from job to job, six months here, a year there, and it was while I was trying to figure out some way of short-circuiting that time-consuming process that it occurred to me that the answer would be to avoid full-time jobs altogether and set up a locum service instead, providing cover whenever and wherever it was needed, a kind of Have Stethoscope, Will Travel. I thought about it for a couple of weeks, talked it over with a few close friends, weighed everything up, then, for better or worse, made my decision.

My bank manager had been reasonably supportive, at least at the outset, but lately he'd begun to show signs of nervousness and had taken to muttering darkly about the People From Area Head Office giving him a hard time – he made Area Head Office sound like a cross between Castle Dracula and Gestapo HQ – but I was unable to offer him much in the line of consolation or succour. I couldn't continue airily telling him that these new ventures were always a bit slow to take off – I'd been telling him that since the second month and by now it had reached the point where we both agreed that 'slow' was a relative term, subjective and vague, notoriously open to different interpretations by different people, look at the case in point. Steele's letter would cheer him up no end. The blood fiends of Area Head Office would be placated, at least until the next full moon.

The letter informed me that P. R. Steele would be going to

America to attend his son's wedding, would be away for nearly two months, and would like me to take over the running of his one-man practice for the duration. The snag was that he was scheduled to fly out in a mere three days' time. He apologised for the short notice, explaining that he had arranged for a stand-in months ago but this plan had suddenly become unstuck when the replacement broke his arm. It was his frantic search for a late stand-in that had prompted him to phone to see if his old friend, John Cunningham, mightn't be able to spare one of his many assistants, and that was how he had come upon my name. He hoped I could take over at such short notice. Either way, could I please ring him at once. Cunningham hadn't had my number, he explained, or he would have phoned, not written . . . He sounded even more anxious than I was.

I got through to Steele and put him out of his misery. He explained that he would be leaving Knockmore early Sunday morning, spending the day in Dublin, and flying out on Monday. This was Friday. I promised to be there by lunchtime tomorrow at the latest so we could have all afternoon for him to show me around.

I suddenly found myself short of time to do all the things I had been planning to tackle at my leisure, mostly small things, but there were one or two important projects, the most pressing of which had cropped up recently and was in no way connected with work. It could have been described as a matter of the heart, but only in so far as my blood pressure was involved; the nobler sentiments which that phrase generally implies were conspicuous by their absence. I hardly knew the girl.

Marnie was Dutch, and a fashion photographer; 'top', 'inspired', 'up-and-coming', 'much-sought-after', were all qualifiers I had heard prefixing her job description. Tall, blonde as sunny August cornfields, eyes blue as sapphires, nose, mouth and teeth all in keeping, it seemed to me that she was at the wrong end of the camera. Someone once told me that fashion models should be flat-chested, so maybe that was

3

why Marnie didn't make the grade, but she moved with a loose-limbed natural flow which would have graced any catwalk. To me she was a creature of wonder, exotic in her accent, mannerisms, profession, dress, attitudes, not to mention the loose-limbed natural flow, and I developed a rapid and serious case of the hots for her. Now I had to rush things.

I'd only met her twice, the first time less than a week ago. She was in Dublin on holiday, attending a festival of Irish traditional music of which she was an enthusiastic fan. I'd happened to find myself sitting beside her at a De Dannan concert the previous Sunday night. I was on my own – tickets were rare but I had been given a complimentary by Frankie Gavin, the fiddle-player and driving force behind the band and a long-time friend. Marnie was part of a group of four – one man and three beautiful girls. She had bought an album in the foyer on the way in and had enlisted my aid in translating the track titles, which were all in Irish. She and her friends were delighted when I took them backstage afterwards but they had to leave early for a prior supper date. Marnie, who spent most of her time talking to me, gave me a list of pubs and clubs she intended to visit during the next few evenings, all of which were hosting music sessions, and left with the hope that we might meet at one of these. This was delivered with a smile which I later decided had been 'significant'. Which was when the hots began in earnest.

By Wednesday evening, I had done the rounds of the pubs and, though I had heard some great music, there was no sign of Marnie. I was about to throw my hat at it, deciding that the smile had, after all, been just an ordinary one and that any significance I had attributed to it had been solely in my insignificant head, when Frankie rang to say the band was doing a gig in Searson's and why didn't I come along.

She was already there when I arrived about ten. With the same people. She saw me almost at once (I, of course, immediately decided that she'd been watching hungrily for me), waved, and fought her way through the throng. She laid a hand on my arm and said it was great to see me. The crowd

4

pressed us together and I asked her what she wanted to drink hoping to prise her away from the group.

'There is room at our table, Frank. Come sit with us. I haff a drink there already. Yust for yourself, get one.' The accent made my toes curl in my Nikes.

She led me back to her table where she insisted that I share the leatherette seat with her, and though she made introductions, the names got lost among the skirling notes of the music and the noise of the crowd. While everyone was tapping feet or rapping knuckles, in thrall to the infectious rhythms of reels which slid seamlessly from one into the next, I was busy reading the omens, poring over the entrails. Unable to fix the man's position within the group when we had met at the concert, I now decided that it wasn't important: had he been Marnie's boyfriend, then I would have been given her seat and her thigh would now be moving up and down rhythmically against his leg instead of mine. I also figured that she could, unless she was trying to tell me something, have shared with one of the girls. The entrails looked very promising indeed, but then, to me, they always did.

It was not to be – at least not that night. Performance over, Helene, one of the friends, who had gone very quiet during the previous hour, announced that she felt like death and had to go home. In fairness, though I cursed her silently at the time, she did look pretty awful, and Marnie understandably insisted on going with her. So the Gang of Four departed.

'Give us a ring,' said Marnie as she left, handing me a phone number, and I told her I'd love to, fervently hoping that the 'us' was used idiomatically and not literally.

That was Wednesday, this was Friday. I had phoned (about twenty times) on Thursday but there'd been no reply, I thought maybe I'd left it too late in the evening and decided not to take the same chance today.

The lady herself answered and sounded delighted to hear from me.

'How's Helene?' (Show what a kind heart you've got.)

'She is very good now thank you. A twenty-four-hour bug.'

5

'Good. So . . .' (Don't overdo the kind heart bit or she may think it's *Helene* you fancy.) 'Any plans for this evening?'

'There's a party. Are you going?'

'I haven't heard of any parties. I haven't been invited.'

'If I inwite you, vill that be good enough?'

'If *you* invite me, I shall be the most honoured man in the world and immediately cancel my dinner date with Jodie Foster.'

'Poor Yodie. . .'

'She'll get over it in time. But *can* you invite me? Whose party is it?'

'I do not know their name but it is not a formal or a fancy party or anything like that.' She laughed flirtatiously. 'If they refuse to permit you in, then I shall not enter either . . .'

She was certainly right about it not being formal. The party, when we eventually located the basement flat in Rathmines, was crammed with people who all seemed to be sniffing, snorting or puffing various prohibited substances – not my ideal scene at all. Still, I decided to stick it out for a while – Marnie might soon decide she wanted to leave, and I didn't want to be missing when and if that happened. Besides, she now had a hostage: my camera. *En route* much to her delight, she had found it in the glove compartment and, despite my unspoken but obvious disapproval, had insisted on taking it to the party. She'd had her way, the hots, by this time, having achieved maximum intensity, I was in no mood to deny her anything, even unto half my kingdom, which was just about what my camera was worth. So I moved about hither and thither, drifting amongst the smokers and the sniffers, the snorters and the puffers, trying to keep up with Marnie without it seeming like I was slavishly following her, and feeling more and more ill at ease.

As I moved aimlessly through the milling crowd and the heavy music, I began to feel eyes upon me; suspicious, wary eyes, following me wherever I went. I studiously avoided catching their gaze, but one quick, unobserved peep revealed that the eyes belonged to two, large, well-muscled young men

6

who, like me, seemed out of place and were taking no part in the action; however, unlike me, it was clear that they had business there – they stood, broad shoulder to broad shoulder, facing the room, almost blocking with their bulk a corner in which a nattily dressed older man sat talking earnestly to two others. One of them spotted me again and I melted further into the crowd. I was clearly giving off uncomfortable vibes which they, equally clearly, were picking up and, presumably, wondering why, if I was so ill at ease, I was there at all.

To get myself out of sight, I squatted down beside a girl who was sitting on the floor, crying. She didn't know why she was crying; in fact she doubted that she *was* crying because she claimed to be very happy, so I didn't pursue the matter. She asked me if I had any good shit on me, to which I replied that I was fresh out. At this news she began to wail loudly, so I left. As soon as I straightened up, I could feel the eyes picking me up again. A minute later, when I'd slipped into another room and was trying to strike up a conversation with a petite redhead who wasn't even vaguely interested, one of the minders appeared at the door and lounged there, openly eyeing me. I went back into the main room through another door. Next time I looked, one of the goons had a partygoer by the sleeve and was pointing him in my direction. I saw him shrug and shake his dreadlocks – he didn't know who I was and, by the look of him, couldn't care less. A flashbulb popped, pinpointing Marnie's whereabouts, and I edged nervously in that direction.

Some time later I went out into the small back garden to relieve myself against the back wall – the tiny loo was constantly occupied. Just as I turned towards the open back door again, zipping up my fly, I saw one of the minders heading my way through the crowd; to avoid meeting him, I moved into the shadows by a shed the size of a phone kiosk. There was a sudden drop in the noise level when he closed the door behind him and suddenly it was just me and him. As his eyes probed the dark space, I felt sure he was looking for me, and when he reached purposefully into his inside pocket, I froze; my heart only stopped thudding when his hand came out holding nothing more lethal than a mobile phone. He extended the telescopic aerial and dialled. 'Harry? It's Les. Listen I want you and Jack over here . . . you've got the address?' There was some indistinct squawking from the phone which I couldn't make out. Then: 'Maybe there's no problem and maybe there's a big problem – that's what you guys are goin' to find out. There's a guy here I want you to . . . have a little chat with. Squeeze him a little : . .' Squawk. 'He's a new face to me, and nobody else seems to know him either. He's no raver, that's for sure.' Several squawks. 'Naw! A cop'd look the part – this one's dressed cas but not cool. Sorry to call you out, but there's just Phil and me, and one of us has to stay with the old man. I think it'd be better to have at least two to tackle this guy – he's pretty big and looks as if he could handle himself well.' Static reply which he had to query several times. 'Say again? Say again, Harry. I'm losing you, you're breaking up. *Half an hour?* Fuck that. Make it twenty minutes. I want to get home. I'm shagged.' A few squawks. 'Yeah. Ten-four to you too, Harry. Twenty minutes, OK?'

As soon as he'd gone back in, I went in search of Marnie. But Marnie was in her element, and wouldn't hear of leaving. Eventually, I did well to get my camera back. She wanted me and it to stay.

'Can't, Marnie. Got to be off.' I didn't tell her I had to be off in something under twenty minutes. 'I was late last night and I've got an early start in the morning.'

'When will you be in town again, Frank?' she asked, inhaling fiercely on the joint she held between thumb and forefinger. 'You sure you don't vant some of this?'

'I'm sure, thanks. I probably won't be back for at least six weeks. Maybe more. It depends. I'd better leave you the film so you can have it developed.'

'I did not finish it. You finish it and maybe you call around with the prints next time you get to Dublin? I like it here and maybe I stay a few months? Look for some vork.'

'OK then. Maybe I can give you a shout when I get myself sorted out? If the tinselly blandishments of the metropolis begin to look jaded, you could take a trip westwards to recuperate and replenish the batteries for the continued struggle.' I smiled winningly, but she didn't answer. On reflection, I thought, she probably hadn't understood a word of it. 'You're sure now you can get home?' I gave it one last go. Hope springing eternal.

'Ja.' She looked around at the sea of admiring male faces turned towards her. 'I'm sure.'

I was sure too. 'OK,' I said. 'See you around.'

As I nosed on to the main Rathmines road, two carloads of grim-faced men turned into the quiet street I was just leaving, their drivers in blue uniforms. I watched in my mirror as they pulled in to the kerb behind the lines of cars of my recent fellow revellers, and shuddered. Half a mile further along, a white Mercedes passed me doing ninety. Though it was only a blur, I recognised the two minders in the front. The back-seat area was blinded by curtains. It slowed briefly, jumped a red light and shot off up along the canal. I checked my mirror expecting to see squad cars in hot pursuit, but there was only emptiness behind.

That night I slept fitfully between dreams of Marnie and Les and Phil and Harry and Jack and how close I'd come to being caught in a dragnet which could have ended up with me being struck off the Register.

2

My tyres swished through evidence of what the radio had
called 'heavy pre-dawn showers in all areas', but by the time I
reached Maynooth, the ominous grey blanket loitering
overhead had been hustled on by an army of small clouds, the
rearguard of which was now swabbing its way eastward,
leaving the sky up ahead a hot dry blue. By the time I turned
left in Kinnegad, there was steam rising from the fields of lush
aftergrass and the long empty road ahead shimmered in haze.

I reached Knockmore and located Steele's house just in
time to join them for lunch and an hour later I'd been
installed in Fernditch, my home for the next while: a classic
whitewashed, thick-thatched, climbing-rose-covered cottage
in an acre of garden – all in all, very much the des. res.
Looking over my shoulder as I followed Steele back down the
lobelia-edged path towards the gate, I reckoned that, if I
could only induce her to travel west, Marnie might very well
be tempted to move in for the duration.

We had a hectic afternoon. First Steele showed me around
the surgery, kennels, cattery, and the loose boxes for larger
in-patients, giving me a quick rundown on the various
inmates. Next came the office, the domain of Eileen who
doubled as nurse, secretary and practice manager, and to
whom, he informed me, I could turn in almost any crisis. As
we headed out on the afternoon rounds, Steele pointed out
important landmarks – crucial crossroads, alternative routes,
shortcuts. I ended up doing most of the work. He didn't ask

me to . . . I just said, when we got to the first case that, if he liked, I'd see to it and he said fine, and that was the pattern after that. As the afternoon wore on, he looked less and less worried about leaving his beloved practice in a stranger's hands.

'Well . . . what do you think?' he asked. We were about half-way through our list of calls.

'So far, it all seems fairly routine,' I replied. 'No surprises in store? I once did a locum for a practice which had a large salmon farm on its books.'

'No surprises. There's one client who runs what amounts to a private zoo but he has an exhaustive knowledge of his animals and he rarely needs attention. And they're the only exotica. Unless of course,' he added after a reflective pause, 'you want to include Catamaran.'

'*Catamaran?* You mean . . . *the* Catamaran?'

'The Catamaran.'

'He's here?'

'Oh yes. Down the road at Bally Ard, Gilbert Norris's place. Where he was born. Norris owns one of the nine shares in Catamaran.'

'An inspired move that, keeping one share.'

'Keeping?' he snorted. 'Not keeping! *Buying!* Catamaran was sold along with the other foals. Norris bought back in.'

'So! I have the great Catamaran as a potential patient! Wow! I'd have presumed he'd be somewhere on the Curragh. Ah well . . . I suppose, when all's said and done, he's just another horse. He must be worth a fortune, though. Never beaten, was he?'

'Never. Never even looked like it. As for what he'd be worth . . . that would be hard to say. He's insured for twenty-five million but he's worth a lot more now.'

'Oh goody, goody!' I said sarcastically. 'Just what I need: Catamaran with a heart attack or an acute fit of the vapours. How's his health?'

'Fine. He had a cut on his nose a few weeks ago but it was nothing much. Anyway we'll be seeing him soon. I want to

11

introduce you to him. And to Norris. As you can imagine, security is pretty tight, and I'd like you to call in at least once a week as I do, just to have a look, so we'd better smooth your passage with Norris and old Jack in the gate lodge.'

We made Bally Ard our last stop. I was introduced to Jack, the gatekeeper, and had my features closely scrutinised and, presumably, committed to memory, as he opened the massive double gates and swung them to.

The house was a grey stone affair set among pleasant gardens and lawns. The driveway, which curved gracefully up from the gate, had, over the years, become a canyon between tall rhododendron hedges which cut off any view of the house itself until we were almost upon it so that it was impossible to see it in its entirety; there was, however, an overall impression of impending dilapidation. Norris, Steele told me, had been widowed some years before and seemed to have lost interest in the place since. I stayed in the car while Steele climbed the steps to the front door and rang the bell. Almost at once, an odd-looking mongrel appeared from around the side of the house and came bounding over to Steele, tongue lolling in welcome. They were obviously old pals and Steele bent, tickling a nondescript brownish ear until the door was opened by Gilbert Norris. He was short and stocky with a shock of white hair and his ruddy weather-beaten features made it difficult to guess his age with any accuracy — fifty-five to sixty-five perhaps. His legs were bowed, indicating a lifetime in the saddle.

They spoke briefly. Norris looked over at the car (obviously Steele had mentioned me), then Steele turned and beckoned. I joined them on the doorstep and introductions were made. Norris turned as if to lead us into the house, mentioning something about joining him for an evening drink, but Steele declined on the grounds that he had to go home and pack.

'That's a pity. But if you can't, then you can't.'

'Some other time, Gilbert. We just dropped by to take a look at Catamaran before I go. I want Frank to see him.'

Norris didn't seem any too pleased at having his evening snifter postponed for some sightseeing. 'But . . . why do you want to see him?'

'Just to introduce them. It'll only take a minute.'

'I don't know, Peter,' Norris protested. 'He'll have settled down for the evening now. It's going to get him all worked up to have strangers around.' He turned to me. 'The stud season isn't all that long over and he's going to get the wrong idea if there's activity in the yard.'

Personally I'd have given up at that point, but Steele was adamant.

'It's really quite important, Gilbert. I want Frank to see that nose wound while I'm here. He has to know what it's like now to be able to judge its progress later . . . No?'

'But that nose thing was ages ago, for God's sake! I'd really rather not disturb him . . .'

I was getting embarrassed. Norris was looking at me as if I was some kind of spoilt brat nuisance demanding to see the horse for no good reason, regardless of the trouble involved for one and all, including the horse. I glanced at Steele to give him an it-doesn't-matter sign but he didn't notice so I shrugged apologetically at Norris, while Steele pressed on. Of course what was really worrying him was the fact that I might be overawed if I did have to attend the great animal; and it was quite likely that I would be. Catamaran was world famous. During his racing career, he had taken on and hammered all comers from all over the world; winning record prize money, he had galloped through the record books . . . Yes, I reckoned I might be in awe of him.

'I think, Gilbert, that the insurance people would expect me to hand him over formally,' Steele said, a bit stiffly.

'OK. If you insist. I'll get my boots.' Norris gave up the argument and, without much grace, went into the house leaving us standing on the step. On the way to the yard, which was down past the house some few hundred yards along a farm road, Norris returned to his theme: 'I really don't think, Peter that this is at all necessary. After all, if Mr . . . eh mm . . .'

'Samson.'

'If Mr Samson does have to attend Catamaran, then I'm quite sure the horse won't be too upset to find that he doesn't have his usual vet in attendance. Sensitive they may be, these thoroughbreds, but this . . .' He shrugged.

'Gilbert, I think it's essential that we introduce them – just so that there are no surprises if they do have to see each other. On either side.'

'I'd still prefer we didn't upset him,' Norris persisted. 'He wasn't quite himself yesterday evening.'

'Why? What was wrong?' Steele slowed, his tone sharpening.

'Well . . . he had a bit of a shiver and he didn't eat his meal with the usual relish.'

'What? Why on earth didn't you call me?' Steele asked, flabbergasted. Obviously a 'bit of a shiver' in a horse of Catamaran's value was enough to set up a tremor of the order of 6.7 on the Richter Scale in his vet. 'My God, Gilbert, you can't be too careful! You know that! The time to get all these chills and flu's is at the very start! You should have called!'

'Well it was so slight, it didn't seem anything to worry about. I said I'd leave it overnight, and this morning he was back to his old self again.'

'Well that settles it. We'll have to take a look at him now.' Steele strode on purposefully, increasing his pace.

We stopped at tall double gates of vertical iron bars which came into sharp points at their tops and while Norris went through the complicated opening process – which included a combination padlock as well as two other padlocks, and an electronic device which was released by the insertion of a plastic card into a slot in one of the pillars – I surveyed the yard beyond.

There was a row of loose boxes diagonally across to the left, about twelve in all, all with the top halves of their doors open, hooked to the wall to prevent them slamming closed in a sudden gust and decapitating any of the occupants that might be having a quiet look around. At the sound of the gate swinging inwards on an incongruously squeaky hinge, a head appeared in one of the doors about half-way down the row. Only one head appeared and, as its muzzle had a bright purple patch on it, I deduced that the head belonged to the fabled Catamaran, the purple patch being caused by a wound dressing containing gentian violet.

'And how's my big fella this evening? Ay? How's the luvly boy?' Norris began baby-talking the horse while we were still a good ten yards away. Liquid dark eyes in a rich bay-brown head regarded our approach with supreme indifference, cocked ears rotating like radar dishes as the strong jaw worked rhythmically without cease on something crunchy. Then, as we got within arm's length, the head withdrew and vanished into the dark interior of the box.

'Oh!' pouted Norris. 'That's not very polite, now, is it? Who's being a naughty boy? C'mon Cat! I've got someone new for you to meet.'

There was the sound of a door closing from behind us and we turned. A man of about my own age and build with a head of copper curls, so bright it was almost orange, came ambling across the yard. He walked slowly, buttoning his shirt as he came, his pace unconsciously measured to arrive as the last button was done up.

'Evening, Mr Steele,' he said in the soft-sharp accent of Cork.

'Good evening, Tom. I'd like you to meet Mr Samson who'll be looking after things for me while I'm away. Tom Kelly, Frank Samson.'

We shook hands, muttering wordless 'pleased to meet you' noises.

'We'd like to have a look at Catamaran, Tom. Perhaps you wouldn't mind taking him out for us.'

'Right you are, Mr Steele. I'll just get his bridle from the tack room.'

'And Tom . . .' Norris called after the retreating figure.

'Yes sir?'

'Bring a rug for him too.'

'A *rug*, sir?'

15

'Yes Tom, a rug.' Kelly looked puzzled for a moment, then turned and continued on to the tack room. 'The evenings are getting a bit chilly, don't you think?' Norris turned to me.

'Well,' I shrugged, 'perhaps a very little . . .' In fact, to me, it didn't seem at all cold. The warm sun was still a good three or four hours above the paling horizon, but I didn't argue. Like their human counterparts, animal prima donnas probably liked to have their petty, precious eccentricities pandered to.

The groom returned, bridle in one hand and a light rug, the equine equivalent of a string vest, draped over the other. Without a word he passed through the door of the box and a moment later emerged leading Catamaran. We stood back, giving the animal plenty of clearance, waiting for him to settle.

'He's always a bit frisky when we take him out, especially at an unusual hour. He probably thinks there's a mare to be covered. The stud season isn't long over,' Norris repeated, 'and the memories survive. He'll quieten down after another few weeks.'

While Norris was explaining this to me, I studied the famous horse. I had seen many pictures of him – at one stage, he appeared in the press more often than did the politicians – but the three-dimensional, live image was a totally different experience. Through the mesh of the light rug, I could sense rather than see solid muscle burgeoning beneath taut brown skin. Whinnying in sharp bursts, he reared and bucked alternately like a rocking horse, looking around alertly for the mare he expected to be awaiting his attentions in the covering shed. At last, helped by the groom's soothing tones, he got the message and settled down. Only then did we approach him gingerly.

Steele examined his eyes, felt the pulse in the artery lying on the curve of his jaw, peered up his nostrils and palpated the glands lying in the fork of his mandible behind the root of his tongue. Everyone was silent during the examination except Steele who said things like 'Mmmmmm!' and 'Huh!' intermittently.

'And he ate perfectly normally today, Tom?' He glanced at the groom.

'A1, Mr Steele. He's in great fettle. That nose thing didn't knock a feather out of him. He was never better.'

'Well he certainly seems fine. I don't think we need bother taking his temperature.' He turned to me. 'That's an ordeal, Frank. He hates it. Here, take a look at this nose.' I moved closer and inspected the purple-sprayed area on the velvet-black muzzle. 'It's almost cleared up now,' he continued. 'It never *was* very bad, only a slice of skin missing – about the size of a fifty-pence piece. The subcutaneous tissues weren't damaged at all, luckily enough.'

'How did it happen?'

'We don't know, really. Probably the tin nailed over the door to stop him from chewing the timber. It only went a couple of inches down on the inside, but the edge seemed flush with the timber so I can't see how he managed to jag himself on it. Anyway, we've replaced the tin with a sheet which goes all the way to the bottom now, so, if that was the problem, it won't happen again.' He stepped back a few paces, viewed the horse overall for a moment, then nodded at the groom. 'That's fine thanks, Tom. You can put him back in now.'

We left soon after, refusing Norris's second offer of a drink.

'Well then, *bon voyage*, Peter. Wish Michael and his new bride every happiness from me.' His argumentative mood seemed to have been left behind in the stable yard.

On the way home, Steele asked me if I was a racing man and I replied that no, I couldn't call myself that.

'Hah! I thought not.'

'What made you think that?'

'A racing man would have been dumbstruck at being so close to Catamaran.'

'Oh I was impressed all right.'

'Yes, but not dumbstruck. And it's better that way.' After a moment's reverie, he continued. 'I used to be a racing man myself. I still go now and then but I gave up betting . . .'

He seemed to be awaiting my 'why' in order to kickstart the rest of the story, so I complied. 'Why?'

'Can't trust anyone.'

'Bookies?'

'No, not the bookies. The bookies are all right. They're as honest as daylight compared to the jockeys and trainers! I gave it up because one day I happened to overhear a conversation between the trainer and rider of a horse, a supposed dead cert I had just lost a small fortune on. "How did he go out there?" asks the trainer. "So-so," says the jockey. "I could have beaten the four ahead of me, no bother, but I'm not so sure about the ones behind." Could you believe that?'

I had dinner with the Steeles, wished them *bon voyage* and, shortly after 9.30, walked the half-mile to Fernditch, which stood on a quiet road on the outskirts of town. It was owned by Marion Steele's brother, who had been travelling in the States for some months. My brief visit earlier in the day had afforded me the opportunity for only the most cursory of examinations but I had liked what little I had seen. Now I explored it more fully and was impressed. The kitchen and bathroom were well equipped and modern but the living quarters were furnished as one would expect of a wealthy confirmed bachelor – lots of old leather and dark wood. The only modern items in the living room were the TV/video unit and the hi-fi/CD system, which were housed in a single high-tech column occupying one side of the heavy bookcase that covered one wall of the room. It was a welcome change from the usual room in a boarding-house or small hotel, or a spartan flat over the surgery.

An inspection of the kitchen cupboards and fridge revealed that someone, presumably Mrs Steele, had thoughtfully laid in essential provisions, and I made myself coffee.

On page six of the paper I had bought on my walk to the cottage, there was a short article about Black Marias having to be called in to cart away all the people who had been arrested during a raid by Drug Squad detectives on a house in the

Rathmines area of Dublin the previous night. They were to have been arraigned in court this morning. I thanked my lucky stars. Though no names were mentioned, I knew it had to be the party I'd been at. The cops couldn't have missed it. The pungent fug that hung above that house must have been like the Star in the East. I turned on the news but it was half over and there was no mention of the raid.

I went to bed and dreamt uneasily of the hard-faced minders. I awoke in the small hours, got up, drew the curtains, went to the loo, had a glass of water, and settled back to sleep, but the goons were still there, waiting for me to step back out through the doors of sleep . . .

Sunday passed uneventfully. There were a few calls and I found my way to them without too many wrong turns – Steele's hand-drawn map made up in local knowledge for what it lacked in scale accuracy. Later, after a refreshing swim off the rocks beyond the town beach, my quartered *Sunday Tribune*, propped against the water jug on the lunch table at a local restaurant, informed me that I could kiss goodbye to Marnie. Under the heading DRUG SQUAD ARRESTS, I found her name – inevitably bracketed by the names of her three friends – among the list of foreigners against whom immediate deportation orders had been issued. At the end of the report there was a veiled suggestion that, though the Drug Squad had rounded up lots of minnows, a prize catch had managed to give them the slip. I knew. I had seen him with his minders in his white Merc. giving them the slip at about ninety, up along the canal. The menace of the night immediately muscled into my head again and, in the broad light of day, I shuddered.

3

Though it was to blow up in my face before evening, Monday began well. When I arrived at the surgery at 8.30 I found a full waiting-room but, with Eileen supplying pertinent information on the foibles and quirks of patients and owners, I cleared the lot in little over an hour. If there is such a thing as a normal morning surgery in veterinary practice, then this was it – a few scratchy dogs, one or two with ear problems, a handful of vaccinations, wormings, and a lame cat. Afterwards, as we sipped coffee, she talked me through the morning round of farm visits, giving directions and drawing little sketch maps as required, and I got through the nine calls almost as quickly as Steele himself would. So far, so good.

On my way back to the surgery, I found myself passing the high wall of Bally Ard and I slowed down; a glance at my watch showed me I had time on my hands, so I swung in. Waiting for Jack, the elderly gatekeeper to answer the bell, I hoped Gilbert Norris would not misconstrue my calling so soon after I had last seen Catamaran as over-anxiety on my part or, worse still, an abuse of privilege by some sort of celebrity groupie. What the hell. I wanted to check out the horse. Steele's orders.

By alternately ringing the bell and blowing my horn, I managed, at last, to attract Jack's attention and he came and peered with myopic suspicion at me for a long time before recognition finally dawned. 'Oh yes! The vet! You're the new vet, aren't you?'

'That's right,' I nodded. I'd been telling him so all along, in varying degrees of loudness, but obviously he was either a man who liked to make up his own mind about these things or he was hard of hearing.

'What's wrong with the stallion? Himself said nothing about sending for you. He'd have told me on his way out. To expect you, like.'

'Nobody sent for me,' I shouted. 'Mr Steele asked me to keep an eye on Catamaran, so I thought I'd call as I was passing.'

'Oh, I see.'

'Mr Norris has gone out, you say?'

'Aye. Near an hour ago.'

'Is Tom at the yard?'

'Tom's gone home. To Cork.'

'Oh . . . Well if there's no one . . .' I began, thinking of the locked yard gate.

'His mother's in the hospital. They broke into her house on Saturday night and frightened the poor creature half to death. Shock, Tom said.'

'Who's they?'

'What was that?'

'I said : "Who broke in?" '

'Hooligans. Thugs! Who d'you think?' He sounded as if he expected me to have known that. 'The poor woman lives on her own. I'd like to see them try it here . . .'

'I hope she wasn't badly hurt.'

'Shock, Tom said,' he repeated.

'Maybe I can call again later . . .'

'Young Hynes from the town is looking after things at the yard,' he said, inserting a key. 'But take your time driving up there. I'll have to phone him that it's the vet that's coming 'cause you're new and he won't know you and if he doesn't know you, he won't let you in and then you won't be able to see the horse.' A man who believed in spelling things out.

He opened the great gates and waved me through. I saluted him as I passed.

'Young' Hynes, who looked a couple of years older than

me, was already at the gate when I arrived and we went through the 'who-sent-for-you?-what's-wrong?' routine again.

'It's just a passing visit,' I assured him as he opened the gate, a far simpler procedure from the inside; he removed the padlock and turned the handle. 'I want to check up on him. Mr Norris thought he was a bit off colour at the weekend. How has he seemed to you this morning?'

'Fine, I suppose. But then, I don't know a lot about horses – I'm not a groom as such. I stay here if there's no one else about, because there's supposed to be someone in the yard all the time and . . .'

He lost my attention there. Even from half the yard away, I could see a change in the horse. His eye lacked the obvious fire of Saturday evening and he didn't retreat into his box as we approached; he regarded me with a calm docility that disturbed me as I stood in front of him, a prudent arm's length away. In the interests of absolute safety, Hynes had pulled up a few steps to the rear. I raised a tentative hand towards the violet muzzle and the horse didn't move; nor did he object when I touched him and began to stroke his face. I peered at the nose wound but there was no sign of a breakdown in the healing process. I checked his eye and it too, seemed fine – not in any way as spirited as it had been, but clear and free from discharge. His nostrils were clean and there was no swelling of the glands under his jaw; his pulse rate was marginally elevated but only just. I peered past him, into the relative dark of the box and immediately noticed the full hay net hanging on the back wall, the sweet grey-green stalks bulging through the mesh.

'Did you give him that hay?' I asked, knowing full well he hadn't. I couldn't see Hynes entering Catamaran's box, even with the distraction of a stuffed hay net.

'No. The boss did.'

'When?'

'I don't know. Before I got here this morning.'

'What time was that?'

'Eightish. Give or take.'

'He hasn't eaten any of it. It's nearly one now. Five hours. At least five hours.'

Catamaran was off his grub again like Norris had reported a few days ago – hardly cause for panic, but still, Steele had been pretty alarmed. I looked again. It was hard to see the horse's body because of his colour – dark skin in a dark box. 'When do you expect the boss back?' I asked.

'He didn't say.'

'Do you think we could take him out of the box ourselves?'

'I don't know. Are you any good with horses?'

'So-so. Maybe we can do it in easy stages, one step at a time. Let's see first if he'll let us put the bridle on without us having to open the door.'

Hynes looked unsure for a moment, then he shrugged: 'You're the doctor.' His tone had more than a touch of Pilate asking for the hand basin. 'I'll get it from the tack room.'

When he came back, he handed me the bridle and stepped pointedly away. I arranged the leathers over my left hand, the bit stretched in the span of my fingers. Catching the horse by the forelock with my right hand, I pressed the bit against his lips and with just moderate resistance, he let it into his mouth and began to chew on it. Slowly I moved the brow-band up along his forehead until I could push the poll-strap over his ears. I fastened the buckle of the cheek-strap and it was done. 'So far, so good,' I said over my shoulder. 'Now for the dicey part.'

'Taking him out,' Hynes replied, and he moved even further away to make sure that there was absolutely no doubt that, if anything went wrong, I was on my own.

Wishing I had gone myself to the tack room to look for something more substantial than the flimsy bridle – like a cavisson – I eased the door open, all the time waiting for the surge of power; but it didn't come, at least not in the strength I was steeling myself for. He came through quickly enough and wheeled me round a couple of times, but soon settled. I held him a while, talking softly and soothingly, tense in case he was only drawing his breath, but the moment when he might have exploded came and went and I knew I had him. I walked him around the yard a few times; he tossed his head and walked crabwise a fair bit, but there was none of the wildness I had seen before and, after four or five rounds, we had settled the matter of who was leading whom. While all this was going on, Hynes was constantly on the move too and, with the skill of a very small referee in a heavyweight boxing ring, he nimbly managed to maintain the maximum distance between himself and the other occupants who might, indeed were *expected* to, erupt in a flurry of violence without warning. At last I managed to cajole him into holding the horse and stood with him for a moment until he felt confident enough to go solo. Then I stepped back and observed my patient.

He looked fine. On physical signs alone, I couldn't fault him. He was a normal-looking thoroughbred stallion (apart from the purple muzzle), well muscled, strong, alert and eager. But he wasn't as fiery as he had been on Saturday evening and he had had a shivering attack only a few days previously and he hadn't eaten his hay and he was my responsibility. Also he was worth millions. I decided to give him the full treatment. As much for my sake as for his.

I checked the heartbeat beneath his elbow, then moved the bell of the stethoscope over his ribcage on both sides, carefully sounding the great lungs for the slightest wrong sounds: wheezes, squeaks, gurgles or pants. There were none. I listened to his abdomen; there was nothing untoward in that department either. That left his temperature, usually the first thing I do, but mindful of Steele's warning of how much this horse hated it, I had left it until last. Cautioning Hynes to hold him tight, I gently slid my hand along the top of his rump. Catamaran wheeled away. I tried again, and this time he confined his protest to some vigorous tail swishing. Slowly I grasped the root of the tail and raised it away from the body. The horse made anxious noises and looked nervous but didn't object beyond that. I reached round the back of his haunches and gingerly probed for the anus. He whinnied anxiously as I inserted the thermometer, but he let me do it. I could have asked Hynes to pick up a foreleg, which would have reduced the danger of my being kicked, but he was too uneasy and was hanging on to the bridle for dear life. A minute later I withdrew the thermometer. 100.5. Perfectly normal. The comfort of this was offset by the fact that he had let me take his temperature so docilely in the first place.

'How is it?' Hynes asked, getting involved.

'Spot on. Normal as can be. I can't find anything wrong but he just doesn't seem himself; he could be getting a flu or some such. I presume he's had the usual vaccinations?'

'I wouldn't know, but I'd say so.' Hynes shrugged.

I stood back again, regarding the horse speculatively, and I was still uneasy. I decided to go a step further.

'Hold him a moment while I go to the Land Rover; I want to take a few blood samples for the lab.'

'A b-blood sample!' The uneasiness came flooding back into Hynes's eyes.

'It's no big deal. Somehow horses never seem to mind it too much.'

I fetched several evacuated vials with different-coloured stoppers, each containing a different anticoagulant; when a double-ended needle pierced, first the blood vessel and then the rubber stopper, blood was sucked in by the vacuum. I also fetched my camera – this was too good an opportunity to miss. I laid the camera on the ground, a safe distance away. Then, having swabbed a few inches of the jugular furrow, I pressed my thumb hard in to stop the flow of blood from the head. Immediately, the vein filled, thick as my middle finger and turgid. I waited for a moment before postively shoving the needle through. Catamaran winced but that was all. One after the other I placed the vials in the holder, pierced them and filled them with the warm red-black blood. I rolled the vials gently between my palms rather than shaking them, to ensure that the anticoagulant mixed evenly with the blood. That finished, I fished out the camera.

'Do you mind holding him just another minute? I'd like to take a few photos. Do you think Mr Norris would mind?'

'Why should he? It'll do no harm, will it?'

'No. I'll take a few of the horse first and then maybe you

can take one of me holding him. After all, I'm never going to have another patient like him, am I?'

First I took a close-up of the nose wound for my 'interesting case box'; admittedly, the wound was no great shakes as an interesting case, but the muzzle on which it had occurred was. Then I took a few of his head, one straight on and one of each profile. To complete the set, I moved back to focus on the whole animal, giving Hynes, each time, a chance to slick back his hair and compose himself rigidly into an attitude of strained casualness.

'OK. My turn now. How are you on cameras?'

'I know as much about them as a hen knows about a bank holiday.'

I gave him a quick run-through, inclining the camera towards him, pointing out the bits. 'You can't go wrong,' I said encouragingly. But, as I turned the wind-on lever, it jammed. 'Aww damn!' I cursed in disgust. 'The blasted film's finished and I don't have another! Ah well . . . some other time.'

I began to gather up my belongings and just as I was about to tell Hynes he could put the horse back in, Catamaran, raising his tail, passed dung. On impulse I thought I might as well pull out all the stops for my priceless patient and eliminate the possibility of intestinal worms too. There was a laboratory of sorts at the surgery, the main equipment being a rather ancient microscope – it would be adequate for my purposes, however; all I wanted was a quick glance. I didn't expect to find any – worms are invariably a sign of bad management. I wouldn't even have considered the possibility had Catamaran's bowel movement not taken place when it did. Using a corner of a plastic bag, I picked up a section of the steaming, pungent waste, and wrapped it.

'Tell Mr Norris I'll phone him this evening some time. And tell him to keep a close eye on the horse.'

I waited until Catamaran was safely back in his box and left. At the main gate, I told the old man that the horse was fine and drove on, hoping that he was.

Beside me, on the passenger seat, was the box containing

Catamaran's blood samples and, wrapped in the corner of a plastic bag, a couple of ounces of rose fertiliser which were going to cause no end of trouble before I was much older.

I had soup and sandwiches at the pub across the road from the office and thought about Catamaran. Back at the surgery, I typed a covering letter for the blood samples, not mentioning the horse's name, and addressed it to the local Regional Veterinary Laboratory. Then I investigated the laboratory equipment. It was pretty basic but I found a bottle of saturated zinc sulphate solution and a McMaster slide, a slide with a raised, grid-ruled chamber which permitted counting of the number of eggs present in a measured amount of faeces.

I broke up the dung and removed some of the larger pieces of matter, including a few short stalks of hay, three or four grains of oats, and two whole sunflower seeds. The rest I added to the solution, swizzling it with the end of a ballpoint until it became a suspension of separate particles. While I washed the McMaster slide, I let the mixture stand, to allow any worm eggs present to float to the surface. I filled the chamber from the surface of the suspension, placed the slide on the stage of the microscope and adjusted it until the blurred circle of light and all it contained came into sharp focus – as I expected, nothing but broken pieces of vegetable matter and shreds of sloughed gut lining. I moved the slide a little – nothing there either. I moved it again and suddenly, to my astonishment, there, trapped in the circle of light, lurking amongst the jumbled organic debris, was the unmistakable dark oval of a worm egg. Catamaran had bowel worms!

Roundworms parasite almost all animals, each species of animal having its own species of roundworm. Though different species parasitise different organs, all share some characteristics, notably their life cycles, and the way in which they spread from host to host. Adult roundworms attached to, for example, the lining of the small intestine of a herbivore, lay numerous eggs which find their way to the outside world via the animal's faeces. Outside the body, they hatch and pass through a number of immature larval stages before becoming infective; only infective larvae can grow to maturity when swallowed by the right animal, and thus complete the life cycle. Larvae are actively mobile and usually crawl away from the dung pat in which they hatch, often congregating at the tips of grass stalks to improve their chances of being swallowed by a grazing animal. And so they spread from one animal to another. Where animals are confined in fields or paddocks, the chances of infective-stage larvae being swallowed are very much enhanced.

For some reason, newly swallowed larvae don't go directly to the target organ. Most roundworms are parasites of the digestive tract so they find themselves 'at home' as soon as they are swallowed. Yet, before settling down, the larvae of many species embark on a tour of other body organs causing damage as they go, the severity of the damage depending on the numbers of larvae on the move at the time. Horse-worm larvae tend to go to the great arteries of the abdominal cavity. They burrow into the walls of these blood vessels causing a dangerous weakening and consequent bulging which, in medical terms, is called an aneurysm. If this ruptures, as it most likely will sooner or later, the animal bleeds to death. In the case of major arteries, death would follow in a matter of minutes. I saw it happen, but only once, and that was in a donkey. The presence of such potentially lethal parasites in Catamaran was inexcusable, and, apart from the dangers to himself, the thought of him spreading deadly larvae on to the very paddocks where, come springtime, foals would graze was horrific.

This time measuring, I repeated the test several times, and came up with an average count of 1,100 eggs per gram of faeces, a significant burden.

Eileen arrived back from her lunch break but I decided against asking her about the parasite control regime at Bally Ard. There was something amiss, but until I could figure out what exactly it was, or who was responsible, the less said the better.

I exonerated Norris, the experienced breeder, and Steele, parasite control would be one of his major concerns. Perhaps whoever was supposed to dose Catamaran, through laziness or fear, only *pretended* to do it; if that was the case, then I was willing to bet it wasn't Tom Kelly. Or maybe, at Bally Ard, a resistant strain of *Strongylus vulgaris* had evolved, a strain resistant to modern drugs? Unlikely, though not impossible. Perhaps Catamaran had learned to hold the dose at the back of his tongue and spit it out when no one was looking; or perhaps it made him sick and he'd vomit it before it had time to kill the worms, though surely someone would have noticed, as horses rarely vomit. Or maybe Bally Ard had bought a defective batch of worm medicine?

The discovery of the worm eggs posed an ethical dilemma. The one thing I was *not* going to do was tell Norris, he would be extremely angry, justifiably so, and in the subsequent, inevitable furore, all concerned would be running for cover and looking for scapegoats. The danger was that P.R. Steele, not being present to defend himself, might end up with the short stick. I didn't doubt for a moment that the large pharmaceutical firms would shaft him without the batting of a corporate eye. Eventually what it all came down to was a question of my own responsibilities and my primary allegiance was to my patient, Catamaran. As soon as I finished my afternoon rounds, I could nip round to Bally Ard and get a good worm dose into him; but where my secondary duty lay was a toss-up. My client, Norris? My employer, Steele? After a brief tussle with my conscience, Steele won. What decided me was nothing more noble than self-interest: if I could be seen, in any way, not to have protected his best interests, then other practitioners would be that much less willing to entrust their practices to me. That made up my mind. There was nothing in any book of ethics which said a man had to commit business suicide. Steele would be the first to know on his return. Still worrying over the problem, I set out on my afternoon rounds.

I don't know when I began to wonder if the red car behind me was following me. Driving a Land Rover without side windows in the back, I rely heavily on my wing mirrors, flicking my eyes at them every few seconds. It probably didn't register in the traffic in town and I don't think it really made an impression until I caught sight of it on the long, deserted mountain road that bucked and wound its way across the transverse folds of the mountainous spine that separated the plains around Knockmore from the southern coastal strip. I tried changing speed, but the gap between us remained constant; the car stayed some four to five hundred yards back.

At the end of a longish stretch, I stopped and got out, ostensibly to check a tyre, and the car came on to the stretch as I bent and pulled over. It was a red Sierra with one occupant. I kicked the tyre a few times and drove off. It kept with me as I did a few calls along the coast, and I was just beginning to wonder if I shouldn't call the gardaí when it vanished. As soon as I crossed the bridge that was the only way on to a chain of islands which stretched for a further twelve miles, I was on my own.

By the time I was crossing back over the bridge a couple of hours later, I'd completely forgotten about the car when suddenly it reappeared. For a brief moment, I worried that someone was going to attack me on the lonely mountain road, then I figured if he intended me any harm, he'd already had ample time. Perhaps he was just keeping an eye on me. Not, mind you, that I felt really great about that, either. But anxious to get back and give Catamaran his worm dose, I decided to ignore him and headed back into the mountains.

On my way to the summit, I began to pick up a weak signal on the radio-telephone – Eileen trying to get me. I stopped twice to eliminate engine noise, but the great bulk of the mountain which reared gaunt, granite strewn and sedge brown between us, prevented any decent reception. In the shallow valleys I could hear nothing at all, but as I crested each successive ridge her voice would come in, plaintive, urgent and indecipherable. With a growing sense of unease I wondered why she was keeping up a continuous broadcast, like the radio officer of a stricken vessel sending out a constant stream of *Mayday*, *Mayday* into the forlorn ether above a desolate sea.

The higher I climbed, the stronger the signal became. Though it was still garbled, I thought I caught the word 'Norris' and suddenly my palms were sweating. Surely it couldn't be Catamaran! Not with an aneurysm! Not on my first day! I tried to respond but my transmitter was not as powerful as hers and I knew from her incessant calling that she wasn't registering my efforts. Replacing the handset, I concentrated on driving.

It wasn't until I breasted the last summit that I could hear her plainly. From that point, I could see Knockmore-on-Sea in the distance. Spread out on the green plain below me, the sun reflecting from its windows, it looked like a multi-gemmed pendant on a jeweller's tray, the silvered river its chain.

'Base to Mobile One, Base to Mobile One, are you receiving me?'

'I read you, base. What's the problem?'

'Oh! Where are you Frank?'

'On my way in. Just on top of the hill. What's the problem?'

'Go straight to Bally Ard. It's Catamaran. The house-keeper has been calling every couple of minutes for the last half-hour. It sounds bad.'

'What's wrong?'

'She's not sure. Mr Norris just told her to say it was very urgent.'

'Call and tell her I'm on my way. And see if you can get any details.'

'OK. There's the phone now. It'll probably be her again.'

With thoughts of all kinds of catastrophes filling my head, especially ruptured aneurysms, I twisted my way down to the valley floor, careered through the town and out on to the road to the north-west which led to Bally Ard. Twenty minutes later, when I was still a couple of miles from Norris's place, I called base again.

'Eileen? Do you read me? Eileen? Eileen?'

'Loud and clear.'

'Anything?'

'Nothing. She just said to hurry.'

'Nearly there. Another couple of minutes.'

'I'll stay on here in the surgery for a while. In case you need anything.'

'Thanks. If you haven't heard from me by six, lock up. But thanks anyway. You're a star. Over and out.'

'Good luck.'

4

The gates stood wide, so I changed down into second and roared through, tyres spinning, almost knocking down Jack who stood immediately inside waving me urgently on. Broad-leafed rhododendron branches slapped along the sides of the jeep as I hugged the right-hand curve of the driveway. I slid to a halt in a shower of gravel on the semicircular parking space. Norris, who had obviously heard my approach, trotted bandily over to me and one look at him was enough to confirm my worst fears. This was no storm in a teacup, no groundless panic by a hypochondriac owner which would disappear magically as soon as the vet arrived. Despair and anguish were etched on his face as if they were there to stay. Mentally preparing myself for a major catastrophe, I opened the door.

'It's Catamaran,' he wailed and, before I could ask what was wrong, he blurted out: 'He's dead!'

Catamaran *dead!* The awful reality began to seep into my shocked senses. Was it an aneurysm? Or had I missed something obvious this morning? Was it my fault? Even partially? If it was an aneurysm, then how could I explain it without getting Steele into trouble? Automatically I was battening down the hatches, going into damage-limitation mode.

'When?' I asked. It came out as a squeak.

'He was dead when I found him. I don't know when.'

At least ('Oh thank you, God, thank you!') I couldn't be reproached for not being available when I was needed. The horse hadn't died for want of medical attention. And now I wouldn't have to do anything brilliant either. An ignoble reaction, but regrettably true.

'What happened?' I asked with a bit more composure.

'I don't know!' Blank-eyed, Norris shook his head. 'How could he have got out? The yard gate is still locked! I've got the only key!'

'What do you mean, *out*?' I asked incredulously, the voice a squeak again. 'Outside his *box*?'

'Outside his box, outside the yard, out running loose in the fields . . .'

'But . . . but how? Who let him out?'

'I tell you, I can't understand it!' He shook his head again.

'Mr Norris. How exactly did he die? Tell me what happened? Where did you find him?'

'In the old quarry pit. He must have fallen into it. How am I going to tell the others?'

While Norris was worrying about that, another flood of selfish relief coursed through me. It was an accident! An Act of God! Hallelujah! I became even more composed. 'Perhaps we ought to go and have a look at him,' I suggested, but Norris seemed too dazed to reply. 'Is it far away?' I waited for him to answer but he remained lost in thought. 'Mr Norris?' I prodded.

'What?' He came back to the present.

'This quarry. Is it far from here?'

'No. About half a mile down the farm road.' He pointed a distracted hand in the general direction of the yard.

'We'd best take the Land Rover, then. Come on.' He walked round to the passenger door, climbed on to the seat and, with a great sigh, pulled the door shut.

On the bumpy drive along the rutted track, some more details emerged. He had been out shooting rabbits. He had been walking for half an hour, shot two rabbits in the lower fields, and, on the way back to the house, Patch, his terrier who 'had a great nose', had gone into the thicket which had grown up around the disused limestone pit, and had started to bark furiously, refusing to respond to Norris's summoning whistles. It was when he had gone into the thicket to get Patch that he had found Catamaran, lying dead at the foot of the old quarry face.

'It was horrible!' He shuddered. 'I grabbed the dog and ran as quickly as I could to phone for you. Horrible!' he repeated.

I didn't have the heart to ask him what he had expected me to do for a dead horse. I put it down to human conditioning – doctors are always called when there's a sudden death and his reaction to finding an animal corpse had been to call the animal doctor.

'Stop here.' He touched my elbow. 'It's as near as you'll get.'

Across the fields, some five hundred yards away, there was a small spinney; I presumed from the fact that it grew against a steep escarpment, that this was where the accident had happened. Some of the quicker growing trees had almost reached the height of the cliff-face which I could just see, grey, bare and scrub-topped, behind them.

We trudged along in silence. Norris tending to lag back. At the line of the first brushwood, he stopped. 'Do you need me in there?'

'No. There's nothing you can do. There's nothing anyone can do.'

'Tchah!' he said, mostly to himself, 'it's got to be faced. Come on.'

We pushed through clinging undergrowth, twisting and turning along some invisible path which didn't seem any different to me than any other bush-clogged route he might have chosen. Suddenly, at the edge of a small clearing, he stopped and, averting his head, pointed straight ahead. 'There!' At the foot of a cliff about fifty feet high, in a pool of muddy water, lay Catamaran.

The first time I saw his chest rise, I thought my eyes were playing tricks on me. Then it happened again and I knew that they weren't. An icy hand clutched my heart.

'Jesus!' I breathed. 'That animal is alive!' I glared at Norris, covering my own panic at being suddenly thrust back into a position of full responsibility, but he was standing transfixed, his dazed gaze following the slow, shallow movements of the stallion's chest. 'Christ!' I muttered savagely and pushed roughly past him.

Having been told the horse was dead, I'd brought no equipment with me; everything was locked in the back of the Land Rover a coppice and three wide fields away – ten to fifteen minutes if I ran there and back, and frankly it didn't look, from what I could see, as if Catamaran had that much time left.

I dropped to my knees by his head, the only part of him clear of the muddy water. His eye was flickering rapidly, almost too quickly to see, the eyeball moving up and down in its socket. On the bare ground, the tongue, unnaturally pale, lay limply, covered in grit. His breaths were taken in slowly, reaching a sudden stop so that each one sounded like his last, and then let out again with a faint snort and flapping of the nostril fold. Tenderly I rolled back the black velvet lip. It had lost most of its mobility and the gum beneath was deathly pale. I pressed my index finger down hard on it and held it for a moment; when I took it away the resulting white round area barely contrasted with the cold paleness of the gum, and it took a long time for it to get its faint colour back again. Catamaran was in deep shock, the blood diverted from the peripheral blood vessels to supply maximum oxygen and nutrients to the vital organs which would now be struggling to keep the last spark of life fanned just a little longer. If he was going to be treated, an immediate essential was massive volumes of intravenous fluids, preferably warmed to body heat . . . That was when I noticed the blood in the water, a cloud darker than the brown muddiness of the pool, which, even as I watched, was growing and spreading sluggishly. It had the ominous look of catastrophe.

I reached into the murky water and gingerly felt along the uppermost forelimb from elbow to hoof. I found nothing amiss and I reached deeper to repeat the process with its deeper fellow. I felt around the elbow, then down the forearm to the knee. Nothing wrong there. I moved my hand over the knee, down along the slim cannon bone, and half-way along, felt my fingers sink into pulped flesh. I felt the warm spurt of blood at the same time as the jagged spike of protruding bone. Compound fracture. The shattered bone, having knifed through the skin, was now irrevocably infected and even with the most modern advances in equine orthopaedics, a successful outcome was a remote hope. I noticed another dark cloud behind the first and then a third at the horse's rear. The second cloud emanated from an almost identical fracture, this time in the left hind leg, but it was the third which proved the real last straw. Inside a few seconds, my probing hand met with a jagged end of broken metal protruding from between the horse's buttocks. I eased it out as gently and delicately as I could but it took a long time in coming. It was some three inches long, two wide and about one eighth thick. The blood washed off as I raised it through the water but some flakes of yellow paint still clung to it. The broken edge showed clean grey metal, freshly broken. I guessed it had come from an old abandoned dumper that stood beside me half in the pool – there was a freshly broken edge on a flange of its front bucket. But what made that bit of metal so important was the *position* in which it had lodged. It had been embedded transversely between the buttocks, and that meant that the structures in that area had been severed across. And they included the root of the penis.

I straightened slowly and turned to Norris. The sludge on the bottom of the pool sucked weakly at my boots, nearly toppling me, and I reached out a quick hand to steady myself against the haunch of the dying horse. In the dirty water, blood swirled and coiled into the sluggish eddies of my movements, clouding into indistinguishability, dust to dust, ashes to ashes, blood to mud . . .

Norris had slumped, dazed against a rock. I waded out of the pool and crossed to him. 'There's no chance,' I said quietly. 'I'm going to have to put him down. He's got two broken legs, both compound fractures . . .' I held up the metal flange, '. . . this was stuck in him. It's cut through his penis. Even if he lived he could never breed again. I'm afraid it's useless. I'm sorry'.

He looked up at me, shaking his head in wordless protest. I waited for him to say something and, when he didn't, I said: 'I'll just go and get something to put him out of his misery. You ought to come with me.' As I made to pass him, he caught me by the sleeve.

'Please!' he implored. 'Can't you do something? You can't just kill him like that! Can't you keep him alive for twenty-four hours? I'll have the best surgeons in the world here by morning! All you've got to do is to keep him alive until then! Please!' His voice was shrill.

'I'm sorry, Mr Norris. Believe me, he's beyond help.'

'Think of the loss to the bloodstock lines of the world . . .'

'I've considered everything. The fact remains, he can't be saved. Now, I'm going to get what I need, and I strongly advise you to come with me.'

Norris suddenly gave in, all resistance flowing out of him. He released my sleeve and his hand dropped to his side. 'You're right of course,' he sighed. 'But, if it's got to be done, please do it at once. I can't bear it any longer.'

'As soon as I get what I need.'

'Can't you use my gun?' He pointed. Against a rock, a double-barrelled shotgun was propped; there were two dead rabbits lying beside it. 'I had to leave it to carry Patch to the house. He was hysterical.'

'That'll do,' I said, picking up the gun and breaking it open. Both barrels were loaded. 'Would you prefer to leave? I'll join you in a moment.'

'No, I think I ought to wait.'

'Whatever you say.'

I settled myself on the mud-splashed ground a short distance from the horse's head, lying to get the best line on his forehead. Then, taking careful aim on the intersection of imaginary lines drawn between the inner corner of each eye and the opposite ear, I steadied myself, took a deep breath, held it, and took up the pressure on the first trigger. I squeezed once and, immediately after, pulled the second.

Catamaran gave one massive, convulsive shudder and then slowly relaxed. A brief trickle of thick red-black blood ran from the smoking hole in his forehead, pumped by the last beat of his great heart. His eye closed once, then slowly reopened and rotated upwards to focus on infinity in the eternal, sightless stare of death.

Silence returned slowly to the clearing. The sound of the shots reverberated for a long time, bouncing from the grey wall of rock to the green wall of vegetation, back and forth until it worked its way up and escaped into the air above. The shrill alarm cries of the birds lessened and died and soon the only sound in the clearing was the rustle of the leaves at the tops of those trees high enough to catch the freshening evening breeze.

I arose slowly from the ground and, propping the gun back against the rock, crossed to where Norris stood, immobile as Lot's wife. No words came to me as, side by side, we stood, staring at the worthless carcase of the once-great horse. I waited for him to decide when it was time, but after some minutes I touched his arm. 'I think we ought to go now.' I picked up the gun and the two rabbits. 'Ready?'

There was a huge sigh before he tore his mesmerised eyes away from the corpse. 'Yes. I suppose so.'

'I've got the gun and the rabbits.'

'You can throw the rabbits into the bushes,' he said hollowly.

'It's no trouble. As you've brought them this far . . .'

'No. I don't eat them. It's just that their burrows are dangerous for horses' legs. Throw them away.'

I swung the rabbits a few times and let them go, watching them arc up and into the dense thicket before I followed his dejected figure along the same invisible path. Half-way across the field, Norris broke the silence.

'But how could he have got out? That's what I can't fathom.'

'Have you asked Hynes?' I asked. Out of the blue, I had a sudden awful thought: had we closed the box properly after we had finished with Catamaran in the morning? Then I knew that we had, and I relaxed. Norris had lapsed back into silence.

'Eh . . . Hynes?' he said at last.

'Hynes. The stand-in groom.'

More silence. 'No actually, I didn't. He left once he knew I was back. I didn't see him at all.' The silence resumed.

Most of the journey back to the house passed in the same silence, but as we approached the last turn before the stableyard, he said to me: 'How do you know Hynes?'

'I met him this morning when I called in to the yard.' When he fell silent again, I added: 'Didn't he tell you I'd called? I did ask him to.'

'No. I told you, I didn't see Hynes. Why did you call?'

'Well . . . I was anxious to make sure that nothing happened to Catamaran while he was under my care,' I finished with a mirthless snort.

'Did you find anything wrong with him?'

'Nothing specific. He didn't seem in the best of form, didn't have the same fire in him that I'd seen on Saturday, the same spirit. So I got a bit worried. Naturally.'

'Naturally.'

'But apart from that, he checked out OK. I was going to call you this evening. I told Hynes to tell you. Do you want to stop to take a look at the yard?' I asked as we were passing the gate.

'No. We'd best press on to the house. I need a drink. Jack never mentioned your visit either.'

'I didn't leave a message with Jack.'

'Still. It's strange nobody thought to tell me.'

I was saved from having to answer by our arrival at the front door.

5

Norris didn't need a drink, singular; he needed several and he attacked the Jameson Crested Ten as if there was a distinct possibility that by finishing it off, he might be able to bring his beloved horse back to life, to un-shoot him, to un-break his legs, to break his fall. He was on his fifth double while I nursed my second, well watered with Canada Dry. I hadn't even wanted the first. He drained his glass at a gulp and looked like he was heading for the bottle again.

'Do you not think you ought to call the gardaí?' I asked. That stopped him.

'The *gardaí!*' There wasn't a trace of a slur in his voice.

I shrugged. 'They'll have to be called.' Obviously the idea had not occurred to him.

'For what?' His tone was indignant, as if I had accused him of dropping the horse over the cliff himself.

'To find out exactly how Catamaran managed to get out of his box and out of the yard.' Surely he couldn't have thought it was all over bar the crying? There was all kinds of hassle ahead: pathologist's examination and reports, police investigation, insurance company enquiries, painful meetings of the syndicate . . . He was coming to terms with the tragedy very slowly.

'Do you know, I hadn't even thought that far,' he said quietly after a long pause. 'I'm afraid my thoughts are totally scrambled at the moment. I don't know what I'm doing. You're right, of course. I'll do it now.'

He went off, freshened glass of Jameson in hand, through a high door to the left of the elegant Adams-style fireplace; he left the door ajar and I could hear him beginning his calls. I didn't envy him. I considered what *I* should do. I could just go home, now that my part in the grim drama was over, but I didn't feel I should. Nor, to be honest, did I want to. It was all too momentous to just walk away from – I wouldn't be able to concentrate on much else. On the other hand, there didn't seem to be a lot I *could* do and all I had managed to think of by the time Norris came back was to contact the pathologist who acted for Norris's insurance company.

'Who is Catamaran insured with?'

'Town and Country. Why?'

'They'll have to know as soon as possible.'

'They'll be closed now,' he said, looking at his watch.

'Do you know who their pathologist is?'

'No. I'm afraid I don't.'

'I ought to try to find out so I can give him fair warning. The sooner an autopsy is done, the better.'

'Will an autopsy be necessary? Surely the cause of death is as plain as can be?'

'Granted. But not the reasons why Catamaran should break out and run amok.'

'Are you suggesting foul play? Ten men wouldn't have been able to throw the horse over that cliff! He'd have killed them!'

'Not if he was doped to the eyeballs.'

'Hmmmph! But how could anyone have got in? The whole farm is sealed off like a security prison! The yard gate is locked with every kind of device. I'm the only one who can open it. Apart from Tom Kelly and he's a hundred and fifty miles away.' A fleeting thought of Norris and Kelly organising a tortuous insurance rip-off was banished by his next words. 'I don't know how I'm going to tell the syndicate members. We're going to lose a fortune! He was insured for twenty-five million, but after the prices his foals fetched at the sales, he was revalued at nearer to forty. The policy falls due for renewal at the end of this month and we were to up the cover then. Fifteen million gone down the drain! By a couple of weeks!' If there had been foul play, I reckoned Norris was not involved – nobody's timing could be *that* bad.

I offered to call my old pathology professor to see if he knew who the pathologist for Town and Country was. In fact it turned out to be Professor Wall himself. I ought to have guessed as much; there was no point in being Head of Department and letting others get the plum consultancies. I gave him the facts as I knew them and he undertook to inform the insurance company. He asked me to ensure that the horse was locked away for the night and arranged to meet me at Bally Ard the following morning at 7.30. He was going to have an early start – Dublin was a good four hours' drive away.

We waited for the gardaí. Norris glanced towards the bottle once or twice, but made no move to pour himself another. He was impatient, drumming his fingers on the cracked leather of his deep armchair. 'I think I'll ring Tom,' he said suddenly, springing up.

I wandered round the room looking at the pictures of horses – nine out of ten seemed to be of Catamaran – which smothered every available surface. Mantelpiece, piano, sideboard and tables . . . even a storage heater had been pressed into service for its summer redundancy, as a stand for two small silver-framed photographs. On the walls were mainly paintings, drawings and sketches, but there were a few photographs, nearly all of his foalhood, the days before the latter-day Stubbses began queuing up to paint him. Many of the foal photographs included a pleasant, plump, middle-aged woman, presumably the late Mrs Norris. The whole house was a shrine to the great horse. The hall, I'd noticed on my way through, was similarly adorned.

Norris had left the door ajar again and I could overhear his conversation with the groom. First he asked about the health of the mother and by the way he kept saying 'Good, good, good', I gathered that he was getting a favourable, if rather long-winded report of the old lady's progress.

'Well that's great news, Tom. Please convey my best

wishes to her, and wish her a speedy recovery.' He paused. 'Tom?' He paused again. 'I'm sorry to say that the news from here is not quite so good. Catamaran had an accident this afternoon . . . Yes, I'm afraid it was – very bad . . . He's dead, Tom.' From a whole room away, I could hear the groom's incredulous squeak. 'We had to put him down.'

'Tom is totally shocked,' Norris said, coming back in, some ten minutes later – Kelly had had a thousand questions. 'Devastated. He loved that horse like a brother. And Catamaran loved him. He wasn't the easiest horse in the world but in Tom's hands he was a kitten. Do you know, if Tom was out in the yard doing something, anything, Catamaran wouldn't take his head in? He'd watch him wherever he went, and if Tom didn't keep talking to him, he'd whinny and neigh until he did. Sometimes, I almost thought that they could understand one another. Poor Tom.' Norris looked vacantly out the window, lost in memories. And he reached again for the bottle.

When the gardaí arrived, Norris was in the study phoning his syndicate colleagues. Hearing the car, I looked out the window. There were three of them, one in uniform, the driver. I knocked on the closed study door and poked my head round.

'They're here,' I mouthed, pointing over my shoulder.

He covered the mouthpiece with his hand. 'I'll be there in a moment. Can you look after them please.'

The housekeeper announced Inspector Potter, who immediately discharged the business of perfunctory introductions. 'Detective Sergeant O'Hanlon, Garda Fitzpatrick. And you sir, I take it, are Mr Samson?'

'That's right.' No handshake. 'Mr Norris is on the phone. He shouldn't be long.'

'Can you tell us what happened?'

I told him as much as I could and he listened, head bowed, nodding from time to time. O'Hanlon wrote in a wire-backed notebook and interrupted once or twice. Fitzpatrick stood by

44

the door as if he expected me, any second, to make a sudden bolt for it.

'Have you looked in the yard?' Potter asked when I finished, looking up for the first time.

'No. Mr Norris thought it better to wait for you.'

He nodded his agreement. 'Who's with the horse now?'

'Nobody.'

'Well then, I think we ought to go there at once. He shouldn't have been left unattended.' Seeing my puzzled frown, he went on: 'Our job is to see if there's been any, what shall I say, hanky-panky . . .' I nodded. 'So the earlier we get to the scene the better the chances are that we will be accurate in our reconstruction of the events which led to it. Also, if there has been any funny business – and I'm not saying for a moment that there has – then the culprit or culprits might be only too delighted with a few moments' grace to cover their tracks. Maybe Mr Norris disturbed them when he went to get his dog. Mick, you come with us,' he turned to his men, 'and Fitzy, you wait for Mr Norris and bring him down in the squad car when he finishes his phone call.'

We let O'Hanlon off at the yard 'to walk around outside a bit', then drove on. 'You know,' I said, pointing towards the coppice, 'the horse was alone for a good hour after the accident happened while Norris was calling me, and it's another hour since I shot him, and he's been alone all that time too.'

'We can but do our best,' Potter said, opening his door as we rolled to a halt.

On our way through the fields, he was on full alert, like a good pointer, straining to detect anything strange. He stopped a few times and listened intently, his head cocked to one side to lessen the sound of the breeze which had become a small wind with the approach of late evening; he peered out towards the west where Bally Ard ran into the sea, now gilding lustrously as the sun appoached it. I looked too, half expecting to see furtive figures in the hedge-rimmed fields, but I saw nothing untoward. Neither, it seemed, did the pointer.

'A fine farm this,' he said at last. 'As fine as there is in the county. That cliff over there' he pointed to a high escarpment which ran eastwards at right angles from the coast and some eight hundred yards behind the smaller outcrop of rock which had been quarried away to form the fatal pit 'is the northern boundary, and over there to your left you can see the river, that's the southern boundary. It's wide and it's deep and there are no bridges. It's also the eastern boundary because it flows over the cliff in a big waterfall, runs south for half a mile or so, and then turns sharp west and straight out to the sea. So Bally Ard is everything between the cliff, the waterfall, the river and the sea. There'll never be a boundary or a trespassing dispute on *this* farm.' We continued towards the coppice. 'And it would be a damn hard place for anyone to get into or out of without using the front gate. The only gate.' His lecture on the local geography wasn't as pointless as it had at first seemed. 'The whole farm,' he waxed agricultural again, 'slopes south to the river, which gives it perfect drainage, not to mention constant exposure to the sun.' Potter resumed his alert silence until we reached the beginning of the thicket, then stopped suddenly. 'They say that the grass grows in those fields along by the cliff right up to January; the cliff shelters it from the north wind and the sun reaches it most days. When there *is* sun.'

As soon as we entered the wood I could tell that he was concentrating on the job, not dreaming of fine farms or southern exposures. I went in front, trying to find the vague path which Norris had led me along, but more than once we had to backtrack when faced with a hostile wall of blackthorn or briar.

The clearing was in deep shade when we finally reached it, the setting sun obscured by the dense foliage; it would, however, be still bright on top – the dying rays gave the cliff face from tree-height up, a rosy tinge. A few late scavenging gulls from the shore flew off at our approach. With a silent reverence more befitting a human wake, we crossed to where Catamaran lay.

'Look carefully,' Potter said to me in a respectful, almost

funereal whisper. 'Do you see anything different to when you left? Anything at all? Take your time.'

'No,' I replied, after a while. 'It's exactly as it was – as far as I can make out.'

'You're sure?'

'As sure as I can be.'

'Good. Now, tell me again exactly what happened.'

I went through the whole story once more, starting at the point when I discovered that the horse was still alive. When I showed him the metal flange, he picked it up and asked me if I wouldn't mind, as I had wellingtons on, wading out to the dumper to see if it fitted. It did and he stored it away in a plastic bag. By the time my story ended, Potter was on his hunkers kneading the animal's stiffened ear. He looked up at me: 'I've been living within ten miles of Bally Ard for years, and I've never seen Catamaran in the flesh before.' He transferred his rubbing to the horse's cold and hardening cheek. 'And this is a hell of a way to meet the poor bastard. He was some animal, that's for sure.' He gave the cheek one last pat, sighed and straightened up.

Facing the cliff, he backed a dozen steps, his eyes sweeping slowly back and forth along the rim. 'Let's get up there and have a look before it gets too dark.'

We pushed through the thicket where it grew against the rock, brushing and snagging our way until we came to a scalable slope and, after a short climb, we came out on to the edge; like the floor below, it was covered in wild scrub, though not as dense. We made our way cautiously along, frequently peering over the edge to find the spot directly above Catamaran; once we'd found it, we moved away from the treacherous rim and began a slow search. There was ample evidence of the horse's passage, broken twigs, long, coarse, black tail hairs snagged on branches and even a clear hoof-print in one soft spot. We followed the trail to the beginning of the scrub, but then lost it. In the next twenty minutes, we searched outwards from where Catamaran had entered the scrub.

'Found anything?' Potter came up behind me.

'Nothing.'

'Me neither. I don't think there's much point in going on. It's getting dark. Maybe the last of the Mohicans could read all this like a book, but . . .' He shrugged. 'Anyway, it's pretty clear he went through the bushes at this point, then on and . . . bang! We'd better go and see how things are at the yard. You take the Land Rover and I'll walk across the fields in case there's anything obvious.'

He was at the yard before me. Norris was unlocking the gate as I arrived and O'Hanlon was saying: 'So it looks as if he actually *jumped* the wall. The ground is all gouged up where he landed and there's a couple of hoof-marks heading off towards the quarry. But the wall is about eleven feet high, so I don't know. No horse could jump that high, especially a flat racer.' He looked questioningly towards Norris.

'If that *is* what happened, then I think I know how he did it. The dungstead comes to within a couple of feet of the top of the wall. We usually keep it cleared away, but this year I was letting it build up. A friend of mine grows mushrooms. He was going to send a truck when there was a decent load.' Suddenly, impatient barking came from a horsebox parked by the gate. 'Oh, poor Patch!' Norris exclaimed. 'I forgot all about you!' He turned to Potter. 'It was the first place I came to on my way to the phone. I didn't have the yard keys with me, so I had to go on to the house. I locked Patch in to stop him from going back down again.' He swung the gate open and stood aside to let us through, but as I was about to bring up the rear he put a hand on my arm: 'Would you mind letting the dog out? But . . . hold on to him. I don't want him running back to the quarry.'

'Sure, no problem,' I said as Norris followed the law into the yard. 'Attaboy Patch, good doggy!' I eased the door open a tad. A flat snout pushed into the crack, and I opened a bit wider, enough to admit my hand. 'Good dog, Patch. Easy on Patch, OK?' I wouldn't normally shove a groping hand into a dark space containing a dog to which I hadn't been introduced, but I assumed Norris would have told me if Patch was a biter. After a brief, cold, wet, investigation of my hand, the snout returned to the crack, snuffling. More confidently, I reached down along his neck and hooked my finger under the collar. Then I opened the door enough to let him through. Patch was the animal that had given Steele the big welcome on Saturday. An odd-looking mongrel, with a flat snout, long legs, a coarse off-white coat with brownish patches that looked as though they'd wash off, he came to an abrupt end in a short fluffy tail. He didn't seem in the least perturbed that he'd never laid a bulging eye on his liberator before; he welcomed me like a brother, and stood, relatively quietly, short tail wagging furiously at one end, short pink tongue lolling happily at the other, seemingly none the worse psychologically for his recent ordeal. I passed some blue baling twine under his collar, and led him into the yard.

The space between the gate pillars was occupied, almost for its whole width, by a trough, some fifteen feet across. At one side there was a narrow walkway to allow for pedestrian traffic during the stud season, when the trough would be filled with disinfectant. Now there was only a couple of inches of sludge in the bottom. As I led Patch across the catwalk, I could see that the sludge was unmarked, no hoof-prints. Catamaran had certainly not come out through the gate – he couldn't have jumped it without leaving landing marks on the road and he couldn't have walked along the narrow concrete walkway.

The group had now gathered in front of the back wall. O'Hanlon was standing on top of the dungstead, a nine-foot high heap of dry horse manure. All I could see of him was the back of his ample trousers as he leaned out over the wall. The others stood silently looking up at him, awaiting his verdict. Floodlights had been switched on to augment the waning daylight.

'The tracks are right beneath here all right,' he said, straightening up and dousing his flashlight. 'That's how he did it.' He came crabwise down the manure heap, delicately avoiding the places where the hard crust had been punctured by the sharp hooves of half a ton of horse.

'It *had* to be that way,' Norris concurred, reaching towards me for the baling twine lead.

Potter nodded. 'Let's see how he managed to get out of his stable in the first place.' And he headed off.

'This way, Inspector,' Norris called after him, correcting his course, and we all trooped off across the yard like a package tour on a guided trip round a museum.

There were black mane hairs snagged on a splinter of timber in the top of the door frame and, inside, the bedding straw had been scooted back so that it was piled up in the middle of the box. As the door was still closed, there was only one inference to be drawn – Catamaran had lunged his forelegs on to the half-door and then pushed so hard with his hind legs that he had forced his bulk through an opening which seemed too narrow to accommodate it. Everyone agreed on that. It was the only thing that made sense.

'But why?' asked Norris of nobody in particular. 'Why would he do a strange thing like that? Something must have set him off. And to jump that wall! He must have been crazy. Do you know of any reason why a horse would suddenly go mad and do the most odd things?' He turned to me.

'Well, apart from rabies or some other form of encephalitis, no; I can't say that I do. Not off hand anyway.'

'But we don't have rabies in Ireland,' Potter protested.

'No. I wasn't suggesting he had rabies. I was just generalising.'

'Oh . . .' He turned his attention back to the locked door. Suddenly there was a deep growl from the dog and the hair along his back erected. Ears pricked, he strained at the bailing twine, leaning towards the door.

'Sit Patch! Sit!' Norris spoke sharply and yanked at the leash. Patch hunkered down briefly but didn't lose his alert expression. In seconds, he was up again, growling threateningly and straining towards the door. '*Sit!* What the blazes is wrong with you?' This time the dog paid no heed and began to bark excitedly as he almost pulled Norris to the door where he began to whine and scratch at the timber. Then we all heard what Patch had obviously heard, a faint rustle in the straw inside the box. At this, the dog began to scratch furiously, scraping white gouges in the maroon paintwork. His barks became excited yelps.

'What was that?' Potter asked, his head cocked to one side. 'Shhh!'

O'Hanlon, who was nearest the door, shone his torch into the box and leaned in to follow its probing beam. 'It's a bloody great rat!' he announced a moment later, turning to us. 'As big as a rabbit, he is! Jaysus, Inspector but he's the size of a small rabbit!'

Norris swore a sudden oath, then buried his crumpling face in his hand. 'Oh *no!*' he moaned, and didn't resist when O'Hanlon took the dog's lead, swiftly removed the twine, and lifted Patch in over the half-door. A minute of scrabbling and barking ended in ten seconds of shrill screams, then silence. O'Hanlon, who had been shouting encouragement during the brief hunt, was now offering Patch congratulations over the door. Potter and Fitzpatrick were exchanging knowing mumbles and nods and Norris was running his fingers through his thick white hair, his eyes screwed tightly closed, his mouth a slash of grief and disbelief. The door was opened and Patch emerged, his limp trophy and much straw hanging from his mouth. 'Drop it, boy! Drop it!' Norris commanded. When the dog complied, he swore again and kicked the limp brown body along the yard, stooping to catch Patch's collar to prevent him from continuing his sport.

Nobody said anything for a while until at last, Potter broke the silence. 'Well, Mr Norris. It seems to be a straightforward case of really bad luck and I'm very sorry about it. A real tragedy.' O'Hanlon and Fitzpatrick nodded agreement. 'We won't detain you any longer. If you'd be kind enough to arrange for me to have a copy of the pathologist's report, I'd appreciate it.' He nodded briefly and they left.

Earlier, Norris had phoned a neighbour who had promised to gather enough help to manhandle Catamaran through the thicket and bring him by tractor to the yard. Professor Wall had insisted that he be kept under lock until he arrived next morning. While we waited in the house for the help to arrive, I asked Norris about the significance of the rat.

'Didn't you know?' he asked, surprised. 'It's well known that Catamaran had a phobia about rats.'

'No, actually, I didn't know,' I said, feeling as if in some way it was an admission of professional incompetence.

'Oh he hated them! Ever since he was a foal. One day, just after he was weaned, he put his head into his feed bucket and there was a rat in it. The rat clung to his nose, climbed up his face and between his ears and down along his back. I was in the yard when I heard his screams and I actually saw the rat, like a brown, furry, moving growth, scurrying up along his nose. He nearly came through the door on that occasion too; we barely held him until Steele got here. He had to keep him sedated for days. He never put his nose into a bucket after that; we had to get a wide bakers' tray for him.' He stopped, remembering, then shook his head and went on. 'Actually, we could have lost the Derby all because of a rat. A certain notorious racecourse bum was caught within a few feet of his box an hour before the race, just before we tacked him up. Luckily, Tom Kelly spotted him and called security. When they searched him, they found a box in his pocket with a rat in it. He claimed it was a pet, and there's no law against that. But there's no doubt about it, if Catamaran had seen the rat that day, he'd never have run. Poor Cat! What an awful way to go.'

There was the sound of an approaching tractor and, having first checked with the answering service that there were no more calls, I offered to stay and supervise Catamaran's removal so that Norris could get on with the business of calling the rest of the syndicate members.

An hour later the broken body of the great horse had been locked away in a large shed, the help had been served hot soup, sandwiches and whiskey, and had left. Norris came with me to the Land Rover. 'Thank you for all you've done. I'd never have managed without you.'

I made some suitably disclaiming reply. In the bushes, in the dark, something stirred. 'That's probably another bloody rat!' Norris growled savagely. 'I wouldn't mind, but I spend a

52

fortune trying to keep the place rat-free. Patch!' he called.
'Patch! Here boy!'

I left them at it. On the way home the thought struck me
that Norris had to have the worst vermin control programme
in the world – despite his expense and efforts, his horse had
worms, his fields had rabbits and his yard had rats.

As I let myself into the cottage, a faraway church launched
midnight's chimes out on to the warm, still night. I lay on the
bed and heard the same church strike one, two and three. In a
bucket in the bathroom, my shirt, jeans and socks, muddy
and bloody, steeped in cold water, leaching out the organic
reminders of the ordeal. Before going to bed, I had washed
and rewashed my hands as fastidiously as Lady Macbeth, but
they still felt stained. I don't know why. None of it had been
my fault.

I can't recall sleeping but I must have – I don't remember
any far-off clock chimes after three.

6

I arrived at Bally Ard shortly before 7.20. The sun was hours up, the morning already promising a warm day. As I rolled to a stop, I felt as though I'd never left at all.

One of the larger BMWs was parked by the steps, its metallic fawn body gleaming in the morning sun which, robbed of its blinding glare, was reflected as a whitish-yellow disc in the smoked glass of the windscreen. I trotted up the limestone steps but before I could ring, the door opened and Norris came to meet me. He looked wrecked.

'I see I'm late,' I said, indicating the BMW.

'What? No. No, you're not. That's Dr Field's car, our local GP. I had to call him this morning because I didn't sleep a wink all night. I've got the most awful headache and I need something stronger than aspirin; I've a feeling today is going to be hectic.'

A tall, carefully groomed man in his early forties rose from a chair beside a small table on which stood a steaming cup. Norris made introductions and poured me a welcome coffee from the glass pot which stood on a warming plate on the sideboard.

'An awful business this,' the doctor commented, when we had all settled down into deep chairs.

'Awful,' I agreed, setting my cup back on its saucer.

'Thank God I don't often come across injuries as bad as Gilbert has described but, when I do, I sometimes envy you vets your facility of euthanasia. In some cases it would be a relief.'

I wondered if he wasn't giving me a gentle dig about the fact that I'd put down the horse so decisively. More than once during the night, I'd had the horrifying thought that the insurance people might try to worm their way out of paying, on the grounds that euthanasia could only be justified when all else had failed. In this case nothing else had been tried, so nothing could be said to have failed.

'But,' he went on, 'if you want the opinion of a mere medic, I think you were right. It must have been a difficult decision. I'd hate to have been faced with it.'

Norris chimed in: 'I agree. You were absolutely right and I apologise for trying to talk you out of it. But you'll forgive me; I wasn't myself at the time. I'm sure you can appreciate that.'

'Under the circumstances, you bore up remarkably well,' I said magnanimously.

Professor Wall arrived at 7.30 on the dot. I knew he would, his punctuality had been a byword at college. He was a tall man with a slight stoop. Luxuriant eyebrows, more like moustaches, overhung his lively blue eyes like hairy awnings. Despite his obsession with time, he was a relaxed man, a man to whom we, as students, could relate easily. 'Ah, Samson!' he said, gripping my hand warmly. 'Good to see you again.'

'It's good to see *you*, Professor. Though I would have preferred it to be in different circumstances.'

'Yes, indeed.' He turned towards Dr Field and Norris made the introductions. The conversation was general while the professor sipped hot, black coffee. Then he looked at me: 'We'd better get started. Can you help me with my paraphernalia?'

I related the whole story as we walked to his car. Out of earshot of the others, he studied me shrewdly for a moment. 'I'd say that right now, you're suffering all kinds of self-doubt?' I gave a vague shrug. 'Well you needn't. Putting down an animal is never pleasant, but when it's a *valuable* animal, there's the added worry of insurance claims, court cases, etc. Some of these things go on for years. From what you tell me, there was no other course open to you. But it was a lonely decision. Very lonely.'

When we went back to the house, Norris said worriedly: 'I hope you won't need me . . . I don't think I'd be able for it.'

'I can appreciate that, but no, you won't be needed.'

Dr Field coughed politely. 'Would it be in order for *me* to attend. I'm quite fascinated by it all.'

'Mr Samson? It's your case. I've certainly got no objections.'

I told Dr Field he was welcome.

Norris led us across the yard towards the locked double doors of the coach house. I carried the professor's case. At the car, he had put on a white lab coat and a white rubber apron and, as Norris unlocked the door, he clipped a dictaphone into his breast pocket and attached a microphone to the lapel. The horse was already beginning to smell. Norris touched a switch and the shed flickered into view in the cold grey-pink light of neon fluorescent tubes. We waited respectfully while he took a last look and then, wordlessly, left.

The pathologist walked slowly around the body on the floor as he pulled on his long rubber gloves, then looked up at me. 'You did the right thing, Samson. No question.' Then he bent and snapped open his case. 'Right,' he said, straightening, 'we can begin. Perhaps we can have the door closed?' Dr Field obliged.

Professor Wall switched on his recorder and gave it the date and time as a test. He played that back and, satisfied, went on in a monotone. 'Findings of autopsy at Bally Ard Stud, County Galway, on the body of thoroughbred stallion, Catamaran, the property of Mr Gilbert Norris of the same address, and others. Autopsy carried out by Stephen Wall and Francis Samson, veterinary surgeons. Superficial examination revealed the following lesions: healing skin wound on muzzle approximately one inch high and half an inch wide. The epidermis is missing but repair has been taking place normally. This wound is roughly rectangular and is situated mainly to the left of the mid-line; it extends into the medial distal commissure of the left nostril. There is already a report

56

of this wound on the file, check and insert date. New paragraph. Two conjoined roughly circular wounds in mid-forehead, each having a diameter of just under an inch. Skin, frontal bone, frontal sinus and cranial cavity with its contents penetrated. Wounds straddle mid-line.' He broke off, covering the microphone with his hand, said: 'Good shooting, Mr Samson,' then continued: 'These, the cause of death, resulting from the horse being shot with a shotgun by Mr Samson. New paragraph. Compound fracture, right fore involving metacarpus at the level of the buttons of the splint bones. Severe trauma to soft tissues in the area of the fracture. Next. New paragraph. Compound fracture of left hind involving metatarsus at the junction of its proximal and middle thirds. Severe soft tissue damage in the area of the fracture. Right. New paragraph. Transverse, stab-like wound in sub-pubic region about five inches antero-ventral to the pubic symphysis. Probing reveals the wound to be almost two inches deep and somewhat more long – about three inches. Structures in the area severed transversely, including penis and its muscles. Bruising at lips of wound and haemorrhage in its depth. Yellow flakes of paint recovered from wound. Mr Samson reports piece of metal found actually in wound and removed by him. Next paragraph. Cuts and bruises of a relatively, underline "relatively", minor nature on the right side of the body all consistent with subject having fallen on that side. No such superficial trauma on left side, compound fracture of hind leg being the only wound on that side.'

At this point, he switched off the recorder and took a knife from the case. Fifteen minutes later, the horse had been neatly skinned and lay, glistening white and red, beneath the humming glow of the strip-lights. When he saw the tiny leakage of blood in the jugular furrow, he paused and looked up. 'This horse has had an IV recently.'

'I took a blood sample a few hours ante mortem.'

'Oh? Why?'

'Just routine. His appetite was a little off one evening last week and he seemed less than greedy yesterday morning –

nothing much. He checked out perfectly every other way. I suppose I was just being extra careful.'

'Oh I see.' Switching the recorder back on, he resumed his monologue. 'Subcutaneous lesions. Extensive bruising all along right side, from facial area to rump. Bruising most severe over bony prominences, jaw, shoulder and elbow joints, ribcage and point of hip. All consistent with subject having fallen on that side. That is, the right side. Left side unaffected.'

The pathologist now took a break, doing callisthenics to relieve his back, grimacing as, hands on hips, he stretched and swayed and rolled one shoulder after the other. He smiled ruefully. 'I suppose, Doctor, you don't happen to have any magic potion to alleviate Ageing Back Syndrome on you at the moment?'

'Unfortunately, not at the moment, Professor.' Field smiled back.

'In that case, we may as well go on. The back isn't going to get any younger. Mr Samson, can you please pass me the saw and the big knife.'

The examination of the abdominal cavity was thorough but failed to show up any gross pathological lesions. I was thankful to see that there were no signs of aneurysms and the only thing that went on the dictaphone was a roll-call of the abdominal organs with the same comment after each: 'Normal position, relations, colour, size and texture.' I hadn't mentioned the worm burden and I wasn't going to. It was of purely academic interest now anyway and there was no way that it could have contributed to Catamaran's death. Field peered over the professor's shoulder, rapt. At one stage he broke in excitedly.

'There's no gall bladder! Look! No gall bladder!'

Professor Wall and I exchanged knowing smiles. 'Horses don't have gall bladders.'

'Oh . . .' Field sounded disappointed. 'I was always told that all animals, humans included, had the same bits and pieces, only varying in size and shape . . .'

'That's broadly true but there *are* differences. For instance

58

the animals that we deal with, the farm and domestic animals, don't have collarbones. We have five digits at the end of each limb, the horse just one and two tiny splint bones; the ox, sheep and pig have two; dogs and cats have four and vestigial thumbs and big toes, the dew claws . . . Cattle have a bone in their hearts. A pig has a bone in the tip of its snout. A dog has a bone in his penis. Cattle, sheep and goats have four very specialised compartments in their highly efficient stomachs, compared to which the simple bags we, in common with cats, dogs, rats, pigs, horses, have been blessed with, are a very basic design . . .' He suspended the lecture in comparative anatomy to ask me for a bottle for the small cube he had just cut from the liver; when he had plopped it in, I placed the capped bottle back with the other samples he had already taken.

Next he tackled the thoracic cavity, sawing through the ribs at their sternal ends; as each one was cut through he freed it from its neighbour and twisted it up to dislocate it from its junction with the spine. When the last rib fell to his saw, he switched on his recorder again and reported all normal in the thorax. He concluded by giving a résumé, beginning in short sentences from which all superfluous words were excised; it only needed the regular interposing of the word 'Stop' to make it sound as though he was composing a telegram.

'End of autopsy. Brain examination not possible as subject shot so cranial contents destroyed. Following samples taken: blood, urine, saliva, stomach contents, intestinal contents, liver and kidney sections. Toxicology and pharmacology only. No recent history any significant illness so histology, bacteriology and virology not necessary. All gross lesions consistent with history. Panicked by rat in box, bolted and fell over quarry-edge, unseen because of bushes. Injuries necessitated euthanasia, carried out by Frank Samson. That's about it, Joan. Wait until we get written reports from Mr Samson and the local police and type it up. Subject to clear lab tests, I record a verdict of death by misadventure.' He switched off the recorder.

While I stored the carefully labelled sample bottles away in the case, Professor Wall stripped off his gloves, apron and white rubber boots and deposited them in a heavy plastic bag which he sealed as soon as I gave him the apron that he had lent me. Then we left the shed, switching out the light and closing the door behind us, shutting away the pathetic bits of the once great horse from the warm, quick world of living things.

As we rounded the corner into view of the side of the house, Norris came through the french windows. He crossed the lawn to meet us, picking his way between flowerbeds swollen with late summer colours, his feet brushing a track through the dew-blue grass which was still shaded from the bright sun by the house's bulk. 'You've finished?' he asked, taking Professor Wall by the elbow and steering him on to the lawn.

'Yes. We have.'

'Good. I've had Mrs Flahive cook breakfast – I'm sure you could do with some after your early start. This way gentlemen,' he added, turning to include the doctor and me. Dr Field pleaded an overdue morning clinic and, wishing us a good morning, continued on round the front of the house to his car. I, being both hungry and interested in seeing the case through to its end, followed Norris and the professor. I had a morning clinic too, but I squared it with my conscience by reasoning that Professor Wall might have further need of my services – if indeed he ever had had at all.

Norris led us into his study, which was more a private sitting room than a study. He indicated one of the two armchairs to the professor and took the other himself. I sat in the middle of a sofa, forearms on thighs, leaning attentively forward.

'Well?' Norris asked.

'Well,' echoed the professor, 'it looks like a straightforward case of accidental death.'

'*Looks* like? Have you found something wrong?'

'No. Nothing like that. It's just that we can't give a final verdict until we run some tests. That's all.'

'I see. What tests?'

'Tests for drugs mainly. Because of the amount of money involved, we must cover all possible angles. The insurance company would demand it.'

'Of course. I understand. One doesn't think of these things somehow.'

'It's almost certainly a formality. There wouldn't have been any sense to it. If someone wanted to kill Catamaran, they'd hardly have left it to chance by choosing drugs – it was just a freak accident that he ran amok into the scrub and over that quarry. And if they *weren't* trying to kill him, then it makes even *less* sense. It seems pretty certain that it happened as the gardaí have reconstructed it, starting with the rat.'

'I suppose so.' Norris lapsed into a short meditative silence, then suddenly pulled himself together. 'Forgive me. I'm sure you both want to wash and freshen up. We'll eat then.' He stood up and so did we. Stooping, I picked up the case. Norris looked distastefully at it. 'Are the . . . samples in that?'

'Yes.'

'You can leave it here. It will be safe, I assure you. The door can be locked if you wish.'

Professor Wall nodded at me. I left the case by the sofa and we went out, Norris locking the door and pocketing the key.

Breakfast was a lavish one, though Norris merely picked at his. Conversation was mainly about racing, which left me a bit out. Shortly after we finished eating, I made my excuses and left.

On my way to town I turned on the radio and just caught the news item about Catamaran. 'Catamaran, one of the most famous racehorses of the century, was destroyed yesterday evening following an accident at Bally Ard stud in Galway.' There was a brief, superlative-spangled résumé of his splendid career, then the news item finished: 'A documentary about Catamaran, "King of the Sport of Kings", first televised last March, will be broadcast again this evening on RTE 2 at 10.15.'

Catamaran was to be given the full treatment, to be mourned by the nation like the true hero he was. Somehow it made me feel uneasy all over again. I was the man who had shot the nation's darling. I'd be infamous.

As I drove towards the clinic, I noticed several heads turning to look at me and when I glanced in my mirror, the heads were still turned, following my progress. It seemed as if I was already infamous – at least locally.

7

Driving into the yard behind the surgery brought me back to the world of normality with a jerk, the mental equivalent of stepping off an escalator. As I put on my lab coat, I gave Eileen the story in the barest detail; from the next room came an assortment of snarls and whines, growls and barks, and an infrequent nervous miaow. Animals kept overlong in the artificial confines of a waiting room don't much like it – the out-of-date magazines mean nothing to them. 'Listen to that,' I said. 'Better get going before there's carnage.' I headed for the white-tiled consultation room. 'Roll 'em in.'

For the next hour I dealt with the usual cases of dogs with skin disorders, ear cankers and impacted anal glands. The only cat had been brought in because it had been constipated for three days; when it arrived on the table, however, a total cure seemed to have been effected and I wondered, somewhat unscientifically, if forty-five minutes among a howling pack of strange dogs hadn't – to put it delicately – had a frighteningly laxative effect. Clinic should have finished earlier but each person wanted to know about Catamaran, and by the time the last one came through I had developed an encapsulated story which seemed to satisfy everybody. It was the same on my morning farm rounds.

By late morning, the reporters had arrived. As Norris wouldn't even talk to them, and old Jack had suddenly become totally deaf, they hunted me down. Three of them tracked me to the pub across from the surgery and, though I got a free lunch out of them, they got precious little in return to add to the skimpy typed handout they had been given at Bally Ard. When I excused myself I left behind me, in the gloom of the pub, three disgruntled-looking newshounds.

Because of the late start to the day, I finished late, not getting back to Ferndtich until after eight. I read the papers while I soaked in a hot bath until my skin wrinkled. I briefly considered making an omelette but didn't – I reckoned that the hectic events of the previous day entitled me to pamper myself a bit so I opted for an excursion to the local takeaway for something unwholesome but filling, for consumption in front of the TV. As I came out of the cottage, it looked as if even this simple plan was about to be frustrated, and I cursed *sotto voce*. In the dusk, the figure of a woman was fumbling for the gate latch.

Hearing the door close, she looked up. 'Mr Samson?' she enquired. Nice voice. I tried to guess what her problem might be. Late, so an emergency. Farm call? Probably not – she would have used the phone. Probably she had a dog in the car, a small bitch trying to give birth to a single large pup. That was it. I placed a bet with myself.

'Yes,' I admitted, more than a touch of the martyr in my tone. The street light outside the gate had not yet come on and, in the dusk, with the remains of the day's light coming from behind her it wasn't at first easy to see her features. Now that I was closer, I noted the absence of a worried expression; I adjusted my bet, maybe a bitch not actually in labour as such, just off her food. That was it. I increased my wager.

'Yes?' I said again, reaching the gate.

'I'm Claire O'Sullivan.'

'Oh . . . Hi,' I replied, taking her extended hand, wondering if the name was supposed to mean something to me. I lifted the latch, opened the gate and emerged on to the path. She turned to face me, bringing the evening light full on to her face and I knew at once that I hadn't met her before – I would have remembered, for she was quite breathtakingly beautiful.

'So,' I said busily. 'What can I do for you?'

64

'I'm a reporter with the *Daily Instructor*,' she began.

'Oh!' (So much for her anorexic bitch and my Holmesian logic.)

'I'm sorry for bothering you at this hour . . .'

'No problem. It could be worse. It could have been work.' It sounded faintly ungallant and I regretted at once having said it, but she didn't seem to notice.

'. . . but I couldn't get here before now. I'm just a substitute, really. Our racing correspondent *was* on his way this morning, but he had a crash somewhere near Ballinasloe and he's in hospital there now with a broken leg.'

'Oh! Tough.'

'Yes. Tough. So, as I wasn't doing anything actually important,' she continued, trying not to sound too pleased at her lucky break, 'my editor ordered me west. And here I ám. I suppose you've had it up to here with reporters since morning?' she queried, gently rabbit-chopping the bridge of her delicate nose.

'I've seen a few,' I conceded. 'Three of them clubbed together in a pub today to buy me a bowl of oxtail and a salad sandwich.'

'Oh my! The *extravagance!* Only those on limitless expense accounts could afford it.' She laughed and the laugh fitted her exactly – clear, fresh, a tinkly, pleasing sound. 'And, for that I presume you had to Tell All and sign a pact in your own blood never to talk to a reporter from any other paper?'

I smiled. 'Hardly. When I left, I thought they were going to ask me for the lunch back.' Once again I was aware of having said the wrong thing, crude this time, so I rushed on: 'Gilbert Norris has prepared a kind of press release, a printed handout . . .'

'And you didn't think you could go beyond that.'

'Not in my position. No.'

'Well am I allowed to ask what was in the press release? Because I haven't even seen it. I went out to Bally Ard as soon as I got here but the place was locked up tight as a drum.'

I hesitated. I hadn't read the flyer but I could hardly refuse to give her any information at all. It'd have to be a synopsis, fleshing out the bones of radio reports and newspapers. She misunderstood my hesitation.

'Oh, I'm sorry! You're obviously going out for the evening. Perhaps if you're not going to be too late . . . I could call . . .'

'No. No. I'm just going out for a bite to eat. If you like, you can come along and we can talk and eat at the same time.'

'Actually I've already eaten, thanks, but I would like to tag along if I wouldn't be in the way. You don't have a date or anything?'

'No. No date or anything. Whatever that "anything" might mean.'

She laughed, another tinkly one. 'Oh – business, family, a night out with the boys, anything that doesn't fit comfortably under the heading "date".'

'No. Strictly a solo performance. I didn't feel like cooking and anyway I'm a lousy cook. I always give myself indigestion and once I nearly committed unintentional suicide with a tuna fish pie.'

As we drove along in the Land Rover, I had to do some quick thinking. I'd left the house with my heart set on some masterpiece of junk cuisine, smothered in salt, vinegar and ketchup, but now that suddenly seemed terribly unsophisticated and I sorted quickly through my limited local knowledge until I thought of a likely place I had noticed on my rounds. It looked far better than it was and its prices were based on its looks.

She sat, toying with an indifferent prawn cocktail, while I worked my way through the set dinner: eighteen quid, service charge not included. Very early on in the proceedings – between the grapefruit segments and the French onion soup – I concluded my report on Catamaran's last moments. There wasn't a lot to tell. I gave her as much as I knew myself which, judging from the spellbound look in her calm, grey eyes, she found fascinating. I didn't tart up the facts or exaggerate my role in the drama, which was most unlike me, given a beautiful woman for an audience, and I left out all references to the suspicious mental exercises I had indulged in immediately after I had put down the horse. Nor did I mention a word of my own reactions during the whole affair; I was still trying to come to grips with them myself. It seemed that within my own self there lurked a craven me, a me which panicked when faced with the big one and felt secret relief when it found out that there was nothing that could be done.

Not, mind you, that I thought I *ought* to have told her any of this but I was beginning to notice, as time went on, how important it was becoming that this beautiful woman with the warm grey eyes which looked so steadily back into mine, should develop an interest in my feelings in the matter, how it had all affected *me*.

'Wow,' she breathed, entranced, and I began to glow inside. I assumed she was wowing me, my heroic courage, my Herculean tribulations, my doughty intrepidness, and I could feel a huge, unstoppable smirk coming on. 'Wow!' she repeated, stopping the smirk like the number 11 bus would. 'A *rat!* All that caused by . . . a *rat?*'

'Eh . . . eh . . .' I stumbled in confusion, switching wavelengths. 'That's right. Incredible, isn't it? My kingdom for a rat, aye?' I explained at great length about Catamaran's phobia and told her Norris's story about the attempted sabotage just before the Derby. 'But you'd better not print that. Libel laws, you know,' I advised gravely, showing, I hoped, how knowledgeable I was in all matters, even journalism. Jesus, I thought suddenly, I'm going goofy!

She nodded in equally grave agreement and her face broke into a delighted laugh which sent tiny crows' feet crinkling out from her eyes when, dropping my voice conspiratorially, I advised her instead to locate a dead rat, preferably of much the same dimensions as a small rabbit, photograph it, and print it in the paper as 'The Rat!'

'Just that! "THE RAT".' I blocked the two words out in the air between us. 'The most famous rat in all history!' I began to warm to my theme, to get into my stride. 'And can you imagine the lure of a dead rat photograph on the front page? The public fascination!' I flexed my arms tightly, bringing the hands up under my chin, bunched fingers extended forward, wrinkled my nose, stuck my front teeth out over my lower lip, and snapped my head back. And it was while I was rigid in that undignified position with my eyes closed as tight as a dead rat's, that the waiter approached and enquired if I was Mr Samson, the veterinary surgeon.

'Yes,' I replied, uncoiling myself rapidly and trying to assume an air of professional dignity.

'Telephone for you, sir. You can take it at reception.'

I knew it would be work because I had given the answering service my number, and it was – the bane of the vet's life, a calving case.

'Emergency, I'm afraid,' I told Claire, getting back to the table and draining my coffee. I was dejected.

'Oh? What's the emergency?'

'Cow calving.' I made writing motions in the air to the waiter.

Suddenly I was desolate. I realised with a shock that I didn't want to say goodbye to this woman that I had met just ninety minutes before, that the thought of it gave me a sense of utter loss. Confused at the intensity of my emotion, I gave her a resigned smile. 'Well I'd like to have had a post-prandial drink but I'm afraid calving cases claim precedence over everything.'

She shrugged and made what to me was definitely a disappointed little grimace. 'Duty calls.'

'As you say. Come on. We'd better get you back to your hotel.'

We were almost there, having driven most of the way in near silence, when she turned to me. 'If you don't think I'd be in the way, I'd love to go with you. I've never seen a birth.'

All I could do was grin at her. I couldn't very well tell her that she had just saved me from the pit of blackest depression. Before chancing a reply, afraid she might change her mind, I did a U-turn and headed back out for the open country. 'No. You won't be in the way,' I said, trying not to sound too thrilled as we passed under the last street light. 'I'm sure of that. Certain. Positive. Absolutely positive.'

Once again, as the velvety night closed in about us, I knew I'd gone on too much. Damn!

Thick, golden corn straw carpeted the floor of the byre and the soft yellow light of an oil lamp showed a quiet old Shorthorn standing peacefully and untroubled, tethered to a ring in the whitewashed wall. She'd been through it all before and was calm and composed, awaiting the moment when the calf would mysteriously appear, and she, hearing its snuffling and sharp cry, would lick it dry, stimulating its first shaky breaths. I glanced at Claire as I soaped my arm, and saw her look of fascination; she was obviously mesmerised, and I hoped it wasn't going to be one of the messier ones. They can put people off.

The cow was roomy and the calf lively, and, when I grasped the little fetlock which lay just out of sight in the vagina, it was jerked back with a force which made the mother look back to see what was going on. I touched the calf's muzzle and he obviously objected to this also because he began to rotate his head to escape my exploring fingers. But that was all there was; the other forelimb had been left behind and was now lying bent backwards along the underside of the little body. Gently pushing the calf back into the uterus, I created enough room to admit my hand and succeeded in grasping the wayward limb between the elbow and the next joint down – the knee. The cow's powerful contractions forced the calf back at me again and I had to withdraw my hand just as I managed to flex its shoulder and elbow joints. I repelled the calf and groped for the leg again, this time getting my fingers hooked behind the bent knee. After that it was just a matter of pulling forward and upward a little and inching my hand down along the leg, repeating the manoeuvre until the fetlock and hoof came within reach. Covering the sharp points of the little hoof with my hand to protect the stretched uterine wall, I flexed all the joints and drew the folded leg forward to join its fellow in the birth canal. Gentle traction did the rest and less than ten minutes after our arrival, the calf flopped on to the straw, steam rising from its wet coat.

'Bull calf,' the farmer pronounced, dropping the hind leg and moving to the cow's head to untie her.

For the first time Claire moved. Walking slowly, her gaze never leaving it, she approached the calf and hunkered down beside it. The farmer delayed untying the cow; some cows don't take kindly to strangers being close to their offspring, but someone whose only experience of cows was probably the view from passing cars wouldn't have known that and, while I was working, he, in his quiet way, had obviously summed up the situation. Anyway, the look of wonder on her face was a real giveaway. Gently she stroked the wet, snorting head, then, looking up at me, smiled. I smiled back. The smiles were easy, as though we'd known one another for years.

It was I who spoke first on the journey back to Knockmore. 'So . . . What did you think of your first calving case, then?' I already knew the answer.

She shook her head. 'Unbelievable . . .' she breathed, then went on. She seemed to think I was some sort of life-giver, somewhere, though not much, this side of deity. In fact it had been a cinch, needing only one of the simpler obstetrical interferences, but I didn't disillusion her – honest I may be, but that much honest is stupid; if she wanted to think of me as one of the lesser gods, then that was perfectly all right by me.

Driving along the dark roads we discussed calving cases in some detail. Claire's fascination with the whole subject was endless, and of course, I was on home turf. After I had explained how to correct some of the more common problems, we got on to difficult ones.

'What happens if the calf is simply too big to fit through the pelvis?' she asked, eyes widening in horror at the very thought of it.

'Dead or alive?' I changed down to squeeze past an ancient truck.

'How do you mean?'

'The foetus. Dead or alive?'

'It makes a difference?'

'Sure. If it's dead, you cut it up inside using a wire saw and take it out in bits . . .'

'Eee-yuck! What about the poor cow?'

'No problem. Stick in a drop of epidural and then there's a

collection of metal pipes we use to protect her insides. Of course if the calf is alive then we do a Caesarean. Same as in humans.'

'No kidding? I was born by section.'

'There you are! Didn't do you one bit of harm, did it?'

'I suppose not.' She laughed. 'It nearly killed my mother, though. Infection.'

'That's always a danger. But somehow cows seem to be able to handle it. If you saw some of the places I've had to operate in, you'd wonder how *I* came out alive, never mind the cow and calf! Muck from wall to wall, flies all over, dust thick in the air. It's Murphy's law in reverse, the only time it works in reverse where calving cases are concerned. Otherwise it goes true to form. With a vengeance.'

'Why's that?'

'Well . . . cows usually pick the most inopportune times, as if they were just *waiting* for a man to start relaxing . . .' I stopped there, backing off from an almost perfect chat-up line – how, when I was just hoping to spend the evening with the most beautiful woman . . . blah, blah, blah. Though I'd only met her that evening and she'd be gone in the morning, I knew with a strange certainty that we'd meet again, and I didn't want her to go away thinking of me as a fast worker, a smooth-talker.

'It must play merry hell with your social life, all these untimely calving cases,' she said. 'Do you have a girlfriend?'

'No,' I said, taken aback by the sudden direct question. 'Do you have a boyfriend?'

She glanced quickly at me. 'Why do you ask?' There was an odd little smile on her mouth.

'Because you asked me,' I smiled back.

'Well, I'm a reporter, remember? So my question was professional.'

'Well, I'm a man, so my question was personal,' I countered in parody. I grinned her a really wide grin to let her know she could take it as a joke if she chose.

'I see you believe in being frank, Frank,' she said, still smiling, but dodging the question.

'I believe in being clear, Claire,' I counter-punned, trying to disguise my insistence. I glanced at her again and did a Groucho Marx with the eyebrows, taking the seriousness out of it. 'But you haven't answered my question.'

She laughed, a delighted, delightful gurgle. 'No.'

'Is that a "No", you haven't answered my question, or a "No", you haven't a regular boyfriend?'

'It's a "No" to both.' She laughed again. 'A double negative.'

'Which makes it positive, right.'

'This is the exception.'

We had reached the hotel, and I turned into the car park.

'Maybe we can have that drink now?' I suggested. I would have found it almost physically impossible just to drive off.

'I'd like that,' she said simply. 'I've got a few more questions too. If you don't mind?'

'Are we coming to the "no comment" stuff at last?'

When I switched off the engine, the strains of 'The Hokey Cokey' came thumping through the night from a row of open windows at the side of the hotel.

'Sounds of revelry from within,' Claire said. 'I wonder what's going on?'

It turned out to be a dinner dance for the entertainment of a party of French travel agents which was staying at the hotel and, after we had sat for ten minutes in the deserted bar, we decided to gatecrash. During the next couple of hours we boogied and jived, waltzed and foxtrotted and took part in the Paul Joneses and congas which are the essence of such functions. There were a few 'Excuse me' dances and I never managed to stay with Claire for more than the first few bars before getting a polite Gallic tap on the shoulder and seeing her being whisked off.

We even won two spot prizes. It wasn't hard, as the French visitors were hampered by a language difficulty exacerbated by the tubby band-leader's broad West of Ireland accent, and a total ignorance of the jargon of 'in' spot prize buzz-phrases. Thus, when the leader announced with a gappy, devilish smile that the prize would go to 'The firsht gintleman up here with a pair o' lady's tights in his hands', the French travel agents looked around, not knowing what was going on, while I picked up Claire and carried her to the stage to claim our prize, a bottle of whiskey and a box of chocolates. Twenty minutes later, I added a bottle of aftershave lotion and a jar of bath salts for being the first to respond to his call for a 'spare seh a' teeth'. To a seasoned attender of dinner dances in Ireland, that means 'a comb', but to the French the whole thing must have seemed like some arcane Celtic ritual, and they responded with generous, if somewhat mystified applause as I went to collect two other gaily wrapped packages. Obviously, the band-leader realised he'd have to internationalise the whole thing to prevent us from making a clean sweep, because the next spot prize was offered to 'the firsht wan up here with a franc'.

'Come on!' Claire tugged at my arm. 'You're a Frank!'

'Hold on! I think this is meant to be confined to the visitors. Give them a crack at the booty. Anyhow,' I said as she sat down beside me again, 'we've already cheated, haven't we?'

'You mean because I'm not wearing tights?' she whispered with an intimate wink which dried my mouth like a tablespoon of Milk of Magnesia. 'Who's ever going to know?' she smiled again. 'Except the two of us.'

We left the ballroom after the third round of hokey-cokey, having had enough of putting our right leg in, our right leg out, doing the hokey-cokey, and shaking it all about . . . As we went out the door, the tubby band-leader, obviously a member of the Irish branch of the Malaprop family, was announcing with great pride: 'In honour of our Frinch gueshts, the orchestra will now play, "Viva Espana".'

We walked in silence to the jeep. I was busily trying to think of some way to postpone the moment of parting; I don't know what Claire was thinking. 'Hey!' I said, suddenly inspired, 'you haven't asked me those other questions!'

'You're right, I haven't. Is it too late, do you think?'

'Not for me, it isn't. How about you?'

'Oh, I'm fine!'

'OK then. Would you like to go back into the hotel and ask

73

or would you like to stand here and ask or would you like to ramble about the town a bit and ask?'

'A midnight stroll sounds just the job to me.'

Under the orange glow of the sodium lights in the deserted streets, she looked green – green but still beautiful. 'You've gone all green!' I mocked gently, again deciding to forgo the comment about being still very beautiful.

'You look kind of seasick yourself,' she smiled.

Her questions didn't amount to much; in fact, they had nothing at all to do with Catamaran. She explained that she was really a features writer, not a reporter as such, and she'd had the idea, during the calving case, that she would like to do a feature on a vet's life. 'What do you think?'

All I could think at that moment was that that meant she would have to spend time with me, but then I'd known all along that we'd spend more than just one brief evening together. 'When would you like to do it?' I asked eagerly, the mask of reserve slipping for the first time.

'That depends on my editor. But would it be OK with you if I was around for a few days?'

'Sure,' I replied with a feigned indifference. 'No problem.'

We had descended a narrow street to the harbour and now we stopped, looking down on the boats tied alongside, rocking gently on the still, full tide. At the end of the harbour the road turned a corner; after this, there were no more street lights and the town was lost to our view. Ahead, the way twisted and climbed, a pale ribbon in the light of the slice of moon which hung over the mouth of the bay and sent a track of silver along the dark water towards us, a gleaming path which shimmered and disintegrated slowly on the tiny swell which slurped lazily among the stones below.

We walked slowly, almost in silence. Claire's few comments were mainly expressions of wonder at the peace and beauty of night in the country. She marvelled at everything – the moon, the stars, the quiet, the bay; it all seemed so new to her that I began to wonder if she ever left the city at all. While she was poetic about the manifestations of nature as displayed in Knockmore, she was scathing about their appearance from the point of view of urban man – I remember the moon over Dublin being described as looking like a piece of lemon lying in the bottom of last night's gin and tonic glass, while the stars in the city sky came off even worse, being likened to 'flecks of dandruff on the cassock of a very old priest'. Rough stuff.

My contributions consisted mainly of agreeing noises – the night *was* beautiful, the moon-streaked bay *was* magical, the sky *was* alive with stars, but I hardly noticed any of it. Unlike Claire, I was used to them, and besides, I was too besotted to take much notice of anything but the lovely creature beside me. Also I couldn't match the metaphors. If put to it, I'd have described the rural Heavens as 'very nice', the urban, as 'not very nice'. Such command of the language is apt to induce prudent silences.

The road climbed steadily and soon we could see beyond the mouth of the bay, out over its headlands, out to the immensity of the ocean – flat, calm and peaceful, it stretched silvery-grey in the moonlight to north, south and west. Suddenly Claire shivered and hugged herself.

'It's getting a bit chilly,' she said.

'Perhaps we ought to be getting back?'

'Anyway you've had a hell of a twenty-four hours.'

I realised with a sudden shock that I had totally forgotten about Catamaran. A few hours ago I wouldn't have believed that possible, but Claire had gently and effortlessly eased him from my mind. 'Oh, I'm fine,' I smiled tenderly. 'But you're right; it is getting chilly.' I removed my jacket and draped it over her shoulders, hushing her protests, insisting that I was too warm anyway, robbing it of any gallantry. 'Honestly! You'll be doing me a favour by carrying it back for me. It's quite heavy and I'm not all that strong, you know. Carrying jackets tires me easily.'

She laughed and snuggled with great exaggeration into the warm garment. 'You're sure?'

'Scout's honour,' I lied, already aware of the chill shrinking the skin of my arms.

When we got back to the hotel, the dinner dance had ended and the place was in almost total darkness. Claire handed me the jacket. 'Well, Frank, thank you for a most enjoyable evening.'

I've heard those same words hundreds of times, yet this time they sounded as if it was the first time, in the entire history of the world, that they'd ever been spoken.

'It was my pleasure,' I responded, trying to sound equally unique, but ending up sounding hackneyed.

'So . . . goodnight,' and she tilted her face towards me.

'Goodnight, Claire.' For one magical instant my lips brushed hers. 'Let me know when you hear from the editor.'

'Yes.' She spoke softly, still standing close, well within kissing distance.

I kissed her again, briefly, like the first time, and she squeezed my arm, whispered goodnight again and turned towards the hotel. I watched her go, the grace of a ballerina in her walk.

'Hey, Claire!' I called after her in a loud whisper. She turned. 'What about your spot prizes? The chocolates and the bath salts?'

'You keep them for me. We can share them when I come again.' She half-turned away, then turned back. 'The chocolates anyway.' With a happy laugh and a wave, she went through the door into the dimly lit foyer of the sleeping hotel.

At 3.15 a.m. my panicking employer telephoned from the States. He had just heard about Catamaran and, understandably, was in shock. The news bulletin which had informed him of the tragedy had given no details other than that Catamaran had been put down and, not unnaturally, he had begun to wonder if he hadn't left his practice in the hands of a complete incompetent or, worse still, the animal equivalent of a homicidal maniac. It took me ten minutes to persuade him that it had all been a tragic mishap and nothing more. After another ten minutes of questions he seemed reassured. 'Apart from that, everything is just fine,' I went on, rather unwisely – it seemed to reduce the incident to the importance of a minor traffic accident in which a tail light has been broken.

A snorted transatlantic 'Hmmmph!' came down the line to me.

He gave me a phone number at which I could reach him 'if anything else like that happens', and said goodbye.

Wondering what exactly he had in mind, or if indeed anything else like that could happen, I hung up, and, pummelling my pillow into shape, settled down to sleep what was left of the night.

8

Life returned to normal. I went about my business without
any sign of being followed by cars, red or otherwise, and
never did get round to reporting the Sierra to the gardaí.
When it didn't reappear, I assumed it had just been one of the
minders double-checking that I really was a vet and not some
kind of undercover Drug Squad agent, and promptly forgot
about it. If I was just a bit surprised that a Dublin thug would
know that a sea-bridge in Connemara was the beginning of a
twelve-mile cul-de-sac, I didn't worry about it – I suppose
being involved in something like the destruction of a living
legend is inclined to monopolise the mind. Catamaran's name
began to fade from the press, and in the end he just about
made the nine-days' wonder which one cynical journalist had
predicted.

His blood test came in by Friday's post – all parameters
normal – and I locked them away in a drawer, pending
Steele's return.

My photographs arrived the following Monday and I
browsed through them after morning clinic. Most of them
showed at least one of Marnie's three companions, more often
all three, all having a whale of a time with various co-revellers.
The best picture was a close up of Jon, the six-foot-eight one,
blue eyes crossed, a joint up each nostril, bushy red
moustache smouldering. Apart from him and the two girls, I
didn't recognise anybody else and, with a tinge of guilty
regret, I noticed there was none of Marnie. The shots of

Catamaran were good, which made me sorrier than ever that I hadn't managed to get even one of me with him.

Claire took up most of my thoughts. I didn't believe in love at first sight but how else could I explain how I felt about her? After four short heady hours? There were times when I thought she was just a dream, brought on by wishful thinking; then she'd phone and I'd believe again. She phoned two nights after she went back to tell me that the editor had sanctioned her idea but that it wouldn't be for another few weeks. I tried to keep the disappointment out of my voice and said OK. She phoned almost every second night after that, ostensibly to check facts for the article she was blocking out, but the professional aspect of her calls began to occupy noticeably less time and soon, with the safety of two hundred miles between us, we began to flirt.

'I bet,' Claire said, 'that you've wolfed our chocolates already. Beset by starvation at 3 a.m. or something . . .'

'Claire!' I gasped, shocked. 'Do you think I'm a *savage*?' I noted the 'our' and felt warm inside.

'Or on one of the evenings when you were faced with a possibly lethal tuna pie?'

'Those chocolates are *sacred!*'

'Oh yeah? I'd say you guzzled them long ago and you'll replace them just before I arrive,' she continued, laughing.

'Oh how can you say such things?'

'Well, just remember! We've to share them together.'

'Could I forget? But speaking of sharing things together, whatever about the chocs, there's no way that the bath salts will be interfered with until you get here.'

Her answering laugh was of a different quality, gentle, personal, for me alone, the half-suppressed girl's laugh you sometimes hear coming through the dark of a cinema or from a quiet room in a house where there's a party going on.

During those weeks, we also managed to meet on a few occasions, mainly in Dublin. With each meeting, I was falling for her ever more and she had to have realised it. The trouble was that, though we got along famously together, there was always some undefinable reserve in her, some hesitation any time the relationship even looked like moving a single millimetre away from what used to be quaintly described as platonic. I was beginning to think she just didn't fancy me and spent one whole, three-hour, early-morning drive back to Knockmore wondering if I could bear being her confidant, treasured companion, great friend, and . . . nothing more. I didn't think so, but if the alternative meant never seeing her again, then I wasn't sure.

I was in Dublin to placate my bank manager who had sent me a nasty letter reminding me that my term loan account had not been credited with the agreed monthly repayments since March. I had replied to his previous letters but this one was couched in more unambiguous terms, 'suggesting' that I call in person, at my earliest possible convenience, Bankspeak for: 'Get your ass in here, now!' So, having arranged for the neighbouring practice to cover for me, I set off, not looking forward to it at all.

By five o'clock, I'd finished my business and went in search of the address Claire had given me. The increasing happiness I felt as I neared her flat banished the memory of my recent awkward interview, just as she had blotted out the memories of Catamaran's death, the first night we met. The euphoria however, hit a brick wall when, on locating the address, I found a shiny black Porsche crouched outside the gate. Its customised registration number proclaimed that it belonged to Paul Markham, a guy I had known vaguely at college and had met on several occasions since, always in the company of a beautiful woman. Handsome as a cigarette ad, rich as Croesus, he was witty, charming, athletic, widely read and even more widely travelled, and, given the choice, he was the man whose car I would least like to find parked outside Claire's flat.

Scowling at the Porsche, I went through the gate, up the short path, and pressed the bell with C. O'SULLIVAN beside it in a little plastic wallet.

'Hello? Who is it?' Claire's voice came through the metal

speaker. Even the crackly, tinny reproduction couldn't disguise its sweetness.

'It's me. Frank.' Or should that be 'It's I, Frank?' I wondered briefly.

'*Frank!*' the box squawked with evident pleasure. 'Come in! Come in!'

'I will! I will!' I said with matching enthusiasm and pushed through the door when it opened with a buzz and a thunk.

Her flat was on the second floor and she met me on the landing with a wide beam of welcome. I remembered she was beautiful, but my memory had blurred into an overall effect; now, as she kissed me on the cheek, the wonder of it engulfed me again, bewitching me afresh. 'Paul is here,' she said unbewitching me pretty smartly as she linked me up the steps.

'Paul?' I asked innocently.

'Paul Markham. I think you know him, don't you? He knows you anyway,' she said. 'I've been telling him about you.'

Paul Markham sat in a high-backed wicker armchair looking as handsome as ever. 'Hallo there, Frank,' he said in his rich masculine bass, unleashing a smile which ought, by law, to have had a dip-switch fitted for the protection of oncoming traffic after dark.

'Hallo Paul! Good to see you!' I replied, returning the opening salvo in what was already a full-scale battle.

Claire, seemingly unaware that hostilities had been entered into, went to make coffee while Paul and I sparred with polite conversation.

'How about you, Paul?' Claire asked, poking her head round the screen which hid the kitchen alcove. 'Another?'

'Yes please, Claire,' he replied, looking into the mug he held in a long-fingered, lean, tanned hand. 'This is nearly finished.'

'OK. Two sugars, isn't it?'

'No,' he laughed. 'Just half a spoon – got to watch the old figure you know.'

'Half a spoon, OK. Frank, you take two and a smidgin, right?'

'Right, Claire. *My*, what a good memory you've got!'

One – nil. In the absence of team-mates, I mentally kissed myself on the back of the neck.

'Paul is helping me with an article I'm a bit stuck with,' she explained, carrying in two steaming mugs.

'Oh? What's the article about?' I was willing to help too.

'Spengler.'

'Eh? . . .' I said involuntarily, scrabbling frantically in my mind to see if there was any little single cell which might have registered what a spengler was.

'You know? Oswald Spengler? The German philosopher . . .'

'Oh, of *course!*' I said, suddenly feeling that I was playing an away match without supporters. I could feel my eyes glazing over, and, whereas Claire went on without noticing, the significance of this wasn't lost on my rival. He sipped thoughtfully.

'There's been such talk lately,' Claire went on, 'about his theory of the cyclical patterns in the rise and fall of civilisations that I thought I ought to do a piece on it, and I was all for it until Paul pointed out a few basic flaws. I can't quite make up my mind whether they make the whole thing untenable or not, but it's certainly food for thought. Throws it wide open. Interesting. Moot.'

'Oh!' I said, wondering if in fact 'moot' meant what I thought it meant. Claire had told me over her shoulder as we danced a conga that she had a degree in Philosophy and English Literature and I remembered hoping at the time that these weren't her only interests, or we were off to a very bad start.

A silence developed which was beginning to look as if it might last to the weekend. They were both looking at me, so I asked: 'And just what *are* your arguments against Spengler, Paul?' I ought, of course, to have admitted neither knowledge of, nor interest in, Spengler, and let them at it, but unfortunately I don't seem to have been blessed with that much common sense.

He began in the beautifully modulated tones of one who knows he's in the driving seat. 'There's a certain irrefutable logic in his hypothesis, I admit, but when one examines it in detail, especially as he has expressed it in *Der Untergang des Abendlandes*, one is, I think, bound to concede that there are a few basic flaws which, to my mind at least, leave the whole argument moot.' *Another* 'moot'! 'Look at it this way. I presume you wouldn't take issue with Spinoza, would you, Frank?'

'Of course not!' I replied, aghast.

'Then if you accept Spinoza's philosophy – and here I draw your attention specifically to the points made in his *Ethics* – I don't see how you can but question the Spenglerian conclusions.'

I pulled meditatively at the lower lip, nodded vaguely a few times, and let my eyes focus on the middle distance in the manner of one not wholly convinced but thinking about it. I was acutely aware of yet another silence, a silence designed to let me have my say.

'I had no idea that you'd taken Philosophy at college, Paul. I could have sworn you did Geology,' I said. Playing for time. I walked into it.

'That's right, Frank. Geology was my subject. Philosophy is just a hobby, but a most fascinating one. One likes to read, to understand, to think for oneself, and, once in a while,' he smiled sickeningly, soupily at Claire, 'to play the iconoclast.'

Disaster! Own goal! Markham 6 – Samson 1.

Luckily for me, Claire butted in, seizing on some point or other and, for the next five minutes the air was criss-crossed by ropes of jargon as they argued the various points, unravelling them strand by strand. I sat, rigid as a pauper at Sotheby's, lest any movement might be misconstrued as a signal that I wished to add my contribution. Words like 'syllogism' and 'empiricism' and phrases such as 'fundamentalist totalitarianism', 'theistic obscuranticism' and 'socioeconomic political naivety' whirled about me and, though I had often discussed these weighty matters in pubs, where nobody else had a clue what they meant either, there was no way I wanted to get involved here.

Claire glanced my way once or twice – obviously her sense of duty as hostess was telling her I ought to be included, and the danger of her doing so was increasing by the second. But when it came, it didn't come from Claire and it didn't come from a sense of duty; it came from Paul Markham and it came from a sense of *coup de grâce*.

'What do *you* think, Frank? You've been sitting quietly there taking it all in and keeping your counsel.' He fixed me with a smile so happy it almost met at the back of his neck, and said I was probably waiting to explode their arguments with 'infinite sagacity'. He ended up: 'So, Frank, you be judge. *The State v Oswald Spengler.* Guilty or not guilty? True or false? Right or wrong?' There was a gleam in his eye as he went through the long-winded rigmarole, the roll of drums as the guillotine was winched up.

'Sorry, Paul,' I said vaguely, suddenly inspired. 'Did you say something?'

'I said: "What do *you* think?" '

'About what?'

'What Claire and I have been talking about for the past five minutes.' His exasperation was controlled, but, to me, obvious.

'I'm sorry. I'm afraid I haven't been listening. I've got a very serious situation on hand at the moment – something which could have grave implications for the bloodstock business. But I probably shouldn't say any more until I'm sure.' I knew that that would get Spengler out of the way – when we'd been making small talk earlier, Paul had boasted, without it seeming like boasting of course, of his brood mares and his yearlings and his horses in training.

'That sounds awful. What is it?' I had him – even at that early stage. It was now just a matter of reeling him in.

'It *is* awful. If it *is* it. A potential disaster for the Irish Horse. As I said, I probably shouldn't say any more. After all it may *not* be it, and I don't want to cause a national panic.'

'What are we talking here, Frank?' Paul asked, getting all friendly and man to man. 'Maybe I ought to know, and I can keep things to myself. Forewarned is forearmed, you know.'

'Neatly put, that. Look . . . I won't be sure until tomorrow, until I get the results of the final tests they're doing now. All the other tests were inconclusive – electrophoretic chromatography, reverse-binding fluorescent photomicrography, auto-immuno assay biometrical titration,' I ticked off on my fingers a list of likely-sounding buzz-words, not one of which, as far as I knew, meant anything, only stopping when I ran out of fingers. As the list rolled on, Paul Markham nodded sagely as if they were *exactly* the tests he would have expected me to do. 'But as I said, all inconclusive. So I had to take samples today for these definitive tests. That's why I came to town.'

'I thought you had to come up to see your . . . on business,' Claire collected herself, not wanting to mention bank managers in front of Croesus.

'I just said that, Claire because I didn't want the press getting wind of it.'

Claire looked hurt for a moment and then asked, sensibly: 'Why didn't you do the tests you're doing now, first, if they're the only completely reliable ones?'

'Because they're so difficult! I was up at four this morning doing biopsies from the cerebral medulla, the anterior pituitary, the adrenal medulla, the mitral valve, the stem of the pancreas, Larsen's Peduncle' . . . I reeled off another list, all fictitious but they sounded great – 'Waterman's Ligament, Garcia's Follicle, Heinemann's Fundus . . .' There were a few more which I can't recall but they were going down so well that I almost chanced 'Handel's Messiah'. All of a sudden I was having a whale of a time.

'Look Frank, what is it exactly that you suspect? You can tell me. Us. We can keep a secret. I'm sure I speak for Claire too.'

'I thought, Frank, that you would have known that about me already,' she said, again the hurt in her eyes and voice – perhaps more confused disappointment than hurt.

'Well, confidentially, it looks like . . . Eumitis. I hope I'm

85

wrong but . . . Do you remember, Paul, some years ago, they had an outbreak in Kentucky? Horses dropping all over the place?'

'I seem to remember reading about it. But I hadn't moved into the US market at that stage so I'm a bit hazy. Remind me.'

'Lucky for them, they managed to control the outbreak by slaughtering all the in-contact animals and burning down the stables. But, here, if it *is* eumitis, it's the less acute form and the horses take up to a month to die and it spreads everywhere.'

'Of course! Now I remember! What was the name of that stud farm that it started on?' He clicked fingers rapidly, frowning hard.

'I don't know.' We spent a while discussing eumitis and I invented a whole battery of horrifying symptoms and appalling mortality rates. Claire was agog.

So was Paul. 'Frank, old buddy . . . Will you tip me off if the tests are positive?'

'Sure. Why not? Tell you what – if you don't hear from me, you can take it that the tests were negative, OK?'

Soon after, Paul left – he had to prepare for a coup he hoped to pull off in Sweden in a few days' time, a hostile bid for a papermill. If you don't mind.

When Claire came back from seeing him to the top of the stairs, she said: 'There's a great story in that eumitis thing, but I think you ought to have trusted me enough to know I wouldn't have published if you asked me not to. I thought we understood each other better.'

I looked at her, wondering how I was going to handle this one. Telling her I'd made it all up was no problem – telling her *why* was another matter. I cleared my throat. 'Claire. I made it up. The whole thing. There's no story. There's no eumitis.'

She looked at me, perplexed. 'You mean there's no danger to the horses?'

'There's not even any such thing as eumitis. Well, there is, in a way, but it's not a disease. It's a silly phrase vets use to cover the multitude of nonsense jobs we get asked about on farms. We get called to a genuinely sick animal and, when we've treated that, as often as not, the farmer will say: "While you're here you might as well have a look at this, that or the other." We call those *eumitis* calls because they always begin with "You might as . . ." ' I shrugged bashfully.

She was looking at me with a puzzled expression and I was just beginning to wonder how to explain the reason for the whole charade when I saw understanding flare suddenly in her eyes. A slow smile began at the corners of her mouth and ended up as a laugh of delight.

'No outbreak in Kentucky?'

'No outbreak in Kentucky.'

'So how come Paul remembered it so well?'

I shrugged innocently. 'You tell me.'

She laughed again then reached up and kissed me.

We met some friends of hers for dinner and afterwards, when I took Claire back to her flat, I declined her offer of a nightcap, a move which, of itself, ought to have made me unique amongst men in her eyes. I drove slowly through the wet night to Knockmore, humming smugly all the way.

During the next ten days I managed to get to Dublin twice. I had no reason whatever to make the seven-hour round trip other than to be with Claire, but on each occasion I pretended that I was up on business anyway and as I had to be in town, perhaps we might go to the theatre, have dinner . . . if, of course, she was free? Not only was she free, but she sounded delighted at the prospect and gave every evidence of relishing my company. Despite this while I was driving home after the second visit I perversely convinced myself that she just didn't fancy me physically. And never would. No matter how long I waited.

A few days later she came to Galway to cover a lunchtime concert at the university. I was late. Vets often are. I heard her laugh before I saw her and found her with a group of students, standing and chatting on the green, sunny quadrangle. 'Sorry about that,' I said, joining them and claiming her. 'Another calving case. Just as I was going out the door.'

'Murphy's law. Well, I can't say you didn't warn me.'

'Never fails.'

She said goodbye to the students and we passed under the archway, Claire asking me a hundred questions about the calving case.

Out along the slow river, out past the end of the city, we walked in the warm sunshine. Swans turned expectantly towards the bank at our approach, then away in regal disapproval when we had no crusts or apple cores to scatter on the dark sliding water, making the transition from hopeful beggars to disdainful aristocrats effortlessly. Further out, coxed eights zipped smoothly upriver, incising the fluid surface with their scalpel-bows, oars suturing the river closed behind them with tiny, transient whirlpools.

Once we had exhausted the topic of calvings, conversation came to a halt, and the only sound was the lazy gurgle of the stream as it slipped by the cut limestone bank, heading steadily for the rushing weir which marked the beginning of its last turbulent stretch before it broke free from the confines of the land into the broad expanse of Galway Bay.

'The shortest river in Ireland,' I said, looking out at the oarsmen.

'Mmm?' Her mind came back from somewhere.

'Ireland's shortest river. The Corrib. The lake is just up there, around that corner, all hundreds of square miles of it, and the bay is just a mile or so downstream.'

We stopped to look out on the shining flow at a point where steps led down into the water. Some twenty yards out was a chain of islands, none of them larger than a small boat. Dark channels separated them, overhung by the scrub with which the islands were covered; in the air between them, clouds of insects hovered and darted in short eye-defying hops, their numbers never seeming to decrease despite the depredations of marauding swallows from above and the ambushes of sleek, unseen trout from below. I took her elbow and steered her down and we sat on the last dry step. Claire took off her shoes and wiggled her toes in the river while, beside her, I sat, balanced slightly precariously, one buttock out in space, flicking small pebbles off my thumbnail and watching them plop into the sluggish current. There seemed to be something bothering her but I didn't ask – she'd tell me in her own time if she wanted to. I couldn't see her face as the curtain of her auburn hair hung between us, so I had no idea of her expression; she sat there and watched her toes making tiny splashes. For the next few minutes, she wriggled and I flicked and that was all that happened. Splash, splash went her toes and plop, plop went the pebbles. I ran out of little pebbles and patience at the same time.

'What's the matter?' I asked gently. 'Are you worried about something?'

Abruptly the toes ceased their wriggling but she didn't reply for a while. 'Nothing really. I suppose . . .'

'Thinking deep thoughts?'

'Something like that.' She wasn't exactly bursting to tell me.

'Perhaps I can help?' I nudged, after a bit. 'Provided, of course, it's not another problem to do with Whojee Shpinkler, the acclaimed German whatsit.'

That broke the spell a bit. She laughed and shook her hair back. 'No, Frank. Nothing as trivial as that. And it's Spengler, not Shpinkler.'

'So what *were* you thinking about?'

I was surprised when she answered. 'Me.' She paused, then added tentatively. 'And you.'

'So was I,' I said. 'As usual.'

'Really?'

'Really. Hadn't you noticed?'

She went silent again, her lovely brow furrowed. 'Frank,' she began at last, 'you're a very special person . . .' My heart sank. It sounded very much like the velvet glove, the beginning of the classic brush-off speech, the one that ended in Victorian novels . . . 'but it can never be . . .' on receipt of which, Frank went off and searched for the source of the Nile or opened a trading post on the Amazon, married a native woman, and died from a mixture of malaria, curare, snakebite, and the produce of local stills without ever discovering that he was the long-lost son of the Duke of Chipping Norton . . .

'And I'm afraid . . . that I'm getting more involved with you than I ought to. I've known you for such a short time.' In a daze I heard her go on. 'Even the way I can *say* these things to you, without embarrassment – well, with relatively *minor* embarrassment – shows how special you are. I can't even begin to *think* of myself being able to talk this freely with any other man I know. Since I was sixteen, I don't think I've ever ended up alone with a man for an evening without having to spend the whole time trying to dodge passes, pretending not to notice the unsubtle *double entendres*, the half-hinted suggestions, the barely disguised leers. You get sick and tired of it. I'm no prude, but there's a time for everything – and that isn't ten seconds after we end up being alone. At least, not for me, it's not. You're different, Frank.' She gave a little laugh. 'I even asked you in for a nightcap the other evening and you said no!'

'Tactics,' I grinned at her. 'Stratagems and fiendishly clever plans. I'm not different. You just make me *act* different. I can't explain it. I'm not even sure I like myself like this. But there's something about you, a kind of trust or openness that appeals to something deep inside me. Whatever it is, I have a longing to know *that* side of you more than the physical side. Or at least as much,' I added with a smile. 'God, but that sounds corny! Does it make any sense to you at all?'

'Yes. I told you you were special.'

'Special? I must be mad!' I growled lasciviously. 'So, what happens now?'

'That's the problem.'

'Why is it a problem? Unless you find me physically repulsive or something . . .' It was time to get it out in the open.

'No, it's nothing like that, I assure you! Quite the opposite, in fact. It's just me. You see, once I knew a man like you. He was simple and nice and kind and gentle and I suppose I loved him. He was also married, though I didn't know that and, just for good measure, he had another couple of ladies to keep him company when I wasn't around. That was four years ago and I've fought very shy of allowing myself to get emotionally tied up with anyone since; and I feel – I *worry* – Frank, that with you, it could happen all over again.'

'What? Find out that I'm married?'

'No! Twit! Be *serious*. I mean that I'd get emotionally involved and then have to cast loose again. For whatever reason.'

'But Claire, you can't go through life choking off any relationship that looks like getting serious – that way all you've got are the good-time boys and the sugar daddies. There *are* no guarantees, but I'd certainly hate to say goodbye now on the sole grounds that it *mightn't* work.'

She considered this a while in silence, then she leaned slowly towards me and we kissed with infinite tenderness, only our lips touching. We sat for a while more watching the river and talking, then it was time to go.

As we walked back, meeting people, other couples, traffic, I gradually readjusted to the real world. 'Claire,' I said, worrying. 'How sure are you that Spengler *isn't* important? I mean I'm not exactly *au fait* with your philosophers and such. Do you think that'll matter?'

'Not in the slightest. I do have other interests, you know.'

'Good. Though I've already made a start on trying to even the field of common interests.'

'Oh?'

'Yes. The other night, after the Spengler débâcle, when I got home, I found a book on twentieth-century poetry. And, as I didn't feel like sleeping, I browsed through it.'

'Did you like it?'

'Do I have to be honest?'

She laughed. 'One woman's meat is another man's poison.'

'Actually, I couldn't make much sense of it. The two most abiding memories I have are that Ezra Pound probably wasn't the full shilling, and, if T. S. Eliot had been christened S .T.

Eliot instead, his name would have been "toilets" spelled backwards. Some highbrow, huh?'

Claire laughed and assured me that my observations had to be the most original ever made in reference to such august figures.

We reached the Land Rover and I rooted in the box beneath the passenger seat and fished out the eight prints of Catamaran.

'Present for you.'

'Photographs?' Claire opened the used envelope which I'd put them in. 'What of?'

'Catamaran. The last photographs of him, taken the day he died. They probably aren't any use to you at this stage as he seems not to be news any more. It's a pity I didn't think of them when you were doing the article.'

Claire was leafing through the prints. 'Wow! Look at the muscles rippling under that skin! What do they feed these animals to develop them like that?'

'There are special formulations all worked out with the same care, or more, than they lavish on the manufacture of baby foods. And, of course, many breeders have their own little secret ingredients . . .'

'Yeah?'

'Sure. A glass of port, a slice of lemon, a spoon of this, a cup of that, you name it. There are as many secret ingredients as there are owners. Catamaran was on sunflower seeds.'

'Norris told you his secret ingredient?'

'No way! These matters are covered by the Official Secrets Act! I found sunflower seeds in a dung sample I took from Catamaran that morning, the same time that I took the pictures. So you think you might be able to use them, then?'

'Maybe I can do another article based on them – I'm sure the editor would go for it. Which ones can I have?'

'Whichever. All, if you want.'

'You're a darling. But suppose they want enlargements or something? Maybe I should take the negatives and leave you the prints.'

'Fine.'

I lifted the passenger seat, removed the Sureprint wallet again, and returned the prints to it. Holding the negatives up against the bright sky, I separated the two strips which, conveniently contained all eight shots of the horse. Claire placed them in the envelope, I put the remaining negatives back into the wallet and closed down the seat.

'It's a pity that you didn't have one of yourself and Catamaran. That would have made a smashing centrepiece for a story.'

'The damned film ran out.'

We had lunch in Hooker Jimmy's, then drove out along the rocky north shore of Galway Bay, talking about work, what was happening in Dublin, general, noncommittal stuff like that. We parked on the grassy top of a range of sand dunes and walked down towards a long, deserted beach, Claire threading her arm through mine. I climbed over a wall which ran across our path and turned to help her. Not being used to dry-stone walls, Claire teetered on top, panicked when it began to wobble, dislodged a few stones, and then half-jumped, half-fell into my rescuing arms.

'Four faults,' I grinned as she clung to me while she found her feet. I didn't actually clutch her to me, but I didn't push her away either – I left our separation up to her.

She stayed while she caught her breath, which took a magical few seconds, then tilted her head back to look up at me. 'They don't go in for cement much in Connemara, do they?'

'No. And now you can see why. It never fails. Avoid crossing walls where you see groups of young lads hanging about – they're particularly rickety stretches.'

She laughed, told me I was full of bullshit and, after a pause, during which she made no effort to step away from me, asked if we were going to stand there all day. I almost said yes, but I was afraid that that might come under the heading of rushing her, so I took her hand and led her off towards the beach. We walked across the dry, crackling seaweed line down on to the cleaner sand.

'I haven't seen Paul Markham since,' she said in a gently teasing voice.

'Who he?' I asked in wide-eyed innocence.

'Spengler he. That who he.'

'Oh! You mean Markham-Spengler! The one and only, world-famous, Hiberno-Teutonic, double-barrelled, industrialist-philosopher!'

She laughed and, after a pause, 'You know . . . he used to pop in for coffee a couple of times a week.'

'Perhaps you make lousy coffee.'

'I do. But it never stopped him before.'

'Before what?'

'Before the evening you almost wiped out the entire equine population of the whole country single-handedly with galloping eumitis.'

'A highly fatal condition that proved to be. For some . . . D'you think he fancied your ass?'

'You're such a poet, Frank. I wish I had a pen to write that down.'

'Don't worry. I'll remember it. Well? Do you?'

'Mmm . . . I think he liked me. Yes.'

I noted the past tense. 'Well then it's obvious what happened. Faced with my *joie de vivre*, my *je ne sais quoi*, my *sang froid* and *savoir faire*, not to mention my *mal-de-mer*, *fait accompli*, *au revoir*, *bon voyage*, *boeuf aux champignons*, *auf Wiedersehen*, and *appellation controllée*, he decided it was no contest and quit the field.'

'I think your conclusion is correct but I also think your reasons are way off.'

'Why?'

'I think he got the message from me,' she replied simply.

'Oh,' I said, and shut up.

'Do you notice anything different about me?' Claire asked after a while.

'Eh . . .' I examined her as she smiled expectantly. 'You've changed your hair?'

'No!'

'I give up. What?'

94

'About my attitude.'

'Attitude to what?'

'My demeanour.'

'No. I can't say I do. Give us a clue. Animal, vegetable or mineral?'

'Forget it. Forget the guessing. Do I seem to you like a woman who has come to a decision and is happy about it, or do I remind you more of a woman who is still letting the ghosts of the past haunt her?'

We stopped and I pulled her round to me. 'I think I need another hint' I smiled. 'And make it obvious . . . like the last one.'

She slid her hand up to the back of my neck and gently pulled my mouth down to hers.

On a small grassy patch above a cove we sat and rested. The sea, without a breath of air to ruffle it, lay in the bay like molten pewter. Offshore, on small rocks, cormorants squatted motionless, necks folded back, wings hung out to each side like supplicants. Along the western horizon a bank of white clouds had marshalled, but without any wind to move them they just lay there, like a lace hem on the blue mantle of the sky, or the snow-capped peaks of Atlantis. In a little while, when the time was right for Claire, we made love.

I drove her to the station and she just managed to catch the train. We ran along the platform towards the last open door. There were so many things I wanted to say to her but there was no time.

'Any chance you might make it down at the weekend?' I asked when we reached the door.

'Not this weekend. I've promised to go to England with my mother – there's an old friend of hers very poorly – dying, actually.' She shrugged sadly, but whether it was for the old friend or the lost weekend, I didn't know. The train gave a lurch. I kissed her quickly and she hopped aboard. Then she was gone, out of sight, out over the sea-bridge which was only a few hundred yards along the line.

I trudged back to the Land Rover, missing her intensely already.

9

The last of the evening half-light was dissolving into darkness as I pulled up outside the cottage late on Monday evening. The squeaky hinges of the gate startled a sleeping bird which, with a great clatter of wings, shot out of the apple tree and flapped off over the cottage, squawking its raucous protest. In the dark porch, I fumbled the key into the lock and passed into the deeper dark of the house. Yawning cavernously, I heeled the door closed and reached for the light switch. In an instant, my drowsiness shattered and the skin shuddered tight along my back, raising my nape-hairs stiffly. In the impenetrable blackness I sensed movement nearby – positive, menacing movement. I flicked down the switch.

There was hardly time to raise a defensive arm before the masked figure rushing at me shoved me backwards. As he wrenched open the door and headed for the night, I overcame my shock enough to have a go. Throwing myself at him, rugby fashion, I managed to wrap my arms around one leg at mid-shin. I heard him swear as he tried to haul me along the rough path and I was grimly concentrating on making a grab for the other leg when I became aware of a rush of footsteps behind me. Glancing over my shoulder, I saw, silhouetted against the bright rectangle of the open door, a figure towering over me. High above his head, he brandished a golf club, which at that moment began to whistle down in a lethal arc. I released my grip on the leg and instinctively tried to get my arms into a protective position – I didn't quite manage and, though the deadly force was somewhat absorbed by my left forearm, the club-head detonated against my temple, scattering my senses in a kaleidoscopic explosion of nauseating pain.

I rolled limply off the path on to the herbaceous border. In my semi-conscious state, I overheard voices from what seemed a great distance: 'Jesus! You've *killed* him!' the first one said in horror. '*Run, damn you! Run!*' the second one urged, panic-stricken. Then there was the squeak of the gate, the sound of feet running on the pavement and car doors being slammed shut. Grimly determined, I hauled myself into a half-stance and stumbled to the gate, forcing my mind to concentrate on getting the car number, or at least a description of it. But it didn't come past the gate – it roared off up the side road.

'Damn!' I swore disgustedly, and leaned against the wrought ironwork, bent double, dry-retching. My head was a shifting mass of pain and each attempt at throwing up only made it worse. After a while, it passed, but I remained doubled over, gulping in huge draughts of cool air and collecting my senses. Then, very gingerly, I shuffled towards the door.

In the split second between switching on the light and being attacked, I had just about noticed that the room was a shambles, but I was shocked when I saw how total the devastation really was. The once comfortable apartment was now a wreck.

The tall, elegant bookshelves had been ransacked, the books thrown about the room; some had had their covers pulled off and they lay scattered everywhere, naked and vulnerable as oysters on the half-shell – on the floor, on the slashed sofa and armchairs and, soot covered, in the grate. Mingled with them were the albums; these had been systematically removed from their sleeves, which now lay in a heap beneath the record cabinet.

The sound system lay face down on a pile of LP sleeves; on top of it, the video recorder, all smoked glass, digital display panels and slide control knobs, canted at a crazy angle, while above the whole mess, seemingly defying gravity, the TV set perched askew on its shelf. More than half of it stuck out in space; from its outer bottom stud the cardboard backing panel hung, exposing its internal organs. I replaced it and pushed the set back to safety.

The rest of the furniture had suffered the same fate. An inlaid bureau was on its back, ravaged, its drawers torn out and left lying among their one-time contents; a large *papier mâché* globe had a fire iron sticking out of it like a spoon in an egg. In the corner by the fireplace stood a tall, slim cabinet which housed a collection of birds' eggs; the eggs had been dumped on the floor but had been spared any breakages that I could see, presumably by their lightness. The boxes in which they had nestled lay nearby, the green baize torn from the underlying wood, and, though the cabinet was still upright, the baize had been ripped from its shelves and back.

I phoned the gardaí and went to check the rest of the house. My bedroom had received the grand treatment too – bed, pillow, mattress, clothes, suitcase, cupboards and drawers had been mindlessly thrown around and the mattress stuffing lay on the floor like drifts of grey slush. 'Jesus!' I thought. 'What a fucking mess!'

They had got in through the bathroom window. It was broken and the plastic curtains with the tropical fish on them billowed gently in the breeze. I dabbed a cold compress on the rapidly rising lump on my head and continued my inspection, wondering who my visitors were and what they had stolen. If anything – I didn't remember either of them carrying anything as they fled along the path. Except the golf club, and they weren't stealing that. The spare bedroom was less chaotic, but the kitchen hadn't been spared – dresser, cupboards, cooker and fridge had been pulled away from the wall; even the freezer section of the fridge had been emptied and the floor covering had been torn up at the corners and edges. I righted a chair and set the kettle for coffee. When under duress, make coffee.

I sat and sipped and nursed my bump and waited for the gardaí and tried, painfully, to think. If their motive was plain robbery, then why hadn't they taken the valuables, the electronics? Or, even more puzzling, why had they wrecked them? Could they have been nursing a grudge? If so, against whom? Me? Then why wreck someone else's property? Against the owner of the house? Maybe he was a murky character, though I doubted the sweet and gentle Mrs Steele had a shady brother, but who knew? Despite the senseless destruction, I couldn't see them as vandals, the one I'd had hold of was not a young man and his tweed trousers and polished brogues didn't fit the bill. Also no self-respecting vandal could have thrown the egg collection on the ground and not jumped all over it – I'd been tempted to pop one or two myself. Could they have been just ordinary nutcases? Two nutcases together didn't seem very likely. Could they have been searching for something? That would explain the lino in the kitchen being torn up, the ripped green baize on the back of the egg cabinet. Something flat. I wandered back into the sitting room and noticed that the inner white sleeves of the records had also been removed – something flat, small enough to be hidden in a book or record sleeve . . .

At this point Potter and the same two colleagues arrived. 'God Almighty!' he said, peering over my shoulder as I opened the door. I stood aside to admit them. 'Holy God Almighty! Would you look at this for a mess!'

As we went from room to room, I explained what had happened. When we got to the bathroom with its broken window, O'Hanlon produced a small case and went to work on the sill, dusting it for fingerprints. The inspector and I wandered back to the living room, me continuing my story. Every few sentences, he'd interrupt with a question or a comment and when I came to the part about the car being parked in the side road, he held up his hand to stop me and turned to the uniformed man. 'Nip round there, Fitzy, and see what you can see – and bring in that golf club when you're coming back.' Fitzy left. 'And don't forget not to touch the handle,' he called after him. 'He's a good lad, Fitzy, but sometimes these youngsters get excited.' He called again, a shout. 'Or the *head*, Fitzy!' Again he turned back to me:

'Your man would have taken it out of the golf bag by the head.'

I nodded. 'I was doing a bit of thinking while I was waiting for you,' I said and told him as far as I'd got.

'I'd say you're probably right. Are you sure you don't have anything of value?'

'I should be so lucky!' I snorted. 'I'm certain.'

He wandered off looking here and there in a way that I suspected wasn't as aimless as it seemed, like our walk through the fields. I continued with my coffee.

He ambled back into the kitchen. 'No wills, deeds, share certificates, nothing of that nature?' He regarded me from under bunched brows.

'No,' I replied. 'But what about the owner? Would he have?'

'He's a very neat man and anything of value would be in the bank.'

Fitzy came back. In one hand, he carried the golf club (by the neck) and, in the other, a pale yellow latex glove. He carried it as if it had been used in some foul operation, at arm's length, his thumb and forefinger barely holding it by the wrist. 'I found this just outside the gate, sir,' he intoned importantly and dropped it on the table with the gravity befitting 'Exhibit A'.

'Only one?'

'Only one, sir, and I went up about three hundred yards.'

'Did you check both sides?'

'Of course, sir!' Fitzy said, hurt.

'Good man yourself, Fitzy. Nip in there now and see how the fingerprinting is getting along. I'll want this club dusted as soon as the bathroom is ready – though I think we'll be unlucky by the look of that glove.' He turned to me. 'Correct me if I'm wrong,' he said in a tone which didn't allow for that eventuality, 'but isn't this a surgical glove?' He poked it with his pen.

'It certainly looks like one,' I said.

'It's not one of your own, by any chance?'

'No. It's a new one too.'

'How can you tell?'

'I can smell the talc. They put powder in them as a kind of dry lubrication.'

'Well then, there'll be no prints *inside* it, that's for sure, and I doubt we'll find any on the outside either, not on stretchy latex.'

'It looks like a quality glove, highly sensitive, just the job for brain surgery. Though the nearest those lads came to brain surgery was with yon mashie niblick.'

'Three iron,' Potter said automatically, obviously a golfer. 'Do vets do brain surgery?'

'Well . . . Not as a rule. I was merely illustrating a point.'

'Oh. The glove complicates matters a bit,' he said, scratching his head. 'It gives an air of professionalism to an otherwise very amateur job. Any half-decent pro would have had that front door open quicker than you could with your key. On the other hand, the bathroom window is the *only* one not visible from the road and, as they must have broken in at least an hour ago to have done this much damage, it would still have been bright, so maybe that's why they came in that way. But I still think they were amateurs – a pro would work alone and would have been long gone before you entered the house.'

'Perhaps I surprised them. Took them unawares.'

He shook his head. 'As I said, except for the bathroom, all the windows open to the front. If they hadn't heard you coming, you'd have seen lights, the house lights or torches, unless, of course, they were working in the bathroom, which is unlikely, as there's nothing in there to search. So they hear or see you pull up and douse their lights immediately; but beyond that, they can't think what to do next, and just stand, frozen, until your entry forces some action on them. They must have had at least a couple of minutes before you entered, and they couldn't even get out the way they'd come in!'

O'Hanlon had been working on the handle of the club. He straightened up. 'Nothing,' he said, disgusted. 'Same as the bathroom.'

'There wouldn't be. Not with the gloves. Well . . . that's

that, isn't it? There's not a lot more we can do here tonight. I think, Fitzy, you'd better stay, in case they decide to finish off the job. I'll send McMahon along to keep you company. Now, what about you, Mr Samson? There isn't a bed fit to sleep in and you won't find a hotel room at this time of night at this time of year. You'd better come home with me.'

'Lord, no! I wouldn't dream of it!'

'I'll give the missus a buzz right this minute and tell her,' he went on as if I hadn't spoken. 'You need that bump looked at and she's a nurse. The spare room is always ready, so it's no problem.' This could only happen in a small town, I thought. Good old forgotten values.

Five minutes later, he was driving me in my own Land Rover to his house. In the driveway of the neat bungalow, I caught the smell of bacon and eggs, and when we went in I could hear them sizzling; suddenly I realised that I hadn't eaten all day and offered no more than token resistance when Mrs Potter said they were for me. My headache subsided as I sat in the kitchen demolishing the food as genteely as I could. Afterwards, we sat talking into the small hours, and in no time we were on first-name terms. At one point my attention was caught by a glass case full of medals, trophies, cups and the other trappings of successful competition.

'Have your children won all those?'

'No,' Potter replied. 'Actually that was Joan and me. We won them.'

'Yeah?' I asked, surprised. 'For what?'

'Ballroom dancing. We used to do a lot of it. We were runners-up in the All Ireland finals twice and semi-finalists six years in a row. We never actually *won* it – unfortunately, our *paso doble* let us down, every time. It was always our weakest.' And he whistled a few bars in a catchy rhythm which I assumed was the bogey *paso doble*.

'Well at least it gives the lie for once and for all to the alleged flat-footedness of the force,' I said.

'I don't know about that,' Potter smiled. 'I'm probably the exception. I take a seven and I think the smallest size they had when I joined was ten. Some of them had boots like young violin cases. Guess what the sergeant used to call me?' He smiled knowingly across at his wife, who was grinning at the memory.

'Twinkletoes?' I hazarded.

He shook his head. ' "The Peter Potter of Tiny Feet". It used to drive me *wild*, especially as I was the youngest recruit in the place.'

We laughed happily at the thirty-year-old-pun. Soon after, he showed me to the spare room and wished me goodnight. Despite the excitement of the evening and the pain in my head, I fell asleep almost instantly and, for the first night in a long time, Claire didn't turn up to fill my dreams. Nothing did.

10

Next morning, I nursed a surprisingly mild headache through a quick and easy clinic, and afterwards set out with my shortest list of farm visits yet. A few minutes after noon, Eileen came over the radio-telephone with an urgent call for Bally Ard, and all that looked like changing.

'What's the problem?' I answered uneasily.

'Mr Norris's hunter. Bad colic.'

'OK, I'm on my way. Over and out.' I swung the Land Rover around. *Déjà vu.*

Colic can be caused by any number of factors, ranging from wind pains at one end of the scale to ruptured stomach, twisted gut, torsion, volvulus, intussusception and other horrendous conditions at the other. The problem is how to tell them apart. Horses are not the stoics of the animal kingdom, and a horse with a build-up of wind can act much the same as a horse in the early stages of one of the fatal colics. X-rays powerful enough to penetrate the bulk of a horse's body are not usually part of a GP's kit, and laboratory tests take time. Some colics have specific symptoms, but generally, definitive diagnosis is difficult. Palpating the abdominal organs per rectum can help, and exploratory laparotomy (opening up to have a look inside) is even better, but it takes time and can be awkward when one is working on one's own, so it's not usually done. Many colics respond well to drug therapy but some require immediate surgery, and major abdominal operations carried out single-handed, under field conditions are often more heroic than practical. With the way my luck had been running lately, I was convinced it would be one of the deadlier ones and I began to have a waking nightmare that I'd have depopulated Bally Ard by the time Steele came back. Then I remembered: Norris only had the hunter left. Damn. I could do it *today*.

I swept through the imposing gates of Bally Ard and drove straight to the yard, knowing that Norris, an experienced owner, would be with the horse. As I pulled up, he led a handsome chestnut gelding across to the gate. To my profound relief, the horse seemed quite normal – no foot stamping, tail swishing, bending the back, trying to lie down . . . But he had sweated up badly and his coat was wet. Exchanging brief greetings with Norris, I checked the horse's pulse and the colour of his mucous membranes; I listened to his abdominal sounds, took his heart rate, respiration rate and temperature, all of which, to my great relief and mild surprise, were normal.

'Amazing,' I said to myself more than to Norris. 'Was he bad?'

'Well I was quite worried when I rang you. As you can see, he's sweated up a lot.'

'I see that.'

'Then about ten minutes ago, he passed a lot of wind and seemed to get instant relief. I was going to cancel the call, but then I thought I'd let it stand and have him checked out anyway.'

'Well,' I said, looking at the horse again, 'whatever it was seems to have gone. Hopefully, anyway. I presume he's had his worm dose? Worms can cause colic you know.'

'Of course he's been dosed!' Norris sounded vaguely insulted. 'We dose regular as clockwork.' He gave me the lecture I'd have given him if he'd said no. 'Can't have worms on the paddocks. Not with mares and foals grazing them.'

'Just checking every angle,' I said placatingly. I didn't tell him Catamaran's sample had been positive. 'I'll just take a sample to check that your dosing is effective; it's no harm to check it out every now and then.'

'It better be effective! It costs enough, that new stuff.'

I gave the horse an antispasmodic injection, just in case, took the dung sample and prepared to leave. Norris, however, would have none of it.

'No, no! You must come in for a drink and talk with me for a while. I insist! We've hardly spoken since . . . that awful day, and I wanted to thank you for being so splendid and for staying with Catamaran to the end.'

'Well . . .' I began.

'Just for a few minutes.'

'Well . . . perhaps a cup of coffee might not be a bad idea.'

'Splendid! Capital!' Superlatives tumbled from him as we drove back to the house. He led me through the hall door, then headed straight for the back of the hall, calling for the housekeeper. 'Mrs Flahive! Mrs Flahive!'

'Yes, Mr Norris.' She emerged from one of the reception rooms.

'Ah! There you are! We'd like some coffee please.'

'Very well, sir. I will bring it to the study presently.'

'Not the study, Mrs Flahive. With your permission we will take it in the kitchen.'

'In the *kitchen*, Mr Norris?'

He turned to me. 'It's much more homely – especially for two men in their working clothes.'

'Very well, sir,' the housekeeper replied in a disapproving tone, passing through the door which Norris held open for her.

We sat at a small table in a little room – a larder or scullery or housemaid's pantry or one of those now-obsolete rooms – which obviously had become Mrs Flahive's preserve, and her displeasure as she spread a red gingham cloth was positively proprietorial. But Norris was impervious; he was waffling on about my sterling presence in his darkest hour. 'Don't know what I'd have done without you. I just do not know.'

I tried, once or twice, to protest his lavish and exaggerated praise, but soon gave up; he wasn't hearing anything I said. So I simpered self-deprecatingly a few times and left it at that. The arrival of the coffee put a stop to his gallop, but only briefly. Half-way through his coffee, he suddenly looked at his watch. 'My goodness! Is it that time already? I've got to make a phone call. Excuse me a moment.' Then he sprang up from the table and was gone.

'Mr Norris is a little overwrought,' the housekeeper said.

'Well, I suppose with what he's been through, anybody would be. I hope my being here hasn't sparked off bad memories.' I didn't think it was that – he'd showed no signs of being upset at the yard, where the memories should have been at their worst. I wondered if maybe the insurance people or the syndicate were giving him a hard time, trying to blame him for being careless . . .

'Oh, no, sir. He's been like that for the past few days now. At first, after it happened, he was fine. I didn't think he'd get over it, he was that fond of the horse. It's only in the last couple of days that it's begun to bother him. Delayed shock, I think it is, myself. This morning he had me take down all the pictures of Catamaran in the hall as if he couldn't bear to look at them.' She shook her head sadly.

'I really ought to be getting back on the road,' I said. 'Do you think he'll be back soon? I'd rather not leave without saying goodbye.'

'He shouldn't be much longer,' she said, leaving it up to me.

'I'll wait till half-past,' I compromised. Six more minutes, a respectful and respectable time. He had already been gone about ten minutes. By mutual unspoken agreement, the subject of Gilbert Norris was dropped and a silence ensued. The housekeeper and I had exhausted our one topic of common interest. Now the silence in the old kitchen was broken only by the ticking of a pendulum clock which slowly and remorselessly whiled away the years from a shelf over the range.

Looking around I noticed that there were brilliantly coloured feathers everywhere – in vases, jugs, empty wine bottles, behind pictures, the calendar. Like other houses have cut flowers, this house had feathers.

'Are those feathers real?' I asked, indicating the displays.

'Oh yes indeed, sir. They're all feathers from different members of the parrot family. Psittacines, I believe the technical word is? Mr Vernon gives them to me. He's a friend of Mr Norris's and he's got one of the largest collections of psittacines in the country. All free flying.'

'Do you mean *loose*? Out in the open?'

'Yes sir. Mr Vernon lives alone, with just his birds for company, in what he describes as a wooded oasis in the middle of the bogs, so there's nowhere for the birds to fly to. My son, Eddie, works with him during his school holidays.'

Norris returned at that point. 'Ah, *there* you are!' he said as if he'd just stumbled on my secret hiding place. 'Mrs Flahive been looking after you, I trust? Good, good, good. Well, I've detained you long enough and I'm sure you've more to do than sit and listen to a silly old man, so I won't keep you any longer. Next time, we must make sure we're not interrupted.' His strange behaviour didn't seem to have changed; he remained standing pointedly by the door. I can take a hint as well as the next man, so I stood up.

'Well actually, I *am* quite busy,' I lied to lessen the feeling of being chucked out. 'Thank you for the coffee, Mrs Flahive. Good-day.'

Following Norris through the hall, I noted the substitute pictures – landscapes and still lifes; dark oils and airy watercolours, originals and prints. 'The king is dead. Long live the prints,' I punned irreverently to myself. At the hall door, Norris thanked me for coming so quickly and shook my hand. Obviously, this was as far as he intended to come.

'Wouldn't you like to have a last look at the hunter before I leave?'

'I'm sure he's fine. You did a good job.'

'Still, I think I'll look in on him. I'd feel better.'

'Very wise. Well, I mustn't keep you. Thank you again. Goodbye.'

'Goodbye and don't hesitate to call if the pain comes back.'

I drove back to the yard, puzzled. I'd never before come across an owner less concerned about a colicky horse; I've known people to stay up all night with a fully recovered horse, just in case. As my shadow fell on the floor of the hunter's box, he turned and looked back at me, the picture of health, chewing his sweet hay.

I stopped off at the surgery to check the hunter's dung sample and, though I did the test three times, there was no sign of worm eggs. Bang went my theory of defective worm medicine; it was back to the merry-go-round: how come the precious Catamaran had worms and his stablemate didn't? Had somebody shirked dosing him because he was so hard to handle? Had he managed to spit it out? Et cetera, et (*ad nauseam*) cetera.

Late the following night I discovered what the burglars had been searching for. I had decided to tackle some overdue correspondence and, a couple of hours later, there was a gratifying pile of envelopes ready for posting in the morning; though I was really tired by then, I decided to finish the job and send off the roll of film I had finished the previous week. I fetched my camera bag and peeled open the Velcro-sealed pouch where I keep my used rolls. It was empty. On a hunch, I checked the camera. The exposure counter window showed empty. Double-checking, I opened the camera. Empty. I sat back and thought.

It didn't need any great brainwork to deduce that what the intruders had been searching for in record sleeves, between the pages of books and under the lining of shelves was a photograph or photographs, and that, having drawn a blank at the cottage – where they had obviously found the three or four wallets of prints in the drawer in my bedroom of no interest – they had moved on to the next most likely place, the camera bag and camera itself. Or was it the other way round? Perhaps they had stolen the undeveloped films first . . . Either way, it didn't matter. They had now been through all the photographs I had taken in the past couple of months and I doubted that what they wanted predated that – surely they'd never have taken the film from the camera unless what they wanted was fairly recent?

I glanced at my watch. The new day was almost an hour old

– too late to call Potter. Anyway, he couldn't do much until morning. It would keep. I stood up and turned off the table lamp. Then I did my last round, checking windows and doors, a new habit I had developed.

As I was brushing my teeth, it struck me that the only possibly compromising photographs were the ones that Marnie had been shooting at the party; they seemed innocent enough, but, as I only recognised her three friends, how did I know? Perhaps she had captured someone who seriously didn't want to be photographed? With a sudden shiver I jerked my head up, half expecting to see the two goons behind me in the mirror. Drying my face, I again considered calling Potter, and again decided against it. Surely I was safe – they now had (or had seen) all the prints I had taken in months and, assuming they were reasonable, rational beings, they would call off the hunt . . . Moments later, as I slid over the threshold of sleep, I wondered what kind of reasonable, rational beings would steal films and leave a valuable camera. They might as well have sent me a notice telling me what they were looking for . . . But it was too late for further thought. The door to consciousness closed behind me with a gentle click.

I had troubled dreams of being chased by a white Mercedes with curtained windows all round, including the windscreen, so that I couldn't see who was in it. Then a black Porsche growled out of a Georgian side street and joined the chase. Finally, Claire turned up at a street corner, we went off for a swim in the Corrib, and my followers vanished.

In my dream a phone was ringing. I let it ring for a while before picking it up. 'Hello?' I said in my dream. Claire asked: 'Is this Frank Samson, the greatest lover the world has ever known?' In my dream I replied, in all seriousness: 'Yes. This is he.' It never would have crossed my mind to doubt it – I suppose that's what dreams are for. The only problem was that during this dream conversation there was *another* phone ringing somewhere in the background and it went on and on with such persistence that my dream became bothered, shimmered briefly, then evaporated, leaving me groping confusedly for the bedside phone. I wouldn't have minded only I was going really well – getting places. I fumbled the receiver, dropped it on the floor and hauled it in again on its cord.

'Hallo?' I said thickly, coughed and tried again. 'Hallo?' I tried to make it seductive, like the voice of the greatest lover the world has ever known.

There was a pause. 'Is that the vet?' Th . . . this was a man . . . Where had Claire gone?

'Yes, yes. This is the vet, yes. Speaking. The vet.' I was coming awake by degrees now, though still on automatic pilot. The other person had fallen silent. 'What's the problem?' I asked, now almost fully awake.

'I'm sorry for calling at this hour, but I've got a young heifer calving . . .' A polished voice. Gentleman farmer.

'How young?'

'She's only twenty months.'

'Is she a big one?' I asked hopefully.

'No. She's not. I didn't even know she was in calf until a while ago. She must have broken into the bull-field, and the bull is a Charolais . . .'

'Oh shit!' I muttered; it sounded like a long job. 'How long has she been calving?'

'Couple of hours now.'

'Has she broken her waters?'

'Over an hour ago.'

'Anything coming?'

'No. No sign. But I didn't handle her – I'd prefer to leave that to the man who knows what he's doing. She's straining a lot, though. And she's down.'

'OK.' I sighed heavily. 'What's the name?'

'John Kiernan.'

'Of?'

'Oak Hill Farm.'

'Can you give me the directions, please?'

'Do you know the "Cave Inn" on the Galway road?'

I made a mental note of his instructions. 'Fine, then. I'll be there in about twenty minutes. You'd better have some boiling water ready – she sounds like she might need a Caesarean.'

With a sigh of resignation I rolled out of bed, dressed in the clothes I'd shed a few hours previously and headed for the bathroom. I splashed cold water on my face and winced, made a comb of my wet fingers and headed out into the mild night. On my way through town, I stopped off at the surgery to get a sterile surgical pack from the cabinet, hoping that I'd be returning it in the morning, its autoclave sealing tape unbroken. I wrote 'J. Kiernan, Oak Hill Farm. Heifer calving 2.30 a.m.' on the call book, switched out the light and pulled the door after me. I tried the radio on the way out the road but could get nothing but the squeaks, squeals and whistles that always seem to possess car radios in the small hours. Soon the Cave Inn showed up in the headlights, and I indicated to the emptiness behind me that I was going left. The directions proved accurate and in a short time I rolled to a stop before impressive iron gates, my tyres crunching in the loose gravel of the semicircular area between them and the road. I sat and waited for someone to open up.

A minute later I was still sitting, waiting, and thinking that at that unholy hour a little consideration wouldn't have gone amiss. Maybe the house was some distance from the gate. I blew my horn once – an announcement that I had arrived, not an imperious summons. My lights, passing through the bars, shone on nothing beyond, no ghostly buildings, and there was no sign of lights further out in the blackness. By now, moths and other nocturnal fliers were performing energetic aerial ballets in front of me. I blew again, a longer blast, and, when this produced no response, climbed out to open the gates myself. I unwrapped the chain which held them together, then stopped to roll back the large stone which rested against them, seemingly superflously, as the chain kept them tightly closed. As the stone turned into the glare of the headlights, I was brought up short when I saw the stem of ivy which clung to it. Broken at both ends, it was fresh and full of sap, and its single three-pointed leaf stood stiff, shining and bright green. It had been broken from the parent plant a matter of hours at most, and a queasy feeling that something was very, very wrong welled up warningly inside me. I suddenly realised, with an awful dawning, that the searchers had *not* found what they'd been looking for – since the day I'd met Claire in Galway, the photographs of the party, along with the prints of Catamaran, lay in the well beneath the passenger seat of the Land Rover. I began to straighten and turn reflexly, just in time to see grotesque shadows leap onto the limestone walls. Over the knocking of the diesel engine I could hear the crunch of footsteps rushing towards me.

I spun to face them but, blinded by my headlights, all I could do was raise an arm to protect my head from the blow which I could sense coming. I raised the wrong arm. There was a dull thud as a club of sorts struck me on the right cheekbone and then I was being borne to the ground under the combined weight of my attackers. Feverish arms wrapped around me, pinning mine to my side; someone grabbed a fistful of hair at the back of my head and twisted it to steady my frantic struggling; a knee pressed down on my ear, and a pad reeking of chloroform found my mouth and nose. Immediately I stopped fighting. I had enough presence of mind to remember that chloroform is toxic to the heart and liver, and a sudden gulp would be dangerous to a heart already under stress. So I breathed as slowly as I could, in, out, in, out, in . . .

Clawing my way up through the swirling blackness, I broke surface into a pitch-dark world of pain. I tried to turn my head, but the agony which burst in it drove me back down again towards the abyss. Next time I surfaced, I didn't dare move; I lay, semi-submerged on the ocean of oblivion, my mind adrift on waves of nausea, aware only of a primitive satisfaction at being alive. Even in that fugged, half-drugged state, one thing was absolutely clear: it was vital that the photographs remain in their hiding place – once they had what they wanted, they'd have no further use for me.

I drifted in and out of consciousness for a while, then began to explore with my senses, still afraid to move.

Smell: dank, unused, mouldy, unclean, chloroform.

Taste: bile, blood, chloroform.

Touch: thin, hard, mattress, on a narrow iron bed.

Hearing: painful breathing, pumping heart.

Seeing: nothing. I was in total darkness, or – a sudden horrifying spark of precocious logic mocked me – I had lost my sight! This worried me obsessively as I checked for injuries.

My legs and arms were working. Moving them caused discomfort only in my head and that, I reckoned, was largely due to the chloroform, and would soon ease. My left thumb and forefinger were painful and swollen – I vaguely recalled them twisting back under me in the struggle.

I thought I heard a faraway noise and stayed my breathing;

the noise became recognisable as the opening of a door, followed by the loudening tread of approaching footsteps. I decided to feign unconsciousness – I had no intention of facing the next part of my ordeal until I'd had time to think.

A bolt drew back, a door opened, then: 'Are you awake?' It was the voice that had summoned me over the phone, calling softly. The light came on, and the sudden brilliance, even through closed lids, made me jerk my head; the man must have decided it was an unconscious reflex, because he repeated the question, just as softly, this time, from right beside me: 'Are you awake?' I almost flinched when he laid a hand on my forehead. I sensed him retreating towards the door, and I stole a quick glance. A stupid move – for one thing, I ought to have known the light would dazzle me and I'd see nothing anyway; for another, he might have been looking back at me as he went.

The light went out and, after he had redone the lock, I heard his steps receding again. I listened until absolute silence settled, then I listened some more. Finally, convinced he'd gone, I sat up and swung my legs on to the floor. When my head stopped throbbing, I set out on an inch-by-inch shuffle towards the door, outstretched arms sweeping the space before me, eyes scrunched tight for their protection. Locating the switch with my left hand, I clicked it down. Once more, the room was blindingly lit. When my eyes adjusted, I took stock.

The only way out was the door which, when I tapped it, had an uncomfortably solid ring to it. At eye level there was a Yale lock and, at the same level, roughly in the centre, a crude peep-hole, newly cut. When I put my eye to it I blocked the light, so I couldn't see anything on the other side; I tried standing back from it, but that didn't work either. Licking a fingertip, I stuck it through, checking for a breeze or draught, but all I learned was that the door was almost as thick as my index finger was long.

The naked bulb lit the meagre furnishings with an unforgiving starkness. I checked the bed irons first, but the base was one solid rectangle of angle-iron rusted fast into position. That was the best possibility of a lever or weapon gone. Disappointed, I let the mattress roll back. Against the wall facing the bed-end was a small, flimsy table, barely large enough for a breakfast tray, and beside it, a rickety wooden chair. Either could serve as a weapon, in its entirety or dismantled – I reckoned I could easily take them apart with my hands. Above the table was a narrow shelf; covered in faded pink oilcloth, it held two little red votive light holders in honour of the picture of the Sacred Heart which hung above it. The glass had a long diagonal crack, which might be another weapon if the going got really tough. And that was it.

Immediate escape was out, so now I had to deal with the problem of what to tell my captors at our no doubt imminent interview. I switched off the light and retired to the bed to think. I couldn't deny that the photographs existed. And I couldn't say that the film hadn't yet been sent off because they'd just ask for the undeveloped roll. Nor could I claim to have mislaid the roll – they'd never buy that, and, even if they did, they might decide that they had no further use for me . . . and then what? They could hardly let me go. Could I say I'd sent the roll to Marnie? But, I thought, they might *already* have got to Marnie – after all, she'd been the one using the camera. So they'd have gone after her first. Come to think of it, she and her friends, were the only ones (as far as I knew) who knew it was my camera. It might even have been Marnie who told them about me. How about saying I'd sent it for development and was awaiting its return? No good – they'd only have to check with the lab. Another washout.

That looked like being the depressingly limited shakings of the bag, until suddenly I had another idea. I was just refining the story when I heard the man approach again. I decided to face him this time – I wasn't going to be more ready. I swallowed hard and painfully as the steps stopped outside the door. Then it opened and the light came on.

I sat bolt upright, as if the light had just awoken me. 'What happened? Where am I?' I mumbled thickly, hamming it up. I'd reckoned on pretending I thought I'd been in an accident and that he was a kindly householder, but one look at him and

I knew I'd have to forgo that bit of window dressing – kindly householders do not come dressed in black balaclavas, black anoraks and reflective sunglasses. And they usually carry grapes or mugs of Ovaltine, not wicked-looking revolvers. I stared at him, awed. 'Who are you?' Face to face with an armed captor, my foggy brain cleared instantly. 'Who are you?' I asked again. 'What's this about?'

He continued staring at me through his mirrored lenses, then coughed nervously and shuffled his feet. I got the distinct impression that he was more uneasy than I was. I thought he was about fifty, more from his hands than anything else because they were all I could see of him. He was well built, a couple of inches under six feet, and broad shouldered. His trousers were tweed, his shoes brogues, and I was willing to bet that those were the same trousers I had wrapped my arms around the night of the break-in. While he stood in awkward silence, I tried to size him up.

'Is this political or something?' I threw in a red herring for what it was worth.

'You . . .' he croaked suddenly and coughed again to clear the frog. 'You will be held here . . . until we . . . complete our business with you. If you co-operate, you will be released unharmed, but if you don't, it will end up . . . nasty.' I was right. He *was* nervous. As a mouse. There was even a tremor in his voice.

I decided to try him. 'What do you want with me?' I waited for him to speak and, when he didn't, said with forced petulance: 'How the hell do you expect me to co-operate when I don't know what you want?'

Instead of replying, he pulled a set of handcuffs from his pocket and threw them on to the bed beside me. 'Put those on. They snap shut.'

Reluctantly I complied, and immediately felt depressed – apart from the physical bind of having my hands bound together by a foot of chain, there was the psychological blow of having followed orders. With the click of the second cuff, my developing confidence took a nose dive; his rose in inverse proportion.

'You've got something we want,' he said, walking to the chair and pulling it into the middle of the room. 'Sit here.'

'What?' I asked, moving to the chair – another submission. 'I told you. You can have anything I've got.'

'You've got photographs.'

'*Photographs*!' I squawked in disbelief. 'That *I've* taken?'

'Yes.'

'Well, take them! Take them *all!* I don't know what good they are to you, and I don't want to know, but you're welcome to them.'

He thought about that for a moment, again seeming hesitant, unsure. 'These would have been taken . . . recently, within the last eh . . . month or so.'

'Well that doesn't leave many. I've been too busy.' Then: 'Was *that* what you were looking for at the cottage? It *was* you, I presume? At the cottage?' He said nothing, so I went on: 'But . . . did you not find the photographs? In the bedroom?'

'They weren't the ones we want.'

'In that case, you must have the wrong man. There aren't any more. Oh, sorry! I forgot. There's a film in my camera bag. And another in the camera. It must be one of those. You'll find them in the back of my Land Rover.'

'We've already checked those and they're not the right ones either.'

'You've already checked them?' I gaped. 'You mean – had them developed!'

'Yes.'

'Jesus! How long have I been here?'

'That is of no consequence. Where are they?' He tried to sound menacing and reasonable at the same time.

'I'm afraid there aren't any more,' I shrugged helplessly.

'Oh, but there are, you know. There's at least one other roll.' I didn't like the way he suddenly sounded more sure of himself.

'I tell you, there isn't!' I insisted. This was it, the big bluff. 'Uh-oh! I think I know where we're getting our lines crossed. Do you know anything about cameras?'

'Enough.'

'Perhaps it's even happened to you.'

'What are you talking about? What might have happened to me?'

'Putting the film in wrong, not winding it on to the take-up spool?'

He began to pace. I waited for him to stop, but he waved me on. 'Go on, go on. I'm listening.'

'That's it.' I shrugged again. 'That's what happened.'

'When?'

'Oh, weeks ago. I couldn't say for sure.' I gulped quietly and felt my palms sweat up.

'What were you photographing during the time you say this happened?'

'Who can remember that far back?' I snorted, trying to ignore the 'you say'. Obviously he was reserving judgement. My heart began to pound. I was afraid he'd hear it booming in my chest and know I was lying.

'Try,' he growled; a warning, not an encouragement.

'I don't know if I can'. I had already decided that this would be an opportunity to introduce a whole shoal of red herrings — the more subjects, the less I'd be likely to remember about any of them. In the next few minutes I invented a whole plethora of subjects; among them, I mentioned the only two subjects actually on the roll — the party and Catamaran — but only *en passant*. When I'd finished, he continued to walk the floor, head down, quietly evaluating my story. I grew more and more uneasy as the silent pacing continued.

When the blow came, it caught me on the side of the head. Apart from the shock of its suddenness, it wouldn't have hurt much except that it was right on the spot where I'd been planked with the golf club. 'That,' he growled menacingly, his mirror-hidden eyes only inches from mine, 'is a damned *lie!* Don't try to make a fool of me again!'

He lowered his arm and gradually straightened, breathing heavily. I sat hunched, wondering where the collapse of my story left me.

'So,' he resumed, chest heaving, towering over me. 'Where is it?'

'It's at the processors,' I said in a small voice, swallowing hard.

'It's at the processors,' he repeated, mimicking me. 'When did you send it?'

'Not long ago. The end of last week, maybe.'

'Why the delay?'

'I was in no hurry.' I shrugged. 'There was nothing important on it.'

'What processing laboratory do you use?'

I thought of lying, but I remembered that all the prints at the cottage were in Sureprint wallets, so he already knew the answer. He was testing me, so I answered truthfully. 'Sureprint. In Cork.' This left me with the problem that he would now check with Sureprint and then I'd be back where I started. I could always insist that I *had* sent it and blame the post, but that would be asking a little too much. 'But not this roll,' I added suddenly, inspired by desperation. His head jerked towards me. 'I didn't send these to Sureprint.'

He looked like someone who was preparing not to believe a word of it.

'At this time of the year, the tourist season, they get overstretched and they can be very slow. Or so I've found in past years anyway. I figured, if they're overworked, they could lose the film or mix it up with someone else's, or make a total bags of the job altogether . . .'

He snorted, then said in a resigned voice, humouring me for the moment: 'So what lab *did* you send it to?'

'That's just it, you see . . . I can't remember.' I knew that would go down like the *Titanic*, so I rushed on: 'It was one of those labs you see advertised in the Sunday colour supplements – very cheap, guarantees, free film, free albums, etc. There are loads of them. Every Sunday.'

'Where was this one?'

'Dublin.'

'I don't believe you,' he said in a challenging tone.

'It's true.'

He looked at me long and hard but failed to think of any way to trip me. He could question and probe until we were blue in the face, but my story was too simple to shake – just a few basic facts and no embellishments. 'OK then,' he said, 'we'll keep an eye on your post, and I hope, for your sake, that they turn up soon. We'll give it a day or two . . .' He began to walk again, and I realised that the interview wasn't yet over. 'Tell me,' he said in deceptively conversational tones, 'how come you made up such a fancy story first?'

'How d'you mean?' I asked, with a sinking heart, knowing full well what he meant.

'The film not being loaded properly. You only found out a minute before that we were looking for photographs, and yet you came up with that pat little tale. Even if you *hadn't* been under pressure, you'd have had quite a job concocting that one.'

I shrugged. 'It just came to me. Once I heard "photographs", it seemed like a good plan. To prove to you that I don't know what the hell is going on.'

He stood in front of me now, staring. 'You wouldn't, by any chance, have got the prints back already, seen their significance – if you hadn't already noticed it when you were taking them – and be considering a little blackmail?'

'*Jesus no!*' This was a completely unforeseen and frightening turn of events. 'I swear! I've no idea what's on that reel that worries anybody. I didn't take any shots that could give the slightest offence to anyone.' This was the nearest I came to dropping Marnie in it.

'Because, if that's your game, it might be as well to make your proposal now. We are men of the world, after all . . .'

'There *is* no proposal. Goddamn it! I've no idea what you're looking for.'

'So, you just thought up that story on the spur of the moment, eh?'

'Yes! I've told you.'

'Amazing. A regular Hans Christian Andersen we've got here.' After another few minutes' pacing, during which he obviously couldn't think of any other avenues of interrogation, he said: 'I'm going now, but I'll be back soon. In the meantime, you can shout your head off, but it won't get you anywhere. There are four solid doors between you and the outside world, and this –' he said, pulling open the door of the room – 'is the most solid of the lot.' He rapped the stout timber with his knuckles. 'As you can see, it's been fitted with a dead-bolt and padlock. What else? Oh yes. Before I come in again, I want you to go and lie on the bed. I'll be able to keep an eye on you through this peep-hole.

'Right. I'm off. I'll check your post, then bring you back something to eat.' He went out and locked the door, letting the heavy padlock fall back against the wood with a significant thud. I listened to his footsteps receding along the passage outside; then there was the sound of another door closing and being locked. After that, a very faint footfall, which I wasn't even sure I heard, and then, nothing. I strained to hear the other two doors, the slam of a car door, the noise of an engine, anything; but there were no further sounds. He was dead right – there wouldn't be any point in shouting for help.

12

I paced a while, then lay on the bed. Thinking back over my interrogation I reckoned that, all things considered, it could have been worse – at least they weren't going to kill me straight off. I tried to recall why I'd felt on several occasions that some of his questions didn't make sense, but only one instance came to mind; he had said it was *I* who had taken the photos, as if he knew nothing at all about Marnie, but perhaps he himself had not been at the party. After a time I began to feel nauseous and dozed off, the chloroform still slopping about in my veins.

I don't know how long I slept, but I awoke feeling much better, and lay on the thin, damp mattress, staring at the stained ceiling, making a list of pluses and minuses. The minuses were, alas, dead easy:

– Claire was away, and, if she phoned at all, would assume I was out working;

– nobody, including me, knew where I was;

– nobody, *except* me, knew about the photos – I'd thought it too late to phone Potter (a fine time to develop a sensitive streak);

– my captor was armed, while my arms were cuffed;

– the room seemed to be escape-proof . . .

There were many more minuses, but, as each one nudged me closer to despair, I gave up and concentrated instead on a search for some silver linings. It was a struggle but I managed a few.

– I had written Kiernan's name in the book and, when I didn't show up for work and Kiernan (if he existed) could throw no light on the bogus calving case, the search would be on at once;

– I had a variety of improvised weapons which could be effective, if I could catch him unawares;

– my captor seemed far from confident, as if all this was as new to him as it was to me;

– time was on my side (I reckoned about a week). They might *doubt* my story but they'd have to give it time;

– collecting my post daily would be dangerous for them, specially with the gardaí looking for me . . .

I began to feel quite buoyed. Once again, the entrails were looking pretty good.

An hour later, an eerie age with no external sounds whatever, my optimism had slipped back towards reality. There mightn't even *be* a search! How did I know how they might have stage-managed my disappearance? My graphic imagination promptly weighed in with all sorts of unhelpful suggestions.

Suppose they had left the Land Rover on one of the cliff-top roads, doors unlocked and light-switch on, wouldn't people think I had fallen or jumped? 'Believe he owed a bank in Dublin *hundreds* of thousands . . . something about a girl . . . Oh he *seemed* happy but, you know what they say, they're the ones to watch . . .' Or suppose they had pushed it off the end of a pier with the windows open: wouldn't the obvious conclusion be that I'd lost my way, driven off the pier, tried to escape through the window, and drowned? 'New to the area . . . wrong turn . . . maybe a few drinks . . . to forget . . . *millions* I heard . . . if they don't find him today, then I'm afraid . . . washed out to sea . . . undercurrents, you know . . .' I shivered. Forget rescue; for all practical purposes, I was on my own – I'd have to rely solely on my own resources.

When I heard him coming back, I dashed to the door and switched out the light. Nobody likes to feel they're being peeped at through a small spy-hole. I lay and waited, and heard him stop.

'Are you on the bed?' The voice, muffled through the balaclava and a few inches of wood, was barely intelligible.

I knew what he'd said but couldn't think why I should make it easy for him. 'What was that?' I asked. 'Did you say something?'

'I said: "Are you on the bed?" ' He called. Louder.

'I am.'

'Put on the light.' Still loud – if he had dropped his voice back to normal, I was going to ask him 'What?' again.

'You can put it on yourself when you come in. I'm trying to sleep.'

'Put it on now. You'll have lots of time for sleeping.'

'What was that?'

'Put the light on! Switch on the light!' Exasperated, he raised his voice again.

There didn't seem to be much point in annoying him just for the hell of it, so, mumbling oaths, I tumbled off the bed slowly and crossed to the door.

'Now go back and lie on the bed,' he ordered, and waited until I had done so. I watched the mirrored lens watching me through the peep-hole all the time he was fiddling with the lock. Then he came in.

In his right hand, he had the gun; under his left arm he carried a cardboard box from which the smell of roast chicken issued. He heeled the door closed, then stopped, puzzled – he had obviously just realised, for the first time, that once he was in the room, the door would be held closed only by the Yale lock, which, even handcuffed, I could easily reach. He stood perplexed for a minute, stymied, perhaps annoyed, by this unforeseen hitch. Then he came up with an answer.

'Get under the bed,' he said.

.'*What?*' I asked, perplexed. 'Why?'

'Just until I get the food set out. I don't want you making a rush for the door . . .'

'Christ, haven't you got a bloody *gun* pointing at me?'

'Go on! I don't want to use this. Things are bad enough.'

'That's for sure.'

'I wasn't talking about you,' he said.

It was an odd comment and I stored it away for later consideration as I rolled under the bed – a retrogressive step, compliance, submission, obedience.

I watched as he set out the food: a whole roast chicken in its takeaway tinfoil tray, a bag of chips, an apple, a banana, a plastic cup of yoghurt and a carton of milk. Despite everything, I was quite hungry.

'You'll have to open the milk for me,' I said. 'I can't use my left hand; it got hurt at the gate. It's a two-hand job, opening milk cartons.'

He finished laying out my breakfast, picked up the carton of milk and looked down at me; he made to put the gun in his pocket, then changed his mind and placed it on the shelf instead, moving one of the votive lights to the end to make room for it. He kept an extra wary eye on me for the short time it took to open the carton, then he retrieved the gun and retreated to the door. 'You can come out now. The key to the handcuffs is on the table.'

It was good to be free, and I did some stretching exercises before sitting down. I could sense his tension, and he relaxed only slightly when I sat. There wasn't much hope that he could be taken unawares; he was as alert as a hunting cat.

'They weren't in your post,' he said after a minute, almost accusingly.

'Oh.' I felt that maybe I ought to have shown more interest – after all, my fate was now inextricably linked with those prints. 'I was afraid to ask. In case they were.' I swallowed nervously: 'What eh . . . happens . . . to me . . . when they do come?'

I waited a bit, then, when he didn't answer, put down the chicken-leg I was holding, sat back in the fragile chair and turned towards him. 'Well?' I demanded.

'That's a bridge to cross when we come to it,' he replied lamely. 'The main thing is to get the prints.'

'Speak for yourself. For me, the main thing is what's the bottom line.' I was heartened by his obvious discomfort and rated it as a minor victory in our developing psychological skirmish – he had the gun, he was in command, and yet there he was, acceding to my demand for an answer; he should have told me to get stuffed. I decided, from now on, to push him whenever I could, as far I could. 'Well?' I pressed.

Again the discomfort. 'Look . . . The prints will most likely show that there is nothing . . . of a . . . compromising nature in them, or at least that you couldn't appreciate the significance of it if there is – in which case you'll be released at once, unharmed. Believe it or not, there's not a violent bone in the body of any of us.'

'Yeah, so I've noticed,' I said with heavy irony, and turned back, with a snort of derision, to my breakfast.

'I got some Sunday supplements,' he announced after a while and fished into the box in which he had brought the food.

I hadn't anticipated being faced with specifics. 'I don't remember which paper. It was an old one I found at the cottage. If it's any help, there was an article on the Galapagos Islands on the same page, photos of iguanas and things.' I painted in some supportive backdrop.

'Well these are all recent, all from the last few weeks.' He went through the four or five magazines, calling out the dates and the names of their parent newspapers. 'But we'll go through them anyway – they probably advertise week in, week out and maybe the name will come to you.'

'Sure,' I said, and raised the milk carton to my lips.

After I had wiped my greasy hands on a sheet of newspaper which he – having first checked it carefully for ads for developing labs – passed to me, I reached one hand towards him. He came forward the few steps to hand the magazines to me – another tiny victory.

'Look through them carefully. Take your time. We've got all the time in the world. And I hope, for your sake, that you find the name.' The veiled threat came as an afterthought in a totally unconvincing tone.

Languidly I turned the pages. Once or twice I paused and repeated a name a couple of times speculatively to myself, just to show that I was trying. There were names like Snappysnap and Phastphoto and Printopronto and Kwikpik, all glib without being really clever. 'I'm sorry,' I shrugged after a decent interval, 'it could really be any of these . . . any of the Dublin ones anyway.' He looked as if he didn't believe me, and, self-consciously, I added: 'None of them rings a bell.'

'OK,' he said at last, 'put the cuffs back on and get under the bed again. It looks as if we'll just have to wait to see what comes in tomorrow's post.'

'And if they don't come tomorrow? What then?' I clicked the first manacle into place.

'We wait another while, I suppose. But,' he added, another feeble attempt at being ominous, 'we won't wait forever.'

'Aren't you concerned that the whole country will be looking for me by now?'

He gave a smug little laugh. 'You can forget that one. This morning I phoned your office and told the girl you'd had to go to Dublin last night on a personal matter, and on the way back, your Land Rover had left the road and that you were in hospital, under observation for a few days. I told her I was your uncle and that you had asked me to phone her.'

'And . . .' I demanded, when he seemed like stopping.

'And she sends her best regards and says you're not to worry. She didn't even ask what hospital you were in. So don't start listening for the bugles of the seventh cavalry coming down the passage'.

I shuffled myself under the bed again, relieved that their story would not cover anything in the nature of a permanent disappearance. They should have done the clifftop one. Bunglers. Little things like that could nail them in the end.

Lying on my back, looking up, I noticed that when he cleaned away the leftovers of my meal, he held the cardboard box to the edge of the table and scooped everything into it; and, most interesting of all, while he carried out this two-handed operation, he again placed the gun, without the slightest hesitation, on the shelf, as if it was already an established routine.

'Stay where you are until I leave,' he warned. 'I'll be back this evening. I'll leave the magazines. If they don't refresh your memory, they'll help pass the time.'

'Gee, thanks.'

'There's no point in making this harder than it is. For anybody.' He paused a moment. 'I'm sure you'd find us equally amenable to ... eh ... arrangements ... if you suddenly remembered anything ... helpful about those photographs.'

'I told you,' I rolled my head backwards and forwards on the floor. 'I can't help.' He looked at me surmisingly until the silence became embarrassing. To cover my unease, which I was afraid he might read as guilt, I joked lamely: 'But if you want to know whether I prefer the stick treatment or the carrot, then my vote is for the carrot.'

Abruptly, he turned on his heel and went out. About five minutes later, as I sat on the bed and read about: 'Jackpot Winner! "It will *not* change my life!" says bachelor Bert Witherspoon (87), Bootle, winner of £3,628,000,' I was surprised to hear his footsteps returning and I looked over at the peep-hole. His lens-covered eye appeared at it, and the door opened just enough to admit an arm holding a plastic bucket, then closed again. From the other side of the door, which was having its padlock replaced, his muffled voice came: 'That's as much as we can do by way of a loo. I'm sorry.' Then he went away and I picked up another glossy and read: ' "I've always loved Bert Witherspoon," declares Mimi (23), "but I've been too shy to tell him." '

During that day, which seemed to drag on for ever, I read the magazines from cover to cover, and dozed fitfully. I spent a long time trying to come up with even an embryonic escape plan, but got no further than working out that my only real chance was to get him when the gun was on the shelf, provided, of course, that he continued to put it there. However, no doubt, I'd be under the bed at the time, so I'd either have to think of a totally different approach or come up with some way of *not* being under the bed at that critical time. Once or twice, I almost captured the elusive inconsistencies of my interrogation, but they continued to float, tantalisingly out of reach in the dark pools of my subconscious, fleetingly breaking surface only when I was thinking of something else. I wasn't doing too well on any front.

That evening, what seemed at first to be another negative development turned out to be a blessing in disguise. When he came, we went through the peep-hole under the bed routine again. He laid out the food, opened the carton of milk – placing the gun on the shelf as he did so – and told me to come out, a repetition of the morning's procedure, except that he was ominously quiet. It was I who initiated whatever desultory conversations there were, and he who killed them off monosyllabically as soon as they began. By the time I had slowly worked my way through supper, I had given up trying to figure out what was bothering him; I couldn't even decide whether it might be good or bad for me.

'Have you finished?' he asked, long after it was obvious that I had.

'Yes,' I answered warily.

'Then put the cuffs on again.' He watched until I had snapped on the first and then said: 'Hold it there!' I looked up at him, leaving the other cuff swinging from my left wrist. 'Go and sit on the bed,' he ordered. The gun was directed at me in a hand which I could see was shaking. There was something big coming up. I did as I was told. 'Go on. Up to the top,' he directed. Even more uneasy now, I shuffled along until I had the pillow under my left thigh, all the time watching him warily. 'Now, pass the chain around the bar,' he nodded at the bed-head, 'then put the cuff on the other wrist.'

'What?' I demanded. 'What for?'

'Because we think you're up to something. That story of yours this morning was just a wee bit too good to be true. So, for the night, my colleagues and I have decided that this is the safest way to guarantee your inactivity.'

'Fuck you and your colleagues!' I blazed. 'What the hell do you think I can get up to in this godforsaken dungeon?' I glared at him in impotent rage. 'Tell me! What am I supposed to do?'

'Look, I'm sorry about this, but I must insist! There's too much at stake. If there was any other way of guaranteeing your ... harmlessness, then I would gladly – I told you already I'm not a violent man.'

'Bollocks!' I snarled, turning my head away.

'So come on now. Do as I say.' When I didn't immediately comply, he continued: 'I can easily arrange another chloroform session, you know, but this way saves everybody a lot of trouble, not least you.'

I had to accept his reasoning and, with as much bad grace as I could muster, I anchored myself to the iron top of the bed.

'Now I've said I'm sorry and I meant it. That's why I left it so late to bring your evening meal. It's now –' he checked his watch, – '9.47 and I'll be back before eight in the morning, so it's not that long.'

I stared obstinately at the ceiling, refusing to acknowledge him in any way, but I knew he was standing half-way between the bed and the door, the gun now held down by his side, no longer needed.

'How about the light?' he asked. 'On or off?' When I didn't reply, he said: 'Very well then. I'll turn it off. Good-night.' He went to the door, opened it, and just before pulling it to, he flicked off the switch. The room was suddenly very dark and very lonely.

'Leave it on,' I said.

'Right then.' He switched it on again, waited a few seconds and repeated his good-night. I continued to stare at the ceiling in sullen, mute rebellion. What the hell was he waiting for? Some kind of *approval*?

It had all happened so quickly that he had gone by the time I got to thinking straight again. There was no sense in my being so completely restrained – one hand chained to the bed would have served their purpose every bit as well and still allowed me a minimum of movement, a very important minimum. I shouted as loudly as I could, hoping he might have delayed briefly in the house but, if he had, he didn't hear me or, if he did, he didn't heed me. Furious with myself for not having had the presence of mind to take advantage of his sincere-sounding protestation that he wished there was some less drastic way to guarantee my immobility, I composed myself to make the best of a very uncomfortable bad lot. Within minutes, I began to itch in the most inaccessible places.

I tried to sleep, a real no-hoper. Apart from the excruciating restriction of my arms and the erratic flights of my thoughts, the backs of my eyeballs felt as if they were being massaged roughly by two giant thumbs – the naked light bulb hanging directly above my face. At last I had to roll off the bed and drag it across until I could reach my leg up and switch off the light with my foot. I tried to sleep again, but only managed some sporadic dozing – each time, my automatic efforts to adjust my unnatural position would jerk me awake again, and I began to occupy myself less with thoughts of eventual escape and more with trying to work out how to avoid another night in such discomfort. Some time in the small hours, the two aspirations crossed paths and fused, and the germ of a plan slowly took form in my head. I examined it in detail as I lay in total darkness and silence.

In the end it depended on his being serious about wishing he could immobilise me more humanely; if he was, I only had to think of another way and persuade him to accept it. I had to provide him with a substantial-looking lock, but one for which I would have a secret key.

And already, I could see the vague outlines of it in the dark.

13

When he came in the morning, my wrists were wealed and raw. He didn't notice at first; he set out breakfast (placing the gun on the shelf as he opened the milk carton) and it wasn't until he approached the bed to free me that he saw the reddened flesh. 'Jesus!' He looked up from my hands so quickly he almost dislodged the sunglasses. I stared at him in silent reproach.

'Oh! I'm sorry,' he said.

'Yeah, yeah. Big deal. If you're so fucking sorry, get these cuffs off and give me a break.'

'Of course . . . I had no idea . . .'

'What did you expect?' I sat on the bed, gently rubbing my blazing wrists.

'I'm sorry. Really I am,' he said from the door.

'So you said,' I replied testily. After a few minutes, I stood, stretched and reviewed the early results. So far, so good. His remorse seemed genuine – he was actually feeling guilty! He had also, in a way, carried out my order to remove the cuffs – he was going to anyway, but I reckoned that, if he had been more self-assured, he'd have made some comment about who gave the orders around here. But he hadn't, and I painted another little cross on my fuselage.

Before starting the self-mutilation, I'd hauled the bed over to the door and, by fishing about with my foot, found the switch and turned the light back on; I didn't want him to know that I'd been able to move about in the night. Then I'd hauled the bed back and, reluctantly, but afraid to postpone it, begun, with grim determination, twisting and grinding my wrists against the sharp bracelets until they burned with raw soreness; not knowing the time, I'd started much too early and had to lie for hours in agonised frustration, eagerly awaiting his footsteps.

Heartened by his remorse, I began to walk, swinging my arms, restoring circulation; he was taut with wariness, but, feeling all guilty, didn't object – the day before, I'd only been allowed the short walk from bed to table and back. I pushed again, mental fingers crossed. 'I presume this establishment doesn't run to first-aid kits for the benefit of its inmates?' I stopped in front of him, though more than an arm's length away. 'A bit of wound salve? A bandage or two?' Getting him used to me stopping close to him was crucial. In the end, it would all depend on him being the creature of habit I suspected he was. When he arrived with my first meal and found himself faced with the problem of how to ensure that I didn't make a run for the door while he was setting out the food, the only thing he could think of was to order me under the bed. I, and almost anybody I could think of, would have put the box on the floor and told the captive to do the rest himself.

He returned some twenty minutes later, knocked, and called out: 'Get under the bed!'

I did as I was told, glad to entrench another pattern. He didn't open the door until I was under the bed; then he threw a first-aid box on to it.

I found some wound cream and applied it liberally. I bandaged my left wrist, but asked him for help with my right. He declined, with apologies, so I made do as well as I could. In fact, being almost ambidextrous, I could have done a near perfect job, but I deliberately made heavy weather of it. I didn't want him deciding I could open my own milk carton in future.

Afterwards we talked for a while, and this time I didn't forget to ask if the prints had arrived. They hadn't. Surprise, surprise.

'How do you do it anyway?' I asked. 'Hang about the gate and ask the postman if he's got anything for me?'

He answered with a snort.

'Break in after he's been and gone?'

Another snort.

'It's got to be one or the other. Aren't you afraid someone'll see you climbing in and out of the window?'

'Why should we climb in and out the window? We've got the key from the bunch in your Land Rover. We check at night.'

Depression and pessimism, never too far away, set in. I should have spotted that one; not that I'd given it any thought – but I hate asking stupid questions. In a while he ordered me back under the bed, placed the gun on the shelf, and, scooping the remains of my breakfast into the box, left.

I hadn't slept properly since the bogus calving case almost thirty-six hours before, and now, despite the excitement of the plan taking shape, and the pain in my wrists, I drifted into a deep, dreamless sleep. My awakening coincided with his return.

'Under the bed!' He rapped on the door.

When he came in he set the food out, leaving the gun on the shelf while he opened the milk carton. By now the routine had become so firmly established that I rolled out from beneath the bed without his telling me. As usual he threw the key on the bed. So far, neither of us had spoken. He watched warily as I windmilled my arms and approached the table with undisguised distaste – I'd done nothing all day but sleep, and the air in the room had become stale. Listlessly I ate a banana. I reached for the milk and raised it to my lips, but lowered it again without drinking, and turned to him. 'I've come to a decision.'

'Oh? What about?'

'You can shoot me or chloroform me or whatever . . . but you're not chaining me to that bed tonight.' Without moving my eyes from his, I took a deep draught from the carton.

'I wanted to talk to you about that.' He sounded like I wasn't going to like what he had to say.

'Well?' I pressed, as a pause developed. 'Go on.'

'We've . . . um . . . decided it's . . . not necessary to . . . to do the same thing.'

Another uncomfortable pause. 'So?' I demanded.

'Well . . . we don't want you roaming about free at night . . . so the best . . . eh . . . compromise would be to lock only one hand to the bed . . .'

'No!' I exploded. 'To hell with that! It's not my wrists – they're bandaged now. It's my legs. Or my hips, to be more precise.'

'Your hips?' I could almost see the frown behind the mask.

'My hips. I broke my pelvis four years ago in a car accident and I've got arthritis in my hips. I'm supposed to walk at least three miles every day, preferably more. If I don't, I get horrible pains.' I let that sink it, thankful that I had thought the plan through, anticipated some compromise, and prepared a reasonably plausible fly for his ointment. 'Even when I do get my walking done, I often have to get up at night and walk some more. What the hell are you so afraid of anyway? What do you think I can get up to?' I sensed him weakening and I added, with a fervent prayer that he wouldn't: 'Please leave me free so I can walk.'

'I can't,' he protested. 'If it was only me, I would.'

'Well then, for Christ's sake, use some other method, use the GI truss . . .'

'The what?'

'The GI truss,' I said, as if he should know.

He shook his head. 'What's the GI truss?'

'It's the method the Americans developed during the Second World War, to tie up POWs. They'd handcuff them but pass the chain of the cuffs down inside the belt at the front then thread the belt so that it buckled at the back. You must have heard of it . . .' He didn't say anything so I went on, word-storming him so that he couldn't examine it too closely. 'It restricts the hands to a circle about six inches around the navel. Obviously, where there was a crowd of prisoners, one could unbuckle another's belt, so there was a kind of heavy-duty staple-gun affair to staple the belts closed at the back. I

137

believe the biggest advantage was that it allowed prisoners to have a piss without having to call the guards . . .'

'How come you know so much about this?'

'War comics. The same as every other kid of my generation. We were almost reared on 64-page war comics. We used to use the GI truss when we played war, not with handcuffs and staple-guns of course, just the principle.' I let him consider it for a while before pressing on again. 'So, how about it? I warn you – I will not be chained, not without a hell of a struggle!' I wondered if I ought to press him further, or if I'd already gone too far. 'There's nobody to release my belt at the back.'

He hesitated a long moment. 'OK,' he said at last. 'Show me then.' His relief at solving the problem was nothing compared to mine, though I couldn't show it. I'm sure there was some element of humanity in his agreement, but equally, the last thing he wanted was the hassle of having to assemble the troops for battle.

I unbuckled my belt, pulled it free of the loops and held it up, like a magician asking the audience to see for themselves that it was just an ordinary belt. Then I fed it through the loops again, starting at the back, and continuing forward along my right side until the loose end reached the back again. There I buckled it, leaving it as loose as I dared. While I was doing this, I pirouetted slowly so that he could see my hands, and continued the distracting patter. 'Now, as you can see, I can't inch the belt round to the front, to where I can reach the buckle, because the loops are too small to let the buckle pass through, and too strong to let it be torn through, right?' By ending each sentence on a question, I hoped to make it impossible for him to concentrate. 'So *voilà*! Now it's just the handcuffs. Do you want to do that part now? I mean, are you leaving soon?'

'In a minute. You may as well do it now.'

'OK.' I picked up the cuffs and fed one bracelet down inside the belt so that they ended up hanging on the belt, a cuff on either side. Then, with a helpless grimace, I snapped them on.

'That's it! Check for yourself.' I walked towards him and he let me come. When I was three steps away, I turned and reversed the rest of the way, the least threatening approach I could think of. He showed very little alarm – he kept the gun on me, but no more menacingly than when I was sitting on the bed or at the table and much less so than when I was moving about, even handcuffed. Reaching out he caught the buckle, tugged it experimentally and tried to pass it through the adjacent loops.

'Satisfied? Am I or am I not harmless?'

He gave a last tug at the belt, turned me round again and repeated it at the back, then pushed me towards the bed.

'Right. Under the bed!'

'What!' I gawked at him.

'I want to clear away the food. I'm leaving.'

'Jesus! What's the point in the fucking GI truss if you think I can still make a run for it! I can't even reach the knob – besides I'd need to use my arms to shunt myself under. I'll lie on the goddam bed, if that makes you feel better.' Again, by taking the initiative, I robbed him of yet another slice of his authority. He looked at me, feeling as if he ought to make a point of having his wishes complied with, but, seeing no practical advantage in it, let it be. While he scooped away the practically untouched food, he automatically laid the gun on the shelf beneath the picture of the Sacred Heart. Then, box in one hand, gun in the other, he went to the door.

'Light on or off?' he asked, lapsing incredibly into habit.

'Leave it on.' I shook my head and rolled my eyes in disbelief. 'I'm free now. I can turn it on and off as I wish. With my nose.'

'Right then. I'll be off. It's 20.26, nearly half-past eight,' he said, rubbing the sleeve of his left arm along the front of his anorak to expose his watch. 'I'll be back in the morning before eight, though there's no chance of having the prints then. It's Saturday.'

'*Saturday!*' I said, as if I didn't know. 'My, how time flies when you're having fun!'

Again, I lay in perfect silence, listening for some identifiable noise, and again, all sound ended with the closing of the second door. I let out my breath and grinned broadly to myself; no wonder he'd never heard of the GI truss — I'd never heard of it myself until I'd invented it the night before. Towards morning, I slept a little.

14

From the moment he peeped through the spyhole next morning, he was a target, an audience for my command performance. Today, provided he hadn't wised up, I'd condition him into believing how helpless I was, how safe it was to allow me to walk about the room. I lay facing the door.

'How are the wrists?'

'They'll survive. At least the hips are OK.' He crossed to the table with the inevitable box of food, the gun going on the shelf, as usual, while he opened the milk carton. He didn't mention getting under the bed.

I stretched for a long time before going to the table. At the door, he was watchful and kept the gun on me, which was fine; the last thing I wanted was for him to get blasé and start leaving the gun in his pocket. I picked a while at the food, then stood up abruptly. 'I can't eat. The air in here is lousy!' It was true; the air was lousy.

'Sit down,' he warned.

'No, I won't sit down! I want to move!' I windmilled my arms again, defiantly.

'Then you'll have to put on the cuffs again.'

'Here.' I extended my wrists towards him. 'You put them on if you like, but I'm not sitting down or lying down either – on or under that fucking bed! I want to *walk*.'

'Have it your own way, then . . . Put them on.'

'Coward!' I said witheringly and picked the handcuffs up

off the bed. Without being told to, I locked myself in the GI truss and was relieved to see him relax immediately.

I kept him talking for ages, pacing up and down, passing him countless times, getting him used to my nearness and my helplessness, using every opportunity to demonstrate the limited range of my hands – bending double to scratch my nose, sidling up to the table corner to ease an itching thigh. On several occasions I stopped in front of him, mere feet away, to emphasise some point; the first time, the gun jerked up warningly, but with each successive stop, his reaction became less marked, until in the end there was none at all. However, as he was clearing away the food, he made me lie on the bed; I was disappointed; I thought he had come to accept I was totally harmless. Still, everything was more or less on course, and he put the gun on the shelf automatically – as always.

The evening session was much the same except that I moved in on him almost as soon as he came in, joining him at the table as he was actually laying out the food. His hand snaked at once towards the gun on the shelf, hovered a moment, then went back into the box. I pretended not to notice. I managed to hold him again, though for a shorter time. As before, I walked while I was talking, manacled in the GI truss. At one time I backed up to him and asked him to scratch between my shoulderblades. ('Down a little, left a bit, just there . . . Aaaah!') He obliged without question.

'Listen,' I said, when he looked about to leave, 'do you think you could bring me something to read? Who knows when those prints will come?'

He looked at me a moment. 'Sure. Why not?'

'And a toothbrush and toothpaste. Another few days, and my teeth will rot.'

'OK,' he replied, and began to clear away the debris of my supper.

Immediately I distanced myself from him but kept up a steady prattle so that he'd know where I was; he didn't order me to the bed, and suddenly I had gained that extra, all-important little freedom – permission to remain standing while the gun was on the shelf. As he made for the door, I reminded him about the reading material and toothbrush, and he went off carrying with him the box, and the impression that I was reconciling myself to a long stay. I wasn't.

I waited the hour I'd already decided on, and it wasn't easy – I didn't really think he'd come back for anything, but I couldn't take any chances. Not at this stage. At last, with a final silent prayer, I began. I knew the routine by heart and it worked like a dream. In theory.

I eased my shoes off, one with the other. Next, I opened the top button of my jeans and pulled down the zip; that left only the belt holding them up and, a few undignified wriggles later, I had managed, by pushing gently down on the chain in front and rubbing my back up along the end of the bed, to coax the belt down over my hips. Phase one successfully completed.

Phase two was modifying the GI truss. Sitting barelegged on the bed, my jeans on my lap, I undid the buckle and, pulling the belt free of the loops, freed my handcuffed hands. Now I went to work with my teeth on the adhesive bandage on my wrist and, when I had bitten one end loose, unwound it carefully until I had a four-inch strip free. This I bit off – I needed it to bind the spike to the buckle; left loose, it might snag into one of the holes later on, which would be disastrous.

When I had finished, I pulled the bed away from the wall. To make an extension to my belt, I needed a length of the two-strand cable which was tacked along the skirting board. The staples popped out easily, and in seconds I had freed enough. I could easily have bitten through it but as it might have been carrying current I turned the bed on its side and, using the sharp angle-iron of the base as a toothless saw, rubbed the cable on it until I had cut a length of about six feet. As I only needed one of the two strands, I separated them; the surplus strand I rolled into a ball and left by the wall before setting the bed back to rights again.

I bit a hole in the end of the belt, gouging at it with my canines until I had worn away a tiny, rough puncture. Then, using my teeth again, I stripped some of the plastic covering from the cable, exposing about an inch of gleaming copper wire at either end. I fed one end through the hole in the belt-end, then pulled it through until its half-way mark, and wound the bare ends together; I now had a belt about seven feet long – half leather, half wire drawstring. Now came the tricky part.

With the jeans lying in a heap on my lap, I threaded the 'wire end' of the belt through the first of the six waist loops, the right back, and then on in the sequence which I had repeated *ad nauseam* to myself: right side, right front, between handcuffed wrists, left front, left side, left back, over buckle with taped-down spike, again through right back, right side, right front. Stop. So far, so good. Now to see if it actually worked.

I put my legs into the jeans, but before pulling them up beyond my knees I used my hands to put on my shoes. Then I pulled the jeans up and closed the zip and top button. With my hands so loosely restrained, I had no trouble in catching the 'drawstring' which hung from the right front loop. By drawing gingerly on it, I tightened the 'real' belt, and felt it pass through the loops with minimum resistance. The last step was to unwind the twisted ends of wire and, by pulling on one, pull all the wire free. Suddenly it was done. That was it. That was what he was going to see – my hands chained, the belt through the chain. Just like yesterday morning. And afternoon. All in order. Except, this time, the belt wasn't buckled.

With a *frisson* of excitement, I clasped my hands together, tensed my body, drew a deep breath and flashed my arms out and up in a smooth arc. The belt snaked smoothly through the loops, coming free with a vicious slap. I repeated the procedure twice more, and each time it worked perfectly. Feeling like the human equivalent of a tautly coiled spring, I settled down nervously to await the morning and the arrival of my captor.

He was almost outside the door when I became aware of his

footsteps. Instantly I was completely awake and completely alert. I rolled to face the peep-hole, stretching full length so that he couldn't fail to see that the chain was still inside the belt. I pretended to be asleep, then stirred as the door opened and he came in.

'Sorry I'm late,' he said. 'Sunday. Had to go to church.'

I let that one pass. 'Can you please open the cuffs? My arms are cramped.'

'Just a second.' He seemed almost happy, and I wondered if perhaps his problems hadn't begun to sort themselves out. Or maybe God had given him the nod at church, told him he was doing His work on earth – perhaps, after all, he was just one of those nutters. 'Toothbrush and paste,' he held them up, 'and something to read.'

'Oh, great!' This was it. I gulped, one last time. If I screwed up . . . 'What?'

He paused when I stood up and glanced at my hands, but, reassured, turned back to the table. 'A few Sundays, *Time*, *Newsweek*, *Private Eye*, *National Geographic*, and a couple of novels,' he read out as he stacked each one.

'Well, they'll certainly keep me going for a while,' I said, beginning a casual drift towards the table. 'Let's see.'

Again his mirror-hidden eyes flicked down to my belt-restrained hands, then to the gun on the shelf. Finding all in order, he began unpacking the food.

Standing beside him now, almost shivering with anticipation, I edged my belly into the table and picked up the top book, a Dick Francis. 'I've read this,' I said, 'but ages ago.' The food was almost laid out. '*National Geographic*!' I exclaimed, trying to keep the quiver of excitement out of my voice. It had to be now. I laid the novel back on the table and turned towards the pile of books; then, locking my hands together, I took one deep breath and yanked out and up, at the same time swivelling on the balls of my feet. With a whiplash crack, the belt snaked through the loops, and my hands continued on upwards in their vicious arc, to explode against his jaw . . .

He didn't know what hit him – his teeth clicked together

like castanets, his head snapped back, the sunglasses shot off, and he teetered backwards, toppling over the end of the bed and ending up sprawled on the floor. Before he'd slid to rest, I had the gun in my hands.

I stood over him and watched his grey eyes flickering uncomprehendingly – for some reason, I'd always imagined they'd be brown. They drooped drunkenly a few times, then zoomed in on the gun, and from there, warily, on up to my face.

I wanted to neutralise him, but the only thing I could think of was hardly original. 'Under the bed!' I shouted. 'On your back! Head and shoulders only out.' After a moment's hesitation, he obeyed, all the time watching me balefully through the holes in the balaclava.

My pounding heart slowed down a bit. 'Now, very slowly, the key to these cuffs.'

He made rummaging movements under the bed; then his right hand emerged with the key and held it up to me.

'Uh-huh!' I smiled knowingly. 'Drop it on the floor, then put your hand back.'

I scooped the key away with my foot, placed the gun on the shelf, and removed my fetters. Briefly I considered making him put them on, but didn't. Crossing quickly to the door, keeping the gun on Kiernan, or whatever his name was, I took a quick look out into a long concrete corridor without any decoration of any kind, not even a skim of plaster. My cell was at one end and the only other door was at the other, at the top of a short flight of wooden steps. It was wide open, and led, from what I could see of the room beyond, into a kitchen. The air in the corridor was cool and fresh and the lure of the bright kitchen was strong, but I paused for a last look back into my cell. From the floor, he stared up at me. It seemed odd not to say something, yet 'goodbye' was hardly apt. 'At least you'll have plenty to read until the cops get here,' I said, and stepped thankfully over the threshold.

I should have just kept going but I didn't; as I was pushing the dead-bolt home, it struck me that I really ought to lock the padlock too; if his accomplices turned up they could spirit him away. Besides, I might need his keys – for another door, his car. Reluctantly, I went back in.

'Give me all your keys. The same way, slowly.' While he rummaged, I had another disturbing thought: what if his accomplices were already in the house?

'Where are the others?' I asked.

'What others?'

'The ones who were with you when you kidnapped me.'

'They're around,' he replied, though not convincingly.

'Bullshit,' I snorted.

The keys dropped to the floor, and again I scooped them away. While he was searching in his pockets, I'd begun to get curious. 'Now,' I said, 'take off the mask.'

He shook his head, watching me warily. 'No.'

'*No?* What do you mean, no? Just take off the bloody mask. I'm not going to shoot you for it . . . but I'm not putting up with any of this crap either.'

Again, a shake of the head.

'OK,' I shrugged. 'If you won't, then I will . . .' I squatted to reach for the balaclava and roared in surprise and agony when the bed suddenly shot violently sideways, catching me a crunching blow on the bridge of the nose and slamming me back against the wall. Through the blur of tears and blood, as I sagged towards the floor, I caught a misty image of him scrambling from under the bed, then pausing in an indecisive crouch.

He might have made it if he'd gone straight for the corridor, but he didn't. I saw him rise, look at the door, then take a step towards me. 'Stop!' I shouted. 'Stop or I'll shoot!' He hesitated, but I couldn't tell if he was obeying my order, getting ready to spring at me, or going to make for the door. I began to inch my way upright, and though my gun hand was shaking badly, he was almost too close to miss.

Suddenly he made his move and everything happened at once – I pulled the trigger and launched myself away from the wall in the same instant that he jumped for the door; the shot hit one of the votive lights on the shelf – if he had come at me, it would have caught him in the chest – but even before the shards hit the floor, I'd curled my fingers round the end of the door just before it slammed snugly into its jamb. Waves of agony shot up my arm as I hurriedly jerked my body along the floor. I braced my knees against the wall, and, sweating with pain, began an urgent pull, hoping to rescue my fingers and substitute the barrel of the gun for them. For what seemed an agonising age, I strained, but I wasn't getting anywhere so I stopped a moment and tried to gauge any weakening in his effort. When I thought I felt a slight slackening of the pressure, I gathered my ebbing strength into one, huge effort and suddenly, the barrel slotted in. Thankfully, I withdrew my pulped digits and let him pull the door to again.

A moment before, this had been the height of my ambition; now it struck me that I was once more in a position of strength. I pulled down on the butt until the barrel was pointing up at where I judged him to be. He hadn't yet noticed the gun and, with much grunting and straining, was going on with his now futile efforts.

'Hey!' I shouted, when there was a temporary lull in the grunts, 'look down! Do you see the gun?' I gave him a few seconds for contemplation. 'On the count of three, I'm going to start shooting.'

'Jesus Christ!' he squealed, as if the door-handle had suddenly become red hot.

'One!' I leaned against the door in case he tried to slam it violently in on top of me. 'Two!'

At once the pressure was gone and I was in the corridor, haring after him. Holding my jeans up with my injured hand, the loose end of the belt slapping against my knees, I shouted 'Stop! I'll shoot you!' I had no intention of shooting him; I just wanted to stampede him – if he beat me to the kitchen and managed to lock the door behind him . . . Aiming at the ceiling, I pulled the trigger. He gave a wordless squeal, seemed about to stop, but then accelerated, panting, and took the wooden steps in a couple of bounds, rocketing through the door. I shot again at the ceiling to keep him moving, but by now I was so close that my momentum would have carried me through.

I almost had him in the kitchen. I reached for him as we raced past the table, but he seemed to sense my stretching arm, and jerked a chair into my path, bringing me crashing down in a tangle of legs. He vanished through a door opposite and a split second later there was the thud of a heavy door and the rapidly fading crunch of running feet on gravel. Picking myself up, regretting that I hadn't shot him in the leg or shoulder or somewhere non-vital, I followed through the door and found myself in the hall. On either side of the hall door were tall narrow windows and I was just in time to see him slam down the boot of his car and dash through a gap in the hedge which formed the border of the gravel forecourt. My heart lurched sickeningly when I saw the rifle in his hands, and it lurched even more when I saw, with a shock, that the car was a red Ford Sierra. Helplessly peeping through net curtains, outsmarted and outgunned, I revised my opinion yet again; I should have just shot him, indiscriminately – head, heart, liver, spleen, anywhere.

Obviously, hot pursuit was now out. I watched for further sight of him, but he didn't show at either end of the twenty-odd yards of hedge, and he didn't cross the lawn beyond it, towards the boundary wall which was marked by a spaced stand of tall conifers between which sparked the calm blue waters of a narrow bay. He was lurking behind the hedge, waiting for me to show. I continued to watch while I painfully and awkwardly rethreaded my belt.

It was no time for weighing options; while I knew where he was, I had to try to work out an escape plan. Another fucking escape plan, I thought in disgust. Pausing briefly to check the phone on the hall table, which was dead, I took the stairs two at a time and did a quick round of the upstairs rooms. There were no other houses in sight but I thought I recognised the countryside. I reckoned I was five or six miles south-west of Knockmore, on a little-used coast road.

From one of the back windows, I got the first bit of good news I'd had in a long time. Some way along a gravel road which snaked up a rhododendron-clad hill, was a garage, and, backed into it, its bonnet bathed in morning sunshine, was my Land Rover! It was like the face of an old friend and I decided to make for it at once and call for help on the radio.

I rushed back to the front room overlooking the hedge – he was still there but he looked as if he was about to make a move. I made for the kitchen and located, in a small pantry off it, a back door. I made such a loud scraping noise when I pulled it open that I thought he had to hear it. Jerking it closed behind me I dashed across the narrow back yard into the rhododendrons. Heart pounding, I waited to see if he would arrive at the double, but he didn't, so I set off uphill. Ten careful minutes later, I was opposite the garage – to my left, the road ran downhill for thirty or so yards, then turned the corner of the house on to the forecourt; to the right, just beyond the garage, it curved out of sight. I watched for another minute, then dashed across into the gloom, where I paused again. At last, satisfied that I hadn't been seen, I tried the door handle – it was locked, but I had more or less expected that. Swiftly I stooped and retrieved, from up inside the wing, the magnetic box containing the spare key; delaying only long enough to disperse the telltale little pyramid of dried mud which accumulated underneath, I climbed into the Land Rover, relocked the door, and reached for the radio. Maybe it was because I was in the garage or maybe the battery was flat but the radio was dead. With that life-line denied me, I climbed dejectedly into the dark of the back, to rethink my position. Realistically, my best bet now seemed to sit it out – the longer I stayed out of sight, the more likely he was to assume I'd got away; very shortly, he'd begin to worry that, if he hung about much longer, he'd be caught red-handed. At that point, knowing that I couldn't positively identify him, the obvious move for him would be to get as far away as possible, as fast as possible. As long as he didn't actually own the house . . . if he did he was a goner either way, so he might just as well stick around.

My seat on the metal side box had rivets and screw-heads sticking up all over, and, as I was facing a long wait, I decided to make it as comfortable as I could. I folded a brown dust-coat into a rough cushion and half rose to put it under me.

That was when I saw his shadow sliding along the road in front of the garage.

I froze, my skin shrinking with dread, as I watched his shadow, lengthening all the time, crawl closer. I was trapped in a half-standing crouch, my right hand in full sunlight, gripping the back of the driver's seat, the gun in the corner behind me. I had to get back into the dark at once, had to get the gun. I made a snap decision that he hadn't seen or heard anything – he'd surely have stopped if he had. Taking the weight on my left hand, I eased myself down on to the side box, and not daring to take my eyes off the bright entrance, groped for the gun.

From this sitting position, I could no longer see his shadow or mark its progress, and the first I knew of his arrival was when the handle of the driver's door rattled suddenly. If I hadn't known he was nearby, I'd have hit the roof. As it was, my heart lurched violently. He moved quickly once he found the door locked. Crossing in front of the jeep he stooped briefly to peer under it, then tried the passenger door. Finding it locked also, he probably assumed that the jeep hadn't been disturbed since he'd parked it – after all, as far as he knew, he had the only key. He looked in, but I could tell that he wasn't expecting to see anything. He didn't wait for his eyes to adjust to the gloom and he didn't cup a hand to the dusty glass to overcome the reflection. So he didn't see me, and he didn't see the gun which pointed steadily at the middle of his balaclava, and he didn't see the whiteness of the knuckle which was squeezing the trigger.

If he had, I'd have shot him.

Suddenly I was all against waiting. That had been too close, and besides, just how was I going to know when the coast was clear? It was probably as safe now as it would ever be – at least now I knew his general whereabouts.

The problem was how to start the Land Rover on the low battery. After several idle days, I doubted the self-starter would do it. I knew she'd start on a downhill roll, but how was I going to push her out of the garage? There was a low concrete threshold across the doorway, which, even in the whole of my health, would have stymied me, especially as I couldn't get a run at it – it was a mere two feet in front of the wheels. I thought for a moment. Then crouching low to minimise my shadow, I crept into the road. He wasn't in sight. Back in the garage, I pushed until the front wheels rested against the threshold then checked the road once more – still no sign of him. I climbed in and sat, in the full glare of the sun, ears straining, preheating the engine. I had to force myself to give it time before turning the key, but I knew at once, from the sick whirring response, that it wasn't going to start. I shoved the gearshift into first, let out the clutch and turned the key again. It sounded even weaker this time, but the Land Rover laboriously hauled its front wheels up on to the threshold. I locked the steering wheel to the right, hoping she'd roll down the hill, but she didn't, she rolled until the rear wheels met the threshold, then stopped again. Cursing her stubbornness, I glanced fearfully up the road and turned the key again. This time it turned so weakly I was sure it wouldn't last. It almost didn't; it died on the turn that brought the rear wheels to the top, but it had done enough. I pressed in the clutch, knocked the gear into neutral and felt indescribable relief as the Land Rover began to roll, slowly at first, then gathering momentum. Suddenly I was running smoothly, coasting freely down between the rhododendron walls. I kept one eye on the road and one on the mirror, and, before I had gone twenty yards, I saw him round the corner above the garage, running flat out. I waited no longer. Pressing down on the clutch, I put the gearshift into third, gathered another few yards' momentum, and let the clutch out. The wheels locked and slid through the dry surface gravel, only catching when they met the drag of the harder underlying material; the engine wheezed for one horrifying second, then caught, turned and suddenly coughed into throaty life. I nursed it for the moment it took to develop a healthy roar, then accelerated as far as the corner of the house, where I had to almost stop to negotiate the ninety-degree turn on to the forecourt. I took a last quick look in the mirror. He was no longer running, and for a moment I thought he'd given up the chase; that is, until I saw a neat round hole appear in the corner of the back window and the left half-panel of the windscreen shatter and disintegrate. In my haste, I nearly stalled the engine.

As I drew abreast of the red Sierra, I reckoned I had just enough time to stop, shoot out his front tyres and strand him there. I braked as I came up behind it and came to rest a few feet in front. Then, as coolly as I could, I leaned through the window, turned back, gun-arm extended and aimed carefully at the left tyre. To my dismay I saw a spurt of gravel kick up some four inches from the wheel. I shouldn't really have been surprised — I'd never shot a handgun before, I was in an awkward, twisted position, the Land Rover was vibrating, my hand was shaking, and my eyes were being constantly drawn to the corner of the house. Suddenly he was there and I gave up all thoughts of a second shot; I let out the clutch and sped off down the drive. If he tried another shot, then he missed too.

Within the first mile, he appeared in my mirror; by the end of the second, he filled it. I knew I had to stay in front — once past me, he could race ahead and set up an ambush. Taking the offensive, I braked suddenly when he was right behind, hoping he'd impale his radiator on my tow hitch, but, as I already knew to my cost, his reflexes were very good; so were his brakes, and he stuck the Sierra to the road. I tried again after another mile or so, but again he stopped easily. In fact, this time it nearly backfired. It slowed me down and, with his superior acceleration, he almost got by; only a desperate side-lunge on my part foiled him. When we hit a gravelled stretch under repair, he dropped back into my dust cloud, and I thought I'd lost him until he came hurtling suddenly out of the swirling dust, and, once again, nearly managed to streak past. Then I saw the sign for the sharp left bend with a temporary sign beneath it saying 20 m.p.h. I passed it doing sixty and kept up speed as the bend approached. In my mirror I could see him right behind, as if I had him on tow. Avoiding the brakes, I coasted the last few yards into the bend, then, ramming the gear shift into second, drove at it — the Land

Rover listed alarmingly but gamely held her track. In mid-bend, I checked one last time that he was still with me, then reached out and flicked on the headlight switch.

The effect was instant. When he saw my red tail-lights, he stood on his brakes, and before he could work out that they were not brake-lights he'd lost the Sierra. At that speed, on that bend, and on that surface, he had no chance. I watched his slide begin, and saw him spin off into the swirling dust. Then I rounded the corner and could see no more.

He didn't reappear between there and Knockmore. I watched the mirror all the way.

15

I headed straight for the garda barracks. Traffic in town was
practically non-existent, most of the cars being drawn up on
either side of the road outside the tall, imposing church. As I
navigated the narrow channel between them I heard, faintly,
the tinkle of the consecration bell.

The duty officer looked up from his Sunday tabloid.
Seeing my brutalised face, he sat up, shocked. 'What
happened to you?' he asked, wide-eyed.

'Where's Inspector Potter?'

'You're Mr Samson, right?'

'Yes. Where is he?'

'Out looking for you. We've all been out looking for you for
the past few days. Hang on a tick – I'd better pass the word.
The radio is in the back.'

'Tell him to check on the Braggan road – three or four
miles out, where they're doing it up – there may be a red
Sierra gone off the road there. It's the man who was holding
me. It only happened minutes ago, so if he hurries . . .'

He was back in a couple of moments. 'He'll be in soon and
said you're to wait for him.'

'Oh, don't worry, I'm not going anywhere. You told him
about the car?'

'I did.' He opened a flap in the counter. 'You may as well
wait in here in comfort. The bathroom's through that door,
first on your right. I'll put the kettle on.'

Now that I could see my whole face, and not just isolated

islands of battered features, as in the mirror of the jeep, I was shocked. It looked ten years older under its covering of rough, dirty stubble, my hair was filthy and lank, and my face stared back at itself, sweat-streaked, and blotched with crusts of caked blood. I looked an absolute mess and felt even worse. I ran the tap and gently dabbed away the superficial blood and grime, but I was still a mess – the skin had burst in a straight line across the bridge of my nose and through the split, soft flesh pushed like a pouting, purple lip; both eyes were receding into mounds of rapidly darkening tissue. I looked like the Lone Ranger without the hat.

Back in the duty room, I drank strong tea and felt better, and gave the duty officer a synopsis. 'I won't go into details, if you don't mind,' I said, 'because I'll have to do it all over again when the others get here. The one telling can do it all. How did you know I was missing, anyway? I mean missing and needing looking for?'

'The lassie in your surgery got suspicious when you didn't turn up. A man phoned to say you'd had a accident near Dublin the night before, but you'd written a night call in the book for 2.30 a.m. We checked all the accidents for that night all over the country and not one involved a Land Rover. So we put two and two together . . . and we've been searching since.'

'Do my parents know?'

'I think they were going to tell them this evening.'

There was a commotion in the hall and Potter came in.

'Christ!' he gaped. 'What happened to *you*? Did your head go through the windscreen?'

'No, that was a bullet.'

'A bullet! You mean they shot at you?'

'That's right.'

'Holy God Almighty! A fraction more and you could have lost both eyes, or even got it in the brain!'

'Not this,' I indicated the pulped nose. 'The *windscreen* was broken by the bullet. This . . . eh . . . this was . . . because I was hit by a bed. On the ah . . . nose.'

'You were hit on the nose . . . by a bed? Maybe you'd better tell us about it from the beginning. Is there any tea left in that pot, Burke?'

'I'll make more, sir. This has gone cold.'

'Do, then.' He turned to me. 'Now . . . I can't *wait* to hear about the bed, but can you tell me anything definite first, like who held you or where – or even why?'

'Well, they were looking for these photographs' – I held up the Sureprint wallet. 'As to who they were, I don't know, but I'll tell you where they held me.' I described the place, which he identified at once as the summer residence of a wealthy German industrialist.

'Get out there, lads. Now. Seal off the whole place, have a quick look inside but don't touch anything, OK? Burke, you get on the blower and tell them to get some roadblocks up for a red Sierra, driven by –?' He turned to me, eyebrows raised.

'A man of five-nine or ten, grey eyes, well spoken, I'd guess in his fifties, but I can't be sure – he wore a balaclava all the time. He has a rifle, and probably the balaclava. I'm sorry, I didn't get the number of the car . . . I never even thought of it. It all happened so fast . . . Oh! And he'll have a digital watch,' I added, remembering his exact times. 'I'm sorry I can't be of more help,' I said, feeling so stupid for missing the car number.

'You're doing fine. It'll come back bit by bit.'

Leafing through the prints, he paused at one or two but could see nothing incriminating in any of them. 'Well,' he said with a shrug at the end, 'they mean nothing to me, but maybe, for the Drug Squad, they'll be like the Open Sesame.' When he came to the prints of Catamaran, he said: 'Are you sure they weren't looking for these?'

'I considered that but I can't think why anyone should get so excited about them. And besides, now there's the link of the red Sierra. Assuming it's the same car, then, OK, it was following me the day Catamaran died, but in the afternoon, hours before the accident.'

'You never told me that!'

'I forgot, in the excitement of that evening. Then, I didn't see it again. Until today.'

157

He went through the pictures of Catamaran once more, then shuffled them together and laid them aside. 'Well, it all checked out at the time – both with us and the pathologist.' He summoned the duty officer and told him to have the police photographer make two sets of prints of Marnie's masterpieces.

An hour later, just as I finished making a minutely detailed statement, the prints arrived back. Potter put one set in his files, sent the other to Dublin by courier and gave the originals back to me. He insisted I avail myself of his hospitality yet again and I didn't argue. On the way, we stopped by Fernditch to pick up some personal things and a change of clothes. His men were already at work on the quiet road, knocking on doors, asking about strangers or suspiciously parked cars which might have been seen near the cottage around the time the postman made his rounds, red Sierras, middle-aged men of about five-ten, anything unusual or odd, anything out of the ordinary at all?

Joan Potter made me as welcome as she had the night of the burglary. After I'd soaked in a hot bath she dressed my wounds, then fed me like a king. Reckoning that I wasn't fit for work, I phoned around and eventually managed to find someone to take over for a few days.

Afterwards, I phoned Claire. As I waited for the age it seemed to take her to answer, it struck me that I had subconsciously blocked her from my mind for almost the whole time I was in the cellar. To think of her would have made my predicament that much worse.

'Frank! Where have you been? I've been trying to reach you for days!'

'Oh . . . I've been busy. How was your trip?'

'Don't talk to me about the trip! It was harrowing. Ma's friend died about two hours after we got there. Which proved, everyone said, that she'd just been hanging on until Ma got to see her one last time, and now, of course, Ma, God love her innocence, feels that Mabel would still be alive if she hadn't gone near her . . . Some logic, huh?' She paused for breath, and then went on, a bit tentatively: 'I was thinking I might make a trip to Knockmore tomorrow . . . I could do with getting away for a few days . . . a bit of sanity. Would that be all right with you?'

'That would be perfect with me. Actually I've got a few days off myself.'

'How come?'

At first she didn't believe me, but then she became concerned, and, despite the various aches, pains and bruises, when I hung up I felt a warm glow of well being inside. It's nice to be fussed over.

I stayed at Potter's for the afternoon. He kept coming and going. He'd arrive in, ask me a few questions, check a detail or two and then race out again. Sometimes he had little snippets of news: the revolver was untraceable, American, over twenty years old and in poor working order.

'It worked for me all right, every time I fired it.'

'We might have better luck with the bullets – they're a new brand. Dublin says they're only sold in ten or twelve shops throughout the country. We'll leave that till tomorrow, and hopefully, by then we won't need it. The only clear prints on the gun are yours; we raised a few smudges but they could be anybody's. Can you remember anything else he might have touched?'

'Not unless he touched the bottom of the loo bucket when he was emptying it.'

'We've dusted that all over and we got a few smudgy prints – not much use.'

Next time, it was the car. Any bumps or dents? Badges or emblems? Clean or dirty? Tow hitch? Spotlights? Radio aerial and if so, front or back, right side or left? The more he asked about the car, the worse I felt. I couldn't answer any of his questions. 'And you can't remember even a single letter or number from the reg?'

'No. I'm sorry. Not one.'

'Was the plate itself white or yellow?'

I concentrated hard, then shook my head. 'Nothing about it registered. For all I know, it might not even have *had* number plates. I'm sorry. I don't know how I missed it.'

'If you hadn't had the gun, you probably wouldn't,' he said, and it struck me that he was most likely right – because I had a gun, I probably felt I should do something fancy. 'Not to worry. Did you, by any chance, notice if the car might ever have been out of the country? Did it have an IRL sticker on the back?'

'Look . . . I don't know. He'd just shot out my fucking windscreen, dammit!'

'Relax, you're doing fine. All you could think of was getting away alive, not trying to be some kind of model witness. I just thought something might have come back now that you've had time to draw breath, that's all. I don't suppose you could go closer to the colour than red?'

'It was the same colour as tomato soup,' I said. 'It wasn't pink and it wasn't scarlet, if that's what you mean.'

'That'll help. The roadblocks haven't had any luck so far, but I'll keep them in place for another few hours, and then move them a few miles back . . .'

'Why?'

'He may be hiding somewhere, keeping a roadblock under observation. If he sees it leaving, he'll probably think we've given up; then he'll move, anxious to get the hell out of the area, and we'll snag him a couple of miles down the road.'

'Aren't you the devious ones?' I said in admiration.

Potter smiled. 'In the meantime, we're checking all the red Sierras in the area and you wouldn't believe how many of those there are. That's why I wanted something to narrow the field down a bit. Not, I hasten to add, that I expect it to be a local car. Knockmore is a bit short on drug barons. We're also checking the newsagents to see if anyone can remember selling the items he brought you this morning, but that's a long shot.'

He went off again and when he returned in the evening, all he had to announce was that, so far, they had drawn a blank.

Despite the Potters' protestations, I went back to the cottage for the night. I wanted to be alone; I also wanted to be ensconced there when Claire arrived. What eventually won him over was the fact that I might be an attractive enough bait for the gang to have another go. So, with Potter's men hidden all round the place, I went to bed and slept like I'd had an anaesthetic.

16

The sun had already passed its zenith when I awoke next day
and I lay for a long time, staring at the ceiling, heavy-headed
from long sleep. The bedside clock said 2.20 – almost
fourteen hours of exhausted, dreamless oblivion. Though it
was sunny outside, the window was rain-spattered, and I
could hear a blustery breeze. I hauled myself out of bed,
showered, padded to the kitchen and made coffee. I stood at
the window and I sipped the hot black brew, there was no sign
of any gardaí about. After I had attended to my battered nose
and fingers, I made more coffee and pottered about,
rearranging the books on the shelves, putting the LPs in
alphabetical order and, with the aid of a library of reference
works, successfully reuniting most of the eggs with their
name-tags on the display trays. Suddenly, with blinding
clarity, the elusive thought that had been tantalising me since
my first 'interview' was there, right in front of me. 'Frank,' I
breathed to myself, 'you're a *fool*!

I was trying to work out the implications when I saw Claire
pull up outside. Mind surging, I went to greet her.

Her sprightly step faltered and the smile fell from her face
when I opened the door. Wide-eyed, she stared at me as if I
was a perfect stranger, and a mean-looking one at that.

'Christ, Frank! You're ruined! I had no idea it was this
bad.'

'Nothing that can't be cured by the kiss of a certain special woman.' I smiled and walked out into the light to meet her. She kissed me as fiercely as her respect for my battered features would allow, then stepped back and surveyed me.

'Either you should change your witch doctor or I'm not the certain special woman. You still look awful.'

'Don't worry. All the damage is visible. The rest works perfectly.'

'I'm glad to hear it.'

'Anyway, you're a sight for sore eyes and here I speak from first-hand experience.' I'd rehearsed the gag a couple of times, but it fell flat. My mind wasn't on it. Taking her elbow, I steered her inside and closed the door. 'It's the horse!' I said.

'What's the horse?'

'The photographs they wanted were the ones of the horse. The party had nothing to do with it! It's Catamaran.'

She looked sceptical. 'Are you sure?'

'Sure as I can be. I tried to bluff my gaoler by claiming that the film hadn't wound on to the take-up spool. Now, that *does* happen – it could happen to anyone – but he knew I was lying. It was the only time he was definite about anything during the whole time I was there. He was sure it hadn't happened, and the only way you can be sure about that is when you come to the end and the film won't wind on any further. And that happened when I was photographing Catamaran, just as Hynes was going to take one of me with the horse.'

She furrowed her brow and thought a moment. 'If you're right, what are you going to do?'

'Don't know yet. Tell Potter, obviously, but I want to think about it for a while first. Try to figure out what it's all about.'

'You think Hynes is involved?'

'No. If there was any reason why I shouldn't have photographed Catamaran, he'd have tried to stop me then. I even asked him if it was all right, and he told me to go ahead.' I shook my head to clear it. 'Come on, let's go for a drive somewhere. I need to get out of here.'

We drove in Claire's car into the mountains, the scattered showers of the plain becoming a steady drizzle which got progressively heavier as we climbed. I told her the whole story as we went, and we tossed it about trying to pick clues or pointers from the jumble, but all we could come up with was that the film's existence had been unknown until a short time ago, to anyone besides Hynes and me.

The summit of the mountain poked through the clouds into bright sunshine and we got out and walked for half an hour, but when the cloud began to creep up towards us, we turned and made our way back through shrouds of thickening, clinging mist to the car.

'Well, we can't move now,' I grinned. 'We can't even play "I spy with my little eye" because there's nothing to spy . . . So how are we going to kill the time?'

'Any suggestions?' she smiled.

'Only improper ones.'

'Oh? Like what?' Her eyebrows shot up in mock disapproval.

'Like, do you want to get into the back seat?'

'No,' she said, snuggling in towards me.

I put my arm around her and hungrily we made up for lost time. After a while, when our breathing was fast and our hearts were racing, I whispered in her ear: '*Now* do you want to get into the back?'

'No,' she said again, shaking her head.

'Whyever not?'

'Because,' she pouted, 'I want to stay here with you!' Then she laughed and reached down to pull the lever which collapsed her seat all the way back.

When we'd put ourselves, our clothes, and the car back to rights, we decided that the fog really wasn't that bad after all, and set off. Claire was silent and, half afraid that she might be having another crisis of confidence, like that day on the bank of the Corrib, I said: 'So your trip to England wasn't great?'

'Don't remind me . . .'

'That bad, huh?'

'That bad. Still, I did manage to sneak into Stratford one evening to the theatre.'

'What did you see?'

'*Henry the Fourth, Part Two*.'

'Weren't you in time for *Part One*?'

She started to laugh, then stopped and glanced quickly at me, not sure if I was joking or not. I looked back blankly and decided I'd have to stop this foolery, stop confusing the woman.

'Just kidding.' I held up a palm of peace.

Potter wasn't in his office and wouldn't be back for some time so we said we'd call back and went for another drive. This time I drove. The evening had cleared and the streets were crowded with people who hadn't been able to get out all day. 'You know,' I said, 'there's only one way to find out if Hynes told anybody about those photographs, and I know where he lives.'

'Frank, that's a job for Potter. Don't mess.'

'I'm not messing, and I'm not taking Potter's job. I'll make my questions so offhand and casual he won't even realise that they *are* questions. If Potter turned up, it'd be all over town two hours later.'

'So?'

'So. I don't know. It can't do any harm,'

I swung the Escort into a short street of neat bungalows just in time to see Pat Hynes emerge from a gate on to the tree-lined path and turn towards the town centre.

'There he is.' I pointed at the retreating figure a hundred yards along. I let the car coast silently up behind him and braked as we drew abreast. A tourist asking directions, he probably thought. I folded myself down in the seat, trying to get my head low enough to be able to see further up than the breast pocket of his flowery summer shirt. 'Howya, Pat?' I called across Claire, my chin almost resting on the lower rim of the steering wheel. He bent down, looked at me for a moment in puzzlement, then beamed in recognition.

'Ah, it's yourself! The hard man! I didn't know you for a minute there with the shiners. God, but they're two right beauties! I heard you were kidnapped and bet up but got away in the heel of the hunt. Fair play to you. What did they want off you?'

'I never rightly found out, Pat. I . . . eh . . . left before we got to that part.'

He laughed and winked at me with a sharp ducking of his head. 'Fair play to you!' he repeated. 'It's the talk of the town. Sure the place hasn't had so much excitement since Alcock and Brown landed out the road! Catamaran a few weeks ago, and now you.'

'Where are you headed?'

'Town.'

'So are we. Hop in.' I reached back towards the door behind Claire and painfully pulled up the lock button.

'Did you get a new car?'

'No,' I laughed. 'It's not mine, unfortunately. It belongs to Claire here.' I introduced them, Claire swinging round in her seat to nod, smile and offer her hand.

'I heard the Land Rover was riddled with bullets.'

'You heard wrong. It was riddled with just one bullet. In the back window and out the front. If she'd been a left-hand drive, I was jiggered for sure. Jiggered.'

'Still. You were lucky.'

'I sure was.'

We drove off. 'By the way,' he said, 'how did those snaps turn out? The ones of Catamaran and me holdin' him? I often meant to ask you only I didn't see you.'

He had caught me on the hop. Suddenly the subject had popped up all on its own. I glanced at him in the rear-view mirror, which only showed one innocent eye, and said as easily as I could: 'They're not back yet, Pat, but as soon as I get them, you can have a look and tell me which ones you want.'

'Thanks. Just even one as a keepsake. You can let me off at the next corner.'

'We're going right into town,' I protested. I had bargained on more time.

'No thanks. I have to call for the girlfriend – actually, the fiancée now. We got engaged a couple of weeks back.'

'Congratulations.'

'Time to make an honest woman of her,' he laughed in embarrassment, one hard man to another.

'Actually, Pat, I was going to call around to see you anyway about those photographs,' I started as he got out.

'Oh? Why?' he turned and bent down, looking in the open door.

'Well,' I improvised, 'the press seems to have heard that I'd taken photos of Catamaran the day he died and they've been hassling me a bit lately. I just wondered how they heard. I didn't tell them.'

'Neither did I. No reporters came to talk to me at all.' He sounded aggrieved, peeved. 'I mentioned it to Jackie – that's the fiancée – but I'm sure *she* didn't talk to any reporters. She'd have told me. Maybe she mentioned it to someone else. I'll ask her. Is it important?'

'Not really. I just wondered. And you didn't tell anybody else?'

'No. Nobody else. Only Mr Norris, and he certainly didn't tell the press. I heard he wouldn't talk to them at all. Anyway, by the time I told him, all the reporters were well and truly gone. Sure it was only last Sunday, a week yesterday, when I met him buying the papers. I'll ask Jackie and let you know, all right?'

'Fine Pat. But as I said, it's no big deal. See you around.'

'Yeah. See you. G'bye ma'am.'

17

'Norris!' Potter gaped. '*Gilbert Norris?*' He raised a sceptical eyebrow.

'Well,' Claire qualified with a hint of reserve, 'it looks very much like it.' She wasn't as totally convinced as I was.

'Never mind looks very much like it, it *is* him,' I insisted. 'Look at the timing. On Sunday he learns that I took photographs of Catamaran a matter of hours before his accident. The very next night, my house is burgled – looking for those photographs. They don't find them, so, the day after, I get this weird call to his place to a hunter with a colic which has conveniently cured itself by the time I get there. Norris gets me into the kitchen, which, also conveniently, is at the back of the house, on the pretext that he must talk to me, but then scoots off abruptly, leaving me with his housekeeper, and, I presume, steals the films from my camera and bag which are in the Land Rover at the front of the house. Next night, when they've discovered that they *still* haven't got the right pictures, I get set up by yet another bogus call, they kidnap me and try the direct approach.'

'That's all very neat, Frank, but it's circumstantial. I can't go out and arrest him on that. It's not even enough to question him.'

'You know I'm right.'

'I don't know any such thing. The most I know is that it's all very neat and plausible. So how do you explain the horse with colic? How could he have arranged that?'

'I only have his word for the colic, there was no colic when I got there. And do you know what this experienced horseman was doing when he should have been walking his "colicky" horse, as every kid with a pony knows? He was changing pictures around! Oh sure, he described symptoms but he'd have seen a thousand colics in his time, so big deal. The horse was wet, supposed to be sweat, but how do I know it wasn't just water he'd sponged over him? If you ask me, the colic was a decoy to get me and my camera there.'

'Why would anybody go to those lengths when they could just as easily break into the Land Rover in the small hours?'

He had me there. 'I don't know. Maybe they thought I wouldn't leave the camera in the Land Rover overnight. Maybe they *couldn't* break into it at night – Fernditch is on the public road and there's a street light outside the gate. And another thing: your men were keeping a close eye on the place because of the break-in the evening before . . .'

He scratched his jaw a while, then sitting forward, tapped the prints. 'Any idea why anyone should want these pictures so badly?'

'Not yet.'

Potter ordered coffee, Claire went off to the loo, and I sat, knowing I was right, and trying to think of ways to prove it. Coffee arrived and Potter asked for the photographer to be summoned. 'I need more copies, and tell him we don't have negatives for these ones, so he's to bring whatever he needs.'

'How would a drugged horse look, Frank?' Claire asked, coming back in.

'Depends on which drug. Do you mean a sedative?'

She shrugged. 'I suppose so. You said Catamaran was much more subdued when you saw him on Monday than he'd been on Saturday.'

'Maybe he'd be carrying his head low, or his lower lip might be hanging a bit loosely or he might be drooling or his eyelids might be drooping or his *membrana nictitans* . . .'

'His *what*?' asked Potter.

'His third eyelid. It's under the other two, and it slides across the eyeball from the inside corner. It might be half-way across if he was doped. But none of these signs is a must, and I can't see anything in these to suggest that that horse is doped.'

'The pathologist found no dope,' Potter pointed out.

'True. But there are hundreds of drugs and he probably would only have checked for the more obvious ones.' We went back to silently studying the prints. 'You know,' I said after a while, 'in spite of the lousy timing with the insurance, it *could* have been a genuine accident.'

Potter looked at me and sighed theatrically. 'First Norris is guilty, though you don't know of what. Now, it's an accident, so no one is guilty. Make up your mind, Frank.'

'They're not mutually exclusive. I never said he murdered the horse. Just suppose he was doing a bit of innocent do-it-yourself on the horse, shoeing or paring his feet or rasping his teeth, and decided to give him a sedative to make the job easier. And suppose the drug had the opposite effect – that can happen, you know – and the horse went wild instead, and from then on, it all happened as we thought it did. I doubt the insurance would pay up if they knew. So Norris might be afraid the photographs would show evidence of his meddling. That's possible, isn't it? The other two might have been members of the syndicate too, whose help he enlisted, and who also stood to lose a lot of money.'

'Somehow I don't see syndicate members driving red Sierras. Rolls-Royces would be more like it,' Potter said. 'And anyway, nearly all of them live abroad.'

'Perhaps he hired local thugs,' I persisted, knowing that my gaoler was no thug for hire, local or otherwise.

'Also, if it was like you're suggesting, he would probably have been using a common drug, so why didn't the pathology tests show it up?'

I shrugged. 'I don't know. I'm only thinking out loud.'

'And why would Norris have been doing that work himself? If the horse's feet needed seeing to, he'd have called the farrier, and if he needed a sedative, he'd have called the vet.'

'Maybe he just likes tinkering.'

'Then what about the rat?' Potter objected. 'We now have

two reasons why the horse went beserk – the rat and the sedative.'

'Improvisation. He put a rat in the box to cover the real reason why the horse went mad.'

'I don't buy it, Frank,' Potter shook his head, 'but let's assume for a minute that you're right. How long would you say the "accident" had happened before you got there?'

'An hour maximum. The horse couldn't have lived much longer with those wounds.'

'OK, an hour. Could you catch me a live rat in an hour? In a place that's supposed to be rat free? And if you didn't know you had an hour? And if you were expecting the vet to arrive at any moment? And if you had to be there to meet him? You wouldn't even waste your time trying. It would take you the first ten minutes to even think of it. I bet you couldn't catch me a live rat in an hour in the town dump, never mind Bally Ard!'

I shrugged and Claire gave me a what-have-you-to-say-to-that look.

Potter went on, sensing victory. 'Or do you think Norris had a rat on standby just in case his DIY job turned into a fatal accident and he might need an excuse?'

'Maybe one of his accomplices caught the rat.'

'Now hold on there! Accidents don't have accomplices.'

'Therefore I'm right. It *wasn't* an accident.'

'You're the one who said it *was*! Maybe Hynes's girlfriend told someone who told someone else, et cetera. Maybe half the town knows you took those shots.'

'But half the town had no connection with Catamaran, and nothing to gain by his death . . .'

'But, you said it yourself, you could call Norris a loser too. A couple of months later . . . Anyway, leave it with me. Whoever it is, we'll get them in the end.'

We didn't speak until we were in the car and driving. I was teasing the problem out in my mind but getting nowhere fast. Claire drove.

'Our friend seems to have some difficulty in accepting

171

Norris as the villain of the piece,' Claire observed, doing a slalom between two dogs and a bike. 'Mind you, I can't say I blame him. We hardly gave him watertight proof, did we? His hands are tied at the moment.'

I didn't reply. An idea was taking shape in my head. 'Maybe Potter's hands are tied,' I said at last, 'but mine aren't.'

'What do you mean by that?'

'I mean that it might not be the worst move in the world for me to call on Norris. Look at it this way,' I hurried on, to stall her protest: 'it would stir things up and perhaps something might float to the surface. Also I could make life a lot safer for me – he'd think I'd never call if I had any suspicions about him, and I could also throw him a red herring by telling him that what the kidnappers were looking for were the photos of the party.'

'Big deal! Suppose he just takes the opportunity of grabbing you again?'

'No chance. For one thing, you'll be sitting in the car outside, and for another, I'll tell him that Potter is expecting me and knows where I am.'

'You've got it all worked out, haven't you?' Claire was obviously dead against the idea.

'No. But the only way for Potter to get more information is to pay a routine visit and ask a few routine questions, and that'll only put Norris on his guard. I can stir things without him even realising that a finger has been pointed in his general direction.' I reached across and flicked on her indicator. 'This is where we turn for Bally Ard.'

'You really think it's wise?' she asked dubiously, but she turned all the same.

'I can't think of a better way to get the ball rolling.'

'Do you not think you've already done your bit? Why not let the wheels of justice grind to their inevitable ends?'

'Because by that time I may have been ground to *my* inevitable end. I've been close enough,' I added bleakly. Claire dropped the subject, concentrating on the road until we arrived at the imposing gates of Bally Ard. Now they stood open, mute testament to the fact that the priceless animal they had once guarded no longer resided within.

'Drive on up to the house and stay in the car. What time is it, by the way?'

'Almost a quarter to six.'

'I'll say I had an appointment with Potter for half-five.'

Norris himself answered the door. There was a flash of uneasy surprise in his eyes which was replaced instantly by his customary urbane expression, a process no doubt helped by the friendly beam I had managed to impose on my reluctant features.

'Hallo Mr Norris!' I said with a jauntiness I didn't feel. 'Sorry to drop in on you like this, but I need to use a phone pretty urgently and I thought, as I was passing, perhaps –'

'Of course, of course! You're more than welcome. Come in,' he said effusively, which I thought was a pretty good recovery. 'You know where it is, I think?'

'Yes, I remember. Through here, isn't it?'

'Yes that's right. In the study.'

'Thank you.' I left the door open so that he'd be sure to miss none of my 'conversation' and pushed the buttons for Ferndritch, the only number I knew for certain would be unattended. All over the room there were pictures of Catamaran – clearly Norris's phase of not wanting to be reminded had passed. I let the phone ring five times and began my monologue: 'Hello? Gardaí? Inspector Potter, please. Samson. Frank Samson. Thank you.' I hummed into the receiver as I waited. I didn't think that, from the other room, he'd be able to hear the Ferndritch phone still ringing but there was no point in taking a chance so I hummed as noisily as was reasonable in a relative stranger's house. I broke off suddenly. 'Oh! I see,' I said. 'Well then, it doesn't matter because I'm late too – I had some car trouble – but if he *does* come in before I get there, tell him I'll be there about 6.30. I'm phoning from Bally Ard and I've got to go back to the surgery to collect the certificates he needs, so, I think 6.30ish. OK? . . . Right . . . Thank you . . . Goodbye.'

'Did you get through?' Norris asked solicitously when I joined him in the next room. As if he hadn't listened to it all.

'Yes thank you,' I replied equally innocently. 'Actually, it turns out that the panic wasn't so big after all – I was to meet Inspector Potter at the station at 5.30, but he's late too, so there's no harm done.'

'Well if you don't have to be there until 6.30 now, can you stay for a drink? Bring in your lady friend.' I hadn't mentioned 6.30 to him.

'That's very kind of you, but we'd best get along. I've got to go to the surgery first.'

'Some other time perhaps.'

'That would be nice.' I felt it was time to introduce the red herring; I also felt it was odd that he had made no comment about my battered face – even in the most formal of circles, I would have thought a polite expression of interest or sympathy, or both, would have been in order.

'I suppose you've heard that I've been in the wars?'

'I did hear something to that effect, yes. Abducted, I believe?'

'Yes. A terrifying experience.'

'I can imagine. However, as they say, all's well that ends well. You're free and that, in the long run, is all that really matters. Was there a hefty ransom involved?' he went on, showing a very nice line in red herrings himself.

'It wasn't a question of ransom – not money, that is. They were looking for photographs.'

'Photographs! My goodness! What kind of photographs must you take to land yourself in that kind of trouble.'

'That's what took me a long time to figure out. Some seemingly incriminating shots I innocently took at a party. I heard later that there had been a big-time drugs dealer there. If I'd known what kind of party it was, I'd have left my camera at home. In fact, I'd have left myself at home. The drugs scene is not my scene.'

'Nor mine, I assure you . . . And did they?'

'Sorry?'

'Did they show anything incriminating? The photographs?'

'I don't know. They haven't come back from the lab yet. But they should any day now. Actually, the thought just occurs to me . . . I've got a few shots of Catamaran on the end of that roll, a few shots I took the morning of the day he died. I must give them to you when they come, unless, perhaps, you'd rather not be remind . . .'

'No, no, no! I'd be quite interested . . .'

I'll bet you would, you bastard, I thought to myself, but all I said was: 'Right, so – as soon as they're back, I'll let you know.'

Thanking him again for the use of the phone, the offer of the drink and everything else, I took my leave. I noticed that the Catamaran pictures were back up in the hall too. He came to the car, I introduced him to Claire, and he stood waving after us as we drove away.

'Stop outside the gate and let me out,' I said to her as I sat smiling and waving back at the smiling and waving figure of Norris. All smiles. All waves. All bullshit.

'What for?' She sounded as if she knew what for, but was hoping she was wrong.

'I want to see what he does now. That was the whole point!'

'I thought the whole point was to prod him and let Potter take over then.'

'That too.' I said meaninglessly, and was spared the need for further explanation by the fact that we had reached the gates and Claire had to stop before nosing out on to the road. I opened the door and stepped out. 'Come back in thirty minutes but don't stop unless I show myself. If I'm not here, give me another fifteen minutes or so – then, if I'm *still* not here, call Potter.'

'Frank . . .'

'Go on now! If he hears us stopped too long, he may smell a rat. It's all right,' I assured her as I closed the door, gently to make no sound. I could hear her disapproval in the way she drove up the road.

I snaked through the gate and into the dense shrubbery

which bordered the drive. A few minutes later I arrived at the edge of a lawn. From across the lawn, the side of the house looked back at me out of its eight windows, four on each floor. I could see no movement at any of them and only the second from the front on the ground floor was open. I thought it was the study window but I wasn't sure – I couldn't remember if the window had been open or not when I made my bogus call. Towards the back of the house, the lawn had several large trees and I worked my way along until I could cross, using their deep shade as cover. Bent double, I crept along the narrow concrete path which separated the lawn from the building, passing under both rear windows and stopping beneath the open one. As I was about to take a cautious peep over the sill, Norris's voice floated out on the still evening air, shocking me into frozen immobility. 'Hallo?' he said. I thought he was talking to me.

I looked up, with the beginnings of a sickly smile, and was surprised to see that he wasn't looking out the window. 'Hallo?' he said again, and I was about to answer when he went on: 'At last! I thought we'd been cut off . . . No – in fact *great* news. Our guest popped in a few minutes ago, innocent as a babe in arms! No. Not a clue . . . To phone Potter . . . Calm down! It was about something else . . . Well then, you can imagine how I felt when I opened the door . . . Certain – he thinks it was about drugs. And he *was* telling the truth – they're *not* back . . . He actually offered to let me have them as soon as he gets them!' There was a longer pause, then: 'We'll worry about the negatives if the prints look dodgy . . . Won't he just! This'll cure his jaw. I'm going out there now to tell him, but I wanted to let you know first . . . It sure is. I feel better this minute than I have since Hynes told me . . . OK . . . Fine . . . I agree fully . . . Yes of course . . . I'll be in touch.' And he hung up without saying goodbye to Tom, Dick or Harry, leaving me with no idea of who he'd been speaking to. I heard the study door close, his footsteps in the hall faintly, then the bang of the front door, followed at once by the noise of his car driving off.

I listened to the stillness for a few moments, then pulled

myself over the sill and into the study. The key was in the door so I tiptoed across and quietly locked myself in. I didn't want Mrs Flahive popping in to dust the desk or something.

The most likely prospect, the grey filing cabinet, was a non-starter – all the drawers were locked. So were the doors of the heavy mahogany sideboard. That left only the desk and, apart from the top left-hand drawer, everything in it was locked too. Somewhat disconsolately, I rooted through the drawer, and among the pencils and paper-clips, rubber bands and staples, I found an old-fashioned key. I knew it wouldn't fit the filing cabinet and I didn't even try. Nor did it fit any of the desk drawers or its flap. It did, however, open the sideboard and I hunkered down to take a look.

There were two shelves. From the upper one, cut-glass decanters and glasses winked at me; a large variety of bottles of all shapes and sizes stood shoulder to shoulder behind them. The lower shelf was Norris's pharmacy – in boxes and packets, it contained the usual assortment of liniments and ointments, embrocations and lotions, bandages and lint, wound sprays and cotton wool; nothing at all out of the ordinary. To one side there was a large box of the worming medicine currently considered the best on the market. I took the box out, thinking of pocketing a tube to send off for analysis, but I immediately lost all interest in worms for behind it was another box and *this* box had no business whatsoever being anywhere other than in the locked dangerous drugs cabinet in a vet's surgery. The box was the unmistakable green polystyrene-moulded half-cube container of Immobilon and its antidote, Revivon.

Immobilon is a powerful general anaesthetic used mainly in equine practice. When injected intravenously, the animal drops literally on the spot. Other anaesthetic agents will do this too, but the main advantage of Immobilon is that an equal quantity of Revivon injected intravenously will reverse its actions at once, and the patient stands up almost as quickly as he flopped down. This does away with the usual protracted post-operative recovery period – a period of great danger when lack of co-ordination can cause an animal to lunge and fall about, possibly hurting itself or bursting the stitches the surgeon has just so carefully inserted.

That is the great advantage. However, as everyone knows, every silver lining has a cloud, in this case the fact that Immobilon is absolutely lethal to humans – even a prick from a wet needle is enough to cause death almost before you can get half-way through a decent Act of Contrition. Worse, Revivon, so efficient in the horse, is ineffective in man. There is another antidote for man and neither I, nor any colleague I've ever come across, would even think of using Immobilon without having a plentiful supply of the human antidote on hand, plus an attendant who was able to give intravenous injections, and keep on giving them as long as necessary.

I separated the two halves of the box and removed both bottles from their snug polystyrene beds. The Immobilon bottle was not full – I reckoned that the amount missing was sufficient to anaesthetise a medium-sized horse – but the Revivon was unused, its rubber stopper unpunctured. So whatever had been knocked out had not been woken up again – which defeated the whole purpose of using Immobilon in the first place. Puzzled, I rechecked the contents of the pharmacy – there was nothing of a vaguely surgical nature, not even a suture needle. It seemed odd that Norris should possess, and seemingly have used, a general anaesthetic when he had no means of doing anything once he had knocked out the horse. Perhaps he had some instruments in one of the locked drawers? And then again, perhaps not.

I'd have given a lot to know *when* the Immobilon had been used. The obvious thing was to suspect it had been given to Catamaran for some unguessable purpose the day he died, but if he had been given it intravenously, he would have gone down at once; intramuscularly would have taken a bit longer but not a lot – certainly not long enough for him to squeeze out of his box, climb the manure heap, jump the wall and gallop almost half a mile cross-country. Also, Professor Wall would have been sure to have tested for Immobilon residues – it would most likely have been the first thing he'd have checked for. Thoughtfully, I replaced the boxes and relocked the sideboard. The Immobilon couldn't have been used on Catamaran; it would have shown up on tests. Maybe it had been used innocently (relatively) on some animal for euthanasia, an animal which had broken a leg or something? That would explain why none of the Revivon was missing. But then, why use only an anaesthetic dose? Why not inject the whole bottle? Or better still, why not use a gun? It would be just as effective, just as humane and far, far safer for the user. Even better again, why not get Steele to do it in the first place, for Chrissakes? None of it made sense.

It was while I was replacing the key that my eyes were drawn to the phone, and I thought back; it was Norris who had made the call – if he had received it, I would have heard the ring. Also, it was the last call he had made – he had left straight after. Therefore, the number should be lodged in the phone's memory. Deciding to pose as a Post Officer engineer checking faults and ask for their number, I pushed the 'recall' button and cleared my throat softly as I listened to it ring. There was a click as it was answered, then a very efficient female voice saying: 'Good afternoon. Dr Field's surgery. May I help you?'

'Eh . . . s . . . sorry,' I stammered. 'Wrong number.' Standing by the desk I tried to work out the significance of this bombshell. At least it cleared up one mystery – I now had someone who could give intravenous injections, monitor the stages of anaesthesia, use surgical instruments. It also explained the surgical glove dropped by the amateur burglars at the cottage.

I caught sight of the clock on the mantelpiece. I had about three minutes to make it to the road. Remembering to unlock the door, I left as I had come, by the window.

'Well?' Claire demanded as I jumped in.

'Drive on! Head for Potter.' On the way I brought her up to date.

'And you've no idea at all how Field was involved?' she asked when I'd finished.

'None,' I replied with some exasperation.

'You said you met him once.'

'He was at Bally Ard when I arrived at the crack of dawn to help with the autopsy. The excuse was that Norris was feeling lousy – which was entirely plausible at the time. The bereaved owner.'

'Well we know now that that wasn't the case, so there had to be a very compelling reason for him to be there. Otherwise, why tie himself in at all?'

'I presume he was there for the autopsy, though I can't think why.'

'What kind of a guy is he anyway?'

'Early to mid-forties, hard to say. Anyone's idea of a typical GP, well groomed, well dressed, well spoken, probably well heeled and totally lacking in any form of inferiority complex.'

'No doubt a pillar of the community.'

'No doubt.'

'Isn't Potter going to be thrilled with this,' she commented drily, reversing into a narrow space outside the garda barracks. 'First Norris, now Field . . . All he needs is for the third one to be the parish priest, and he'll have a hat trick of the local paragons.'

But, once again, Potter wasn't in and wasn't expected until eight. We said no thanks we wouldn't leave a message, we'd call again later.

'So, what now?' Claire asked across the top of the car. 'Don't tell me!' she held up a warning hand. 'You want to mosey over to Field's surgery and burglarise the joint.'

'How about finding somewhere to eat.' I ignored her sarcasm. In spite of the fruitful harvest, she still did not approve of my visit to Bally Ard.

'A much sounder idea. I haven't eaten since morning.' And she smiled sweetly at me, and slid in behind the wheel.

18

I rested my elbows on the counter of the Riverbank Hotel and watched the receptionist's bangled hand jangle across the long page of a multi-columned book, dipping the pen here and there. She looked up as her hand continued across the last few columns, and brown eyes, rimmed like Nefertiti's, widened in transient surprise at the battlefield of my face, then sweetened professionally. 'Good afternoon, sir. May I help you?'

'We'd like a meal, please,' I smiled, vaguely indicating Claire who was mooching and looking at knick-knacks in a glass case by the door.

'Certainly, sir. Grill or dining room?'

'Eh . . . Grill, I think.'

She made 'go round the corner' motions with her hand. 'Just follow the corridor round to the left and you'll find it on your right – next to the Garden Bar.'

'Thank you.' I collected Claire and we followed the directions. As we passed through the door, my eye caught the name above the frosted glass. 'Take a peek!' I grinned, catching her elbow and backing up.

'The Catamaran Rooms! I bet you chose this place deliberately!'

'I didn't even know it existed!' I protested, but I don't think she believed me. There was a dubious set to her shapely shoulders as I followed her into the dim room.

We slid into the mock-leather seats of a narrow booth by

the hessian-clad wall. All about were Catamaran memorabilia. The place was a veritable museum to Knockmore's most famous son – if the term may be applied to a horse. There were photographs on the walls and the support pillars, mostly the finishes of races with Catamaran frozen at the winning post showing varying amounts of daylight between his noble rump and the nose of the nearest also-ran. One wall was practically papered with newspaper cuttings, and a glass case in the middle of the room was stuffed with what looked like scale models of his trophies. The cashier's desk near the door was marked by a winning post.

A waitress brought menus, gave the table a perfunctory and unnecessary wipe as she squinted sideways at my battered countenance, then retreated. 'It's a wonder she wasn't wearing jockey's silks – or at least jeans, a polo neck, wellies and a riding hat,' Claire joked over the top of her menu. 'They certainly haven't skimped on cashing in on the famous nag, now have they?'

Any shortcomings in the matter of the waitress's attire were more than compensated for in the layout of the menu. The front cover was a black-and-white photograph of Catamaran, looking proudly at the camera, as though he was aware of just who he was; on the back, there was a potted life history – details of his bloodlines, foalhood, progress through the sales rings, unbeaten racing career, races won and the incredible amounts of prize money, his retirement to stud, syndication and triumphant return to the place of his birth, Bally Ard. It gave the names of the syndicate members, but the only one I knew was Gilbert Norris's. Inside, the theme continued – overdoing it, I thought. The 'Starters' section was headed, 'Under Starter's Orders'; 'Main Courses' had '(Race)' inserted between the two words; what would have been 'Desserts' became 'The Final Furlong'; 'The Home Straight' headed a list of cheeses, and 'The Winner's Enclosure' was where you looked for tea, coffee, etc.

The waitress returned and took our orders. Claire went back to studying Catamaran's biography. 'Aha!' she interjected triumphantly. 'So *that's* why he was called Catamaran!'

'Why?' I asked.

'Well, it's says here: "Sire – Ship o' the Line, Dam – Tropical Kayak," and what do you get when you put two boats together?'

'A regatta?' I hazarded, playing dumb.

'No, idiot! A catamaran!'

'You'd be a *horse* of a woman if you were fed!' The phrase is a compliment in our part of the world.

The starters arrived, crab claws in garlic butter for me and Queen Scallops for Claire. She fed me a few of the tasty shellfish from her fork and I passed her a couple of claws; I also acceded to her request for permission to dunk some bread into my molten garlic butter and ended up having to sacrifice my napkin to mop up the trail of butter-blobs which appeared on the polished deal of the table-top directly beneath the flight path of her saturated bread. She finished her starter (and half of mine) and excused herself. 'I want to see if they've got an evening paper at reception. There should be an article of mine in it.'

It was while Claire was gone that the penny finally dropped with a resounding clang. By the time she came back I was trying to impose some order on the tangle of facts which were seething and swirling through my head.

'Are you all right?' she asked, noting my furrowed brow and closed eyes as she slid into the booth.

'Shhh!' I held up a palm. 'Just a minute. I'm thinking.' A lesser woman would have told me to get stuffed.

In fact, it was more like three minutes. Then, still struggling with the implications, I said to her: 'I'm not exactly sure what fits where – yet – but do you want the headline of your life?'

'What? "Genius Comes Down from Mountain and Talks"?'

I shook my head and smiled. 'Better. "Catamaran Alive and Well".'

'*Mad* Genius Comes Down from Mountain and Talks Gibberish.'

'Hear me out, OK?'

She shrugged. 'You have the floor.'

'OK. First fact. I shot a ringer, a double.'

Claire looked shocked, then sceptical. 'How can you tell?'

'The horse I shot had a large untidy forehead whorl and – look at the menu – that whorl's tiny, hardly noticeable.' I pointed to the little eddy of hairs.

'You can remember that far back?'

'Can I remember?' That's what I took aim at! I saw it clearly then and I've seen it clearly in a hundred dreams since. Anyway, the photographs will soon tell us. Give us the keys.'

The difference in the whorls was unmistakable. Even their positions were different. The whorl on the horse I shot (as per my photographs) was dead centre on the forehead whereas Catamaran's whorl (as per menu) was slightly eccentric, high and to the right. No doubt at all.

Claire whistled. 'But *why?* Why would Norris do it?'

'I don't know, but I'm certain he did and I think I've figured out *how* he did it. The broad picture anyway. See what you think of this.'

'For some reason yet to be worked out, Norris, Field and the rest decided to fake Catamaran's death and to make it seem like an accident. To do that successfully they had to find a ringer, or at least a passable likeness, and they had to make sure that those who knew Catamaran well enough not to be fooled, were out of the way – namely Steele, his vet, and Tom Kelly, the live-in groom.

'They knew, months ago, that Steele would be going abroad for his son's wedding and that there'd be a locum taking over. I was supposed to meet Catamaran's understudy for the first time, lying broken at the bottom of the cliff, but I ended up making two unscheduled appearances. The first was when Steele took me to Bally Ard and I met the *real* Catamaran – I remember Norris did his best to prevent me from seeing the horse and, when he couldn't, had the groom cover him with a rug to hide as much of him as possible. The second was when I called on Monday morning, the day the horse died, and met the ringer. On that unforeseeable occasion, the three understudies came together: me, Hynes, and this unfortunate horse who only had hours to live. No doubt this was the last thing Norris would have wanted, but, even if he *had* known I'd called, I'd say they'd have gone ahead anyway; they had to get it done and be rid of the body before Tom Kelly returned, because he knew Catamaran better than anyone.'

'They broke into Kelly's mother's house themselves and roughed her up, didn't they?' Claire interrupted, jumping the gun slightly.

'Either that or they hired thugs. It wouldn't have been left to chance.'

'Jesus! An old woman living on her own.'

'People have done far worse for far less.' I paused and we observed what turned out to be the best part of a minute's silence in the sobering contemplation of the depravity of our species. 'Finding a substitute for Catamaran,' I resumed, 'would have been the hard part even though bays are the most common colour, and clean bays – that is, without any white markings – are fairly common amongst bays. They couldn't have hoped for an absolutely identical animal as the whorls always differ. Like fingerprints. In fact if a horse has no other distinguishing features, the whorls are the main means of indentification. There's some talk of them starting blood-typing, but, as far as I know, it hasn't begun yet. In fact, it can't have – if it had, the whole scam would have been impossible, a non-starter.

'So. Assume they've managed to find the sacrificial lookalike. Their big problem was always going to be the pathologist, whom they knew would have to be called in – he'd have Catamaran's file with him and *that* would have his passport, a document with all his distinguishing features (in this case, his whorls) marked in; for all they knew, an autopsy might begin with a comparison of whorls, etc., in which case they were bunched. They couldn't take that chance, so they devised an elaborate plan to get over it. The body whorls weren't a problem – they could be caked with mud – but the forehead one was a different matter. The ringer had a large whorl which would have been hard to hide. The answer was to have it removed altogether by having the horse shot. I imagine only a vet could legally shoot a horse without the insurance people trying to wriggle out of paying up, so that's where I came in.

'The trickiest part now began. The horse had to be injured so badly that treating him would be out of the question, but, not so badly that he'd die before the vet got there to shoot him. That needed very careful timing and that was why my friend with the red Sierra tailed me all that afternoon – to radio in my whereabouts.

'They also had to make sure that I'd have nothing with me to put the horse down, like a lethal injection, so I'd have to use the shotgun which, lo and behold, just happened to be lying propped against a rock.' I paused, annoyed with myself. 'I ought to have twigged that there was something odd about those rabbits. Norris told me to throw them away, and I never wondered why, if he didn't want them, he hadn't just left them where he'd shot them.

'Anyway, Norris said the horse was already dead, so of course I didn't bother to bring any medicines with me. When I found he was alive, I thought he must have been in such deep shock when Norris found him that his breathing had slowed way down. Or else that Norris was so shocked, he didn't notice him breathing.' I shook my head. 'It worked like a dream, didn't it?'

Claire kneaded a bread pellet and was quiet for a moment. 'It sounds very logical, Frank. But what would have happened if the horse had died before you got there? What about the forehead whirl then?'

'Whorl, not whirl. I don't know. Maybe Field hid in the bushes so that if the horse died, he could then shoot it, and claim he'd found it while *he* was out shooting on his friend, Norris's farm.'

'Would they have got away with that?'

'Possibly, when the extent of his injuries was known. Or maybe they'd organise a "break-in" to where the corpse was kept overnight, decapitate him, and claim it was the work of trophy hunters.'

Ten minutes later we left the restaurant, still deep in discussion, Claire carrying a hot menu, Potter's proof, under her folded jacket.

But Potter still wasn't back. What's more, he wasn't expected until very late – there was a mountain fire somewhere, and all available manpower had been called up. I debated telling the story to the duty officer but decided against it. For one thing, I didn't know if Potter wanted it known, and, more importantly, I was afraid that, in a small town like Knockmore, word might leak out to Norris and Field.

19

'What now?' Claire asked as we came out on to the footpath.

'I feel like a long walk.' I still needed to work off the claustrophobia of my incarceration. 'But not around town. Let's head for the hills.'

'Again?' She arched an eyebrow. 'Are we expecting more mist?'

I cocked an eye at the cloudless evening sky. 'We can but hope.'

Driving mostly in silence, we headed south into the mountains on what turned out to be a voyage of discovery. By the time we eventually got back to Knockmore in the small hours of next morning, we had discovered just about all that could be discovered at that time, one thing leading to another like collapsing dominoes. I slouched in the passenger seat, thinking darkly about my role as gullible cat's paw, and feeling much put upon; soon I was mercilessly castigating myself for mistakes made, inconsistencies unheeded. The answer to the discrepancy in the dung samples was simple, but had I thought of it, even fleetingly? I mentioned it to Claire.

'Worms? What worms?'

'I checked a dung sample from the ringer and it had worm eggs in it.'

'You told me about the dung sample but you said it had sunflower seeds. You didn't mention worms.'

'Well, you were just a nosy reporter then. It could have looked very bad for Steele.'

'Stick together you vets, don't you?'

'No more so, I imagine, than members of the NUJ.'

'So where did the worm eggs land you?'

'The hunter had no worms and I invented that many tortuous hypotheses, my head was spinning. The *obvious* one was that 'Catamaran' was from a different place, under different management. Whoever had him in the days before his transfer to Bally Ard had been feeding him tasty little titbits like sunflower seeds. Very touching.'

Claire, who had obviously been looking for flaws, seemed in no mood for kissing my bruised ego better, so I kept any other misgivings to myself. 'Tell me again, Frank, how you say, they managed it. Blow by blow.'

I told her – let the dungstead build up; when Steele and Kelly were out of the way, swap the horses. Then on D-day, ride the hunter up on to the dungstead, jump the wall, head cross-country to the quarry rim, snag tail hairs on the scrub, next, lead the ringer out of his box, ruck up the bedding, put scuff-marks on the concrete floor, snag some mane-hairs on the door frame and put the rat in the box; then shut the dog up in the horsebox to make sure he was on hand to sniff out the rat; lead the ringer across the bridge over the trough, remove the bridge, go on down to the quarry floor, where Field was waiting, and place the gun and fresh-shot rabbits beside the rock. I paused for breath. 'OK?'

'Go on.'

'As soon as he hears from the red Sierra that I'm on my way in from my afternoon rounds, Norris phones the surgery – Catamaran is in big trouble, he needs the vet double quick. He tells his housekeeper to keep phoning, and goes back down to the quarry. Field anaesthetises the horse and they smash a couple of legs with a sledge-hammer or something.' At this point, she wrinkled her nose in revulsion. 'Field cuts between the hind legs with a scalpel and taps a piece of metal from the dumper into the wound, then they hammer up and down one side to cause bruising consistent with a fall and, their work complete, manhandle the horse into the mud pool so that only his head is out. They do that by rolling him over so that the side they've bruised will be the side on which he'll be found lying, then they pull him the rest of the way.'

'Would two men be able to pull a big horse like that?'

'Remember they were pulling him through deep mud, so he'd half-float and half-slide. OK?'

When she nodded, I went on: 'When they come out of the pool they leave muddy footprints, but it doesn't matter – last one out throws buckets of mud all around, both to cover the footprints and to simulate the effect of half a ton of horse falling fifty feet into a mud-hole. Then they remove the sheet of plastic or tarpaulin on which they performed the "surgery" – to avoid getting blood on the ground – take off their waders or whatever protective clothing they've had on, and hide the lot for removal later. Then they leave and Norris goes to the house to wait for me. And that's it.'

'Are you sure they used drugs? I mean could they have managed, say with the ubiquitous sledge-hammer. . . A tap on the noggin with that . . .'

'No. For several reasons. If you didn't flatten him with the first swipe, he'd go berserk and kill all around him. Two, it'd leave a mark on the head, split the skin, crack the skull. Three, you might kill him and what about the forehead whorl then?'

'Then how come the pathologist didn't find traces of the anaesthetic?'

'Maybe they used some fancy stuff, like a human preparation. Which brings us back to Field. And the autopsy . . . If all they wanted to know was if they'd managed to fool the pathologist, then Norris could have attended, so there must have been a *medical* reason. But I can't think what – he didn't try to interfere, he didn't need to be there to get the result, and he was hardly there to learn how to do an autopsy on a horse . . .'

'So what's left?'

'The samples? A medical man would be best to see what

samples were taken – how much of each organ, what part of the organ, that kind of thing.

'Christ!' It suddenly dawned on me. 'There must have been another animal: they must have switched the samples! Field came to see what samples were taken, and while Professor Wall and I were having breakfast, he substituted them for the samples in the professor's bag which Norris had asked him to leave in the study. There was another animal. Any equine would do! Even a donkey or a mule, as long as it was about the same age and dead for roughly the same length of time as the ringer. Jesus! They're frigging amazing!'

My mind was suddenly back in the warm sunlight of that morning. Professor Wall, Dr Field and myself, the autopsy finished, rounding the bend from the stable yard, coming into view of the side of the house. Norris immediately coming through the french windows and crossing the lawn towards us, hurrying the professor and me into the house keeping him away from his car.

'But what if the case was locked or if he locked it in the car?' Claire persisted.

'I presume one of them had become an expert locksmith. After all, they managed to pick the lock on the Land Rover the day of the bogus colic. And if you're going to argue that they had to break in through the bathroom window at the cottage, Potter reckons that that was because it was the only way in which was hidden from the road.'

We parked by a gate into a conifer plantation, climbed a log stile, and walked along a gravel road through the young trees. There were huge brown puddles in the road, leftovers from the earlier rain. I took Claire's hand and was quite willing to give the whole subject a rest; further picking at it seemed irrelevant – we already had more than enough cause to nail Norris and Field and, presumably, within a few hours of their arrest the details would emerge. But Claire was in full investigative journalist mode, running even the most trivial minutiae relentlessly to earth.

'I presume, when Catamaran cut his muzzle, Field would have been able to duplicate the wound on the other horse?'

'No bother. They were so lucky! That nose wound actually helped them. How many bay stallions with purple muzzles would you expect there to be?' I draped an arm across her shoulders.

'But what were they trying to achieve? And why was it so elaborate?'

I shook my head. 'I've been trying to figure it out, but it doesn't make sense. If it was a straight insurance rip-off, they made a total bags of it. They've lost millions by not waiting a couple of months.'

'Well they didn't have much choice. They could hardly have organised the date of Steele's son's wedding, asked him to put it off until they'd upped the insurance.'

I smiled at the mental image. 'But it *still* doesn't make sense. If it was for the insurance, why not actually *kill* Catamaran? He's worth nothing now – he's supposed to be dead so they can't sell him, stand him at stud or anything. They could use him on their own mares but it takes two to produce a world beater and they wouldn't have mares of good enough quality. And even if they had, there's still no guarantee. They stood to profit much more, legitimately, over the horse's breeding life.'

'Could Catamaran have some fatal illness or something that would reduce his value enormously or the value of his foals?'

'Then there'd be even less reason to keep him alive. A terminally ill horse?'

'Well they must have some way of either selling him or breeding him. Otherwise they could just have killed him and spared themselves all the hassle.'

'If they sell him, it'll have to be as a pet, a point-to-pointer or dogmeat, and that will net them from a few hundred to a few thousand, max. As for breeding, sure they can breed him – to ponies and draught horses and Grade C hunters – for a couple of pounds a go, just because he *looks* nice. They can't wangle him into the stud book. That's run by Weatherby's, and it's about ten times more carefully guarded than Burke's Peerage.'

'Does Weatherby's cover the whole world?'

'No. Just Britain and Ireland. Other countries have their own stud book authorities.'

'Then what about selling him abroad? To some country where the register is not so tightly run?'

For the first time a vaguely tenable theory had come up. It didn't by any means breach the solid wall of contradiction; it was no more than a brick around which the mortar might be suspect. There was nothing to actually support the theory – all you could say for it was that it couldn't be rejected out of hand.

'You know, you could have something there. There's no proof, but that'll come when Norris and Field start answering questions.'

'The lawyers are going to make a fortune out of this,' Claire mused cynically. 'He's probably insured against everything imaginable except straightforward theft. It could take forever to work out – the syndicate will be trying to prove he's dead, the insurance people that he's alive . . . The only way to settle it would be to find Catamaran, but he's probably a million miles away by now with a completely new identity.'

I had a sudden feeling that I shouldn't accept *that* conclusion without examining it in detail. Smuggling a thoroughbred stallion out of the country would always be a difficult task; when the animal was a national institution, it would be almost impossible. The larger airports and ports would have strict veterinary inspections and careful examination of identity documents. Clearly, Catamaran's real passport couldn't be produced without his name being noticed, and he certainly couldn't be sneaked through on the dead ringer's papers – there'd be no way of disguising the whorls this time. Bribery would be out, not because my colleagues to a man or woman were above accepting backhanders, but because an offer would immediately arouse suspicion. An honest port vet would call straight away for the law; a dishonest one would probably demand an exorbitant 'fee' and continue blackmailing for ever. The smaller airports wouldn't take planes large enough to carry the horse and loading him on to a ship in a small fishing port would cause so much comment that speculation would be rife. Sooner or later, a link would be forged with the recently deceased national hero. If he was sedated and loaded aboard in a crate, then the crew would begin to put two and two together – he couldn't be kept in the crate for the whole sea voyage.

'I think Catamaran in still in the country,' I said.

Claire looked speculatively at me. 'Why?'

I explained the problems of getting him out. 'If it was me, I'd hide him for a while. It would be much wiser to wait because (a) there's nobody searching for him, he's supposed to be dead; (b) he's still too fresh in the public mind, but, most of all, (c) he'll still have that nose wound and it's probably still purple – that spray is a devil to get off. That would immediately spark off memories in anyone who happened to see him – the papers were full of it when it happened. If you ask me, then I reckon he's where the ringer was kept before the substitution.'

'You may be right,' she smiled. 'But where was that? That's the problem, isn't it?'

We were back in the car, heading for town, and hopefully, Potter. I was musing idly on the mentality which could care enough to dicky up the feed of an animal and then watch, presumably dispassionately, as it was taken off to a cold-blooded and cruel death, when it struck me that, yet again, I might be going for the complicated solution. Maybe the sunflower seeds hadn't been fed by some weirdo – they could have been picked up accidentally by the horse from its surroundings, the stable floor or whatever. There were places, though not many, where sunflower seeds were used routinely and might be scattered about. Like, for instance, a feedmill. But a feedmill was a most unlikely hiding place – too many people about. Or a health food shop. Again, a high street location didn't seem a good bet. Or a pet shop, where sunflower seeds were used as food for parakeets and other psittacines.

Psitta . . ? Psittacines! The thought had almost passed through before I recognised its significance . . . The kitchen at Bally Ard. Feathers, the wild, free-flying parrots in the wooded oasis in the middle of bogs, miles from anywhere, Norris's good friend, Mr . . .

'Vernon!' I shouted, startling Claire. 'That's him! I bet that's the one who kept me prisoner!'

Claire wanted no part of it. 'I think you're *crazy!* Why can't you just leave it to Potter now? There's no reason to think the horse won't still be there in the morning. Wasn't prodding Norris enough for one day?'

'Maybe the horse *won't* be there in the morning. Maybe they'll decide that the whole thing is getting chancy now – me escaping, calling on Norris, telling him we know they want photographs. Maybe they're afraid Potter will get them from another angle – the Sierra, fingerprints in the house, witnesses who saw Vernon coming or going from the house. Anything could panic them. Suppose Norris happens to run into Hynes again this evening and hears I've been asking questions about the *horse* pictures? Maybe this, maybe that, maybe the other. Who knows?'

'What do you intend to do?'

'Scout around. That's all. I swear,' I added when she looked dubiously at me. 'If Potter goes to Vernon's place tomorrow, he'll have to do it legally, search warrant and all, the same as if he had gone to see Norris today, and, if Catamaran *isn't* there, he'll have given the game away and they'll be able to spirit him away from wherever he is. And that'll put paid to any chance of ever finding him. They'd kill him first. All I want is a quick look. Ten minutes, in and out. Fifteen, max.'

She looked as if she didn't believe a word of it; yet she had to concede the logic of finding out if the horse actually *was* there. 'Where does Vernon live?'

'Someplace out in the mountains or on the bogs. A wooded

oasis, miles from anywhere, according to Norris's house-keeper, but I can't very well phone her for the address.'

'It'll be in the phone book.'

'He doesn't have a phone.'

'Now, just *how* would you happen to know that?'

'I heard Norris telling Field that he was going to drive out to tell the third man about my visit to Bally Ard. If he had a phone, Norris wouldn't have had to drive. Great brain, huh?'

'So how'll we find his address?'

'Any man who keeps all those parrots flying free must be pretty well known locally. I'm sure he comes into town now and then to shop or have a drink or whatever. The shops will be closed by now so we'll ask in a pub.'

We passed by the first four pubs we met after arriving back in Knockmore, on the grounds that they didn't seem like the places that Norris and his friends would frequent, referred snobbery which was going to cause big trouble before the night was out. At last we pulled up outside the Oyster Beds lounge bar, studied it for a moment and decided that it was a much more likely prospect. Claire would do the asking as I was too well known, and we didn't want people wondering why the vet who had shot Catamaran, who had been kidnapped himself, and almost shot as well, should be looking in a pub at this hour of the evening for the address of Vernon, the parrot man. Claire would be a friend of a niece, who wanted to call on him as she found herself in the area.

I watched her cross to the bar with its pale neon lights trying to make an impression on the evening light. Five minutes later she was back with detailed instructions on how to get to Clashard, Vernon's isolated domain. 'One guy even offered to come with me to make sure I didn't go astray in the dark,' she laughed, sliding in behind the wheel.

'I'll bet he did,' I retorted drily.

Claire's directions were good and as we drove west into the sinking sun, she picked off her landmarks one by one. Just short of ten miles from Knockmore she indicated right and announced with satisfaction: 'This is it. The second right after the third house beyond the shop with the telephone kiosk across from it. Simple.' At least she seemed to have shed some of her misgivings.

For the first half-mile, there were houses and small fields surrounded by drystone walls, but once we breasted the first rise and began the descent into the first shallow valley, these vanished, and the only signs that man had ever been there were the road, and the long rank of poles which marched beside it carrying current to Clashard. To our right, the bog rolled eastwards in dark waves to merge with the evening sky, while to the west it lapped against distant mauve mountains which pushed like a fist of knuckles into the turquoise skyline. The sheer immensity and emptiness of the place soon began to gnaw away at Claire's resolve and I could see her doubts return.

'No heroics, Frank. OK?'

'No. Of course not.'

'Of course not, of course not. That's what you said before at Bally Ard and you went and broke in!'

'This is just a quick look-see. I *have* to see if Catamaran is there and I want to get a look at Vernon. Balaclava or no, I'll know if he's my man.'

In silence, Claire steered around huge lichen-bearded boulders which looked as if they should have been sucked under aeons ago. We skirted tiny lily-covered lakes, blobs of liquid sapphire, nestling in every hollow, and crossed the slow brown streams which tried vainly to drain the sodden landscape, until at last, cresting a final rise, we found ourselves looking across an empty valley at the serrated tops of the conifers of Clashard.

20

We hid the car behind a long turf-reek and crept to the top of the rise. Clashard occupied a triangle between two narrow lakes which converged from the north and almost met below us; it stretched back some five hundred yards and, beyond that, the bog stretched away miles to a dark spruce forest. A short river linked the lakes, the road spanning it on a little stone bridge before vanishing into the ubiquitous rhododendrons which flourished on the boggy, acid soil. The road stopped at Clashard. In the fading light, bright bursts of plumage flashed between the few hoary old conifers which poked up through the shrubbery and younger trees, parrots finding roosts for the rapidly approaching night. Crouching in the sedge, we took stock.

We couldn't see buildings, but a pencil-thin column of turf smoke climbed unwaveringly into the still air, marking the position of the house. There was a whoosh as a flock of doves rushed by low overhead, flying in from the west. I watched them settle some distance beyond the smoke.

'That'll be where the stables are,' I whispered. 'There, where those doves landed.'

'How do you know?'

'They're in for the night now, and doves wouldn't roost in trees if there were buildings about. If there *are* sheds, that's where they'll be.'

Several minutes later, without either sight or sound of

activity from below us, Claire said: 'Maybe he's gone. Got the wind up and took off without even putting out the fire.'

'I doubt it. He'll have had the good news by now. Anyway, I'm going down to check.'

'I wish you wouldn't. I think we should try Potter again.' When there was no response, she tried another angle. 'What if he has a dog?'

'Naw!' I said with reassuring scorn, though I, who spend my life keeping a wary lookout for farm dogs, hadn't even thought of a dog. 'With all those birds?'

'Why not?'

'They might eat the birds. Natural enemies.'

'Then why don't dogs eat sheep? They're even *more* natural enemies.'

'That's different.'

'Why is it different?'

'Well . . . sheep are sheep and parrots are . . . parrots . . .'

'And bullshit is bullshit. I think he *has* got a dog. Because of cats. Cats eat birds and climb trees – they're *really* natural enemies. And dogs discourage cats – they're natural enemies too. So, my enemy's enemy is my friend and therefore he probably has a dog. Or two. Or a whole slavering *pack* of them!' I think she thought she had me convinced.

'Claire. I'm going in and that's that.'

'Then so am I.'

'Someone should stay here, just in case, to go for help.'

'I thought you said there was no danger.' She looked at me defiantly. 'If you go, I go.'

'OK,' I sighed. 'Give me a couple of minutes head start. But, if there's any sign of trouble, you stay put. Agreed?'

'Don't worry. One hero is enough.' She squeezed my arm: 'Promise you'll be careful.'

'I promise. See you down there.'

Working my way through the sedge until I met the river, I dashed across the bridge, slipped into the bushes, and, half-fearing the howls of outraged dogs, crouched down. But the only sounds were the gurgling of the river and the drumming of my heart. A short while later, moving like a wraith, Claire materialised by my side.

'That white dress of yours is very visible,' I whispered. 'You'd better stay well back in the bushes.' We set off deeper into the shrubbery, our progress muted by a muffling carpet of old leaves.

Silhouetted against the dying dusk-sky and the last, lingering reflection of the lake waters, the single-storey building was a plain, rectangular converted, smallholder's cottage. Looking from left to right, there were two dark windows, then a third, which poured light in a pale yellow splash on to the gravel of the forecourt, and, at the end, beyond the lighted window, a dark door, ajar. I watched the lighted window for some time but there was no movement.

'I'm going to sneak across for a look,' I whispered and felt Claire stiffen. Pushing silently through on to the narrow lawn, I stood at the edge of the forecourt, just outside the rectangle of light. The room was a kitchen, but I could only see part of it. After listening carefully for a few seconds, I tiptoed across, pressed myself against the wall, and peeped in. Nobody. I retraced my steps, skirted the light, and crept back in on the other side, between it and the door. I was edging forward to peep in when I froze. Coming down the road, I heard the same tread that had ominously approached my cell twice a day during my captivity.

I flattened back against the wall, trapped in a patch of dark – he was up the road to my left and the light was spilling out from the window to my right. If I ran for the bushes, I'd be clearly outlined against the light, and if I moved up the road to get my head below the bright patch I'd run right into him. I did the only thing I could; I slid into the tiny dark porch and, fists bunched, waited for him to appear in the doorway.

When the footsteps were almost at the door, they stopped. For a moment I thought he'd seen me, though he'd given no indication – his measured pace hadn't changed as he approached. Then came the sound of heavy boots being cleaned on a metal scraper and I relaxed. I still had the advantages of surprise, weight, height and years. And I'd already knocked him out once. I waited in the tiny dark space, ready to do it again, only regretting that I hadn't had time to check that Catamaran *was* here. If he wasn't, and Norris or Field had got wind of Vernon's 'arrest', they might decide to cut their losses and destroy the horse, the only really concrete evidence against them; there'd be no exhumation, the ringer had gone straight to the knacker's.

As the scraping continued, I wondered if I mightn't chance going on in through the house and finding a back door. At first, I dismissed the idea because I reckoned the moment I opened the inner door, a flood of light would stream through. Then I noticed that the inner door had no slits of light marking its edges and no exclamation mark of yellow shining through the keyhole which I could feel with my exploring hand. I gently depressed the handle and eased the door open the faintest of cracks. Still no light came through. I pushed it far enough for me to slip through and, closing it gently behind me, found myself in yet another porch, this one so small that it could have had no other function than as a kind of draught excluder against the wild winter winds which would lash, unchecked, against the cottage. This time, the inner door was clearly outlined in light and I went quickly through. Outside the scraping continued unabated.

The kitchen was small and sparsely furnished; I could see at a glance that there was nowhere I could hide and no back door. The only exit led towards a corridor and I headed for this, careful not to pass between the central ceiling light and the window. Half-way along the corridor there were two doors, one opposite the other. From my observations from the bushes, I knew not to bother with rooms opening to my left – they had no outside doors. The right door opened into a bathroom, but it had no outside door, so I closed it gently and pressed on. The scraping stopped as I entered the end room, a sitting room.

There were two windows in the end wall, and two doors, one to the left, the other to the right. Ignoring the door leading to the room on the left, I pushed the right one open a tentative crack, then paused uneasily – there was no sound from the kitchen and I had the impression that Vernon had not yet come into the house. Could he have seen Claire? Spotted her white dress? Then came the sound of the kitchen tap running. Reassured, I stepped into the room and pulled the door to. He'd probably just been removing his boots, which would explain the delay and why I hadn't heard him walking in the kitchen. He was now in his stockinged feet, or had put slippers on. Whichever, his footsteps weren't audible. I'd have to be extra careful.

He was preparing his supper; crockery clinked and cutlery rattled, a fridge door opened and closed, a kettle began to sing, there was the scrape of a chair being moved and the sawing thrusts of a breadknife. Taking advantage of his industry, I closed the door fully and switched on the light.

There was no outside door and the window was small and deep-set. Its sill, crammed with a collection of old, odd-shaped bottles, was useless as an escape route. Beneath the window was a small table on which stood a brass lamp and several magazines. Facing the door, beside the table, a low bookcase stood against the wall. Above this, spaced pegs held three split cane fishing rods and a landing net. Further along that wall was a tall darkwood cabinet. The back wall was covered by a large handwritten genealogical table and on the fourth wall was the door, the light switch, me, and a large glass case of stuffed parrots. There was no way out and nowhere to hide. As I couldn't hear Vernon any more, I switched out the light and retired to the back wall to ponder my ironic predicament – I'd only just escaped from being held in a room by Vernon, and here I was, once again, in the same fix, albeit this time, unknown to him. As yet.

Should I rush him as he was eating his supper? Should I wait until he came into this room? *Would* he come into the room? Should I sit it out, wait until he went to bed before making my escape? If I did, and he stayed up for hours, would Claire wait, not knowing what was going on in the house? If not, what would she do? Go for help? Come in search of me? . . . The questions were endless. A toilet flushed.

Perhaps I *ought* to tackle him – get it over with, citizen's arrest. The chances of Norris and Field finding out that Vernon was in the hands of the gardaí would be remote. Catamaran would be safe . . .

The light in the sitting room came on, sending a sudden patch of yellow under the door, like water from an overflowing bath, illuminating the room just the faintest bit. Then came a click, the voice of a newscaster, and seconds later a flickering bluish light, flowing under the door to mingle with the steadier yellow. I reached a snap decision – I would take him, but make sure there were no cock-ups this time.

It suddenly struck me, looking across at the fishing rods, that Vernon, living where he did, was very likely to own a gun, and, if so, that he probably kept it in this room. I eyed the tall cabinet speculatively, then edged towards it in the deep gloom. What faint light there was, was totally blocked by the out-swinging door, so I explored the interior with slow, careful hands. In seconds, my cautious fingertips were sweeping gingerly across shaped, polished wood, the stock of what proved to be the first of four shotguns. I grasped the last one and tugged it gently. With only slight resistance, it came free. It was empty, which wasn't surprising. I explored the floor of the cabinet and found nothing, but in a drawer underneath there were boxes of cartridges. I loaded the gun, snapped it closed and put a handful of cartridges into my pocket.

Now Vernon was in the sitting room again; I heard him place a tray on a table and turn up the volume as the theme music of *Coronation Street* started up. I hesitated a moment, putting the finishing touches to my plans, but, before I could move, the door opened, the light came on, and Vernon walked in.

At first he didn't see me. He crossed to the table beneath the window and picked up a magazine. Flicking through the pages, he turned towards the door and, just as I was about to say 'Good evening, Mr Vernon', or something equally inane, his head jerked up as if his neck was spring-loaded and he stared at me in horror. Eyes and mouth wide open, he tottered backwards, the magazine falling from his nerveless fingers to the floor.

'Good evening, Mr Vernon,' I said.

21

He was trembling and panting alarmingly, and for a moment I thought he was going to have a heart attack. Not wanting to push him over the top, I stood quietly and, with more than a touch of pride, studied the livid jaw which was highlighted by the waxy pallor of the rest of his face.

'Time to go,' I said, when his breathing slowed, but he ignored me and continued leaning against the table. I didn't trust him – my aching nose was a painful reminder of the last time I thought I'd outwitted him. I waved the gun towards the door. 'It's over. Let's go. Now!'

When I raised my voice, it registered; he looked blearily at me, then said in a broken voice. 'Give me a minute, please. Just a minute. I don't feel well.'

'You've had your minute,' I said, but didn't push it.

In a short while he seemed to have recovered enough strength to push himself, with some difficulty, away from the table. I backed into the sitting room, keeping out of arm's reach, and ushered him towards the corridor. As he passed the chair in front of which his supper tray was set, he sank into it, and seemed to pass out.

'Get up!' I commanded sternly, but his head remained lolling back and his eyes stayed closed. I backed to the TV set and turned it off. 'Catamaran is up at your sheds, isn't he?' I asked, dropping my voice in the sudden quiet.

'Catamaran is dead.'

'How did he die?' I asked, feeling a slight chill, despite knowing he was lying.

'You shot him.'

I snorted in relief. 'The horse I shot was a ringer, and you know it. You or Norris or Field shot another horse for his bits and pieces, but nobody shot Catamaran.'

'I don't know what you're talking about.' The voice wasn't any stronger but it was defiant; it was also a bit strangled, courtesy, no doubt, of the *coup de grâce* of the GI truss.

'I'm talking about conspiracy to defraud, cruelty to animals, breaking and entering, assault on old Mrs Kelly and me, kidnapping, attempted murder . . . Won't Inspector Potter get a nice surprise when he finds out what three of his leading citizens have been up to? And I'll bet he can think of lots more . . .' Crouched pitifully in his chair, Vernon seemed to shrink physically. 'Let's go and have a look at the horse,' I said. 'I'm sure it'll count for something if he's being looked after well.' Actually, it probably wouldn't matter a damn but Vernon clutched eagerly at the specious straw.

'I fed him just a while ago. He's fine!' He rose from the chair, suddenly anxious to show me just how well he had looked after Catamaran – as if I had some say in the matter. 'Come with me.' I still wasn't willing to take any chances, so I kept the gun pressed firmly into the small of his back as we shuffled along the corridor towards the kitchen.

We never made it. As we passed the doors in the corridor there was a metallic click from either side, one from each room, and a voice, strangled with menace, growled: 'Drop the gun, Samson. *Now*!' It was Field's voice, though barely recognisable. With a sick feeling, I did as I was told. Vernon continued on to the kitchen as if nothing had happened, then sank in to a chair by the table and lowered his head onto his hands. 'Don't move. Not an *inch!*' Field hissed. 'You so neatly reeled off all our "crimes" just now, it seems that blowing your nasty, interfering brain to bits couldn't make things much worse. Where's the girl?'

'What girl?' I stammered from between clamped jaws.

'Look, Samson,' he made a massive effort to be reasonable.

'We're . . . under *severe* pressure right now. Do you know how that feels?' He obviously expected an answer so I nodded. 'The *fuck* you do!' His voice began to break but he got it, and himself, back under control. 'So . . . don't give us any bullshit. Answer quickly and truthfully. OK?' Again I nodded. 'Good. Now, where's the girl who was looking for directions an hour ago in the Oyster Beds? Beautiful, tall, white dress, looking for "Mr Vernon who keeps parrots".' He raised his voice to a squeaky falsetto in a vicious caricature of a woman's voice.

'I left her in Knockmore.'

'OK!' The fragile control snapped. 'That's it! I warned you.'

'Easy, Vincent!' Norris spoke for the first time. 'Take it easy, for God's sake! What good will that do? Look, Samson, you were both seen coming up the road. Your girlfriend was driving, so she's *not* in town. Now, tell us where she is and we'll try to sort this out amicably.'

'Amicably?' Field barked with a hysterical laugh. 'Amicably, my *arse!*'

'We'll find her sooner or later, you know . . . Desmond! Where are you going?' Norris broke off as Vernon got up from the table, and, totally confused, headed towards the outer door. 'Don't go out there, Desmond. Sit down like a good chap. Just for a moment.' He waited until Vernon had sat down again, then turned back to me. 'Well? Where is she?'

'Probably gone for help. She was keeping an eye on the gate from the hill out there.'

'Well,' Field took over again with triumphant relish, 'if she *is*, she won't get far because we found your car and let the air out of the tyres. If she walks on the road, we'll get her; if she walks off the road, the bogs will get her. Maybe she's already up to her charming titties in a swallow-hole! Maybe you should tell us where she is before she goes under.'

'I honestly don't know where she is at the moment,' I said, knowing that Claire was far too sensible to tackle such hostile territory in the dark.

'Hey!' Field suddenly called. 'Vernon! Is Samson's woman

207

in the house? Hey, Vernon! Did you hear what I said? Is she in the house?'

But Vernon's head had gone back down on the table.

'She's not in the house,' I said quietly.

Field looked at me and laughed, another sharp bark, as if it was hilarious that I should expect him to believe me.

'Perhaps you ought to take a look,' Norris suggested.

'Oh I intend to! But watch this bastard. Maybe I ought to search him first in case he's still got Vernon's gun on him.'

As Field pocketed his gun I said, 'Potter has a letter explaining everything to him. He could be on his way now.'

'Come, come, Samson,' Norris tutted impatiently. 'You distinctly told Desmond that Potter would be surprised when he found out what three of his leading citizens had been up to.'

'I meant "surprised" when he opened the letter,' I tried lamely.

Field finished patting up and down my trousers, even feeling in my socks; now he started on the side pockets of my jacket. 'Don't mind him, Gilbert. It's just another of his stories. You made good time getting here,' he said conversationally, searching through the contents of my left pocket and replacing them one by one.

I said nothing.

'Made it without a stop, I expect?'

'That's right,' I answered dully.

'Which means you'd left this . . . letter for Potter before you came to the bar? Isn't that right?' he insisted when I didn't answer at once.

'Yes,' I said in a small voice, seething at having been caught out so simply.

'Then why come to the bar? You could have got directions from the cops. Everybody knows where Clashard is.' In the dim corridor, he smiled at me. 'D'you know what I think? I think you haven't been near the cops at all.'

I was spared the need for answering by his sudden exclamation. 'Well, well! What have we got *here*, then?' He gave a low whistle as, from my inside pocket, where it had been since the restaurant, he slowly pulled the wallet of prints they had been hunting for so long. 'Jackpot, Gilbert!' he gloated. 'I think we've just hit the bloody jackpot! Cover him very, very carefully.' He began to leaf hurriedly through the sheaf of photographs, becoming more and more anxious as he came on one shot after another of the party. Suddenly he stopped and let out a long breath of relief. 'They're here! They're here! At long last . . .'

'What are they like?' Norris asked impatiently.

'They don't seem to be *too* bad . . . Here's one of the head which might have proved awkward. I'll give them to you in a minute.'

Field dropped the prints of the party on the floor and started again through the photographs of the horse, this time more thoroughly.

'We've got the photographs, Desmond,' Norris called but Vernon's mind was off somewhere else.

Field was counting '. . . six, seven, eight. Did Hynes say how many shots were taken?'

'No. He wouldn't have known.'

'I wonder if there are any missing?'

'Are they all here?' Norris turned to me.

'Don't *mind* that bastard!' Field scoffed.

'Count them,' Norris said.

'I just did. Eight.'

'No. Count them all. Those ones on the floor too.'

Field bent, scooped up the scattered prints, and began to riffle through them. Suddenly he was beaming. 'Thirty-six! A full roll. All present and correct.' He turned to me, his face wearing a triumphant smirk. 'You can't expect us to believe in a letter waiting for Potter now, can you? Only a certifiable idiot would have left a letter and not included the photographs. Whatever else you may be, you're no idiot. In fact, Samson, you are what I would call . . . a loose end.' Staring at me, he reached slowly into his pocket, and withdrew his gun. This time, there was no interruption from Norris.

There was no way out. If I tried to tackle one, the other would surely get me; if I tried to make a run for the kitchen, they'd both get me. With a curious, numb detachment, I hoped that Claire was, by now, well hidden or, better still, far away, so that she wouldn't have to hear . . .

'Admit it, Samson; there is no letter,' Norris said, still the cautious one.

'Of course there isn't!' Field interrupted testily. 'Look, Gilbert . . . if there was, he'd have left the photographs too, or at least a few of them! But they're all here! As for copies . . . if they'd had copies made we'd be in prison by now, wouldn't we? Come on. Let's get this over with. I don't like it any more than you do, but what the hell else can we do?'

'Now, why don't you count the negatives,' I heard myself say. I still don't know where the thought came from, what made me suddenly remember that Claire had taken them to Dublin, weeks ago, for her editor. Shaking inwardly, I imposed a superior smile on my unwilling features and held it grimly while Field, looking suddenly dubious, pulled the celluloid strips from the wallet. It was obvious he was worried as he started to count.

'Seven. Seven strips.'

I nodded. 'Four frames per strip, seven strips, twenty-eight negatives, thirty-six prints. Where are the eight negatives of the horse?' There was a sudden air of doubt in the corridor. As Field made to hold a strip up to the light, I said: 'You needn't bother checking. They're not there. They're with Potter's letter, along with a menu from the Catamaran Rooms at the Riverbank Hotel.'

'Oh Jesus Christ . . .' Norris breathed.

'Shut up, Norris!' Field snarled. 'Let me think! It's another of his fucking lying tricks!' But his outburst lacked conviction.

Norris heard the hoofbeats a split second before I did. He stiffened and cocked his head. They grew louder and louder until they drew abreast of, then raced by, the cottage. His head turned, following their passage as if he could actually see through the wall. 'Catamaran!' he said in shock. '*The bogs!*' he cried, and, all else forgotten, legged it for the kitchen.

Field was no less stirred. 'The *horse*! The bitch has let out the fucking horse!' His voice was a croak, as if this was the last straw. As he still had his gun pressed hard into my ribcage, I stood stock still, dreading his next move.

Suddenly the gun was gone. He took a few steps towards the kitchen, remembered me, checked, and began to turn. I didn't see him complete the turn because I was already in the bathroom pushing the bolt of the door home with clammy, sweaty hands. A cord brushed against my cheek and I pulled it. With a click, the light came on.

The next few minutes were chaotic. Field ran distractedly between the kitchen and my door, calling on Norris, when he was in the kitchen, to come back and help recapture me, and, when he was outside the door, ordering me to open up, and threatening me with grisly retribution if I didn't.

It suddenly struck me that the bathroom, far from being a safe haven, could actually be a deadly trap – if Vernon woke up enough to stand guard with a gun in the corridor, while Field went round to the window, I was as good as dead.

'Samson!'

'What do you want?' I answered him for the first time, to keep him occupied. I took an almost empty shampoo bottle off a shelf over the bath. I'd have to break the window – apart from a narrow, hinged top flap, it was fixed.

'I *know* you're in there . . .'

'How did you work that out?' If it wasn't so serious, it would have been farcical. I uncapped the bottle and held it under the tap to give it weight – the bubbled window glass looked tough.

'So you'd better come out . . . *right now*.'

'Piss off!' I screwed the cap back on tightly and hefted the bottle in my hand.

'I'll shoot!' he warned.

'Shoot away,' I said, wondering if he had picked up the shotgun.

'Fuck you!' There was a sharp report, a thunk of wood, and

a little splintered area appeared in the door at about eye level, but the bullet didn't come through.

'Fuck you too!' I shouted defiantly and threw the bottle as hard as I could at the window. The heavy glass shattered, leaving a jagged hole into the night. Pulling sharply on the light-cord, I plunged the room into darkness and rushed to the window.

Field hammered on the door, even more panicked now as he realised what was happening. 'The window! He's getting out the *window!*' I wondered, as I pushed out the remaining shards with my jacket-covered elbow, if he was talking to himself or whether, in fact, Vernon had re-entered the fray. As I put my leg over the sill, I heard his pounding feet, racing into the kitchen, heading for the back of the house.

Seconds later, just as Field arrived panting, I gained the sanctuary of the shrubbery and crouched in the dark, scarcely daring to breathe. A matter of feet away, Field stood, alert for any telltale sounds of my retreat. I stayed as I was, frozen in immobility, trying to still the pounding of my heart. The only sound was Norris, forlornly calling: 'Catamaran, Catamaran,' off in the distance.

What seemed like an age later, Field's impatience began to simmer. Angered by Norris's incessant plaintive cries, he started shifting uneasily from one foot to the other – I could tell by the crunching of glass fragments – then suddenly, unable to contain his frustration any longer, roared: 'Damn you, Norris! Get back up here you stupid bastard! We'll get the horse in the morning!'

But the desolate cries went on unabated, and eventually proved too much for Field – there was a clamour of breaking glass mingled with whining ricochets as he fired two frustrated parting shots into the bathroom, then, muttering fierce oaths, left. I waited a long time in an increasingly uncomfortable crouch; there was always the danger that cunning might reassert itself in Field's distraught mind, and, knowing that I couldn't have got far, he might be lurking nearby.

My main worry was Claire. Having seen Norris and Field's

surreptitious arrival, and subsequently heard the three shots, she'd have to be thinking that I was dead or at least badly hurt, and would be distracted with anxiety. Waiting no longer, I cupped my hands to my mouth and shouted: 'I'm OK, Claire! Don't go near the car! Stay where you are!'

Now that there was no further profit in silence, I crashed through the shrubbery and legged it for the front of the house, trusting that night would make a snap shot difficult. Bent low, I streaked across the forecourt and into the bushes where we'd first hidden. But Claire wasn't there. I called her name softly, but no answering whisper filtered back through the undergrowth. Worried, I tried to second-guess her. I didn't think she'd have hidden up by the stables once she'd let the horse out – Catamaran had passed at a flat-out gallop and it didn't seem likely that he'd do that, in the dark, unless there was someone chasing him. Simply released, he'd probably be content to sniff about. For one instant I wondered if he might have been galloping because Claire was on his back, spurring him on, but I dismissed the notion – Claire was no horsewoman. Unless she had decided to go for help and found she had four flat tyres? No, Claire was much too sensible for such long-shot heroics; she'd still be hiding in the bushes. If she could see the door from wherever she was, she'd know where two of them were (assuming Field *had* actually left), but she couldn't know that Vernon was *hors de combat* (if he was) so she couldn't stir. I began to edge towards the sheds.

Suddenly, I saw her dress. Diagonally across from me, a wraith-like figure materialised from out of the dark wall of bushes and hovered a couple of feet above ground; seemingly legless, armless and headless it pulsated in levitation.

'Claire!' I whispered loud enough to reach the apparition, which promptly dematerialized back through the leaf-wall at great speed. I rushed across the intervening space and found my ghost shaking and sobbing just inside the cover of the leaves. I held her tightly in my arms and whispered to her until her shaking subsided and she clung to me as if she was never going to let go.

'Oh God, I thought you were dead,' she sobbed.

'Shhh. Not so loud. Didn't you hear me calling?'

'I didn't know if it was you or if they were trying to trick me. It might have been someone trying to imitate you.' She sniffed loudly. 'What happened?'

'I was almost a goner. They found the photos in my pocket.'

'Who got shot? Vernon?'

'Nobody. Those shots were just Field chancing his arm. He's gone off the head. Raving. Vernon is too, but in a different way. He seems to have collapsed completely. He's still in the house, as far as I know. You didn't see him come out, did you?'

'No. Just Norris and Field.'

'We'd better stay quiet. I can't hear any shouting now.'

For the next hour, Claire and I played the mice in a deadly game of cat and mouse, moving as infrequently as possible and only at the onset of padding, surreptitious footsteps. Early on, we came into a low dell with a shallow trough of soft mud in it, and I smeared Claire's dress liberally; later, when one of them – we couldn't tell which – passed within a few feet of us, her camouflage was all that saved us. Once or twice, at the beginning, we disturbed roosting parrots, but my initial fear that their flapping and squawking would betray our position proved groundless because the alarm spread quickly through the woods, and soon the whole place was a hum of vaguely complaining psittacines. It was both a blessing and a curse – it helped mask the inevitable tiny sounds of our movements and whispers but it also made it harder for us to hear them.

As the night ground on relentlessly, the strain became almost unbearable and we held a whispered discussion. We both felt that our luck couldn't hold.

'If they get more torches, we're done for,' I whispered. They had started out with pencil torches but the batteries had long since died.

'If they could have, they would have,' Claire whispered back. Reasonable enough.

'Still, I think we ought to make a move.'

'A move to where?'

'The lake at the back of the house. It's fairly narrow this end; we could swim it and then just sit them out on the bogs.'

Feeling our way in the dark, we began our slow move, but we had covered only the first few yards when all at once there was the sound of a car. We lay low, hiding from its lights, as it approached, turned in the forecourt and stopped; over the hum of the idling engine we could hear voices; not whose they were or what they said, but there was no mistaking their urgency.

Moving much more quickly now, we edged forward towards the glow of the red tail-lights until there was just one layer of leaves between us and the open space in front of the house. The car – Field's BMW – faced away from us but the headlights were on so we could see, in clear silhouette, everything that happened.

First there was only Field standing beside the car. I could almost see the desperation surrounding him like an aura. Suddenly he looked towards the house and pulled open the back door. Norris came out leading Vernon by the elbow, talking to him in a pleading, reassuring tone, as if he was trying to convince him that everything was going to be alright. They put Vernon into the back seat where his dejected figure promptly lay down (or fell over) and was lost to our view. Field went and sat behind the wheel while Norris returned to the house; a moment later, the kitchen light went out, Norris re-emerged, locked the door, and, crossing in front of the BMW, got in at the passenger side. That was it. Seconds later they had gone and Claire and I were alone in the darkness of Clashard. Breathing great breaths of relief, we stood, arms around each other, listening to the fading sound of the car. In the quiet of the moor night, we could hear it for a long time, maybe for miles and not once did the engine noise falter, not once was its smooth purr interrupted: it just got fainter and fainter.

'Well,' I said, 'if anyone has got out again, they've had to jump from the moving car.'

When we could hear the sound no more, we moved quickly towards the house. I found a stone in the herbaceous border, smashed the window of the room opposite the bathroom, and climbed through. In the corridor, I switched on the light – the shotgun was still propped where I'd left it. I headed for the gun cabinet, chose a second gun, pocketed a box of cartridges to replace those Field had confiscated, and returned to the kitchen.

There was a labelled key-board by the door. The first hook, 'House' was empty. I ran my finger along and unhooked a small bunch from 'Garage', then continued past Feed Store, Breeding Shed, Loose Box, Boat House, Pump House. The last hook, 'General', held a large bunch on several interlocking rings that looked as difficult to undo as a Chinese puzzle, but the car key stood out as it had a black plastic finger grip with the Ford logo. I took the whole bunch.

'Any noises?' I asked Claire as I climbed back out through the window.

'Not a whisper, but I'm glad you're back all the same.' She gave me a brief reassuring hug. 'What now?'

'We head for Knockmore and try to get the law to head them off.'

'They'll be hours gone. We've got four flat tyres, remember?'

I held up the keys and rattled them. 'We go in Vernon's car.'

On our way to the sheds, I said: 'I noticed a key in the kitchen for the loose box. Was it locked?'

'Yes. It was.'

'Then how did you get it open?'

'An iron fence-post. I worked it loose from the ground. I used it to lever the hasp of the lock off the door jamb. That's what took me so long – surely you don't think it took me *that* long to think of letting the nag out?' In the dark, I could sense her smile.

'Just how long did it take you?'

'Five minutes? I'm not sure. Why?'

'It can't have been silent work.'

She didn't answer for a moment, then she shrugged. 'Well . . . no. Not exactly . . .'

'And you had no way of knowing if those cut-throats weren't homing in on the noise?'

Again, I sensed a little enigmatic smile. 'Well you keep getting yourself into these messes, so somebody had to do something. Plus you had the car keys so I couldn't run. Also, I think it's good for the damsel in distress myth to get turned on its head once in a while.'

We found the garage and felt our way up along the car. The plastic grip made the key easy to find by touch and I unlocked the door. When I opened it, the interior light came on. The red Sierra.

'I hope it starts,' Claire said.

'I can't see anyone living in a place like this, having a dodgy battery. It'll start.'

I gave Claire the box of cartridges. 'In case they're waiting for us somewhere. You load and I'll fire.'

'Do you think they might?'

'No. At least, I hope not.'

But the road was clear all the way, and twenty minutes later we pulled in at the garda barracks in the main street of Knockmore.

'You know, Frank,' she said as we walked to the door, 'I've just remembered. I meant to give you those negatives today – I had them in my bag all ready, but when I saw the mess you were in, they went clean out of my head.'

'I don't want to hear this,' I said and shivered.

22

Shortly after Claire and I had intruded on the napping night-duty officer, Potter and his men arrived back, red-eyed, smut-stained and exhausted. He took one look at us and blinked tiredly. 'Is that the red Sierra outside?'

I nodded.

'Whose?'

'Desmond Vernon.'

'The *parrot fellow*?'

'That's the one.'

'God Almighty! What's *he* got to do with this? Vernon from out on the bogs?'

'Yes. We've had an eventful time since we last saw you.'

'You'd better tell me about it.' He led the way into his office and, before closing the door, called: 'Could somebody please make some coffee – strong.'

Potter kept shaking his head throughout, but it was no longer a matter of hypothesis – now there were hard, irrefutable facts, eyewitnesses, a live Catamaran out on the bog, photos, a menu cover, no loose ends. But it was Field's involvement which capped it all, the last straw. Potter treated it almost like a personal betrayal. 'Vincent Field! Christ above, I play golf with the man most Sunday mornings! A fourball – we both play off five!' Obviously it was hard for him to credit a five-handicap man with such goings-on. I knew Claire would be thinking: one law for the rich and one for the poor; one for the five handicappers, one for the pitch and putt merchants, but, obviously making allowances for the inspector's exhaustion, she gave not even the slightest sign of disapproval.

'What have you done so far, Murray?' Potter asked when the duty officer brought the coffee in on a stained and rusted tray.

'Radioed the squad car and phoned all the stations around. I gave them Dr Field's number – the BMW, not the Volvo. That's all so far, sir.'

Potter looked as if he considered this action somewhat peremptory, and Murray went on defensively: 'Mrs Field's called three times already tonight, sir. The doctor left home for a drink at the Beds but she had to phone there because there was an urgent call, and they told her he'd already left around nine. She hasn't seen or heard from him since. It ties in with what they're saying, sir.' He indicated us with the least perceptible inclination of the head.

'I'll have to speak to Thelma Field. Does she know?'

'I don't think so, sir. She hasn't rung since they –' another nod – 'came in.' He acted as if he and Potter were speaking a language Claire and I didn't understand and were trying not to let us know that they were talking about us. I couldn't see what the point of it all was.

When the conspiratorial officer left, Potter phoned his wife and, once more, pressed their boundless hospitality on us. Neither of them would hear of us looking for a hotel, and Fernditch was out because my locum, the *locum's* locum, had moved in.

The red Sierra was impounded so we opted to walk the half-mile to the house, while Potter went round to visit the unfortunate Mrs Field. When he returned nearly an hour later, Claire and I had both showered and were being fed by the tirelessly hospitable Joan. I'd put on the same clothes again but Claire's mud-smeared dress was totally unwearable and, while it churned round in the washing machine, Joan Potter had dug up a T-shirt-cum-nightdress of her daughter's, and Claire now sat in the clinging, slightly too small, jersey garment; it stretched across her breasts and came almost half-way down her long thighs, and carried a picture of the Pink Panther in repose, eyes closed, nose emitting a waving line of Zs which climbed towards a crescent moon.

'How's Thelma?' Joan asked anxiously as Potter opened the door. She had gone silent as soon as we heard his car pull into the driveway.

'Not too good, I'm afraid.'

'Should I go over?'

'No. She'll be all right. I waited until Jim and Doris came. They'll stay the night.'

'I'll ring her, then.'

'I wouldn't. She knows you're concerned. Leave it till morning.'

'Oh God, it's awful. The poor woman.'

There was some sporadic, listless conversation, carried on in short, shocked, and often unfinished sentences. Claire and I kept silent; we couldn't even pretend to be sympathetic as the fugitives – *especially* Potter's golfing buddy – had, over the last few hours, being doing their damnedest to murder us.

Then Potter got his second wind and we went over the story again and again, fact by minute fact, detail by tiny detail. At last Claire asked to be excused; as she turned to close the door, her eyes looked into mine, then she raised her hand briefly, said goodnight and went out. After the best part of an hour, Potter, who must have been numb with tiredness by then, yawned and switched off his recorder. 'You're tired, Frank. We both are. Let's get some sleep.' He stood up, drew a glass of water and, carrying it carefully, crossed to the door. 'Goodnight,' he said.

I headed for the sitting room to make do as best I could on the sofa, and I was sinking into a deep, deep sleep when I felt gentle brushing on my cheeks and lips, and heard a soft, siren's voice whispering: 'Frank? Frank, are you asleep?' I awoke grudgingly, wanting to stay with my dream of Claire, and was momentarily disorientated when the first thing I saw, lit softly by a street light, was the Pink Panther. My eyes followed the wavy line of Zs up to the crescent moon, then beyond, along the graceful line of her neck, her small determined chin, gently smiling lips, delicately sculpted nose and stopped when they met her smiling, grey eyes.

'Are you awake?' she whispered softly, leaning down to brush my lips with another kiss.

'I am now. What's wrong? Can't you sleep?'

She smiled. 'Oh, I can sleep all right; the trick was to stay awake. I wanted to say goodnight to you properly, not . . .' she raised a hand in a repetition of the wave she'd given me earlier.

'That was the sexiest wave I ever saw.' I reached out and pulled her towards me. Her hair tumbled down on my cheeks, as her mouth found mine.

Then she pulled her head back and mocked gently. 'Of course, if you're *tired* . . .'

'*Me*? Tired? I was just about to do fifty chin-ups on the door frame when you came in!'

Claire clasped a hand to her mouth to prevent a giggle from leaking out into the sleeping house and pushed until I made room for her to stretch out beside me.

'Does this mean we're engaged?' I grinned at her in the faint light.

'I didn't think it was a leap year.'

'Perhaps it is. See if you can find a pen, some paper, and a calculator, and we'll divide by four.'

'Shh! You'll waken the house.'

'Right now, the only danger I see,' I nibbled her earlobe, 'is that we might wake the Pink Panther. Do you not think it might be wise to put him on that chair over there and let him continue his sleep?'

'I suppose, if he does wake up, he'll make an awful racket . . . De-dum, de-dah, de dah . . .' she hummed a few bars, as she stood. Her eyes never left mine as she walked to the chair and, with one smooth, breathtaking move, pulled the T-shirt over her head. Heart pounding, mouth dry, I reached towards her and, with the grace of a real panther, she came to me. As I was about to kiss her, she put a finger to my lips.

'Do you think we should, Frank? What about the Potters?'

'I'm sure they'd be all for it but, if you like, I'll go up, wake them, and ask them for their votes.'

'Stop teasing!'

'Seriously, I'm sure they'd be all in favour – they're only human, after all. And did you ever wonder why they never managed to get their *paso doble* to championship standard?'

'What?'

'Tell you later,' I said, and buried my face in the soft fragrance of her hair.

Next morning, I set about trying to put names to the ringer and his previous owner. As soon as offices were open I rang Bord na gCapall, the Irish Horse Board. One of my best friends at college was now its breeding manager.

'Declan Forbes, please,' I told the girl who answered.

'Who shall I say is calling?'

'Frank Samson.'

'Hold the line please,' she sang. 'I'll see if he's available.'

I waited and hoped that he was. Declan had an encyclopaedic knowledge of, and a consuming interest in all things equine. During our college days, while the rest of us, if put upon, might perform a song or two, Declan's party-piece was to grab an empty Guinness bottle by the neck, hold it like a microphone, and, closing his eyes, begin, in a perfect impression of the voice of Peter O'Sullevan: 'Good afternoon ladies and gentlemen and welcome to Prestbury Park . . .' He would then regale the company with a full and accurate commentary on one of the Arkle Gold Cups with hardly a pause for breath, complete with the appropriate voice changes for the betting news from the paddock, all the statistics involved, and commentary from 'our country camera'. The climactic last furlong could glue a whole pubfull of people to their seats.

'Hey, Hair!' Declan came on the line. 'How's it going?' 'Hair' had been my nickname at college. Samson, Hair. Hardly very original or inspired.

'Great, Dec. How's it going yourself?'

'The usual. I've been wanting to have a chat with you – the

man who shot Catamaran. Fair dues to you. I'd hate to have been faced with it.'

'You'd have done the same thing without blinking. You should have seen the poor bastard! It was the easiest decision ever. No choice. Dec? I need a favour done, no questions asked.'

'Well, unless you've changed, you're not going to ask me for anything that'll cost me my job. What is it?'

'Do you have a list of all the thoroughbred stallions in Ireland on your computers?'

'No. Weatherby's deal with the thoroughbreds. They'll have them. Why?'

'What d'you mean "why"? You promised! No questions. Do you know anybody at Weatherby's? Well enough to do you a favour, like?'

'Several. Depending, of course, on the favour.'

'What I need is a list of the stallions nearest to Catamaran in age, height and markings.'

I could feel the pregnant silence at the other end as Declan put two and two together, but he stoutly confined himself to: 'Catamaran had no markings.'

'Who are you telling?' I laughed, a mirthless one. 'What I mean is, clean bays like him and pretty much the same height and age.'

'That shouldn't be a problem, Frank. But I'm beginning to regret agreeing to no questions.'

'I'll tell you as soon as I can. How long should the check take? It's pretty urgent.'

'Give me your number. I'll call you back in ten minutes.'

He called in less than five. 'I don't know if it's good news or bad, but there aren't *any* stallions in that category. I went two inches either side of his height, a year either side of his age and the only clean bay thoroughbred stallion in that bracket was Catamaran himself.'

'Are you sure? Not even *one*?'

'Not even one. In case there was one that had died or gone abroad or whatever, I asked them to go back over the last two years and – nothing. Zilch. If there was one, they'd have him for sure.'

'What about imported stallions?'

'If they're thoroughbreds, it doesn't matter whether they arrived in Ireland by stork, plane or boat, Weatherby's will have them on record.' He waited for my next question and, when there wasn't one, nudged: 'Does that help you at all?' I knew he was itching to question me.

'It thickens the plot, Dec, but thanks all the same. I'll be on to you as soon as I can and I'll explain all. Right now, it's more or less *sub judice* – that is, provided I'm not barking up a wrong tree altogether.'

Declan's news had left me perplexed. I thought back through the deductions of yesterday and tried to spot where we had taken a wrong turn, but there didn't seem to be one, and the living proof of this was alive and well, and being rounded up on the bogs above Clashard this morning. I needed to stretch my legs and think.

I walked along a narrow side road near Potter's house, up towards a gold-encrusted hill of flowering gorse bushes. Bonzo, Potter's geriatric, retired police-dog, scraped arthritically along in front. Deaf as a post, he had seen me go out the gate, and struggling dutifully to his feet, lumbered after me, pink tongue lolling. Now, he was leading me by a couple of lengths – useless ears erect from habit, nose sweeping the ground ahead like a mine-detector, he scraped along, his nails scuffing over the rough surface of the road. As we topped the rise, I reckoned if anywhere was going to banish mental cobwebs, then this was the spot. In contrast to the unusually dry and warm weather of the previous few weeks, the morning was bracing. During the night there had been a little rain, and the countryside had a clean, fresh-washed look about it. Along with the rain had come the first autumnal breeze, and this was still playing about the hilltop, dropping the temperature, singing in the telephone wires and causing an agitated rattling in the yellowing leaves of young sycamores by the road. The sun was as bright as ever but there wasn't anything like the same heat from it and, low in the clear-washed sky, small clouds bustled by. I shoved my hands deeper into my pockets, and, hunching down in my anorak, squeezed my arms tighter against my sides.

How could Weatherby's have said there wasn't a ringer for Catamaran? I'd seen both horses and I'd certainly have noticed any discrepancy in either height or colour. I would also have spotted any significant age difference; I'd seen the ringer's teeth when I put the bit in his mouth on Monday morning and, later that same day, when he lay dying and slack-lipped at the foot of the cliff.

I wondered briefly if the ringer might have been smuggled into Ireland but that would have been complicated, chancy and expensive, and I scratched the idea. Perhaps he'd been got off the register by reporting him dead? But Declan had gone back two years and hadn't been able to find a match, and it was highly unlikely that the plan had been two years in the hatching . . . The ringer had to be a registered horse, and, if that was so, then, because no ringer existed on computer, the ringer must have been altered in some way to *make* him a ringer.

I sat down on a large rock, shielded from the chilling wind by an even larger one. Bonzo watched for a moment to see if I was going to settle, then deciding that I was, positioned himself over a comfortable spot, rotated creakily a couple of times, collapsed like a stringless puppet, and fell asleep.

Of my three criteria, age and height were immutable. And besides, Declan had allowed a wide margin of variation for them, so the ringer must have matched age-wise and height-wise. The third parameter, colour, was the only one that could be tampered with in any way, so, by a process of elimination, the ringer could not have been a clean bay; he had to have some white on his face or legs, the only places I had ever seen white patches on a bay horse. So how would they hide the white? Would they chance dyeing a leg that was due to be immersed in muddy water? If it washed off or changed colour weren't they done for? Dyeing a white patch on the face would be even more chancy – matching the colours exactly would be a tall order, failing to do so, a disaster . . . In the end I was almost ready to concede that, with their customary thoroughness, they had indeed managed to find a perfectly fast dye.

Almost as an afterthought, I considered the only other colour one might find on a bay horse, flesh marks – pink areas of unpigmented skin on the muzzle. I reckoned that dyeing these would be out of the question as, every time the horse drank, he would wash off a little more of the dye and in no time the pink would be back through. The only way to remove flesh marks would be by surgery, and even then . . .

Surgery! I suddenly realised the simple answer – the ringer had had a flesh mark which Field had removed under local anaesthesia. He had then duplicated the operation on Catamaran! Small wonder that Steele had been racking his brains, trying to figure how the 'accident' had happened. The wounds just had to be approximately similar as, according to the plan, they would never be compared – I was not supposed to see Catamaran, and neither Steele nor the groom would ever see the ringer. I jumped up, nudged the deaf Bonzo with my toe and we jogged briskly back down the hill to the house. I rang Declan again.

'Listen,' I rushed, not giving him time to speak. 'One more favour, a big one. Can you have that run through again, the same parameters, only this time allow a fleshmark?'

'Can it wait? I'm on my way into a Breeding Committee meeting. Oh hell,' he said, 'it'll only take three minutes. You at the same number?'

He rang before I had finished the coffee that Joan Potter had brought me. I nearly spilled it as I grabbed for the instrument. 'Yes?'

'Hair?'

'Yeah. Any luck?'

'Five.'

'Five!'

'Five. Do you want them all?'

'No. Just the ones with the flesh mark confined to the upper lip.'

There was a moment's semi-silence as he whispered his

way down the list. 'Two,' he announced. 'Passarato and a horse called Second Fiddle. Never heard of him. Have you?'

'No,' I answered, thinking that I had probably met him, though. It certainly couldn't have been Passarato – after Catamaran he was the second most famous stud horse in the country. 'Who owns Second Fiddle?'

'It says here, a Michael Halligan in Waterford . . . but there's a C.O.O dated 12 April . . .'

'A what?'

'C.O.O. Change of ownership. C for change, O for of, O for –'

'I thought you had a meeting. Stop messin' and get on with it!'

'OK, OK. A C.O.O to a Desmond Vernon, Clashard, Knockmore-on-Sea, County Galway. Which, coincidentally just happens to be where Bally Ard is! What the hell is going on Frank?'

'Can't you guess?'

'I *am* guessing, but I don't beliéve it!'

'Believe it. I can't say any more.' Into the stunned silence at the other end, I said: 'Thanks Dec, and give my apologies to the Breeding Committee,' and hung up.

Before going to join Joan Potter for the eggs and bacon which I could smell and hear sizzling in the kitchen, I phoned Bally Ard and asked a tearful Mrs Flahive if she could arrange for her son to go to Clashard to look after the birds. She had heard the rumours and found Norris absent when she went to Bally Ard in the morning, but she still couldn't believe it was true. I couldn't give her much solace. Potter had warned me not to tell anyone anything – a man was innocent until proven guilty.

Potter arrived a few moments later. He was driving Claire's car and brought in the overnight bag which he had found in the boot.

'Isn't she up yet?' He looked at the ceiling.

'The poor girl's had an awful night of it,' Joan said defensively. 'Out on the bogs, being chased around in the dark, and it must have been two o'clock this morning when she got to sleep!'

'You could add an hour to that,' said Potter, winking at me.

'Did they get Catamaran?' I changed the subject.

'No. There's still no sign of him, but it's big country up there.'

'How about the . . . eh . . . fugitives?'

'Not yet. But there's a nationwide alert out for them.'

'The horse I shot was called Second Fiddle. Aptly enough, wouldn't you say?'

He stopped buttering a slice of toast. 'How did you find that out?'

I told him. 'He was bought in Waterford. By Vernon. Last April.'

'Well, would you believe it?' Potter swallowed a thoughtful mouthful of strong tea and, with his tongue, worked a wad of food loose from between his gum and his cheek. 'That seems to be that then, doesn't it? The missing link. Now all we need to know is what in the name of God they intended to do with Catamaran, a horse that's supposed to be dead. Ah well,' he reached for another slice of bread, 'no doubt that'll all have to wait until we catch them . . .'

After breakfast I took the bag up to Claire. She was still fast asleep.

'Hey! Wake up, Sleeping Beauty!' I whispered, bending to kiss her. 'It's half-past ten.'

She stretched sinuously, arching her neck, extending her arms to the limit behind her. The Pink Panther rippled and twisted as she moved. 'Go easy,' I warned. 'You'll wake the Pink Panther.'

She stopped in mid-stretch and fixed me with a mock-cynical eye. 'Frank!' she warned.

I kissed her again and straightened up. 'Here's your case. The car's outside.' I walked to the door. 'See you down there.' I went down the stairs thinking that Claire was getting more beautiful by the minute.

I sat across from Claire in the sunny breakfast alcove of the kitchen, and brought her up to date.

Joan Potter came in. 'Phone for you, Frank.'

'For me? It must be Declan. He's the only one who's got this number.'

But it wasn't Declan. It was Lord Roscahill, one of the syndicate members. He explained, in a voice as dry and rustling as paper, that, as the member of the syndicate nearest the scene of the ... eh ... the scene of the ... incident, that is, as it were, eh ... the other members had asked him to oversee the rounding-up of Catamaran. 'Not really on, Samson. Eighty-three next June, you know.'

'Oh, I see,' I answered, wondering why he was ringing me.

'I'd like you ... if you would ... to take over the business. I gather the gardaí haven't yet succeeded in doing so?'

'Not unless they've done so in the last hour or so.'

'Well, with Norris ... ah ... ah ... ah ... absent,' I couldn't tell whether he had a stutter or was just searching for a nice word for 'on the run', 'he *is* likely to be absent for the foreseeable future, would you think ...?'

'That's really not for me to say.' It was the nearest I could get to 'No Comment' which didn't sound too curt.

'Of course. *Sub judice* and all that. Very proper of you. Put it this way, Samson. As his vet, with responsibility for his welfare, would you consider that it is in Catamaran's interests that I take over looking after him?'

'Emmm. Yes I think you could say that.' Here was an eighty-two-year-old peer who knew several ways to skin a cat.

'Good. Then, will you do it? I might add that expense is no object – for you or all the help you may need, and I shall send my helicopter at once.'

I thought for a second. With a helicopter and all the help I wanted, it shouldn't take more than a few hours. Claire and I had talked about a few days' break somewhere, but she was going to be busy filing her story, so today was a write-off anyway. Then there was the satisfaction of finishing off what I had started. 'I'd be delighted,' I said.

'Good man! I must say it will be a great comfort to know that, when he *is* rounded up, Catamaran will be under the supervision of the best vet in the country.'

This was going a bit far, I thought. 'Well, I'd hardly say . . .'

'Did you not raise him from the dead, Samson? Aye?'

I laughed.

'The helicopter will be there in about an hour. Cooke, the pilot, will give you all the information you need to contact me as soon as you've finished. Thank you again, Samson. For all you've done. Believe me, you won't find the syndicate members ungrateful or unappreciative. Goodbye and good luck.'

'Thank you.' I hung up and must confess to a small knot of avaricious wonder in my belly. I hadn't thought about rewards before, but now that the subject had come up, I couldn't help wondering what a group of nine multi-millionaires might consider a fitting way to prove that they weren't ungrateful or unappreciative. Eight, actually. Norris was hardly going to chip in.

I went back to the kitchen and told Claire and Joan Potter that I was staying on to organise the round-up. A few minutes later, Claire managed to get Potter's permission to call in her story. She vanished back to the spare room and was soon clacking away at the keys of Joan's portable Olivetti. I got an absentminded peck when I went to say goodbye before heading off on a borrowed bicycle to join the helicopter which had clattered in over the town, circled a few times, and finally set down on the football pitch of the local school.

23

The pilot introduced himself as Kevin Cooke as we lifted into a blustery sky, watched by the entire staff and student body of the school, plus a sizeable section of the town's population. Seated wide-eyed in the plastic bubble, trying to hide my excitement and delight, I watched the upturned faces below grow ever smaller as the flimsy machine swayed alarmingly on its vertical ascent, and hoped I wasn't going to be sick. The queasiness didn't pass until we picked up speed and began to move horizontally.

'Where to?' Kevin asked.

Prudently deciding to forego speech, I pointed over my shoulder, and my discomfort became outright terror as he banked the machine in a tight turn which placed him about three feet higher than me, and left me hanging in what suddenly seemed a very flimsy harness, the only thing preventing me from crashing through the fragile perspex and hurtling to the ground, spinning unnaturally zillions of feet below. I didn't dare grab anything to steady myself; in the narrow confines of the bubble, everything looked to have a vital purpose – with my luck, I'd surely grab the ejector-seat button (for the pilot's seat), the brakes, or the self-destruct knob.

'First time up?' Keven grinned. Presumably, he found my ill-concealed nervousness amusing.

I paused a moment before answering, as if not quite sure – nonchalant like. 'Yes.'

It didn't work. 'Don't worry. Most people get a bit woozy the first time. You expect it to be like a regular jetliner to Majorca or Malta or wherever, but it's not. Not a bit, really.'

'No, it's not,' I agreed.

'How far is this place?'

'Not long now – we should be able to see it any minute. If it's not over this hill, it will definitely be beyond the next one. We can't miss it – it's the only thing on the bogs for miles and miles.' I was beginning to enjoy myself, grinning with childish delight as he pulled her up to clear an approaching hillside.

For once, my sense of direction hadn't let me down, and as we clattered over the summit, and the far slope dropped precipitously beneath us, we could see Clashard a few miles off to our left. Dark and abrupt on the immensity of the pale, sedge-brown bogs, it was as obvious as a lump of coal on a fawn carpet in an empty room.

We searched our way up to it, in long zigzags at about a hundred feet. Then we hovered over Clashard itself in case Catamaran, never having experienced real freedom before, might have returned to the security of man-made structures. A uniformed garda came out on to the bridge and waved; it was a friendly wave, as opposed to a beckoning wave, so we waved back and continued our search out over the bogs to the west.

The terrain below was treacherous. Hollows and tussocks, undetectable under a blanket of heather, soft quagmires beneath deceptively green, grassy surfaces – the moor could be a dangerous place, even for the ponies which spent the whole summer roaming at will over it. For a total stranger, like Catamaran, it was fraught with all sorts of traps, and I began to have visions of him, once day broke and he could see that he was free, laying his ears back and taking off in a joyful gallop, assuming that this ground was as firm and even as the Curragh or Epsom, or all the paddocks, training grounds and practice gallops he'd ever been on.

We found him in a narrow gully. He had located a herd of semi-feral Connemara ponies – all mares and foals as far as I could make out, and, not only had he not been injured, he was actually at work, and the unknown owner of a scrawny and creaking white pony mare was getting, for free, what a select handful of highly privileged owners had paid hundreds of thousands of pounds for in the stud season.

'Whoo-eee!' Kevin whooped. 'Nookie in the mountains!'

'Pull over to one side, out of range,' I said, laughing. 'We don't want to scare the mare at this delicate stage. If she suddenly took to her heels now . . .'

'Ouch!' Kevin made a face of exaggerated agony and the helicopter slid away from the bunch.

We landed on a reasonably firm patch some half-mile away, and made our way back on foot. I carried the rope which Kevin kept under his seat, fashioning it into a crude halter as I walked. I knew I was being overly sanguine, but equally, I'd have felt a right twit if I *had* managed to get a hand on his forelock and then had nothing to slip over his head. Catamaran, back on all fours now and dubiously sniffing a gorse bush, jerked up his head as soon as we broke the skyline, and, with a sharp snicker of alarm, led his new-found family at a brisk canter up on to the open bog and away to the north. We didn't even try to follow.

Clattering back to Knockmore to pick up help, we passed over a man unhurriedly leading a grey pony across the bogs.

'I'll bet you a fiver that that's a mare, and another that she's in season. He's headed straight for where we landed. We pinpointed Catamaran for him. Galwaymen! Cute hoors every one of them. They'd mind mice at a crossroads.' Kevin said.

'So it would seem.' I shook my head in amazement at the brazenness of it.

'And the cute hoors in the west are cuter hoors than the cute hoors in the east . . .'

'Where are you from yourself?'

'Galway!' he replied and bellowed with laughter.

Though I didn't know it, and wouldn't have believed it if you had told me, the flight back to Knockmore marked the end of the success phase of the round-up – at least for several days. *Mea culpa*. I accept responsibility – but only for the first day's fiasco. I underestimated Catamaran's determination to hold on to his freedom, and I didn't arrange enough help to deprive him of it. After several short-lived efforts to drive him towards Clashard, the only place within miles where he could be cornered, we gave up. He would co-operate for a while, walking with his herd within the loose frame of the overstretched human cordon, then, with a contemptuous toss of his lordly head, lead his family at a smart, unstoppable trot through a gap, and head back north to the point from which we had just carefully driven them.

Next day, I brought six more helpers, which should have been more than enough. The ponymen, now numbering five, also lent a hand. I ought to have known better – it was naive to expect them to make meaningful efforts to round up the famous sire before he'd finished covering their mares.

The first drive ended in shambles when, as we neared Clashard, one of the pony-owning fifth columnists dropped to one knee to tie a bootlace while his accomplice immediately in front rushed forward to 'tell Jim something', as he later (with almost credible shamefacedness) explained. It was enough for Catamaran; seeing the welcome gap, he swerved suddenly towards it, the herd flowing after him, and thundered through. My apoplectic indignation was borne with innocent sheepishness.

Two hours later we were back to within four hundred yards of the bridge into Clashard. This time I watched the ponymen like a hawk, shouting warnings if I thought that there was any sabotage afoot. Some of the serious helpers were equally vigilant, but only those who didn't have friends or relatives amongst the ponymen. The serious ones were also turning grumpy, because, as the day wore on, clouds of midges rose from the heather and their torments were almost insufferable. Besides, they were on a fixed rate for the job, and the sooner it was done, the better. Scarcely daring to breathe, I watched Catamaran place a testing hoof on the rough surface of the road, not forty yards short of the bridge. He stopped and the unquestioning herd stopped with him. So did we. He looked about at the now solid wall of silent, watching men surrounding him on three sides. The road to the right was blocked, the way to the bog across the road was blocked and, behind him, half a dozen men cut off any retreat. Reluctantly, he turned towards the bridge and led the way across into the rhododendron-clad grounds of Clashard. We piled through after him. Accelerating slightly, he moved up past the house towards the stables. It was only at this point that I felt I could relax; even if he went on past the stables, he would soon come to the back fence of Clashard and there we would corner him, halter him, lead him back to the safety of his stable and lock him in. Then I could leave Potter in charge, phone Lord Roscahill and take off with Claire for our longed-for break. She had gone back to Dublin the night before and, as I followed the horses up towards the sheds, my mind was already thinking of pulling up outside her flat, not even caring if Paul Markham's Porsche was outside this time, running up the stairs two at a time, folding her in my arms . . .

'Oh *shit!*' I heard one of the serious helpers moaning, and jerked my attention back in time to see Catamaran, at the head of the herd, streaking through a cut-out section of the back fence of Clashard, heading exuberantly, once more, for the wilderness. I sagged listlessly against a hairy granite boulder and watched in fury as the herd surged across the bogs. Catamaran, keeping his pace to what was an all-out gallop for the ponies and foals, only slackened off when he had led them free of the confining embrace of the lakes.

Wearily I headed for the helicopter with two of the more honest men, leaving the saboteurs to their celebrations. The chopper could only carry four, three plus Kevin, and he'd be busy for the next hour or so ferrying in the posse. If I had my way, I'd have let most of them walk in the hope that the midges would eat them alive.

'What now?' Kevin asked as we took off.

'It'll have to be tomorrow. Did you see where they stopped *this* time? Right up beside the goddam forestry! Anyway,' I added grimly, 'is there any point with that bunch of no-good bastards?

After we landed, I went straight to the garda station and stormed into Potter's office, emerging fifteen minutes later, somewhat mollified. Three gardaí would go out with Kevin, first trip in the morning, to supervise the drive. From a public phone, I called Lord Roscahill's number to report yet another failure and was lucky enough to escape the embarrassment of having to tell him in person; he was out, but his secretary promised to pass on the message.

While Kevin was away collecting the second-last load, Tom Kelly walked into the hotel bar, where I was having a calming beer. He had come as soon as he heard that Catamaran was alive and he was as fussy as an old hen about the plight of his beloved charge. His pale face went almost white when I told him that Catamaran had been covering nearly every pony mare in Connemara over the last two days. Even his brilliant red hair seemed to pale.

'I tell you, he'll come to me!' he insisted.

'Don't be too sure,' I warned. 'He's changed a lot since you saw him, Tom. He's been locked up in a shed in Clashard for a long time, and now he's gone native and become a family man. Any experience he's had with men in the last while won't have done anything to make him trust us. That horse knows we're out to get him and stick him back in a stable.'

'I tell you, he'll come to me!' he repeated dogmatically.

Consequently, when Kevin arrived back at the football field, Tom and I were waiting for him to go out for one last try. Tom had bought a blue plastic basin and a half-stone of oats.

'Blue is his favourite colour,' he explained.

Kevin scratched his ear. 'Bejasus now. Can you beat that?' he said quietly to himself.

Without actually touching the soft ground, Kevin left us at a point a little distance from the horses.

The ponymen were back on duty, each carefully watching to see that his mare was covered. Now there were only three. We had flown over two, who had waved, cheekily and cheerfully, up at us, as they made their way back towards the road. Kevin, sensing the enraged disapproval of the red-headed groom, refrained from comment though I could tell he was dying to make some remark. He was on the side of the ponymen — he had helped as much as he could with the attempted round-ups but he found it hard to see any harm in Catamaran siring a crop of Connemara pony half-bred foals. So, for that matter, did I, and if it hadn't been for the dangers posed by the treacherous terrain, I'd have been laughing openly too.

Under the close scrutiny of the knot of men who sat a little distance off, the groom and I approached the herd. Sending fierce scowls in the direction of the men, Tom began his soft overtures to Catamaran. I stood well back. Talking sooth-ingly and constantly, he edged towards the wary horse, inch by inch. Catamaran must have recognised him, because he didn't take off at once; neither, on the other hand, did he come trotting up all full of welcomes. In fact, it was probably the blue plastic basin more than Kelly. Having eaten nothing but dry sedge and stemmy heather for the past few days, the Pavlovian responses awakened by it were probably the main reason why he didn't bolt. Nearer and nearer Tom inched, never once ceasing his soothing murmur. Neck fully extended, Catamaran sniffed at the basin in the outstretched hand. Gradually, Tom pulled the basin back. Catamaran's neck stretched until it could stretch no further and then, with only the slightest hesitation, he stepped forward a pace, coming almost within reach of Tom's free hand. The hand began to move, very very slowly, towards the horse and I found myself holding my breath. Just as pale, freckled hand and velvet, violet-tinged muzzle were about to meet, a low-sized black and white sheepdog darted past me and ran straight at the mares and foals. The commotion was instant — they scattered out of the path of the streaking animal and took to their heels, followed at once by Catamaran. He caught up with the main bunch in a few strides and, pushing through the field, as he had so often on the track, led them off towards the forestry miles away.

In cold fury, Tom berated the ponymen. I never ever heard such abusive and insulting language used in the second person *plural*. Two of the men were profusely apologetic, the third said: 'Moss! Come to heel, Moss! Yer a bad dog, Moss! Sit!' But his heart didn't seem to be in it.

For his part, Moss sat as ordered and looked totally confused.

24

The next day there was no sign of Catamaran. I would have been worried except the ponies and their owners had also vanished. We made several flights during the day, including sweeps over the forestry, a young plantation which stretched for miles in a straight line along the foot of the mountains, but it wasn't until the last run, just before dusk, that we found them. The herd was back to its original size, and the ponymen had left.

'What do you think, Frank?' Kevin asked, circling the busily grazing horses; they'd had nothing to eat in the forestry; nothing grows under densely stocked conifers.

'Hardly much point now.'

'After all he's been through, another night isn't going to make things any worse,' Tom Kelly replied grudgingly. He still hadn't got over his outrage at the sabotage of his near miss, or the blasphemy of Catamaran being used on pony mares. 'At least those ignorant bastards have gone,' he added savagely. 'I hope all their mares miscarry!'

'Head for home, Kevin. I'll get Potter to round up a *decent* crowd for tomorrow, and we'll make sure we get it right.'

Flying over Clashard, Kevin surreptitiously nudged my knee and, with a tiny nod, directed my attention towards the road. I craned my neck as he obligingly banked the helicopter and, in a moment I saw it – a decrepit blue Land Rover with a horsebox on tow, moving towards Clashard. Another one. Neither of us had the heart to tell Tom.

As soon as we landed, I phoned Lord Roscahill and, once again, just missed him. The man never seemed to be at home. Then I went in search of Potter.

'Well?' he asked.

'No luck. But at least he's out in the open, and the local Breeders' Association seems to have called it a day – the usual lads anyway. There'll probably be a fleet of them queuing up again by morning; the first of them was on his way up the road as we came in.'

'Old blue Land Rover? Grey horsebox?'

'Yes.'

'That's Nick O'Beirne. He went through an hour ago. In fact, he stopped to check with us if Catamaran was still loose.'

'Christ!' I said, amazed. 'Are you *sure* you can't stop these guys from bringing their mares?'

'The bogs are commonage, Frank. All the townlands around graze them during the summer. In fact, it's Catamaran who's trespassing because unless a farmer uses the commonage at least every third year, his right lapses by default, and, needless to say, Bally Ard never used the bogs. It's your stallion who's breaking the law.'

'So go out and arrest him,' I grinned.

Potter grinned back.

'Seriously though, Peter, what if one of these smart guys caught him and held him for ransom? It could happen y'know.'

'But first, they'd have to catch him, wouldn't they? And if you and your helicopter and your army of helpers and Tom Kelly can't . . .' He shrugged. 'But if anyone has a chance of doing it, it'll be Nick O'Beirne. That fellow would have six different thoughts thought while you and I were struggling with one simple one. Six complicated ones too. But if he catches your horse, he'll have him outside the door of the station here an hour later. I'd stake my life on it. Anyway, I've put together a team of "genuines" to help in the morning, and I'll send three of my men out first trip, to prevent any more vanishing into the forestry. That's about all I can do.'

'Thanks, Peter. By the way,' I asked, turning in the doorway, 'any news of Norris and the others?'

'Not really. I heard they phoned Norris's solicitor in Dublin, but he's refused to make any comment other than that he doesn't know where they are. Of course, I'm more or less out of it now. For the big-time stuff, the powers that be have taken over.'

'That's not really fair, is it?'

'Fair or not, I'm just as pleased. I know the three of them well, especially Vincent Field. I used to play a fourball with him every Sunday morning.'

'I know. You told me. You both play off five.'

I'd moved into the local hotel, and Kevin, Tom and I arranged to meet in the dining room at eight. Immediately after dinner they both left. Kevin had a date, though it was beyond me how he had even managed to *meet* someone, let alone arrange a date, as he had been in the air or on the bogs every minute between sunrise and sunset every day. But he had, and he borrowed the Land Rover from me and went off, whistling and reeking of aftershave. Tom went out to Bally Ard. He had arranged a lift and decided to stay the night in his old quarters. I promised I'd collect him at five, while Kevin was ferrying the first load out.

'Be up!' I warned as he left.

'I'm always up by 4.30,' he replied, and I got the impression that he was implying that anyone who wasn't was a lazy slacker.

That left me on my own. I bought an evening paper in the foyer and went through to the bar to have a pint and a go at the crossword, but I didn't get very far – I kept thinking of Catamaran on the bogs, and wondering how much longer he could escape serious injury. After a few minutes, I drained the pint, abandoned the crossword, and went to bed. Claire phoned just before I dropped off, and, when she asked what was wrong, I said there was nothing wrong. Then she said there was, she could tell, so I said I was tired and worried about getting Catamaran off the bog. Then she said she loved me and I said I loved her too and she asked me how much and I said this much. Then we hung up and I slept fitfully until the alarm-clock attacked my ears at 4.02 a.m.

Bleary-eyed, I drove out to Bally Ard, hoping to catch Kelly still in bed, but he was up, and looked as though he had been for hours. 'You get used to it when you've horses to look after. I like to get up about sunrise,' he said sanctimoniously. 'Anyway, you know the old saying: "The early bird catches the worm".'

'That's all very well if you happen to be partial to worms,' I said drily, turning into the first streets of the still slumbering Knockmore. 'Look. The empty milk-bottles are still out! If it's before the milkman, it's too early.'

We sat in the concrete shelter in the schoolyard. The morning was blustery and still held the chill of night. The sky behind the school was alive with light changes, but the sun had not yet climbed above the building, and we sat in cold shadow. I huddled down into my anorak and, after listening a while for the helicopter, began to drift off into an uncomfortable doze.

'We better get him today,' Tom said, 'before the rain comes. The bogs will get soft inside a day.'

I stirred and eyed the sky. Apart from a few small wisps of cloud, it was clear. 'You think it's going to rain? The sky seems clear enough.'

'It's not the sky, it's the dust. When you see it behaving like that – running around in little circles all over the place – it means it's going to rain. When the dust acts excited, the rain is on the way.' He pronounced this with a kind of superior finality.

I eyed a little eddy of dust speculatively; I'd never heard that dust behaviour could be used to forecast rain – in fact I'd never heard that dust could 'behave'. Half-dozing again, I wondered if Kelly was an animist or animalist or whatever you call those people who believe there are spirits in all objects, rocks, water, earth, fire – and dust too, presumably – and if there was a god of the dust and, if so, if his name mightn't be Eddy . . . A few moments later, Kelly nudged me in the ribs. The helicopter had already landed, and I hadn't even heard it.

'Do you guys get up for a few hours every day, whatever the weather?' Kevin laughed in greeting as he sent the machine straight up.

'You were a long time on the first run,' I yawned as we banked into the huge sun, towards Clashard.

'I did a quick look round after I dropped off the fuzz. Catamaran wasn't with the horses.'

'What!' Tom and I exclaimed, almost in unison. Icy-footed spiders scuttled across my back.

'He wasn't there. Just the ponies on their own.'

'And the ponymen?' I asked anxiously.

'None, though that Land Rover we saw going up the road last night is still there, half hidden in the shrubs near the gate. But there's no sign of the owner. According to one of the cops he's a guy named Nick O'Beirne. His mare is there all right – the same cop says he knows the mare because she beats *his* mare at all the shows – but there's no sign of your man at all.'

'Are there any other mares beside Nick O'Beirne's? Any new ones?'

'I don't think so.' He thought for a moment. 'Maybe another guy came with a mare and took Catamaran off into the forestry, along with his mare, and they'll be back out soon?'

I knew that that wouldn't be so and so did Tom.

'No,' he said. 'The other horses would have followed because Catamaran is their leader now. They'd go where he went. If they could,' he added darkly.

'And if that's the way it was,' I reasoned, 'then O'Beirne has gone with this other man and he'd surely have taken his own mare along too, wouldn't he?'

'I suppose so,' Kevin admitted. 'Specially as he was first in the queue and all.'

The three gardaí were standing together a little way away from the ponies, long shadows attached to their feet. As we passed over the herd, I counted the ponies; there was only one extra, a grey mare – well muscled and beautifully groomed, she stood out amongst the shaggy mountainy animals almost as starkly as Catamaran had. She seemed a bit lost in the wilderness.

We touched down just long enough to let Tom off, in case Catamaran should suddenly show up, and immediately took off to search the bogs.

'A brown horse on a brown bog,' I said. 'That mightn't be easy.'

'I'll spot him,' Kevin replied confidently. 'It takes a while to get used to seeing things from this height, but I won't miss him.'

'I'm glad to hear it. I think we should just fly around the ponies in a widening circle. If he was lying injured somewhere, the herd probably won't have moved far away. In fact, I'd have expected them to stay with him, even if, God forbid, he was dead. For a day or two anyway.'

'You think he might be dead?'

'No. As I said, the herd would stay with him. And that's what worries me. I think he's gone.'

'*Gone!* Gone where?' He glanced quickly at me.

I shrugged and continued to peer out my side.

'I was just wondering,' Kevin said after we had been circling for a few minutes and were now more than a half-mile from the herd. 'Maybe he went off on his own for a rest. After all the screwing he's been doing over the last few days, and all that bad grub he's been eating, maybe he's just tired out and taken a day off?'

'If he was tired, and he probably is, he'd just give up screwing until he felt up to it again. There's nobody forcing him.'

We flew on in silence, losing hope as the circle widened. We were now well out of sight of the horses.

'There! Below' Kevin said suddenly, as we passed over a tiny, gorse-covered hillock.

'Catamaran?' I asked urgently, craning my neck to see out his side. 'Where?'

'There. A pair of shoes.'

'Horseshoes?'

'No. Men's shoes. You can just see them sticking out from under the furze. D'you see them?' He pivoted the helicopter around on its nose so that my side faced the hillock, and held it, hovering. At last I saw them – two black boots, heels together pointing up; either they'd been propped up like that or somebody was still wearing them.

'I see them. Can you land?'

'Not right here because of the slope, but over there looks OK. Do you reckon it's Nick O'Beirne?'

'Could be. Probably is.'

'He wasn't moving, Frank. And he wasn't trying to hide from us either or he'd have pulled his feet in after him. It looks to me like somebody shoved him in there.' He landed, a bit bumpily.

Grabbing my emergency bag, I waited for Kevin to do whatever he had to do so that his machine wouldn't take off on its own, then we ran across the soft bog and climbed the hill.

'Nick! Nick!' I called his name and stirred his feet with my shoe; there was no response but at least the feet hadn't gone stiff. Kevin and I looked unsurely at one another, then, taking an ankle each, we gently pulled the dead weight out from under the low bush, stepping back and hauling carefully until the long, wiry body was lying in the open. The pulse was weak and thready and the respiratory rate slow. He had lost a lot of blood from a wound on his temple – it had blackened and congealed all down the side of his face and neck, sticking his hair down. By contrast, the other side of his face was chalk white, cold and clammy. I took my stethoscope from the bag, opened his shirt and listened; the heartbeat was not strong but it was steady. As the human animal was pretty much a stranger to me in terms of physiology, I wasn't quite sure about his heart sounds, but they sounded a bit ropy to me.

'He needs a doctor,' I said, jamming the stethoscope into my pocket. 'Let's get him to the chopper.'

It was hard going – the ground was rough and choked with prickly gorse bushes, often without enough space between them to allow us to walk two abreast with the unconscious figure between us, and it took us a good ten minutes to cover the short distance to the helicopter and manoeuvre the long loose limbs and torso into the back.

'It'll have to be Galway,' I said. 'Knockmore's answer to Albert Schweitzer is on the run. How long will it take?'

'About twenty minutes. I'll radio ahead. Hang on.'

The chopper roared into the sky, engine protesting. At the sound, Nick O'Beirne's eyes fluttered open momentarily, then closed again. Tom Kelly and the three gardaí were halfway along to where we had landed. As we shot over them, all the time gaining height, they stood still, looking up and I could plainly see their panting chests and the mystified expressions on their faces. Having seen us land, they had obviously thought we had located the horse. Kevin waved down to them, then reached into a side pocket and pulled out a walkie-talkie.

'Come in, come in,' he said in a professional monotone.

'Where are you going?' the half-angry question came up to us.

'We've found Nick O'Beirne. He's badly injured and we're taking him to hospital in Galway. No sign of the horse. You guys stay on here and I'll be back as soon as I can. Good luck.' Without waiting for further questions, he switched off. He turned at once to the regular radio, switched to the emergency frequency and advised them of the problem. They asked him his present position and what time he expected to be at the hospital, and signed off.

'Can't keep those boys talking too long,' he remarked as we entered a long valley between two mountain ranges. 'Just as well we got to them when we did. Reception would be lousy in here. How's the patient?'

'The same. Holding his own. I think.'

There was an ambulance waiting beside the landing pad and, within seconds, Nick O'Beirne was being whisked the few hundred yards to the door marked CASUALTY in large red letters.

'What do you want to do now?' Kevin asked as we stood by

the helicopter looking across at the ambulance being unloaded.

'Have a cup of coffee?'

'I was hoping you'd say something like that.' He grinned quickly as he locked the helicopter.

'You can't possibly think somebody might *steal* it?'

'Believe it or not, it has happened, but I'd be more anxious about kids messing about and screwing something up.' He stretched luxuriously in the bright morning air.

In the hospital, I bought two cups of lousy coffee from a machine, and two soggy cheese sandwiches wrapped in clammy clingfilm, from a lady inside a tiny cubbyhole booth. Twenty minutes later, Kevin went off to return to the search. Now it had become Potter's business again – Catamaran had probably been stolen and a citizen had been almost murdered by whoever had stolen him. I decided to stay at the hospital in case Nick O'Beirne came to.

On my own, with time to think, I got depressed. I had spent days trying to capture the horse and failed. I was doing the job – correction, I was *supposed* to be doing the job – with the full co-operation of the owners and the gardaí and I had failed. Spectacularly. Then some fly-by-night rustler comes along in the dead of night and walks off with the horse.

No wonder I felt lousy.

25

I followed the trolley with the still inert form on it, along a corridor where everyone's shoes squeaked, and into the service lift which was supposed to be for hospital personnel only. The orderlies looked at me as I squeezed in, but made no objections.

'How is he?' I asked, after the door had sighed closed. The face had been cleaned and the head bandaged, and he looked as if, though still in its general vicinity, he had moved a step or two away from death's door.

'Are you a relative?'

'Not really. Just a very close friend,' I lied.

'What happened anyway?'

'I'm not quite sure. Do you think he'll come round soon?'

'Where did it happen?'

'Out on the bogs in Connemara. What did the doctor say?'

'He certainly walked into no door out on the bogs,' he smirked.

'That's for sure,' replied the other, the first time he had said anything. In that fashion, my questions being parried, we arrived at the fourth floor, and squelched along the polished corridor, which, not being subjected to the wear of constant traffic, as in Casualty, actually sucked at my rubber-soled runners like the bogs. At the door leading to the Intensive Care Unit, I was firmly turned back; not even the orderlies could enter – they rang, waited, stated their business over an intercom, and handed over the trolley to two others who made a brief appearance in the doorway. I retreated to a window alcove across the corridor, and settled down to await news of the patient. Luckily I managed to buy a paper from a man with a trolley who came by a few minutes after Nick had vanished through the door.

I must have been a couple of hours there. At one stage, a nurse came looking for personal details of the patient, and was quite annoyed when I couldn't help. She had obviously done a course in How To Give No Information too, and, when she left, I was none the wiser about what was happening in the inner sanctum of ICU. I'd almost finished the crossword when I became aware of positive, proprietorial footsteps approaching along the corridor; it was a man of patrician bearing, in a brown suit, walking briskly, followed by several others in white coats. Without a pause, they passed into the ICU. When they came out I was waiting for them, almost blocking the door.

'Excuse me. Have you just been to see the patient with the head wound who was brought in by helicopter this morning?'

'May I enquire why you ask?' The consultant gave me a vaguely hostile look.

'I found him and brought him in. It's very important that I talk to him as soon as possible. It's garda business and it's confidential.' I wasn't going to mention Catamaran because of Field's involvement – in his nearest hospital, colleagues might also be friends. So I said it was confidential to avoid questions.

'Are you *with* the gardaí?'

'I'm acting undercover. Believe me, if we had any other way of finding out who attacked this man, I wouldn't have sat here for the last few hours.'

'Do you have any identification?'

'No. As I said, I'm undercover.'

'It's all pretty irregular,' he said. One of the young doctors behind him nodded disapprovingly in agreement.

'Look,' I said, sensing a chance. 'I don't want to do anything to harm him . . .'

'Nobody is suggesting that!' he snapped. He thought a bit

249

more. 'I don't know . . .' he mused to himself dubiously, weighing it up; the sycophant in the white coat shook his head in sympathy with the great man's dilemma.

'Well,' I said, 'at least it's good to know he's improving.'

'And just how would you know that?' the consultant asked sharply. Behind him, the toady looked affronted and raised a nasty eyebrow at me.

'If he wasn't on the mend, you'd have just sent me packing. No?'

That seemed to sway him. 'Give him ten more minutes to get himself orientated and then you can talk briefly to him. Will your questions take long?'

'A few minutes, five at most.'

'Very well then. As long as you don't overtax him. Sister will be on hand to keep an eye on you. I'll have her informed that you're to be admitted for a short visit.' He turned to instruct one of his retinue, but the door was already swinging closed behind the toady.

'Thank you,' I said humbly; consultant neurosurgeons like the favours they dispense to be properly appreciated.

In an anteroom, I donned a cap and mask, and had a disposable paper gown wrapped around me. I pulled on a pair of plastic shoe and leg covers and went on into the quiet of ICU. The silence was cathedral-like, the only sounds being the bleeps and pips of electronic monitoring instruments, televising the vital ebbs and flows of the inmates, and the odd moan or cough from one of the cubicles. Nick O'Beirne was in cubicle seven. He looked up as the door opened, his eyes every bit as aware and alert as my own.

'Hello there,' I muffled through the mask. 'How are you feeling?'

'Fine now, thanks. Bit of a headache, but otherwise OK.'

'I'm Frank Samson.'

'I believe I owe you my life.'

'That's putting it a bit strongly. We were searching the bogs for Catamaran and just happened to spot you. If you want to thank anyone, thank the pilot – I could have flown over a thousand times and never noticed you.'

'Just my luck. I've always wanted a go in a helicopter and when I get it, I have to be *asleep* for the whole trip. But thanks anyway.'

'Would you mind if I asked you a few questions?'

He gave a sharp laugh. 'As long as they're not damnfool questions about my next of kin and religion and all that, fire away. I've just spent ten minutes answering a load of rubbishy questions for that little nurse out there.'

Suddenly, I felt less guilty. If his medical attendants could browbeat him in the interests of bureaucracy, then surely, in the far more noble interests of justice . . . I decided to go for broke. 'What happened, do you remember?'

'Oh, I remember all right. I presume you won't approve, but I took my mare up to the bog yesterday. I'd have gone up earlier but she wasn't rightly on – I was hoping every day that you lads wouldn't capture him before she was covered.'

'And was she?'

'I think so, but not until after dark. Anyway, I decided to wait the night to make sure she got covered this morning. I thought I might catch the stallion too.'

'And just how, might I ask, were you planning to do that?' I asked, a trifle patronisingly.

'Hold the mare while he served her, then throw a rope on him while he was still on her.'

Chastened, I wondered why I hadn't thought of that. 'After he'd finished, no doubt,' I grinned, a bit useless with the mask.

However, he caught it from my eyes. 'Of course!' he grinned back. 'So, I left the mare with the others, had the bit of grub I brought with me, and went to sleep in the back of the jalopy. She was backed well into the bushes, just in case anybody was trying to drive into Clashard at night – I didn't want to block the road. Anyway, at about three or a little after, I woke up because I could hear an engine coming up the road. Then I saw lights go by and this Toyota Hi-Ace pulled up at the gate, just a little beyond where I was. I opened the window and I could hear all these voices talking in a foreign language.'

'Could you tell what language?'

'No. I don't think I ever heard it before. It sounded a bit rough to me. Anyway, there was a lot of door-closing and yap, like someone giving orders, and then they set off out on to the bogs. I could see torches and a few very powerful lights, probably car headlights being worked off a hand-held battery, the same as they use for lamping foxes or rabbits. Well I was thinking that a bunch of foreigners on the bogs in the middle of the night were probably up to no good, so I decided to see what they were doing.

'It was nearly black dark – there's only a tiny moon these nights – but I couldn't use the torch because they'd see it. I could just about make out the number plate on the van because, lucky enough, the moon, small and all as it was, was shining on the back of the van. The number should be in my jacket pocket. Give the nurse a shout there and she might know where my clothes are. Did I have my jacket on when you brought me in?'

'Yes,' I rose to push the bell-button beside his bed.

'Then, unless they searched me, it should be there still. I couldn't see anything else in the van except a pack of cigarettes on the dashboard. It was a gold-coloured box with a strange name on it . . .'

'How come you were able to see the cigarette box and the writing if the moon was shining on the back of the van? Did the roof not shade the dashboard completely?'

'I angled the wing-mirror to reflect the moonlight along the dashboard.'

'Smart move.' I remembered Potter's words. It seemed he hadn't been exaggerating. Nick O'Beirne had come up with a likely plan to catch Catamaran single-handedly; he had improvised scant resources in an effort to identify the mysterious visitors; he had also, I thought wryly, taken the number of the van.

'Anyhow, all I could make out were these cigarettes. Sorry,

nurse,' he broke off as the door opened, 'but could you possibly find my jacket for me; I need something out of it.'

'You're not allowed to smoke in here!' she said sternly.

'Well now, I *know* that! It's only a bit of paper I need.' When she'd gone off, he continued: 'Anyway, where was I?'

'Cigarettes.'

'Oh yes. Well, there was no more to be learned from the van so I followed them out on to the bog, travelling slowly in the dark. Those bogs can be dangerous in the day, never mind the night, but they aren't too bad right now because of the long dry spell. I suppose it must have taken me half an hour to get as near to them as I was intending to go, and by this time they were all together and there was fierce commotion. At first there were lights all over the place like will o' the wisps, but by the time I got there they'd come more or less together and the horses were in the middle. I lay down behind a rock to see what was going on, though I had a fair idea. They tightened in the circle of light until the horses were pushed together in a close knot in the middle. I could see your stallion in the bunch looking all worried and confused, but he was blinded by the lights and kept turning around in circles. Suddenly, one of them threw a rope over his head, then another, and another, and I'm not sure if there wasn't a fourth. He went mad, lepping and bucking and squealing like a pig and started pulling like hell. Unfortunately, he pulled them down towards me and I was in two minds what to do. If I moved, I most likely wouldn't find more cover in the dark, and, if I stayed, they might be on top of me in a moment and it would be too late to move. When they were about a hundred yards off to the west, they managed to calm down Catamaran and I thought I was safe, but, however it happened, didn't one of the buggers just happen to shine a light straight at me! It must have been pointing towards me when he switched it on, because before that, any time a beam seemed to be swinging in my direction, I was damn quick to get my head out of sight. They saw me and there was an immediate hullabaloo. I ran, but I fell three times in as many yards. Next minute there was a load of them on top of me and that's as much as I can remember.'

'That's a lot. That number plate should do it. You've been a great help and I hope your mare has a fine foal.'

'Oh, she will. If she holds, she will. The breeding is in her – from her side anyway.' We both laughed. 'You've been through the wars yourself, I hear . . .'

'You can say that again. It hasn't been the easiest couple of weeks for the good guys, has it?' By the time the nurse came back with his jacket, I had told him the whole story.

I phoned Potter. He was surprised when I told him where I was and why, and more than a little annoyed that he hadn't been informed. 'Kevin talked to your men on the radio,' I protested.

'Which men? The three out on the bog?'

'Yes.'

'And how were they supposed to contact me? By smoke signals?'

I apologised, convinced him that it been a genuine mistake, and reassured him that I wasn't trying to go it alone.

'So there were no gardaí with you when you questioned Nick?'

'I didn't question him. I *talked* to him. Look, I've said I'm sorry, and I meant it. Now, do you want to know what Nick told me or not?'

'OK, Frank,' he said after a pause and a sigh, 'go on.'

I told him as much as I had got from Nick O'Beirne. He asked me to stay put for a while, in case there was anything else he needed; I said where would I go anyhow, gave him the number, and hung up.

I waited by the phone for a long time. It was a pay phone in the corridor and nightied or pyjamaed patients kept shuffling up to it, putting their few bob in the slot and talking for ages to their loved ones as if it might be the last time ever, which, on reflection, was not beyond the bounds of possibility. At last, worrying that Potter might be trying to get through and getting nothing but the engaged signal, I took my place in the queue and, when my turn came, faked a long conversation about Uncle Jimmy's rupture, the complications arising therefrom, and his fifty-fifty chance of pulling through – all of which had the people behind me enthralled; it probably did them no end of good therapeutically, as none of them could have had *half* the troubles Uncle Jimmy had. In the meantime, of course, I kept my finger on the little buttons and, when the phone suddenly rang while I was explaining about his *third* haemorrhage, several of them looked puzzled, but said nothing. I suppose they didn't want to cause any more grief to a man whose Uncle Jimmy was already going through hell on earth. I covered the mouthpiece. 'Excuse me please. Won't be long, but this part is private.' With sheepish looks, they dispersed and became absorbed in looking at holy pictures.

'Frank? Frank? Are you there?'

'Here. What news?'

'Oh, I thought we'd been cut off. First the reg. It belongs to a self-drive firm operating from Shannon. They rented it yesterday to a group from the Hamra Islands which landed an hour or two before, on a private Lear jet. The pilot is Danish. He's been back and forth to the plane a few times so he doesn't seem to be involved. I asked Shannon to have him call me when he shows up next. They've no address for him. The plane is registered to a Cayman Islands company, but who the ultimate owner of *that* company is will take a while to trace. Unless, of course, the pilot knows. That's the main thing I want to ask him. I also want to ask him if he knows anything about the reason for the trip. The other thing is that Norris and his mates have turned themselves in in Dublin. Without prejudice, if you please.'

'Without prejudice, my ass! Anything from them?'

'No. And I wouldn't bank on it, either. They're surrounded by an army of hot-shot lawyers and God knows how long it'll be before we get to even *talk* to them.'

'Catamaran might be gone by then. To the Hamras, I presume.'

'We'll keep after him independently.'

'Is this jet big enough to take a horse?'

'I don't think so, but just in case, I've put an impediment of departure on it, so, even if they do get Catamaran aboard, they won't get clearance for take-off. Shannon told me that the pilot ordered so much fuel he must be nearly empty. It hasn't been fuelled yet and, just to be *doubly* safe, I've told them not to without my personal permission. Either way, they're grounded.'

'Good. Is there anything else you want me to ask Nick?'

'I don't think so. How is he, by the way?'

'He'll live. He seems pretty OK to me.'

'That's good. How're you going to get back to Knock-more?'

'Bus it, I suppose. There's one at 1.30. See you then.'

'Right so.'

When I hung up, there was a race for the phone, those without crutches having a distinct advantage.

I went down to the second floor and found a canteen where I bought a cup of tepid, weak tea – it wasn't quite as bad as the coffee. As I sat on a bench and sipped it, I noticed a sign over a door a little way along the corridor. It said LIBRARY and, on impulse, I went along. The cranky little librarian wouldn't let me in because of my polystyrene teacup, so I drained it and dropped it in a waste bin. Warning me that I wouldn't be allowed to borrow, he grudgingly admitted to having an encyclopaedia and pointed it out to me. Ten minutes later, I knew that the Hamras numbered seventeen, all but two inhabited, spread out over a few hundred square miles of the Indian Ocean. They had been ruled, at one stage or another, by all the European empire nations and by the Arabs – mainly to dislodge pirates who used to infest the area. The islands were dirt poor until two years after independence. In 1949, a small earthquake dislodged a slice off a mountain and uncovered the richest seam of diamonds in the world. Then offshore oil deposits, originally considered small and unworkable, turned out to be vast and easily recoverable with modern technology. There were half a million Hamranis but two million foreigners working in the oil fields. Water was their main problem; they kept digging artesian wells but all they ever seemed to come up with was oil, and there was more grass on the front lawn of Fernditch than in the whole blessed country. The ruler was a king and the government consisted of his sons – all thirteen of them – each of whom was minister for something or other. Apart from the ruling family there were lots of very wealthy men; lesser nobles and the like.

I tried to get my deductive faculties going again; they had lain dormant for the last few days while I dealt with the totally non-abstract business of trying to round up Catamaran. Claire and I had already reached the conclusion that Catamaran was to be spirited abroad for breeding, and there didn't seem to be any reason to change that; it was as good a place as any to start from – a wealthy Hamrani who was also involved in thoroughbreds in a major way. But, as most of the citizens of those islands seemed to fall into that category, I had to narrow the field down somehow, and the right man to ask about that was Declan Forbes. Checking the change in my pocket, I made for the phone again.

I came straight to the point. 'Declan? Frank here. Can you tell me if there are many Hamranis involved in the bloodstock industry, I mean in a big way?'

'A few. Why?'

'Tell you later. Who are they, do you know?'

'Well, as I said, there are a few, but only one who's involved in a *really* big way.'

'Who's that?'

'Prince Alaramos. Known to his friends as Al. He's Minister for Sport and Recreation. He's also a member of the Catamaran syndicate.'

'I don't remember that name on the list,' I said, thinking back to the menu.

'The share is probably in the name of Spanish Park Stud, but it's the same thing. He owns *it* – along with a dozen or so others here and there around the world. It's strange you should ask about him today . . . Because he's flying in this afternoon to go racing at the Curragh. I have to go down and cater for his every need. I always get that job when there's an important owner in town, and it's screwed up my schedule.'

'Why? Is his visit unexpected.'

'Most. All the big names arrive for the classics, but today is just a Mickey Mouse meet – only a couple of thou for the feature race.'

'I see.' At this point I felt I owed Declan an explanation, especially as it looked as if I might now need his help. There were people nearby so I became circumspect. 'Dec. You know that thing I was chasing on the bogs?'

There was a silence. 'Are we talking about Catamaran?'

'Yes. He vanished during the night. Someone caught him. People from the country under discussion, and it looks a good bet that your friend could have him now.'

There was a longer silence. Then he breathed: 'My God . . .'

'What does your duty to Al involve?'

'Sorry, Frank. I'm finding this a bit overwhelming. My duties? I join his party at the course, stay with him till the end, and then we usually have dinner afterwards. Are you *sure*?'

'No. But maybe you could pay extra attention to duty today and stick to him like a poultice – you know, go to the loo with him and all that kind of stuff.'

'Well . . . within reason.'

'If anything's going to happen today, it's going to happen at the Curragh. I imagine HRH will want to be directing the traffic personally – he'd hardly have come over otherwise. Wouldn't you think that Spanish Park would be a quieter place?'

'Jimmy Farnley runs Spanish Park and he's as straight as a die.'

'Maybe that's it.'

'What are you going to do, Hair?'

'I haven't really thought that far ahead. Probably go to the races – take the afternoon off. So I may see you there.'

'OK.' There was a pause. 'D'you know, I've just thought of something. A while back the word was that the prince was trying to buy out four of the other shareholders . . .'

'Which four?'

'Any four. It didn't matter. What he wanted was a controlling interest in Catamaran, which would have given him the voting power to decide where he'd stand at stud. I presume he would have whisked him off to his stud in the Hamras. He's got this enormous, incredible, controlled-environment stud there – I've been in it. Anyway, true or false, the story went that he offered the first four who'd sell to him a fantastic price, the idea being to cause panic, because, if he succeeded, the value of the remaining shares would fall drastically.'

'Why?'

'Because the horse's value would fall.'

'Why again? I don't understand this business.'

'First, because sending a mare to the Hamras would mean a long and expensive journey; second, keeping her there would be very costly because of all that controlled-environment stuff; and third, his brother, Prince Something-or-other-else is Minister for Agriculture and has the power to arbitrarily refuse animals entry into the country.'

'No shit, huh? But why should he want him there so badly? This bad, like?'

'To breed to his own mares. He's got a lot of very useful mares right now, as good a bunch as there is in one place anywhere in the world.'

'Then why not move the mares to Ireland and save all the hassle?'

'It's not that easy. Each owner is allowed to send only two mares to Catamaran and even they have to be vetted by the other members, to see that they're of sufficiently good breeding to warrant the nomination. The remaining nominations go to other breeders. If Alaramos had a controlling interest, he could change all that. I heard he'd wanted a minimum of five mares per member at the outset, and a clause stating that a member who couldn't take up all his nominations would have to give first refusal on the remainder to the other members at a set price, but, as he was the only one with five mares actually good enough for Catamaran, the others voted him down. My guess is that he could have up to thirty mares good enough, maybe more. In the past four years, he's bought heavily and gone into breeding in a huge way, all computerised, top geneticists, et cetera.'

'Maybe he's coming over to buy now?'

'You're not the only one to think that. Word is already out that he's on his way, and half the owners will be going around in a greedy frenzy. Al is rich and spoiled and people know he'll get what he wants, no matter what. But he rarely, if ever, does his own buying; he's a good judge of a horse but he always gets agents to act for him. Filthy rich he may be. Stupid he is not.'

'Did you happen to hear how many members were willing to sell to him?'

'Some said two, others three. The syndicate was scared but, apart from those two, or three, closed ranks. When he couldn't get the majority he needed, the prince withdrew his offer.'

'Did you hear who they were?'

'I heard first that it was Norris and Cuthbertson, the brewery man, but another contact said it was Norris, Samuelson and Georgie Karyanikis. So take your pick.'

'At least both had Norris.'

'Well, he's not in the same league as the others at all. He had to sell all his mares and mortgage Bally Ard to the hilt – and I still don't know how that got him enough to buy in. I mean you're talking *millions*.'

'Perhaps that's where Field and Vernon come in – as extra backers.'

'I never heard of either of them before but you may be right. They'd have to keep it quiet because the syndicate frowned on mini-syndicates as members. Too complicated and could lead to trouble at voting time.'

'OK, Declan. Thanks. I'd say we're on the right track. I'll see you later.'

I tried to work out the sequence of events that had led up to the whole elaborate charade. Norris was probably feeling the financial strain of his investment and, when the prince's offer to buy at an inflated price came up, he jumped at it. When it fell through, he must have been disappointed, to put it mildly. He could, of course, have offered to sell his share at face value but that wasn't the same as getting the much bigger price which he had been offered; he might even have stood to lose money, what with interest rates etcetera. Having almost tasted the big money must have whetted his appetite to get out from under his debts. At that stage, he would have begun to dream of some way to get the deal back on course and what he had come up with had been almost foolproof. It would also have been more lucrative. If Alaramos had been willing to buy four shares at an inflated price, all Norris had to do was offer him *all* of Catamaran at a *fraction* of that – say for the price of two shares or three. As Alaramos wasn't troubled by the problems of how to get the horse on to the register in his own country, and was being offered total ownership for less than he had been willing to pay originally for a mere majority share, the offer would be extremely attractive to him. There would even be an added 'cushion' for both – Norris could add his share of the insurance pay-out to his price, while Alaramos could deduct it. Only the insurance company lost and they would have laid off so much to various underwriters anyway, that, in the long run, it would be hard to find anyone who would actually go hungry because of the scam. It was so neat, it ought to have come off.

I phoned Potter and brought him up to date.

'I'd prefer you were there yourself, Peter.'

'I can't go freelancing around the country, Frank. I look after my own neck of the woods and the Kildare bunch watch theirs. I'll get on to them and bring them up to date.'

'I just hope they don't storm the place. If HRH *is* the one, but the horse isn't at the Curragh, then we can kiss him goodbye – he'll be dogmeat within hours.'

'Don't worry, there'll be no storming. They'll probably just keep him under observation; I have a suspicion anyway he has diplomatic immunity – some sort of roving ambassador. I'll check it out. I think I'll get the Tipperary lads to keep a discreet eye on Spanish Park too.'

'As long as it's discreet.' A thought struck me. 'I hope he hasn't heard that his jet has been grounded by you lot. That'd screw things up nicely.'

'Not much we can do about that now. If he has, he has.'

'I suppose you couldn't lift the refuelling ban, tell the people to keep their mouths shut, and sabotage the jet? Steal the steering wheel or something?'

'No Frank, I couldn't.'

'Just a thought. Ah well . . . I've been hired to do a job, so I'm off to the races. Can you get Kevin on the radio and call him in?'

Potter was a bit dubious at first – he knew I wasn't going just to watch the races. So I promised him I'd clock in with the Kildare gardaí as soon as I arrived, assured him I wouldn't do anything 'daft', and swore blind not to do anything more than observe. 'If they do find the horse, I'll have to be there to check him out,' I clinched it. 'That's part of my deal with Lord Roscahill.'

Shortly after 1.30 I heard the rotors of the approaching helicopter and went to the asphalt square on which we had landed. It had a large white 'H' in a white circle in the centre and I meant to ask Kevin whether it was H for Hospital or H for Helicopter, but I forgot.

26

Just before three o'clock we touched down in the helipark. There were four helicopters there already, all different makes, and room for many more. As we walked towards the entrance gates, the public address system began to call out information on the next race and we shuffled along in the queue which I hadn't expected to be so big. Declan had dismissed the meeting as 'Mickey Mouse' and I wondered, not being a racing man myself, what the attendance at a big meet would be like. I paid my money and passed through the turnstile.

Inside, Kevin and I held a rapid war council. Straightaway I decided to break my promise to Potter and leave checking in with the gardaí until after the race. There wasn't a lot they could do – Kevin had brought word that the prince did, in fact, enjoy full diplomatic immunity. And I didn't want to waste time. The best chance to find Declan would be during a race; between races, he might be off anywhere. I went to find a position from which to view the stands, while Kevin wandered off into the crowd.

Out on the track, the first horses were already being loaded into the starting gates. I took up position along the rail, some way short of the finishing post, and let myself be pressed against the white barrier by the crowd.

'They're off!' blared the Tannoy, 'and first to show is . . .' The field, bunched close, thundered towards us, drawing only muted shouts from the crowd. As they vanished round a corner, those of us who had been leaning over the rail watching the order of their disappearance, straightened up and began to listen intently to the loudspeaker's commentary and, when it announced that they were coming back into view, we all leaned over again. This time, the excitement was palpable and a swelling roar ran along the rails, like a bow-wave, surging ahead of the horses. The leaders passed us, foam-flecked mouths emitting crunching breaths, hooves rippling on the firm turf, sweat-soaked shoulders responding to the last urgings of the whip. The roar of the crowd urged them to greater effort and heads turned as one to follow the last flying gallop of the contest. But my head turned farther than any other as, raising Kevin's binoculars, I began a steady search of the cheering crowd in the stands.

Assuming that the best seats would be directly in front of the winning post, and that that was where the prince would be, I tried there first and soon located Declan, his boyish face flushed with the excitement of the finish. The seats to his right were empty. On his left, an elderly lady in a fur coat and white gloves waved her race card vigorously, eyes bright blue beneath bright blue hair. Next to her an elderly man whose face I knew but couldn't put a name to, sat back stiffly chewing a gnarled knuckle, gaze riveted on the finishers. Beside him was a beautiful woman in her thirties, her dark, Mediterranean features animated with the thrill of the race, brown hands clasped high in front of her bosom and, beside her, a darkskinned man of indeterminate age. He was paying no attention whatever to the race; he was staring straight at me, his gaze coming down through the prisms of his field glasses into mine. Totally flustered, I jerked the binoculars down, and tried to pretend to be absorbed in the order in which the last couple of stragglers wobbled past the post.

The crowd broke away from the rails and headed off towards the bars or bookies, depending on whether they'd lost or won. I hung around for a moment, ostensibly lost in a study of my race card, trying to act nonchalant, fearing that, if I left too soon, the prince might think I was bolting. That was an error – it would have been far more natural for me to leave with the crowd. In the next minute, the error was compounded when Kevin joined me in my visible-for-miles isolation at the rail. Dejectedly, I told him I had now probably blown his cover and almost certainly had blown mine, and we leaned on the rail and stared out at the empty track. 'He must have suspected something, but I don't know what or how. Everyone was glued to the winning post and I was so *sure* it was safe to have a look! Fuck it anyway!' I said in disgust.

'Which one is he?'

'Don't look now, but there's a group of five sitting about half-way up the stand, straight in front of the winning post. One of them is an elderly lady with blue hair. The one nearest us is the prince, Declan Forbes is the one at the other end – beside the blue rinse.'

'Probably the best thing now is for us to find somewhere we can see him but he can't see us, and then just try to tail him when he leaves.' I couldn't think of anything better, so after another few minutes, during which I could almost feel the prince's eyes boring into my back, we decided to leave separately and look for different exits from the stand.

'Right,' said Kevin. 'Time to tail His Royal Highness. I've never had a bit of royal tail before, so it'll be a first.'

I envied him his irrepressibility. 'Good luck,' I forced a grin.

'Yeah,' he grinned back, 'you too,' and he pushed himself away from the rail. 'Wow!' he said as soon as he turned, 'would you look at that for a piece of ass!' He knocked about four syllables out of 'ass'.

With a sinking heart, I saw Claire advancing across the ticket-strewn ground towards us. It was too late to signal her to go back and I could only submit to her kiss, and hope that the prince had turned his attention away – the fewer people he could associate with me, the better. Everything was going wrong.

'Claire,' I said, 'this gentleman here is Kevin, the pilot. Kevin, this piece of ass here is Claire, the lady love. His words, not mine,' I explained in answer to Claire's raised eyebrows.

Not in the least perturbed, Kevin bowed gravely and said: '*Enchanté.*'

'Is this a coincidence?' I asked.

'No. I phoned Knockmore and Potter told me you'd gone to the Curragh, so, as it's only half an hour's drive, I thought I might as well pop along and say hallo. So tell. What brings you here?'

While Kevin explained the latest developments, I surreptitiously surveyed the stand. They were still seated, the prince engaged in conversation with the woman with the blue hair. As I slid my eyes away, I noticed his head beginning to turn in our direction again. Claire said she'd go with Kevin and find another exit from the stand that she could cover, and a few moments after they left, I followed, looking for a phone.

The switchboard girl knew Declan – his job made him a well-known figure throughout the industry. She told me that yes, he was at the races – he'd been in the office earlier to arrange for refreshments for a VIP. She didn't specify who, but she made it sound mysterious. She asked me to hold while she paged him, and warned me to give him time to get to a phone. I waited, listening to the announcement, until at last Declan came on and said a very cautious 'Hallo?'

'Only me.'

'Christ, Hair, he's on to you! I thought you said he didn't know you! He pointed you out to me and Jack Murphy and asked us if we knew you. I said I didn't.'

'Relax. He doesn't know me. He's just worried right now about anyone who shows an interest. Unfortunately, I picked the finish of the last race to study him through the binoculars. I thought he'd be caught up in the excitement, like everone else, but wasn't he looking straight back at me! Then, like a fool, I made it worse by acting guilty.'

'I think you're right about you know who. He's preoccupied with something big, that's for sure, and he's taking no interest at all in the races. He hasn't stopped looking around him since we got here.'

'Did he offer any reason for why he flew in for such a small race meeting?'

'No. But it's a real flying visit because he's already apologised for the fact that he won't be able to host the usual post-races dinner at Chez Pierre. He's got to leave soon.'

'Did he say where he was going?'

'No, but earlier, in the bar, I happened to see travel tickets in his girlfriend's handbag when she was looking for cigarettes. I could only see R-O-S-S-L, but I presume they're for the Rosslare ferry. I reckon they must be going straight on there afterwards, otherwise she'd hardly have the tickets with her, would she?'

'You couldn't see which boat they were for?'

'No. All I could see were those letters.'

'Does he, by any chance, own a stud farm or stables in France or the UK?'

'Uh-huh! It won't help, Frank. He owns two in France, but he owns two in England as well.'

'You're playing a blinder, Dec. Keep it up.'

The next race was about to begin and, the crowds having gone to the rails again, the rest of the enclosure was almost deserted. I wandered round the back of the stands. As soon as he saw me, Kevin beckoned excitedly. 'He's just gone back up into the stand, Frank! He came down, on his own, about ten minutes ago. I tried to follow him but he kept looking back, and I had to stay well back. I saw him go into the VIPs' car park but, by the time I thought it was safe to follow, he'd vanished. I came back here to wait.'

'Have we enough juice to get us to Rosslare if we have to?'

'Rosslare? Is that where he's headed?'

'Possibly. Is there enough juice?'

'Buckets. What's the next move?'

'We wait, I suppose. I just hope I haven't arsed it all up. If he changes his plans at this stage, who knows *what* he'll do?'

I left to look for another exit to cover, but as I walked along, I began to doubt the wisdom of our being split up, with no way of signalling each other; the farcical situation could arise where one of us would be faced with the dilemma of having to follow him solo, or going to tell the others and losing him. A far better idea would be for one of us to wait in the VIP car park to see what kind of car he had, while the other two sat outside on the road in Claire's car; then, when he came out, we could all follow. I stood behind a tractor with CURRAGH RACECOURSE written on it, and watched an exit through two panes of dirty glass. The roar of the crowd told me the horses were in the home straight, and moments later, the area behind the stand filled again; several people came down from the stand but none of them was the prince or any of his party. I decided to go and put my revised plan to Kevin and Claire.

Would Dr Francis O'Hare of Cartfield, Illinois please go to the nearest telephone. Repeat, Dr Francis O'Hare of Cartfield, Illinois to the nearest telephone. Thank you.

I almost didn't spot that the cryptic loudspeaker summons was for me. It had to be Declan – it could hardly have been a coincidence. Hair was my nickname and Cartfield was the name of my parents' house – Declan had often spent weekends there when we were at college. I headed for the nearest phone, picked it up and said in an exaggerated drawl: 'Dactur O'Hayy-ah heey-ah . . . You gotta call fo' me?' It was pure Texas, but I didn't know what an Illinois accent sounded like. Nor, obviously, did the operator.

'Just a moment sir, and I'll put you through.'

'Hair?' Declan's voice was urgent and excited.

'Yeah. What's up?'

'He's just bought a horse!'

'*What?*'

'He wasn't there when I got back from talking to you last time, but he arrived a few minutes later. Just before the last race, Tom Cratchwell arrived and sat beside him and they talked all through the race. I couldn't hear what they were saying but I've seen enough horses bought and sold to know that that's what was going on. Anyway, Cratchwell has just left with a glazed expression, clutching the walls for support. He must have got a mad price.'

'Where's he gone?'

'To fetch the horse's papers. His place is just down the road, three minutes' drive.'

'Don't tell me he's going to try *another* switcheroo!'

'Not this time. The horse he bought is a grey, and a mare. She's in the stables here. She was to run in one of the later races, the Mickey Mousest of them all, a kind of novelty thing, confined to local Curragh horses. You get all kinds of things running in it every year, though this one's not a bad mare really.'

'Is she good enough for him to want her for breeding?'

'No way,' he replied, aghast at the very idea. 'I can't understand it. As I said, he nearly always gets others to do the buying.'

'This must be a *real* emergency. I suppose Tom Cratchwell couldn't be involved?'

'I doubt it very much.'

'He's not, by any chance, a friend of the prince's?'

'Hardly. The prince is a very cultured, civilised man.'

'And Cratchwell isn't?'

'My dear boy,' Declan affected a camp, bitchy tone, 'if you stood Tom Cratchwell barefoot on a branch, his toes would ins-*tinct*-ively curl around it.'

I laughed. 'So can you think of any reason why he should want *this* particular animal?'

'No. She's a nothing. Granted, last time out she won, but that was another Mickey Mouse affair. In France.'

'He sent a horse all the way to *France* to run in a Mickey Mouse race?'

'He had room in the box. He was sending over two good horses for two good races, so he sent the mare as well. He knew she'd win and that would at least cover his expenses. Just as well he did; the other two weren't even placed.'

'Back up there,' I said, beginning to see some light. '*When* was this race in France?'

'Last week. Why?'

'So her papers are still in date, right?'

'I thought of that but you can't send a bay stallion out on a grey mare's papers.'

269

'No,' I said. 'You can't.' But my mind was already shuffling ahead: the mare had been bought solely because she could go to France straight away, presumably through Rosslare. And, what if Catamaran was scheduled to be sneaked out in the same horsebox? That could only mean a hidden compartment. So why the mare? Why not just declare the box empty? Then it struck me. If the box was supposed to be empty, Catamaran would have to be kept silent, and the only way to guarantee that would be to give him a general anaesthetic. This would involve risk to the horse, plus the co-operation, and guaranteed silence, of a vet. The risk would be more than doubled on the other side as he'd need a *second* anaesthetic when the 'empty' vehicle was being offloaded. With the grey mare tied in the stall, nobody would question horse noises. Catamaran would need to be sedated to render him indifferent to the mare's nearness, but that was nothing like as dangerous as an anaesthetic and anyone could give the injection.

'That's it, Hair! That's it!' Declan enthused when I told him my theory. 'There's no way they'd chance knocking him out *twice* in twenty-four hours!'

'I think I should go down to the stables and have a look at this mare.'

'You do that. If there are any other developments, I'll contact you again in the same way, only this time I'll page Mr Tim Carmody from Sligo. He's my nephew.'

'You're a natural cloak and dagger merchant. But what was all that Illinois stuff?'

'An extra red herring. To fool the people. Deep, huh?'

'It damn near fooled me,' I said, and broke the connection, anxious to go and look for the prince's lastest acquisition.

27

On my way to the stabling area, I stopped to tell Kevin about the grey mare. We agreed that the best policy now seemed to be to follow the mare. 'Are you going to clock in with the local cops?' he asked.

'Not until I know where Catamaran is. I know I said I would, but if one of them got over-enthusiastic . . .'

'I think you're right. There's nothing happening anyway, so what can they do? I only asked in case you'd forgotten. I'll go and get Claire and meet you back here.' He went off and I headed for the stables to locate the mare.

I consulted my race card and picked the name of a trainer at random – I knew there'd be security at the stables, and that I'd need a story to get in. Luckily, from the morning's escapade with Nick O'Beirne, I still had the ultimate prop in my pocket: my stethoscope.

'Afternoon,' I said brightly to the man in the booth who began to stare suspiciously at me when I was still ten yards away. 'Michael Reilly asked me to have a look at Honeycomb before he goes out. Can you tell me which box he's in?' I picked up the bell of the stethoscope and wagged it absentmindedly at him.

'What's wrong with Honeycomb?'

'Nothing. I hope. I shouldn't really say, but he had a bit of wind trouble last week on the gallops and I want to make sure he's AOK before he runs.'

'Where's Mr Collins today?' The question was more conversational than suspicious.

'Wedding. His sister's getting married.'

'Mr Collins has a sister young enough to be getting married?'

'Widow,' I swerved around the yawning pitfall, wondering why the hell I always had to make things so complicated. Why couldn't I just have said 'at a wedding', never mind whose.

'Box 56,' he said. 'Near the end. Even numbers on the left.'

'Thanks.' I passed on into the quiet of the stables.

I could have been unlucky. If Honeycomb had been in one of the first few boxes, I might have found it hard to explain why I was wandering off down the passageway looking to left and right. By the time I reached Box 56, I had seen every colour of bay and a few chestnuts, but only one grey, and it was a gelding. I nipped into Box 56, patted Honeycomb on the nose a few times and came back out. I glanced back towards the doorman's cubicle but, against the daylight, I couldn't tell if he was watching. I walked the rest of the corridor – there were only a few more boxes anyway and most of them were empty. None of the horses was grey. I hurried back to the door.

'How's Honeycomb?' the keeper asked.

'If I were you,' I winked, 'I wouldn't put anything on him today. I'd say that grey mare of Cratchwell's is the best bet of the day. She won nicely in France last week, you know.'

He snorted. 'You haven't backed her already, have you?'

'No,' I answered. 'Why?'

'Don't. She's been sold. Cratchwell came in a while ago and took her out.'

'Sold?'

'Aye. Just like that.' He snapped his fingers.

'Wouldn't you think he'd have let her run at least?'

'Wouldn't you? I'd say he must have got a big price for her. He had a couple of black lads with him and I wouldn't be surprised if they were Hamranis. I hear Prince Alaramos is here. If *he* bought the mare, then Cratchwell got what she was worth times over. I never thought that mare would be Alaramos's type.'

'Blast it anyway,' I improvised, 'I was half-thinking of putting in an offer for her myself. I heard he was willing to sell. In fact, the main reason I came today was to see her run.'

'She's all right, mind you. There's nothing wrong with the mare; she's strong and she's honest, I mean to say, but she's not in the class the prince deals in. Sangster or O'Brien or Firestone wouldn't cross the road to look at her, but she'd be all right for the small man. No offence.'

I smiled. 'Sangster and O'Brien and Firestone were small men once too. We've all got to start somewhere.'

'True, true. Too true.'

'Well, that's the quickest bit of work I ever saw,' I said, shaking my head. 'When did they take her?'

'You just missed them.'

'Maybe she's still outside. I'd like to have a look at her – to see what I missed. I'm a devil for punishment.'

'She's gone. They loaded her straightaway on to the transporter.'

'Jesus, that was quick!' I snorted. 'Ah well . . . maybe I'll drop by Cratchwell's place. If the truck is there I might pull up for a look. What kind of truck was it?'

'I didn't see it myself. I'm not allowed to leave here until the last horse is gone.'

'Of course. Then . . . how do you know she was loaded?'

'Cratchwell's lad. He told me when he came back. I don't think he was too pleased at the way she went. He helped them load her, so he'd know. We'll ask him – he's just down the passage. Georgie!' he bellowed. 'Georgie!'

A blond head popped out from a box down along the right. 'Me? Were you callin' me, Patsy?'

He beckoned with his head. 'Yeah. C'mere son. I wantcha minute.'

We didn't get much from Georgie. The mare, which went under the lofty name of Nimble Nimbus, had been loaded on to an ordinary horse transporter which was immediately driven off by a 'coloured chap'. He hadn't even noticed what colour the truck was because he was that upset at the time. 'I still am!' he whined, and sounded it. 'I got her ready for this race for months and she'd have won. The boss couldn't even wait an hour!'

'She won her race in France,' I pointed out.

'I wasn't there to see her.'

'Maybe you'll see her winning again soon.'

'But I won't be the one who's looking after her, will I?' Georgie was determined to knock maximum mileage out of his gloom.

'Did she go off with other horses?'

'No. She was all alone.'

'Was it just a single box, then?'

'No. A truck. A transporter. A big one.'

Leaving Patsy to console the inconsolable Georgie, I went off to join Claire and Kevin, but they weren't there. I'd waited a few moments when suddenly the public address system spoke out, stopping me in my tracks with a shiver.

Attention please! Attention please! There is an urgent message at the administration room for Mr Frank Samson of Knockmore-on-Sea. Mr Frank Samson, Knockmore-on-Sea. Urgent message at the administration room. Thank you.

It had to be trouble. Hoping it might be the Kildare gardaí wanting to know why I hadn't clocked in as promised, but knowing that it wasn't, I ran towards the administration block on legs that had suddenly become rubbery. Who would use my real name and Knockmore address? Not Declan. Potter would never have had me publicly paged. It couldn't be Kevin or Claire – they knew where to find me. So, it had to be the only other person who knew I was at the races: Prince Alaramos. Filled with foreboding, I pushed through the glass doors and made straight for the receptionist. 'Frank Samson. You've got an urgent message for me. It was on the public address just now.'

'Oh, yes sir,' she replied. 'Here it is,' and she handed me a small manila envelope.

Trembling, I opened it. In awkward capitals, it read:

SAMSON.

YOUR LADY FRIEND HAS COME FOR A DRIVE WITH US. SHE
DOESN'T KNOW WHEN SHE WILL BE BACK BUT WISHES THAT YOU
GO TO CHEZ PIERRE AND WAIT FOR HER PHONECALL. SHE SAYS
YOU SHOULD THINK THINGS OUT AND NOT DO ANYTHING HASTY.

I read it again, and as I stood trying to marshall my
thoughts, Kevin burst through the door. I almost pushed him
outside again. 'Alaramos has got Claire,' I said bleakly, as
soon as we were away from the prying eyes and ears of the
staff.

'I know. When I went to get her, she wasn't where we'd left
her. I waited, in case she'd gone to the Ladies, but when she
didn't come back I asked around and one of the ground staff
told me he saw a woman of her description going out the gate
with three foreigners – dark foreigners. Then I heard the
announcement and came straight here. Is that it?' he asked,
nodding at the paper in my nerveless fingers. I handed it to
him without a word.

'What's this Chez Pierre?' he asked.

'The restaurant where Alaramos usually eats after the
races. It's probably the only place he knows around here. I'm
going to go and choke the bastard right now, this minute, till
he tells me where she is.'

'He's gone, Frank. He must have left while I was searching
for Claire, or else he came out another exit – but he's gone.
They all are, Forbes included.'

'Christ!' I swore. 'What the hell do we do now?'

'Do you know where Chez Pierre is?'

'No. It'd be easy to find out, but I'm not going to sit in any
fucking restaurant . . . He probably won't even *call* there. He
just wants us tied up, out of the way. Maybe, if we radio
Potter, he can get a local cop to sit there and take any calls for
me. I've never spoken to Alaramos or any of them, so whoever
rings won't know but that he's talking to me. In the
meantime, we'll try to find them from the air. Then, if we do,
we'll just have to play it by ear, I suppose.'

*

275

A few minutes later, looking balefully down on the receding oval of the Curragh racecourse, I broke the grim silence. 'How do you feel about diplomatic immunity?'

'Do I look, or act, like a diplomat?'

'I don't give a shit either. I'm going to choke the bastard.'

As we straightened up to follow the main road south, the position looked hopeless – a lot of road and, on a racing day, a lot of horseboxes. Picking the right one wasn't going to be easy.

Kevin reached for the radio. 'We'd better get the time of the next ferry from Rosslare.' He made his call-sign. 'If it's soon, they'll have to drive straight through and stick to the main road. If they've got loads of time, then God only knows where they can go. Anywhere!' The radio crackled into life; Kevin listened, said thanks, and signed off. '8.15 to Fishguard. 9.15 to Le Havre. If they want to make either of those, they don't have a lot of time.' He looked at his watch. 'A little over three hours for the Fishguard one – they're cutting it fine already.'

We reckoned the best chance of identifying the truck was to pass over a few suspects and drop me off to check the drivers as they went by; if there were no likely-looking prospects, we'd leapfrog over the next few, and so on; it was full of ifs and buts – for instance, what if the Hamrani driver had been replaced by a local? – but we had to narrow it down somehow; otherwise, it was unmanageable.

'What makes you think,' Kevin asked, reasonably enough, 'that we'll find the prince if we find the truck? He's hardly riding with them.'

'Even if he's not, I reckon we'll find Catamaran and then we can trade. Just as well Potter isn't here – I don't think he'd be over-keen on me bargaining with a horse that isn't mine.'

We passed over the first likely suspect. Kevin sent the chopper over to one side so that we were paralleling the road, about three hundred yards away from it. Through the field-glasses, I checked that it wasn't just a delivery lorry or furniture removals truck. It wasn't.

'Want to land?' he asked.

'Let's go on a bit. See if there are any more on this stretch.'

We found two more. Speeding up, we rushed ahead and landed in a field of stubble about a mile ahead of the leading lorry. I got to the road and was just in time to check the occupants, a florid-faced Irishman, slightly balding, and a young lad so like him he had to be his son. I turned and shook my head. I drew blanks with the other two also and dashed back. 'No good. Let's go.'

We identified the three trucks we had checked and raced on. In the next ten miles we passed over five. We both had a feeling about the third one and watched it a while before moving on. It seemed to be in more of a hurry than the others, changing out of the slow lane often to pass other heavy vehicles which were going only slightly slower than itself. Kevin set down in a field screened from the road by a thick hedge and, with a sense of rising tension, I leaped out and hared to the gate.

The first truck passed, driven by a blond man accompanied by a blonde woman and two blonde children drinking Coca-Cola from cans; a couple of minutes later, the next one laboured along, being driven in too high a gear by an old man in a battered hat. It left the smell of cattle hanging on the air behind it, and the smell was still there when the third one began to bear down. It had made up a lot of road on the first two and I could hear the urgent whine of its engine when it was still a good quarter of a mile away. This was the one. I just knew it. I could *feel* it.

The whitethorn hedge whipped in the slipstream as the lorry thundered past, and the gate was still rocking as I vaulted it. The three men in the cab were dark-skinned and dark-eyed, and the truck was a left-hand drive with French number plates. We were up and away before I got the door closed.

'That's it, the one just gone by! Green cab and varnished wood body. We've got them!'

We picked it up within minutes, climbed to two hundred feet and kept pace.

'Now what?' Kevin asked, looking down at the miniature traffic.

'Maybe he'll stop for a coffee or something. He's probably well on time. He's almost certainly going for the French ferry, so he's got until 9.15'.

For the next ten minutes we followed the truck as it raced through the rich green country, all the time racking our brains for some way to stop it without having to involve the gardaí. We thought of the most outlandish plans, each one more desperate and ridiculous than the other – hiring or 'borrowing' a truck or tractor to block the road, scattering nails in front of it, and others even worse. Kevin reckoned we'd been watching too much television.

The cars below passed out of our sight into a tree-lined section of the road some half a mile long. From our height, it looked like the traffic had suddenly plunged underground. Maintaining a steady speed, we flew to the end of the wooded section where the traffic reappeared, and hovered, waiting for our quarry to emerge. It didn't.

'What the hell is going on now?' I said, developing an immediate tightness in the throat. 'Surely they can't have spotted us!'

'I don't see how they could have,' Kevin replied.

Anxiously I waited for the lorry to show. If Claire was in it, and they knew they were being followed, they wouldn't want to be caught with their hostage, and, if they had stopped . . . A cold sickness crawled through me, spreading out from my heart.

'Put me down here, Kevin. I want to see why they've stopped . . .'

He looked sideways at me.

'Now, dammit! Put me down now!'

'All right, Frank. But only because it's the best thing to do. Take it easy.'

'Jesus Christ! Land, will you!' I clamped my lips in impatience and watched the ground drifting gently up to meet me.

'I don't think she's in the truck at all,' Kevin said quietly, calmly.

'Why not?' I asked, hoping he had a more concrete reason than a desire to calm me down.

'Well, the truck left long before Claire . . . eh . . . got taken and they wouldn't have been able to transfer her from one vehicle to another, on the main road. Not with all that traffic . . .'

'Five minutes in a side road,' I countered aggressively. 'Two minutes!'

'But why would they want her in the truck? She can be just as effective a hostage here as she can in France, with only a fraction of the danger of being found. Believe me, she's *not* in that truck.'

I sighed. 'I suppose you're right. Just as well one of us is thinking clearly. Anyway, I'll get off here and see that they don't come out this end, and you'll . . . what? Go up and see if they've turned back or turned off on to another road?'

'That's what I reckon. I'll do a big circle; if they have changed route, they can't have got very far. Then if I don't find them, I'll come back here. You signal me if they haven't come out this end, and I'll go and land at the other; then we'll both make our way along the road and meet in the middle.'

'Fine. By the way, if the truck is parked, I won't approach it – they might recognise me. I'll hunker down in the woods a few yards short of it on the opposite side of the road, OK?'

Kevin raised his thumb. 'Gotcha.' I slammed the door and ran aside as the helicopter zoomed up.

A short while later he was back; he dropped to treetop height and hovered questioningly until I shook my head; then he pointed towards the other end and made walking movements with two down-pointing fingers. I nodded and began to look for a place to push through the thick hedge.

28

As soon as I stepped out on to the road, I could see that there was no lorry pulled over – there was nothing but rushing traffic. As I waited for Kevin to appear, I scanned the shaded sides for an opening – a side road, gateway, farm track – but the thick hedge stretched unbroken. When I saw him framed momentarily in the far entrance, I set off at a brisk jog. The comforting logic of his reasoning was wearing thin, and a small ember of panic was beginning to smoulder inside me again.

'There's a gate back there,' he said when we met. 'That must be it – I couldn't see any sign of them, but there's nowhere else.' He caught my arm as I went to push past him. 'Hang on . . . I think we should try and get through the hedge here. They may be watching the gate.'

I turned and forced my way through right where we were, regardless of thorns or spikes, scrapes and scratches, and found myself in a kind of scrubby wasteland, choked with head-high undergrowth. A short distance away, there were some large trees. The traffic, mere feet away, suddenly sounded muted and distant. Kevin joined me and pointed towards the trees.

The undergrowth of briars and whitethorns rustled and crackled as we crept stealthily forward, alert for the tiniest warnings of danger. Then we heard it. Muffled but unmistakable, off to the left, a horse neighed. It was hard to judge distance – the horsebox and the undergrowth would muffle the sound – but I sensed it was close. I picked up a length of fallen timber and turned to follow the sound. Glancing at Kevin, I was amazed to see a gun in his hand. It wasn't a large gun, as guns go, but it made the one I'd taken from Vernon look like something out of a Christmas cracker. Later he told me he always kept it under his seat, 'in case of hijackers'.

The neigh came again, only this time definitely close by, and straight ahead. A few steps further on, we came to the edge of a clearing. Across from us, parked tight against the greenery, was the truck. Scarcely daring to breathe, we crouched and waited and watched.

Almost at once, we spotted two of them. Hiding in patches of scrubby undergrowth, intently observing the woods, they had their backs to us. They'd probably seen or heard the helicopter land and, reasonably enough, expected us to approach from that side.

Kevin nudged me. 'Weren't there three?'

I nodded. 'I hope the other's not on this side.' We peered around nervously.

In the cab, a radio-telephone sprang into noisy life and was immediately answered by the third man. Though the words were totally foreign to me, there was such deference in his tone that I felt sure he had to be talking to Alaramos. I'd have given a lot to know what they were saying.

'I'll take the one on the left,' I said, my voice now safely drowned by the radio. Now that we'd located the third man, it was safe to move. 'But let's wait and see what they do after this message. If they leave, it might be better to follow them. They can't wait too long if they want to catch that ferry.'

The conversation was now all incoming, our man's only input being two much-repeated phrases, one of which must have meant 'Yes, Majesty' and the other 'No, Majesty'.

The two men lurking in the shrubbery never moved. Not once. They seemed oblivious to the racket from the radio, not worried that it would be a dead giveaway of their position. They looked to be almost physically straining to listen for sounds of approach and to see through the shifting green wall of foliage which chopped off their view twenty feet in front of them. You had to admire them – in their own country, their visibility would be limited only by a horizon shimmering ephemerally in a heat haze, or by ranges of yellow-grey, sun-scorched mountains.

The conversation went on.

Kevin became impatient. 'I think we should take them now while the radio covers any noise. We'll leave the guy in the cab until he finishes.'

'I think we should wait. Give it another minute at least . . .'

Kevin shook his head in disagreement but waited the minute – sixty impatient seconds.

'C'mon,' he said.

'Hang on,' I said.

'Claire might be locked in that truck,' he said.

'Well, damn me . . .' I said, scarcely able to credit his duplicity, but I knew I couldn't hold him. 'OK, then. On the count of three.'

Straightening from our crouched positions, we rounded the bush into the clearing. Once in the open, we ran at them. My man turned just as I reached him, his fear-widened eyes staring in horror at the raised club, but he had time neither to cry out nor to move before I brought it down on his skull with a force that sickened me. It flattened him. He pitched sideways out of the bushes into the open, rolled over once and lay still. I have no idea how hard to hit a person on the head with a wooden club in order to cause the required depth and duration of unconsciousness, and, hoping to God I hadn't killed him, I searched his pockets. In his back pocket there was a very small penknife; it was old, rusty and probably blunt, but I threw it into the undergrowth anyway. I saw Kevin stand up and move quickly to the back of the lorry, and, a second later, I was at his side.

The ramp was secured by wing-bolts, which in turn were secured by padlocks. Neither of the felled men had had keys on him, so they were probably in the cab. Incredibly, the radio conversation was still going on. 'I wish to God they'd shut up!' I growled, and glanced impatiently around the corner towards the cab. Immediately the man in the cab began to shout in alarm, and, to my disgust, I saw brown eyes staring in fear at me in the wing mirror. 'Aww *shit!*' I swore in self-reproach, inwardly sick.

The man in the cab kept gabbling excitedly to his attentive audience.

'Let's get him quick and get the keys!' I shouted, and we both rushed to the cab and yanked the door open.

'*Out! Out! Out!*' Kevin screamed at the terrified man, with violent waves of his gun.

The man went silent, dropped the handset, gulped painfully and slid across to the door.

'C'mon! *C'mon!*' Kevin grabbed him and hauled him out so quickly he almost fell. The man was in terror – he probably thought we'd already killed his missing comrades. Leaving him to Kevin, I reached in, caught the radio handset, which was swinging forlornly on its coiled cable, and pressed TRANSMIT.

'Listen closely,' I said. 'This is Frank Samson speaking.' I released the button and waited. Nothing happened. I went on: 'I know you've got Claire, but I've got Catamaran. If you hand her over, unharmed, you and your men and your animals can leave. You can have three hours' grace before I contact anyone. What do you say?' Nothing. 'Over,' I prompted hopefully. The set remained as dead as ever.

'Answer me, damn you!' I was getting more worried with every second's silence.

'Hey, Frank,' Kevin called. 'Leave it. He'll be back on, don't worry. C'mon! Give me a hand here! Search him.'

Either the man understood some English or he had seen lots of American TV shows. At my approach, he turned to face the truck and spreadeagled himself against it. I ran my hands over him and stepped back, but as he began to turn round Kevin hit him with the gun, and he fell forward in an unconscious heap on the shadow-stippled ground beside his truck.

While I got the keys from the ignition, Kevin checked the other two. 'They're still flat out,' he said, reaching back to stuff the gun, barrel first, down the back of his shirt collar.

'Isn't that dangerous?' I asked, as he flicked his longish hair out to cover the gun-butt.

'No more than sticking it in your belt. I saw it in a film once – up here, it's less likely to be found in a quick search, and it's also fairly easy to get at unnoticed when you've got your hands in the air or on top of your head. You didn't search *his* collar, I noticed.'

'No. Maybe I ought to check it now?'

'I already did.' He grinned at me.

I chose the correct key straight off and opened the first padlock. My hands were shaking – maybe Claire *was* in the truck; maybe the prince hadn't answered because he knew we'd find her, so no deal was needed. There'd be nothing to talk about. From inside the box came horse noises, and once, I thought I heard a movement lighter and more gentle than a horse could make, but I wasn't sure. The second key was proving more difficult and I was on my third try when Prince Alaramos suddenly appeared.

The prince, his features disfigured by frustration and anger stood a little away from the side of the truck, pointing a gun unwaveringly at us. 'You should have gone to Chez Pierre. That was the arrangement. Now anything could happen.' He paused as if he wanted to hear what I had to say to that, but I was speechless. Then he shrugged, as if it didn't matter one way or another, and went on: 'I thought I recognised you this afternoon, but I wasn't sure – I only had a hazy press photograph to go on. I pointed you out to our mutual friend, Mr Forbes, and asked him if he knew who you were – in a small country like this, with only one veterinary school, it would be odd if two veterinarians of approximately the same age didn't recognise each other. But that's what Forbes claimed, though not, I must say, very convincingly. I suspected he was lying, but before changing my plans, I thought I'd better make absolutely sure so I went for a walk. That was when this gentleman here,' he nodded towards Kevin, 'followed me. When I saw Roscahill's helicopter, I knew that you were at the races – he's been telling everybody, *ad nauseam*, how he has placed it at your disposal. But that *still* didn't prove Forbes was lying. Perhaps he *really* didn't know you – perhaps one of you graduated abroad. From my car phone, I called my vet and asked him to check the register to see when you had graduated. Then I asked him if you mightn't be about the same vintage as Forbes, and what do you know? – he told me that you had been classmates! And that, Samson, was when I knew I needed some bargaining power. So I took her. And very beautiful she is too. A hundred years ago, I would have carried her off to my harem, but, unfortunately, times change . . .' He shook his head nostalgically, regretting the passing of the good old days. 'You must miss her terribly.'

'Where is she? What have you done with her?' I growled with as much menace as our relative positions would allow.

'*I'll* ask the questions. But don't worry – your charming lady friend is safe, and will be, as long as my plans go forward. Put it this way,' he said with a sudden bright smile, 'you don't interfere with my breeding programme, and I shan't interfere with yours.'

I couldn't think of an apt retort in time, so I just glared contemptuously at him. He ignored me totally.

'When I saw you standing by the roadside, I could hardly believe my eyes. The same hundred years ago, I would have thought you were the Djinn of Nemesis or something, and had you put to the sword for being in two places at one time. But of course, the helicopter explained all.'

'You were in the lorry?' I asked despite myself.

'Of course not!' he interjected. 'I was in the Mercedes in front of the lorry. When I saw you, I knew at once what you were up to, saw the helicopter following us, came ahead to find somewhere we could stop, so that you would have to land and we could talk. And here we are! I've got a full house; you, the pilot, his machine, the lady, and Catamaran.' He looked about at the recumbent figures of his subjects. 'We didn't expect you to come upon us so quickly. I miscalculated. I thought you would approach with extreme caution. You haven't killed any of them, I trust?' It didn't seem to worry him too much either way. 'Now let's go and get Pitru to open this contraption and fit you both inside. This way, please.'

'Where's Claire?' I demanded.

The prince shook his head slowly, and made tut-tutting noises of disapproval. 'All in good time, Samson. All in good time.'

He herded us past the truck and along a path between the trees. Some fifty yards on we reached a smaller clearing, not much bigger than the silver Mercedes which was parked in it. I shook my head in disgust — the radio/telephone had suggested *distance*. The young Hamrani who stood by the car jumped when he saw Kevin and me, his eyes widening in terror until he saw the prince behind us. Alaramos ordered us to put our hands on the car roof and spread our legs wide; then, closely directing the operation himself, had his servant search us. But they didn't find the gun.

'You may turn around now, but keep your hands up!' Watching us closely, he gave instructions to his young servant. The word 'horsebox' came into it a few times and there were several mentions of Karali, Huasa and Uwani, and I took these to be the names of the three felled ones. Once, I thought I heard him say 'helicopter'. However, I reflected it might just as easily be Hamrani for 'dig two shallow graves'.

Suddenly, I heard Kevin say, very quickly: 'When I count to three, run.'

The prince heard him too, but not what he said. He looked sharply at us. Kevin had lowered his hands on to his head.

'Just keep quiet,' said the prince. 'No talking.' He glared at us for a moment or two, then resumed his instructions.

I stole another quick glance at Kevin. The butt of the gun was already in his hand and I could see his index finger reaching for the trigger-guard, clearing the hair away. I steeled myself for the countdown, pushing away from the Mercedes. Alaramos finished his orders and, with a bow, the boy left, running.

'Where are all your men, anyway?' Kevin asked the prince. 'We know there are at least twelve, and yet, here, you've only got –' he took his left hand and began to count his fingers against the thumb – 'one . . .'

I tensed, and in an odd, detached way I admired Kevin's craftiness – by lowering his hand, he dragged the prince's wary gaze down with it, giving his right hand a better chance to pull the gun unnoticed and me a better chance of reaching cover.

'. . . two . . .'

I coiled for my fire-drawing dash.

'. . . three . . .' Kevin said, and I was off, streaking for the bushes, head and neck telescoped like a human tortoise, bracing myself for the bullet.

Behind me, there was a shout, a shot, and, as I threw myself flat, a cry of pain.

29

It was only when I heard the cry that I was sure that *I* hadn't been shot – I hadn't felt anything but I'd read that you don't, not for the first few seconds anyway. I turned as I hit the ground, and, in my anxiety for Kevin, almost bounced into a crouch. I was unutterably relieved to see him standing, unscathed, though understandably looking a little shaken. He was stonily regarding the prince who lay writhing on the ground, clasping his shoulder with a hand through which blood was seeping. I dashed back almost as quickly as I'd left.

'You all right?' I asked Kevin, scooping up the prince's gun.

'Yeah. Fine,' he answered quietly. 'I'll be OK.'

I couldn't hear Pitru calling his comrades now. Although he'd probably assume it was Kevin or me who'd been shot, I was afraid he might take a quick peep; if he found out the truth, he could easily make radio contact with the ones who were holding Claire . . . a cold claw squeezed my heart. 'Pitru!' I shouted imperiously in as near an impression of the prince's voice as I could manage, and raced for the track.

I ducked behind a bush when I heard Pitru's headlong approach – obviously he was used to complying unquestioningly with the prince's summons. As he dashed past, I sprang at him, but he was going at such a lick that I had to run a few steps before I could reach his head with the butt of his master's gun. With a surprised grunt, he lurched into the bushes and lay still, his legs staying on the path. Jumping across him, I ran back to the clearing.

The prince had sat up now. He was clasping his shoulder tightly with his left hand and the cracks between the fingers had filled with narrow lines of drying blood. I squatted beside him and considered him for a minute, coldly staring into his pain-filled eyes. 'Where is she? You'll tell me sooner or later, and it's best for all if it's sooner. So . . . where is she?'

He returned my stare, contemptuously. I could see that, in his eyes, I was a commoner and a foreigner, and on those two counts alone, I deserved neither respect nor co-operation. Then he dropped his stare and shot a glance towards the car.

'The car? Is she in the car? My God. She's not in the boot?' The prince said nothing. I ran to the back of the Mercedes but the boot was locked. I tapped the lid with the flat of my hand. 'Hang on, Claire! It's me, Frank,' I called and raced to the driver's door. Yanking the key from the ignition, I rushed back, fumbled it into the lock, and sprung the lid. For a second, I couldn't believe that there was nothing but the spare wheel and a picnic basket. I'd been so *sure*. A short nasty laugh came from the grass. At that moment I hated him. Gently, I closed the boot and stood for a few seconds, breathing slowly and deeply, my hands resting on it. Then I turned towards him.

The bleakness in my eyes wiped all traces of laughter off his face. Swallowing nervously, he watched me approach and come to a halt, towering directly above him. 'You rotten bastard,' I growled, and with great malice, kicked him hard on the shoulder.

He screamed and fell backwards, rolling about on the ground, humming in repressed agony. I watched him unfeelingly, waiting for him to sit up again. When he did, his face had a grey sheen to it; sweat beads stood out on his forehead and ran in streaky rivulets down his face. His lips were pulled back, exposing perfect teeth, clenched; his eyes were screwed closed. When at last he opened them, he looked into mine: mean, narrowed slits, only a few inches away. This time he didn't look away.

'If that woman has come to the *slightest* harm, then you're for it, my friend. Do you understand?'

'Yes!' he gasped, his features twisting again.

'Good! Now,' I said in businesslike tones, 'let's go and search that horsebox of yours. Secret compartment and all. You didn't think we knew about that, did you?'

Having regained his feet, the prince also seemed to have regained some of his composure. 'I enjoy diplomatic immunity,' he announced.

'Oh golly*gosh!*,' I looked in mock horror at Kevin. 'What have we done?' Then I grinned at the prince. 'I'm sorry to have to break this to you, but neither of us is in the slightest bit diplomatically inclined. What's more, you'll see no diplomats – or police – until we've finished with you. Now, get going!'

I made him take one of Pitru's ankles while I took the other, and we dragged him behind us with Kevin bringing up the rear.

The three men were pretty much as we had left them. My victim was sitting on a log, swaying, and supporting his bent head in his hands; when he became aware of us, he lurched to his feet, took a few drunken steps in several directions and collapsed again. We dropped Pitru among his fallen comrades.

I undid the second padlock of the horse transporter and, as the ramp descended slowly on its hydraulic rods, we moved to the sides, out of the firing line – if there was anyone in there to fire. The ramp hit the ground with a soft thump, but the only sound that came from inside was the anxious stamping and whinnying of a horse which sees fresh air and green grass and wants to get at both.

'Push the prince into the opening,' I called across to Kevin. 'You!' I said to him. 'Tell them to hold their fire.'

'There are no guns,' he said.

'Oh yeah? Well you just pop your head round the corner there, in case you're wrong and someone in there has a reflex trigger-finger.'

With a look of contempt the prince stepped on to the ramp.

Nothing happened except that the mare became quiet, no doubt expecting him to let her out.

In the box there was just the grey mare, Nimble Nimbus, and a Hamrani even younger than Pitru. He stood wide-eyed at the mare's head, gripping her halter for support, and stared from me to the prince's shoulder. If I'd had horns, cloven hooves and a spear-tipped tail, he couldn't have looked at me with more abject terror – I had wounded his prince, probably the most grievous crime he could imagine. I made a sign for him to come to me but he stood transfixed, his eyes darting to the prince every few seconds.

'Tell him to open the secret compartment,' I instructed Alaramos. 'I presume he doesn't understand English?'

The prince seemed to be at a loss for words. 'I don't expect either of you to understand . . .'

'Sure, give it a whirl anyway,' I said. 'Have a stab at it.'

'I cannot be seen to take orders. These men believe my family to be . . . almost divine. Men take orders, gods don't. I'd rather die than do what you so obviously have commanded me to.'

'Fair enough,' I said. 'I've no desire to shatter the lad's illusions. Just tell me how the secret door works and *I'll* do it.'

'You are a reasonable man, Mr Samson. Perhaps we may yet make another bargain.'

'Forget it!' The line between deity and wheeler-dealer seemed to be a narrow one. 'How do I open this?'

He told me, in words so conversational it was obvious he was still trying to disguise the fact that he was in an inferior position. When I had led down the grey mare, pulled various levers and pushed several knobs, the front wall split in two and pivoted on the central forward roof support, both halves swinging back to rest along the central division. In the small, transverse, forward compartment, was Catamaran. He was doped to the eyeballs, and didn't even lift his head when the light flooded his narrow space.

The cramped area had been soundproofed with material like egg cartons. There was an extractor fan above his head, and a canvas sling under his belly connected by soft ropes at each corner to steel hooks in the ceiling. However, he seemed able to support his weight on his legs, so I unhooked his cradle and led him, wobbling, into the main body of the box. There I tied him loosely to a ring in the side wall.

Continuing the polite tones, I told Alaramos I wanted to lock his men in the compartment until the gardaí came. I explained that I couldn't leave them in the main body of the vehicle as I wanted them kept separate from Catamaran – just in case. I hoped he would co-operate by asking them to follow my instructions.

'What are your intentions towards me?'

'You'll come with us. As a counter-hostage. The deal is, you for Claire – a god for a mere mortal. They'll have to go for it, the bargain of the week.'

The young lad hadn't moved. He stood stiffly, wild-eyed and uncomprehending. When I took his arm to lead him outside, he resisted in terror, looking imploringly at his prince, who ignored him totally. Bastard, I thought, but I was thinking like a westerner. I half-dragged, half-pushed the lad into the sunshine, and felt him go rigid when he saw the others sprawled about. I tried a reassuring smile, but that only made it worse – he probably thought I was gloating in gleeful anticipation of knocking him out too.

I indicated that I wanted him to help me support the wobbling figures into the horsebox and, in the end, he understood. He even helped a little. When the four had been propped against the real front wall, I began to close the false wall back into position. Just before I closed the second half, I touched the young lad on the shoulder and pointed to him to go through. Straightaway his eyes flooded with terror and he looked as if he wanted to cry. He looked in panic at his prince, but seeing only indifference on the royal features, bowed, turned, and, shaking uncontrollably, went in.

I locked the door behind him, picked up a bit of rope, patted Catamaran on his doped rump, descended the ramp and, pushing it up again, replaced the padlocks. I placed the keys behind one of the wheels and covered them with a few handfuls of grass. They'd be there for the gardaí to find.

The prince had sat himself down on a log. The pain was probably getting worse and he was shifting about uncomfortably as he clasped the injured shoulder. Kevin was right behind him.

'Now then,' I said, standing over him, 'do we continue in this reasonable fashion or do we have a bloodbath? It's up to you.'

'Oh, I'm sure we can come to some mutually beneficial arrangement.' He looked up at me, almost smiling.

I shook my head. I was almost smiling too. 'You don't understand. What I'm saying is, are you going to tell me where Claire is *now* . . . or do I have to beat it out of you? None of your people are about. You don't have to be godlike any more. Where is she?'

'If I told you that, there would be nothing to stop you from getting her back and turning the stallion over to the authorities. I'm not used to negotiating from a positon where I might end up with nothing.'

'Look, get this straight. If you leave this country a free man, it'll be thanks to your diplomatic immunity, not because you do some kind of deal with us. There *is* no deal. The horse stays where he is and Claire comes with us. The *only* deal on offer is: tell us where she is and you don't get any further abuse.'

'What about the horse?' he asked calmly, though the half-smile had gone.

'Jesus!' I glanced in disbelief at Kevin, and wearily shook my head; then with a heavy sigh, I turned back to the prince. 'Forget the damned horse!' I shouted irritably. 'The horse doesn't come into it! Just Claire! And you.'

'I can make you both rich men. All you've got to do is leave for an hour. Pretend you never found us. By tomorrow evening, you have my word that your lady friend will be released unhurt and that you both will be the richer by whatever sum you may care to mention.'

'Do *you* want to listen to this bullshit?' I asked Kevin.

'He's not going to be reasonable, Frank. You may as well give him the works.'

The prince regarded me placidly, almost smiling again, as if he believed I was just trying to up the price a bit, that the bargaining, far from being over, was proceeding along standard lines.

'You just don't listen, do you?' I said, and hit his shoulder. 'That's your trouble – you just don't listen.'

There was a brief look of incredulity before his face screwed up in pain again, then he began rocking back and fro, biting his knuckle. 'Listen to me,' I said insistently, 'listen a minute. If you're going to be stubborn about this, I'm going to shoot your balls off.' The prince went rigid. 'And don't think for an instant that I won't. I'm a vet, remember? I castrate hundreds of animals every year. No taboos in it for me. No taboos at all.' I gave him an evil grin. 'Just like this!' I pointed the gun towards his groin, lowered it so that the muzzle almost touched the log in the angle between his legs, and pulled the trigger.

He jolted as if ten thousand volts had passed through him, his eyes wide in terror. Kevin, too, jerked. 'Christ, Frank! . . . You didn't . . .' he breathed.

'Or you can prevent the whole business. So. Last chance. Which is it to be?'

He coughed nervously and swallowed a few times.

'Frank,' Kevin said, 'I'll have no part in any castrating. If it comes to that, you're on your own.'

'No one's forcing you to stay. Go now if you want to.'

'She's at the house of my cousin near Newbridge,' the prince said, his voice shaking.

'Well, at last!' I said. 'Where are the rest of your men?'

'At the house.'

'How many?'

'Six.'

'Armed?'

Silence.

'Armed?' I repeated in a threatening voice.

'Not all. Three of them. I think.'

'You think? Don't you know?'

'No. Not for sure.'

'And the woman?'

'I told you. She's at the house.'

'Not her. The woman who was with you at the Curragh.'

'She's there too.'

'So everybody's at your cousin's house?'

'That is correct.'

'Right then. Let's go. But by God, if you're lying . . .'

On the way, we radioed the Kildare gardaí and told them where to find Catamaran. Kevin told the astounded officer that he was only passing a message on for Peter Potter.

'Newbridge below,' Kevin announced a short while later. He tapped the prince on the knee. 'It's up to you from here. North, south, east or west?'

'Whichever road leads to Naas . . .'

'That one.' Kevin pointed at a thread wending through the rich countryside. 'How far?'

'I'm not sure.'

'Approx. One mile? Three? Ten?'

'Three miles would be maximum. The house is on the left.'

'Then we should be there in no time. Keep a good lookout.'

I was in the back, behind the prince. I had the gun vaguely pointed at him though it wasn't necessary as I had tied his hands together in front, securing them there by tying the long ends together behind his back – a variation on the GI truss.

I was worried: it was all very well knowing where Claire was, but how were we going to get her out? We were outnumbered and out-gunned. At first I could think of nothing more brilliant than marching up to the door, the prince between us, a gun in each of his earholes, and demanding her, but this plan would almost inevitably develop into a stalemate – at some stage, the handover would have to take place and, once the prince was out of the firing line, what then? . . . It was even possible that a couple of them might be crack shots; and we might be picked off as we stood beside the prince. Another problem was the language – there was nothing to stop them from openly orchestrating a rescue effort.

The prince said suddenly: 'That's it, down there. That house behind the trees.'

I raised the binoculars. The house was a decent-sized country house of the last century, square, solid and two-storeyed, not unlike Bally Ard. A long driveway curved round a dense stand of trees which obscured the house from the road and the gate. There was no sign of occupants, no smoke from the chimneys, no windows or doors open, no cars on the forecourt.

'It looks empty. You're sure?'

'Of *course* I'm sure,' he snapped. The old hauteur was coming back.

I did a last sweep of the grounds, then lowered the field-glasses. 'Could you put me down just inside the gate, Kevin? Behind the woods?'

He studied the terrain a moment. 'Yeah. I reckon I could. Then what?'

'Take off again immediately.'

'What are you going to do?'

'Go up to the house and ask them for Claire.'

'Just like tha'?' Kevin asked in a Tommy Cooper voice.

'Never!' said the prince. 'She will *not* be released unless I am there. I shall have to go with you.'

'You'll go with Kevin.'

'Go with me where?' Kevin asked.

'Just fly about for ten minutes. Then come and hover in front of the house. When you get there, I'll go in, and, if I'm not out in five minutes, *with* Claire, radio the nearest cops. They won't harm me, I hope, because you'll have HRH here in the sky, and they certainly won't harm you because he might get killed in the resulting crash. And here's an embellishment which ought to add a little spice.' I threw a noose over the prince's head and tightened it with a jerk as he recoiled violently. 'Watch it!' I hissed, and he went quite still. 'I've tied the other end to the frame of the seat, so, if you fall, or decide to start feeling godlike again and *jump* out . . .' In fact, I hadn't tied the other end to anything; that's how accidents happen. And all I needed to complicate the peaceful rescue of Claire was the simultaneous, accidental, public hanging of Prince Alaramos of the Hamran islands, from a helicopter, above his cousin's lawn, in front of an armed audience of his own adoring subjects.

Coming in fast, Kevin dropped the machine on to the driveway ten yards inside the closed and locked gates.

I slid open the door and squeezed past the petrified figure of the prince. The coarse noose of horse-smelling rope had quietened him into a state of near catatonia. 'Leave the door open, and when you approach the house make sure HRH is well displayed. Good luck.'

Kevin gave me a thumbs-up, and climbed.

I squared my shoulders and started slowly up along the driveway, arms by my sides, palms open to show I was unarmed. I assumed no one was going to shoot me on sight; however, the nearer I came to the blank but sinister windows, the more I began to worry.

I was observed all the way, and, from the point at which the drive opened out to become the large parking space in front of the house, I began to locate them, standing deep in rooms, well in the shadows. I saw movement at a window to the left of the door; then, there was a flash appearance at the window above the door, but, whoever made it had vanished before I could focus; I caught another glimpse in the next upstairs window to the right, and I reckoned the same person could have made both – the interval was about right. As I mounted the first of the three steps to the hall door, a lace curtain twitched in the window immediately to the right. I jerked my head towards it, and was momentarily shaken to see a pair of expressionless, muddy-brown eyes regarding me coldly. In spite of a crawling sensation at the back of the neck, I felt a certain relief – so I wasn't to be shot on sight.

My three knocks on the polished brass knocker were answered at once by Alaramos's beautiful companion.

'Hallo,' I said, suddenly stuck for words.

'What do you want?' Her English was slightly accented.

'Do you know who I am?'

'I think so.'

'Then you know what I want.'

'No.'

'I think you do.'

'Tell me.'

'I want the woman who is here in this house. Claire O'Sullivan.'

'Who said that there is a woman in this house? Who told you there was a woman here?'

'Prince Alaramos. He phoned me at Chez Pierre, said I should come here to get her, and that I should tell you he'd caught the boat.' At the mention of the prince's name, two of his men suddenly appeared behind her; each held a rifle, neither threateningly. They looked briefly at me with the same lack of expression as the one who'd been looking through the window, then, with anxious eyes, began to scan the grounds, as if they expected to see the prince out there. The woman looked at her watch, did some quick calculations and reached a decision.

'I do not believe you,' she said defiantly, although worry was creeping into her dark eyes; nothing much, but it was there, like a tiny flaw in glass.

I shrugged. 'How else would I have known where to come?'

She figured that one out too. 'Where is he?' she demanded, too worried for guessing games.

'He'll be along in a few minutes. That's the truth. And he'll want you to hand over your prisoner, so why not fetch her here now?'

'I don't know what you're talking about. I think we'd better wait until he gets here. That is if he *is* coming. Would you please come inside?'

'If you don't mind, I'd rather wait here until he arrives. He shouldn't be long now.' I strained my ears for the sound of rotors.

Two more men, faces as inscrutable as statues, drifted into view and joined the others behind the dark-eyed woman.

An awkward silence developed. 'Are you the princess?' I asked, after a while, as another man came down the stairs, gun at the ready; he lowered it when he saw there was no confrontation.

'No.'

Her features were southern European – Italian, I thought – though her accent didn't sound Italian. 'Are you Hamrani?'

'No.' The worried look was becoming more obvious now; she turned and said something to the men. She must have told them what was happening because there was an agitated outburst and the confusion of everyone trying to talk at the same time.

'You seem to speak the language very well.'

Then I heard the pulsing thump of rotors. 'Ah! This will be the prince now,' I said. A moment later, coming low, the helicopter edged slowly around the copse and drifted towards the house, swaying gently, flattening grass and flowers in its downdraught.

'That is not our helicopter!' She looked at me accusingly. She hadn't yet noticed the prince; the sun was directly behind the helicopter and it was just a featureless silhouette. She had to raise her voice and lean towards me. She held both hands stiffly along her thighs to stop her skirt from billowing up in the draught.

'No. That is *my* helicopter,' I shouted back. I thought claiming the helicopter might give me a bit of status. 'But His Highness is in it.'

Again she turned and spoke to the men and they all crowded forward to stare. Seeing them shielding their eyes, Kevin realised the problem and moved over to the left, angling the helicopter so that the prince was clearly visible. Immediately, an excited babble broke out.

'Why does he not land?' she demanded, tearing her gaze away from the machine which hovered above the lawn like a monstrous dragonfly.

'He will, I assure you, just as soon as I walk out through this door with Miss O'Sullivan.'

'Who is that man with him, the man who is flying the helicopter?' Her words were almost carried away on the downdraught and throbbing roar of the rotors.

'He is the brother of the lady in the house. He is one of six brothers. She is their only sister.' She looked at me again, trying to judge if I was spinning her another line. 'I wasn't happy about leaving the prince alone with him, but I think I've convinced him not to injure His Highness further – as long as his sister is released, unharmed.'

'The prince has been *injured*.'

'I'm afraid so. He was shot in the shoulder before I could stop it. He was lucky. Kevin, the brother, was aiming for his heart. Here,' I said unslinging the binoculars, 'see for yourself.'

Clamping the hem of her dress between her knees, she pointed the binoculars and did minor adjustments with the focus.

'It's his right shoulder,' I offered helpfully.

She lowered the glasses and turned to me, eyes wide with horror. 'There is a rope round His Highness's neck!'

'*What!*' I grabbed the binoculars, focused quickly, then jerked them down again almost at once. 'He *promised* me he wouldn't! Jesus! If the prince should faint again or if the helicopter lurched over suddenly! We'd better get her out here, where he can see her, as quickly as possible. I don't like the way he's opened the prince's door . . .'

She closed her eyes, thought for a very short moment, then looked up at the helicopter again. 'Follow me.' Turning abruptly, she elbowed her way through the mesmerised throng, handing the glasses to one of them as she went.

I followed her closely. 'He told me he'd wait five minutes after I'd gone into the house. Five minutes, but no more.'

We rushed upstairs and along a corridor until we came to a door. 'She's in here. She's not hurt but she tried to escape so she may be sleeping,' the woman explained, fishing into her cleavage and hauling up a gold chain with a stainless steel key hanging on it. I caught a faint whiff of chloroform. 'I assure you she is not hurt though she may look ... eh ... untidy,' she whispered, suddenly becoming solicitous, anxious to give no further trouble. She obviously reckoned I was the one person who might be able to divert the lunatic brother from his murderous design. 'Shhh!' she whispered, and eased the door open a crack. Beyond, the room was in total darkness.

Tiptoeing forward, she was reaching for the light switch when, in a sudden blur, a pair of hands clamped on to her wrist and yanked with such force that she flew out of sight into the dark, and crashed with a thud and a little squeal somewhere inside. In the same instant Claire rocketed from the room, bent double, and, without a break in stride, head-butted me solidly in the solar plexus.

'Claire!' I croaked, half winded, as she raced along the corridor, straightening as she went. 'Claire! It's me! Frank!'

She hesitated, then stopped and turned, puzzled. 'Run, Frank! We'll make it!' she urged, stretching a hand back towards me like a last-leg relay runner, starting to move forward again.

'We *have* made it,' I said, massaging my belly. 'It's all over!' Her captor had got it right – she did look 'untidy'. 'Did they hurt you?' I asked.

'Not really ...' Her eyes opened in alarm when her erstwhile gaoler came limping rapidly from the room and started to tug at my elbow. I shook off her hand. Claire looked from me to the lady and back again. 'Will you *please* tell me what's going on, Frank?'

'Later. Kevin is hovering about twenty feet above the lawn out in front, with a hangman's noose around His Highness's neck, and a foot in the small of his back. He'll hang him, if you and I don't appear outside within the next couple of minutes.' I turned to the woman. 'We need a car. The helicopter won't land until we're away from here, and, I assure you, we're not going to walk!'

'There isn't a car.'

'Oh yes there is,' Claire said. 'I heard one earlier. It pulled up under my window. I couldn't see out because of the locked shutters, but I definitely heard one. There's a car all right.'

'We don't go another inch until you produce a car. Not an inch.' I leaned against the wall.

'But he may *kill* the prince!' the woman implored.

'Not our problem,' I said. 'Call a taxi if you must, but get a car. No car, no deal.'

She looked at me appraisingly; then her lovely mouth set in a grim line. 'Come with me.'

As we descended the stairs, the woman began to call rapid instructions, but the throb of the rotors drowned her words, and it wasn't until she was among the men that she managed to make herself heard. I held Claire back on the stairs and counted heads. Six. Full house. No tricks.

One of the men went through the door at a run and the others turned back to stare helplessly at their prince. Time seemed to have been suspended; the helicopter was in exactly the same position, the prince still sitting rigidly in the open door, and his loyal subjects were gazing up unblinkingly in rapt horror.

I gave Kevin the thumbs-up and he answered with a wiggle which sent a horrified gasp through the group. Suddenly I wanted to be outside. If anything went wrong . . . Looking at their adoring faces, I just wanted to be outside.

I nudged the woman. 'Let us through. He has to be able to see us all the time. He has to see that his sister is safe.'

'He *has* seen her,' she argued, but moved aside anyway.

I pushed through the throng and led Claire out on to the forecourt. The helicopter pivoted rapidly, bringing Kevin's side to face the house. He was grinning hugely as he pointed towards the corner of the house. In a moment, the classic radiator of a Rolls-Royce nosed its way round and halted condescendingly in front of us.

'Aha! You see?' Claire crowed, and couldn't resist a triumphal look at the woman. 'No car, aye?'

I moved towards the driver's door but the young man behind the wheel glared at me and sat sullenly there, looking towards the house for further instructions. This was neither the time nor the place to start something so I left it to the woman to sort him out. She made beckoning motions but he stared blankly back at her, pretending not to understand. Exasperated, she turned to one of the older men, who promptly came across, opened the door, and ordered the rebel out.

'Now go and open the gate,' I said to the older man, making appropriate signs.

He looked at me and nodded slowly.

'And come straight back here when you've opened it.' I couldn't think of good enough signs for this part, so I steered him across to the house and told the woman what I wanted.

'I want the gates closed again,' she objected. 'The gates are always kept closed. Always. He will stay at the gates and lock them after you.'

I shook my head. 'No. He opens the gates and comes back here. I want to be able to count six men *and* you, standing here before I leave. I also want them to hand me their guns now.'

She looked long and hard at me, then, with obvious distaste, gave the order. There were only three rifles – had the prince not given me the same figure, I'd have thought they were holding out. I cradled the guns in one arm. 'Is this all?' I asked, deciding to give her a hard time anyway.

'Yes,' she answered, tight-lipped.

'No more?'

'No more.'

'Yeah. Like there was no car.'

She said nothing.

'You'd better remember that the prince is still hanging up there in the air. No funny business. All of you stay here, in full view of the pilot, until we've been gone five minutes. Now, tell him to go and open the gates, then to come straight back.'

I went back to the Rolls and threw the guns inside. Then I stood by the driver's door until the gate opener returned. Claire was already at the passenger door.

'Ready?' I asked her.

'Ready,' she nodded. 'I'll keep an eye on them; you just mind the road.'

I looked up and gave Kevin a wave; I could almost hear his delighted laugh – it would appeal to his sense of humour, escape by hijacked Rolls-Royce.

'Then let's get the hell out of here'. As I let out the clutch I glanced at the group in the doorway but not one of them even looked at us. Their attention was riveted on their prince, and Claire and I passed unnoticed out of their sight and out of their lives.

I was nervous all the way down the long drive. I didn't know what I was expecting to happen, indeed what could happen at this stage – I just didn't believe we'd have a free run. Claire was riding shotgun, so nothing was going to sneak up on us; still, I watched the receding house until we rounded the first bend and it slid off the edge of the mirror, then worriedly probed the copse ahead for dark, running, armed figures. When we came in sight of the gates, they looked closed, and, for a few skipped heartbeats, I was sure we had driven straight into a trap; but it was just a trick of the angle, and, moments later, I steered the great car between them.

'Right or left?' I asked, nudging on to the main road.

'Do you know where we are?' Claire asked, still looking out the back window. 'Because I don't – I was blindfolded.'

'Somewhere outside Newbridge. Three or four miles. But I'm not sure which direction.'

She gave a nervous cough. 'How about getting as far away from here as possible first, and *then* deciding?'

I swung to the right.

A few almost silent miles on, we were still wary as cats – Claire continuing to mind our back, me dividing my attentions as best I could between rear mirror, side mirrors, the road, and the occupants of oncoming cars. It wasn't until a convoy of three squad cars passed us, heading at full speed towards Alaramos's cousin's house, sirens pulsing and wailing, crammed to the gunwales with gardaí, that we relaxed. Claire flopped back in her seat and expelled a long relieved sigh.

'Obviously, Kevin got through to the law.'

'Yep,' I breathed deeply and whistled. 'Jesus! What a *day!*'

'That, Frank,' she said, after a moment's consideration, 'must enter the annals as one of the great understatements of our age. Of *any* age.'

'Still,' I said, ignoring her, 'barring a puncture, we're home and dry.'

'Practical to the last.' She smiled at me indulgently.

'Well, by God! There's no justice.' I pretended to be hurt. 'Here we are, after one of the greatest rescues in history, and you're complaining about my conversation! And me ferrying you along in the luxury of a bloody great Rolls-Royce!'

'Oh I'm impressed all right, very, very impressed. But I would have preferred a blue one. Powder blue.'

'The powder blue one is at the panel-beater's. Still, you have to admit it's a class act. Do you think Paul Markham would ever have rescued you in a Rolls?'

'Very likely. Only I'm sure it would have been his own.'

I laughed. 'You're probably right.' I slapped the steering wheel. 'I've never even been *in* one of these mothers, have you?'

'No. Although this time last year, I was having the devil's own job keeping *out* of one.'

'How come?'

'Hotly pursued by a sugar-daddy. He used to send his Rolls around every day with the most outlandish gifts. It could have been the same car, the same colour and all.

'Maybe it is. Wouldn't that be some coincidence? Maybe he was Alaramos's cousin?'

'Not unless the cousin's name is Fergus O'Lafferty, five feet nothing, very pale, lots of freckles, thinning salt and pepper hair . . .'

'You never know,' I said. 'Did he have a strong Hamrani accent and a load of oil wells, diamond mines and race-horses?'

'No. A strong Meath accent, a couple of pubs in Navan and

Trim, a farm or two somewhere in between, and did a bit of building on the side.'

'That might be only a cover for tax purposes. Was he a man of regal mien, of obvious blue blood?'

'He was an unashamed, grasping, political grassroot.'

'He didn't shower you with gold, spices, sandalwood and whatsit from Samarkand?'

'He didn't get the chance. I was introduced to him at a party, spoke with him for about three minutes, and the very next day, began to get presents of the most *outrageously* tarty underwear . . . you wouldn't believe!'

I looked at her, really seriously now. 'Do you still have it?'

And we both burst out laughing.

Coming into Newbridge, I saw a telephone box and pulled over. I thought I ought to make Lord Roscahill's day for him – the poor man had had enough bad news from me.

I heard the number ring, the receiver being picked up, and the coins drop. 'Hallo?' I said.

'Hallo?' came the shaky reply.

The man himself.

Everything was turning up good today.

Other titles available from Arrow

MALLORY'S ORACLE

Carol O'Connell

When Kathleen Mallory was ten she was a street kid and a thief. Then a cop called Markowitz took her home to his wife to civilize her . . .

Now Mallory is in charge of a complex database and a police officer herself, and someone has just murdered the man she considers her father – the only man she has ever loved.

More used to the company of computers than people, Mallory descends into the urban nightmare of New York, to hunt down a cold-blooded killer.

Mallory's Oracle is a dangerous chase through the city's underworld, down the fibre-optic cables of hi-tech computer networks and behind the blinds of genteel Gramercy Park – and an investigation into the chilly heart of its damaged and elusive heroine.

'Something close to a masterwork'
The Times

'Sgt Kathleen Mallory is one of the most original and intriguing detectives you'll ever meet'
Carl Hiaasen

'A stunning debut'
Daily Mirror

'A deeply satisfying read'
Time Out

THE MAN WHO LIED TO WOMEN

Carol O'Connell

Fifteen years after Inspector Louis Markowitz adopted the wild child, no one in New York's Special Crimes section knew much about Kathy Mallory's origins. They only knew that the young cop with the soul of a thief could bewitch the most complex computer systems, could slip into the minds of killers with disturbing ease.

In Central Park, a woman dies, while a witness watches, believing the brutal murder to be a prelude to a kiss. Mallory goes hunting the killer, armed with under-the-skin knowledge of the man's mind and the bare clue of a lie.

Mallory holds on to one truth: everybody lies, and some lies can get you killed. And she knows that, to trap the killer, she must put her own life at risk, for this killer has taken a personal interest in her . . .

'Mallory's progress is enthralling . . . beautifully observed in fine, controlled prose'
Mail on Sunday

'Carol O'Connell is a gifted writer with a style as quick and arresting as Kathy Mallory herself'
Richard North Patterson

PRINCIPAL DEFENCE

Gini Hartzmark

Katherine Millholland has a reputation of being a brilliant and ambitious lawyer. She may be a privileged heiress, but that has never stopped her from taking chances and working hard for her money as a mergers and acquisitions lawyer in Chicago's most aggressive law firm.

When the highly profitable pharmaceutical company owned by her sometime lover, Stephen Azorini, is under threat from a hostile takeover bid, Kate takes on the case and is determined to stop it from happening.

But the stakes are higher than she thought, and a dangerous angle to the case appears when Stephen's teenage niece is killed. Kate suddenly finds herself investigating the vicious murder and uncovering the deadly reality behind the corporate doors of Chicago.

Working against an impossible deadline to find the killer, family fights simmer and mob connections threaten to smother. But the closer she gets to the answers, the closer she moves to becoming the latest victim of a corporate murder scheme . . .

In the bestselling tradition of *Presumed Innocent* and *The Firm*, *Principal Defence* goes beyond the courtroom to take a revealing look at a world where mergers can lead to murder.

FINAL OPTION

Gini Hartzmark

Grey suits, red ties . . . and murder

When lawyer Katherine Millholland arrives at the home of Bart Hexter, one of Chicago's most powerful players in the futures market, she finds him behind the wheel of his Rolls Royce, clad only in a pair of red silk pajamas, with two bullets in his head.

As Kate sorts through the tangle of the dead man's complex financial dealings, she finds herself dangerously drawn into his affairs, and into a virulent web of potential enemies. And as she zeroes in on the killer she realizes that she may be the next victim . . .

With riveting suspense, *Final Option* takes us deep inside the cut-throat world of the commodities exchange, where life is expendable and making money is the only game worth playing . . .

BULLETIN FROM THE STREET

Eugene Izzi

The murder count has been high for a Chicago winter, and when a black woman is elected mayor it looks set to increase.

A fanatical preacher, The Reverend Afrikaan, is stirring the black population into a racist frenzy while a group of vicious white supremacists seize the opportunity to get even. A race war of apocalyptic proportions is about to explode.

Barry Henry, Denise Durkin and her homeless friend, Booker, are struggling to survive the rising heat of violence. No laws can protect them now, and Henry should know, he's about to get kicked off the vice-squad for using the only laws that work – his own. If they stay off the streets they might pull through. But it isn't that simple. An insane doctor has moved from euthanasing AIDS patients to spearing hobos, and now he's zeroed in on Booker

'Eugene Izzi is a pro, one of the very best in the crime field.'
Elmore Leonard

SAFE HARBOUR

Eugene Izzi

Tommy Torrelli, a New York wiseguy and right-hand man to the boss of bosses, goes for the score of his career, the one that will get him out of crime and into a normal life for him and his son. But he gets busted and when the mob threaten the life of his son he talks, and enters the Witness Protection Programme.

Now, fifteen years later, he has escaped the Programme with a new identity thanks to a sympathetic Fed. Tommy has become Mark Torrence, with a wife, three kids, a home in Chicago, a job helping reform young offenders – and a new character. He thinks he has left the past behind. But knows he's fooling himself.

The people he shopped years ago have not forgotten him. Photos of his new home have started to appear on someone's desk in New York, and the most ruthless hitman in America, a killer who doesn't even consider himself human, smells revenge . . .

'Eugene Izzi is a pro, one of the very best in the crime field.'
Elmore Leonard

ALL ARROW BOOKS ARE AVAILABLE THROUGH MAIL ORDER OR FROM YOUR LOCAL BOOKSHOP AND NEWSAGENT.

PLEASE SEND CHEQUE/EUROCHEQUE/POSTAL ORDER (STERLING ONLY) ACCESS, VISA OR MASTERCARD

EXPIRY DATE............... SIGNATURE...

PLEASE ALLOW 75 PENCE PER BOOK FOR POST AND PACKING U.K.

OVERSEAS CUSTOMERS PLEASE ALLOW £1.00 PER COPY FOR POST AND PACKING.

ALL ORDERS TO:

ARROW BOOKS, BOOK SERVICE BY POST, P.O. BOX 29, DOUGLAS, ISLE OF MAN, IM99 1BQ. TEL: 01624 675137 FAX: 01624 670 923

NAME..

ADDRESS ....

....

Please allow 28 days for delivery. Please tick box if you do not wish to receive any additional information ☐

Prices and availability subject to change without notice.